MAJESTIC

sands press
Brockville, Ontario

MAJESTIC

PETER PARKIN & ALISON DARBY

sands press

sands press

A division of 3244601 Canada Inc.
300 Central Avenue West
Brockville, Ontario
K6V 5V2

Toll Free 1-800-563-0911 or 613-345-2687
http://www.sandspress.com

ISBN 978-1-988281-12-4

Cover concept Anthony Turner, Lanturn Design
Formatting by Kevin Davidson
Publisher Sands Press
Author Agent Sparks Literary Consultants

Publisher's Note

This book is a work of fiction. References to real people, events, establishments, organizations, or locales, are intended only to provide as a sense of authenticity, and are used fictitiously. All other characters, and all incidents and dialogue, are drawn from the authors' imaginations and are not to be construed as real.

For information on bulk purchases of this book or any book published by Sands Press, please call 1-800-563-0911.

1st Printing March 2017

To book an author for your live event, please call: 1-800-563-0911

Sands Press is a literary publisher interested in new and established authors wishing to develop and market their product. For more information please visit our website at www.sandspress.com.

CHAPTER 1

It was as if there were diamonds floating on the surface of the lake. The midday sun reflecting sparklers off the calm waters was a sight to behold, and Wyatt Carson made certain that he beheld it as long as he could.

He knew he had to get back to work, but a few more minutes enjoying the eye candy that was Kootenay Lake wouldn't cause the world to collapse. Work could wait. After all, he was the boss, so it could either wait or someone else could just handle things in his absence. He had a good team.

He slid open his patio door and stepped out onto the massive cedar deck that embraced the spectacular lake view. Then, he stretched out on a chaise lounge and sighed.

Suddenly, he cursed—he'd forgotten his cup of coffee. He dashed back inside and then emerged once again, steaming cup in hand.

Wyatt reached into his shirt pocket and pulled out a pack of cigarettes and lighter. His doctor had told him he needed to quit these things because his breathing was showing early signs of COPD—but he wasn't too worried. For now, he still enjoyed it—especially at moments like this; a jewel of a lake, a warm summer day, and a cup of java.

These were moments to treasure and for some strange reason a cigarette made them even more relaxing to him. He wasn't stupid, though—he knew it was just in his mind. The opposite was more likely true—that cigarettes actually made him more tense than relaxed.

He blew out a long stream of smoke and watched as a bald eagle soared overhead. Spying some unsuspecting creature on the forest floor, it dove at breakneck speed until disappearing into the trees. A few seconds later, predictably, the powerful predator accelerated upwards once again, the legs of some hapless little animal twitching feverishly while the eagle's lethal beak was clamped securely around its neck.

Wyatt's eyes wandered, settling on the log structure of his house. He knew the logs could probably use a re-staining, but it was such a massive job that he'd probably procrastinate on that until next summer. In the meantime, they still looked pretty good. Good enough.

In fact, everything looked good. His lot was one of the most desirable ones available along the shores of the lake. Although not close enough to be able to actually dive into the water, the view from his deck was spectacular and created the illusion of the lake being closer than it really was.

Wyatt's house was probably a good 150 feet above the surface, which gave him a panoramic view up and down the long snake-like body of water. Kootenay Lake was 104 kilometers long, three miles across at its narrowest, five miles at its widest. A fabulous lake for boating and fishing...but swimming was hit and miss. If the summers were warm, the water might heat up to twenty degrees Celsius at best, but it was usually no more than eighteen degrees on a typical day. Brisk for swimming, for sure. Guaranteed to make blood retreat to the body's inner sanctums.

Wyatt rested his head back against the integral pillow on his chaise mattress and gazed out at the panorama that towered over the lake surface. The Selkirk Mountains—unbelievably intimidating in the summer, and breathtakingly stunning in the winter.

He took a moment to thank his lucky stars that his parents had moved to Nelson, British Columbia forty-five years ago, while he was just a mere lump in his mom's uterus. Born in Canada, he had automatically become a Canadian citizen.

His dad came to Canada in the midst of the wave of draft-dodgers, or as they were affectionately referred to—'conscientious objectors.'

But, while his father tended to liken himself to a draft-dodger, he wasn't. Not really. He just followed the herd of dodgers back in 1970, determined to not sit back and watch that brutal conscription happen one more time. And, that no child of his would ever have to endure what he endured back in 1950.

It was the Korean War, and 1.5 million American men had been drafted. He rose to the rank of Lieutenant and served two full years in the four-year war. He hardly ever talked about it—a short war, but a particularly brutal one. A war that claimed 5 million lives, half of those being civilian Koreans.

His dad had hoped he'd never see it again, but then along came

Vietnam in 1970. The drum beats were sounding, and the draft was once again instituted. His father would have been too old by that time to be conscripted, but that didn't matter to him. He'd had enough—didn't want to live in a country that did that, so he packed up his pretty little pregnant wife and drove north to Canada. Purportedly just to visit for a little while—at least that's what they told people. But, they found a way to stay. Along with 125,000 other Americans who were just as disgusted as they were.

The Americans spread across Canada, most disappearing into the major cities. Then, when the Vietnam war ended four years later, half of them returned to the U.S. under various forms of amnesty.

But, the town of Nelson, B.C. didn't lose any. Several thousand Americans had claimed that town as their home, and it was so beautiful and peaceful that they vowed never to leave. Instead, they helped create the artsy heritage community that it became renowned for.

A town that was as eclectic as it was charming. A town that was as stoned as it was sober.

Nelson was a thriving artistic center now, with a mountain sports reputation that was unrivalled. In 2012, it was voted best ski locale in North America by California's *Powder Magazine*. Not bad, especially to be honored as such by an American publication. Obviously, they harbored no hard feelings towards Nelson's prominent residents for having abandoned their native country half a century before.

The town was now a city, albeit a small one. With a population of only 11,000, it still had the charm that one associated with small towns. And, it had a laid-back style that some attributed to the scenery and lifestyle, but still others attributed to the profitable and rampant marijuana production. Still illegal, but most people just snickered and looked the other way. After all, the most prominent residents of Nelson, although getting on in years, were really still hippies in their hearts and anti-war activists in their souls.

The city was also made famous by the Steve Martin movie, *Roxanne*. After that film achieved critical acclaim, people flocked to Nelson to see firsthand some of the famous locales, such as the iconic fire hall and all of the heritage buildings. The tree-lined streets inspired people into thinking that was what 'living the life' should look like. It was good publicity, but, while residents loved that the movie put their city on the map, they also resented the intrusion of 'riff-raff' and city folk who were hoping to move there and citify the lifestyle.

No one wanted Nelson to change, pure and simple. And Wyatt couldn't really blame them. Life was good.

The descendants of those draft-dodgers kind of took after their parents. Most of them still lived in Nelson and couldn't imagine living anywhere else. They'd adopted their parents' laid-back approach to life and their opinionated ways. Once a draft-dodger, always a draft-dodger, and that usually resulted in rebellious and independent-thinking offspring.

Wyatt was one of those offspring. And, he usually just looked the other way when hotline tips rolled in to him about marijuana farms and processing centers. He couldn't care less and, as long as they behaved themselves and didn't try to sell the stuff to kids, he was okay with it.

As the Chief of Police for the City of Nelson, that was a delicate position for him to take. But, he managed it—somehow, he managed it. The city's residents knew that tolerance had its limits. If they played ball with Wyatt, he'd play ball with them.

So far, it had worked just fine. In the ten years since he'd been appointed police chief, the crime rate in Nelson had dropped dramatically. In fact, most incidents of theft or violent crime were committed by tourists, or transients just passing through. Nelson got a lot of those types, just because it was a magnet to travelers, and to people hoping to find a different way of life. The setting of the city was magnificent, and most people who came to visit never wanted to leave again.

That was the biggest challenge to Wyatt and his twenty-person police force: getting the non-residents to respect the peace and relaxed lifestyles of the ones who had earned the right to live there.

He stretched, and then reluctantly forced himself up out of the chaise lounge for the walk back into the kitchen. Lunch break over. He enjoyed coming home for his lunch hour. He lived only about ten minutes outside the city, but it seemed like more than that. Coming home was a true break from the day's routine tedium.

Sighing with trepidation at having to leave his little piece of paradise, Wyatt snapped his gun and holster onto his belt and slipped on his jacket.

As the chief, he had the choice of wearing his official uniform or just going plainclothes. He always elected to work in his civvies, unless it was some formal event like the Mayor's Ball. Otherwise, he just felt more comfortable in his own clothes and he knew they put his staff and the citizens at ease, too.

He fingered his cell phone and saw that he'd missed a call.

Mom.

Wyatt remembered that today was the day his dad was having a CT scan done at the hospital.

He was eighty-seven years old now, while Mom was still just a 'spring chicken' at sixty-five. Both his parents were in great shape—the fresh mountain air and stress-free living were kind to both the body and soul.

And, he suspected they still smoked the odd joint as well, which probably helped keep them young—at least in their minds and souls.

His father had fallen down the front porch stairs earlier, and the doctor had recommended a scan just to make sure he hadn't broken a hip or something else. He protested, saying that he'd never had an x-ray in his entire life. But, the doctor—and his doting wife—won out in the end.

His mother was probably just phoning to give him an update.

Wyatt decided to get back to her before heading to the office. She answered on the first ring.

"Oh, thank God it's you, Wy."

She always called him 'Wy.' *Why not?*

"Hi Mom. What's wrong? How's Dad?"

There was an awkward pause. Then, her voice once again, sobbing this time.

"Please come to the hospital. I don't know what to do."

Wyatt felt a knot in the pit of his stomach.

"It's okay, Mom. I'll be right there. Something wrong with Dad?"

More sobbing. Then, her soft voice came back on the line, almost a whisper.

"They don't know what to say, or do. I can see right through him."

She was distraught, and not making any sense.

"Of course you can see through him, Mom. You've known him forever. Just calm down—I'll be there in a few minutes."

Wyatt clicked off, grabbed his car keys, and headed out the side door to his police cruiser. The Kootenay Lake District Hospital was only five minutes away, located down on View Street.

He turned on the siren and made it there in three.

Parked in the front circular drive, he dashed in through general admitting, saw the sign towards the x-ray department and half-ran, half-walked, the rest of the way.

He was worried, but he was also well aware of the fact that when people reached the age that his parents were at now, they tended to build little things into major crises.

Sometimes, it was just too overwhelming for them, trying to handle all the details. Even just paying attention to a doctor's explanation or instructions could be a daunting experience for them.

He cursed himself for not going with them this morning, but his mother was insistent that she was capable of handling it. And, she had probably indeed convinced herself that she was. She was a fiercely independent lady, who at the very least didn't want her son to think he had to take care of them like little children.

They had both been assertive like that since hitting their senior years, and Wyatt understood. He knew he'd be the same way.

He saw her—alone in the hallway, pacing back and forth, wringing her hands.

She saw him, too, and rushed up to greet him, wrapping her frail arms around Wyatt's big frame and squeezing as hard as she could.

He squeezed her back, then looked into her eyes. They were bloodshot—he could tell she'd been crying.

"Tell me what's wrong, Mom. What's wrong with Dad?"

Her lips quivered, and her eyes started blinking rapidly.

"I can see right through him. It's horrible, Wy."

"You said that on the phone. What do you mean? What's horrible?"

Suddenly, there was a man in a white coat standing beside them. Wyatt recognized him, but couldn't place his name.

"Hello, Chief. You may not remember me—I'm Doctor Simpson, the radiologist. I don't know what your mom has told you, but we have a very unusual situation here."

"What's so unusual? He came in for a simple CT scan. What's happened?"

The doctor took a deep breath and then spoke. "We can't explain it, and we've never seen anything like it. He seems to be okay otherwise, but…"

"But what? Spit it out!"

The doctor shuffled his feet. "It's better that you see for yourself. We have your father in a containment room just down the hall." He pointed. "Follow me. Please just brace yourself. As I said, he seems okay otherwise and we have him under observation. And his condition does seem to be improving."

The doctor led the way. Wyatt called out to him, "What condition? It was a simple fall!"

Doctor Simpson stopped at a window that was shielded by blinds from the inside. He rapped on the window. "It's best that you just see for yourself."

The blinds opened and Wyatt quickly took in the scene that assaulted him from the antiseptic room beyond the glass.

Three attendants were dressed in what looked like hazmat outfits, hovering around the bed. There was only one bed in this 'containment' room.

Wyatt stared at what he thought was his father. He heard his mother gasp, and was aware of her turning her head away. Wyatt wanted to do the same. The doctor was silent.

His dad was naked on the bed except for a pair of boxer shorts.

And Wyatt could see right through him.

There was a subtle glow surrounding his body, almost like a haze. His eyes were open and, remarkably, he seemed to be conscious and alert. Remarkable, considering that he looked like death.

Only one word came into Wyatt's mind to describe what his father looked like. 'Transparent.' His father was transparent. His skin was intact, but it looked shockingly thin, almost like plastic wrap.

His face was barely recognizable—a thin and feeble apparition. It was, more or less, just a skull.

Beyond the sickeningly eerie sight of a skull staring back at him from the bed—eyes blinking, mouth moving—Wyatt could also see every bone in his dad's body.

CHAPTER 2

His name was William, but everyone called him Willy.

Her name was Helen and everyone called her...Helen.

Willy and Helen were the couple everyone in town seemed to know, one way or another. Either through personal friendship, or by knowing someone else who knew them.

They owned a large heritage home on a crescent right off the main drag, Baker Street. They'd raised their only son, Wyatt, in that home—in fact he'd been born there; upstairs in the third bedroom on the right.

The house had a large covered party verandah, and they loved to entertain. Even at their advanced ages now, they still held a party for their neighbors and friends at least once a month. And, all of their parties seemed to gravitate out to the verandah, which extended a full twelve feet in width and wrapped around the entire house. Their view was spectacular—they could see both the lake and the downtown in one quick glance. And, the hot Kootenay summer nights permitted those parties to extend into the wee hours of the morning.

Most people would groan and roll their eyes if someone told them that a bunch of seventy and eighty-year-olds held a loud party the other night. But, those would be people who didn't live in Nelson. And those eye-rollers wouldn't be considering the fact that these elderly people were the ultimate hippies—the ones 'back in the day' who always did what they said they'd do—went to Woodstock and romped in the mud, made love in fields of daisies, opposed any kind of violence or gun ownership, stood up to Nixon's thugs at Kent State, carried signs protesting the Vietnam war. And, when the signs were ignored, those same hippies said 'to hell with it,' and snuck off to Canada, never to return.

They were the creators, the artists, the free thinkers, the happy spirits—grass and hash helped them see the light, but they never overdid it, and they tended to avoid booze like the plague.

A lot of those things were still true today, even at their advanced ages. They were Americans by birth, but Canadians by choice. When asked, they never slammed their former country—they would just shrug and say they didn't give a shit. That America didn't reflect their values then, and it sure didn't reflect them now.

They were all believers of 'live and let live,' and of the right to enjoy your one and only life the way you want to live it, without apologies to anyone.

In quiet moments, Wyatt sometimes caught himself contemplating his parents' attitude towards life, and the values of peace they had instilled in him. He was so proud of them and so very glad that he had parents like them. He found it easy to forgive their still occasional indulgence in getting a wee bit high.

Wyatt thought that the world could use a few more hippies. Why hadn't that movement sprung up again? Where were the free thinkers? The challengers? The shit-disturbers? The rebels? That was probably why the world was in such sad shape, because there wasn't a national conscience anymore, anywhere. No one cared, and no one seemed to speak up for peace and honesty. Not even the media. And, when no one spoke up, anyone could get away with anything.

Wyatt held his sobbing mother and refused to allow his gaze to swing back to the 'containment' room window. He didn't want to see that image again.

His poor father. William, the sculptor, who had spent his post-military life carving heads and bodies out of solid chunks of rock and ice. Created masterpiece images of how the human body should look, had his work on display in parks and museums all over North America. He participated in the annual Lake Louise ice sculpture competition and had won the event four times.

But, Willy had never ever created anything that looked like the abomination of himself that was lying in that bed. He would have crushed such a creation to pieces and started all over again.

Wyatt was aware of the doctor standing off to the side. He gently pushed his mother out of his arms and eased her down into a chair in the hallway, facing away from the 'containment' room window. Then, he hooked his finger at the polite and respectful radiologist, motioning him farther down the hall away from his mom.

When they had moved halfway down the corridor, Wyatt turned the handle of a storage room door and motioned the doctor inside.

He closed the door behind him, then, with one quick move of his right hand, he shoved the doctor up against the wall. Bringing his face to within mere inches of Doctor Simpson's face, he said, "Start talking to me, fast! What the fuck is that all about? What did you people do to him?"

Simpson stammered, "N...nothing, Chief. He...had a CT scan, that's all."

"There has to be something wrong with your machine!"

"I...don't know about...that. We'll have it checked. But...nothing that I can imagine would cause...cause what we just saw."

Wyatt pulled his hand from the doctor's chest and backed away from him.

"My dad is transparent. How is that medically possible? Did his skin thin from the radiation?"

Simpson shook his head. He seemed calmer now that Wyatt had backed off. "No, we've examined him. His skin has not lost any of its thickness—it seems as if the pigment has temporarily disappeared."

"Temporarily? You mean he'll be okay?"

The doctor nodded. "Yes, he's already improved over the last hour. It looks like a temporary condition. I'm sure he'll look normal in no time at all, and his vital signs are all strong. There appears to be nothing *medically* wrong with him."

Wyatt shook his head and frowned at the doctor. "That's an idiotic thing to say. There's obviously something medically wrong with him. You just don't have a clue as to what it is."

"Yes, I hear you. Wrong choice of words."

Wyatt leaned up against the doorframe. "Doctor, I've never seen anything so hideous in my life. I don't know what effect this will have on my mother, but you need to perhaps prescribe some sedatives for her. This is the man she's spent almost fifty years of her life with, and right now he looks like he's been in a coffin for that long. It breaks my heart—that's my father in there. Someone has to have some answers."

Simpson nodded. "I'll prescribe something for her. And, we're going to search for answers. My specialty is x-ray technology, as you know, and I can attest to the fact that there has never been a case like this before, a reaction like this to any kind of radiation. Even extreme radiation poisoning from exposure to nuclear meltdowns hasn't produced symptoms close to this."

Wyatt lowered his eyes to the floor, not knowing what else to say.

Simpson crossed his arms over his chest, and cleared his throat. "Chief, did you know that your father has never had an x-ray for anything his entire adult life?"

"No, I hadn't known that until my mom and I convinced him to come in for the CT scan. I was surprised about that—he's been pretty lucky over the years, I guess."

"Highly unusual. And the CT scan shows no signs of osteoarthritis, which for his age is also unusual. In fact, his bone structure looks as healthy as a man forty years younger."

Wyatt shrugged his shoulders. "He keeps himself in shape."

"He doesn't wear glasses."

Wyatt shrugged again. "Must eat all the right stuff."

The doctor persisted. "He has a full head of hair."

Wyatt nodded. "Yes, he's quite the specimen for his age, no doubt. He'll probably outlive us all."

Simpson took a step closer, and lowered his voice to almost a whisper. "Are you aware that your father has every single one of his original teeth? And that his dental charts and records show the last filling he ever had was back in 1949?"

Wyatt's mouth went instantly dry. "No, I didn't know that. But, why were you looking at his dental charts?"

"He comes for dental checkups at the clinic here, which is part of the hospital. His records are part of his medical file."

"No fillings, no false teeth, no crowns or root canals? Nothing at all?"

Simpson shook his head slowly. "Nothing at all. All he's ever had done were regular checkups and dental hygiene."

"Jesus."

"Have you ever noticed your dad's tongue?"

Wyatt could feel his heart beating faster with each question. "No, not that I can recall. I mean, who takes notice of things like that? He doesn't exactly go around sticking his tongue out at people."

"It's scaly. Like fish scales."

"Oh, c'mon, doctor. It sounds like you're trying to invent diversions from what really happened here today. Scaly? You've got to be kidding."

"No, I'm not kidding. Find a reason to take a look—ask him to stick his tongue out and say 'Ah.'

"You should know also that he vomited after just a couple of minutes of the scan. We stopped the machine and pulled him out. While he was in there, he sat bolt upright and just vomited all over his chest. After we cleaned him off and prepared him to go back in, we started noticing the change in his skin texture. That's when we moved him into the containment room."

"I've never known my dad to be sick even one day of his life. He must have been nervous about the scan."

Doctor Simpson put his hand on Wyatt's shoulder. "He kept saying over and over again, *'It's too bright. Can't see, can't see.'*"

CHAPTER 3

Willy Carson could see very clearly. His eyes had always been perfect, eerily perfect. Well, okay, a bit of an exaggeration. They hadn't always been perfect—only really for the past sixty-five years of his life.

Ever since...

Despite the state that he was in, he could see clearly through the little window out into the hospital corridor. And, it broke his heart.

Willy didn't need a mirror to tell him what his face looked like. His son's expression said it all. Wyatt's face was the only mirror he needed.

He watched as Wyatt stared at him, mouth agape, his handsome features contorted into a mask of horror. Then, just as quickly, he turned away, holding onto Helen. Helen had only allowed herself a half-second glance and that had been enough to bring her to tears once again. It had been the second time in the last hour that she'd looked at him, this time only slightly shorter than when he came out of the damn CT scan.

He had been told to never have any x-rays done. But, that was so long ago now, it was just a distant memory. He was told that he probably wouldn't need them...ever.

Ever since...

He was told that his bones would be so strong that a break was highly unlikely, unless he did something really stupid.

Well, he finally did something really stupid—falling down the steps off that damn verandah. And, it had hurt like hell. He thought that maybe, just maybe, he had broken something this time.

Despite that, he still didn't want to go to the hospital, remembering the advice...or, more like orders...that he'd been given sixty-five years ago. But, Helen had persisted, and she'd gotten their son on the phone to help her convince him. He relented, more because he didn't want to let the two of them down. And, he had to admit, his left hip hurt like hell. It didn't now, but it did then.

He should have just waited. Listened to his own instincts...and listened to the orders that still rang in his ears after six and a half decades. Orders that he was told had no expiry date, even throughout whatever decades of life he had left in him after leaving the military. He had been an officer, a Lieutenant, with obligations of honor and secrecy. Obligations like that never expired.

They had visited him several times over the last few decades—he didn't even really know who 'they' were. Different people each time, always in dark suits, even the women. They chatted with him, asked how he was doing, feigned concern about his health...all designed to get him to open up about what he'd done or what he'd said. They were always interested in any unusual symptoms that might have made an appearance. There hadn't been any, other than the obvious things that they already knew about. Nothing else had happened, and they seemed relieved to hear that.

And in parting, they always made a point of reminding him of his obligations of honor and secrecy. Even though he was a Canadian now, they reminded him that his citizenship did not make any difference whatsoever.

Willy glanced down at his hands, arms, chest and legs. No wonder Wyatt and Helen had been horrified—he himself was horrified. He could only imagine how his face must look. He pulled up the elastic on his boxer shorts, and took a peek down below. Funny, his penis seemed to be the only part of his body that looked normal.

But...encouragingly, it appeared as if the skin on the rest of his body was starting—slowly but surely—to regain its integrity. He could still see his entire bone structure, but it wasn't as visible as it has been an hour ago.

Willy looked around at the three white-garmented attendants who were doing all sorts of little duties at his bedside, none of which seemed all that important. One was checking the tube that had been inserted into his right forearm, another was pushing buttons on a beeping machine that was apparently monitoring something wired to his head. And, yet another was standing at the foot of his bed reading a chart.

The way they were dressed, covered from head to toe, they must have thought he had some kind of communicable disease. Willy chuckled to himself. That would be so much easier—at least they could maybe cure that. What he had could never be cured. And, they would never know that it couldn't be cured.

He smoothed the fingers of his right hand over his left forearm. Strange, the skin felt exactly the same as it always had—the same thickness, the same elasticity. It was just see-through now; that was the only difference.

But, the reality that Willy couldn't ignore was that it was worse this time around than the first time. Much worse. How bad would it be if this ever happened again? If the reaction was this accelerated after a sixty-five-year absence, what on earth would happen the next time?

He would just have to be careful to make sure that there wasn't a next time.

That thought caused him to close his eyes and remember back to the first time:

It was a cold and brutal day in November, 1950. Willy had already been in Korea for almost six months, and had advanced quickly to the rank of Lieutenant.

He liked to think his promotions were because of his university education and his skill at leading men, but he knew deep down inside that because so many officers had been killed they were scraping the bottom of the barrel now.

Thousands of American soldiers had already been slaughtered in the Korean War and it was only six months old. Willy was twenty-two years of age, and he was surprised that he'd lasted as long as he had. It was his first war, and he hoped that it would be his last. It was labelled as being more rapidly brutal than even WWII. Probably because they were fighting against the Chinese now, too, not just the North Koreans.

Gallantly defending South Korea against Communism, the Americans were convinced the cause was a noble one. The Chinese had warned the Americans that they would jump into the war to aid their North Korean allies, if the battle came too close to their borders. The American generals ignored the warning—and of course it happened just as the Chinese had threatened.

Willy was attached to the 1st Marine Division, and commanded a small platoon of four Marines. All of them looked up to him as their leader, despite the fact that he didn't really have a clue as to what to do or how to do it. He had only been a Marine for a few months, but in war he guessed that was a lifetime. You were a veteran after just a few days, because so many were dropping like flies.

The 'Battle of Chosin Reservoir' was where it happened.

They were in retreat, trying desperately to get back to the coast. Winter had struck in full force and more Marines than he could count were being hauled off with severe frostbite. Luckily, Willy and his small platoon had managed to not lose their winter clothing as so many others had. Retreat had a funny way of causing soldiers to run for their lives and leave their belongings behind.

The Chinese were ferocious—they weren't the least bit tolerant of retreat. Their barrages continued despite the fact that the Marines had already been ordered to get their asses out of there.

But, they were now hunkered down in the Chosin Reservoir; nicknamed 'Hell Fire Valley,' and it had that name for good reason. It was indeed hell.

Willy and his four-man team were crouched in a culvert. Rifles in hand and as alert as they could be after having been awake for the last forty-eight hours. The Chinese were just over the next ridge. Coming hard.

Their orders were to resist until reinforcements arrived. Thousands of Marines and infantrymen were hiding in similar culverts all along the valley, waiting desperately for a break so they could continue their retreat.

It was a pitch black night...and then suddenly it wasn't.

Willy looked up. The lights from an aircraft were beaming down close to their position, moving along the ridge, scanning the terrain.

He knew that if they fired upon the aircraft it would be fruitless, and would only give away their position to the Chinese troops coming over the ridge.

His men followed his gaze upward. Willy continued to stare, allowing his eyes to adjust to this new light in the pitch-black night. He'd never before seen lights of this kind from any airplane or helicopter. They were...different.

Then, the lights shifted away from their position and Willy could more easily discern the shape of the craft.

He gasped. His men gasped with him.

It was unlike anything he'd ever seen.

Willy had heard of flying saucers before and always laughed off the reports. But, this thing came pretty close to the descriptions he'd read. It was definitely oval, but also had a crown—a crown that rose quite high above the oval base. From the crown came the lights that were probing and illuminating the terrain.

Willy ordered his radioman to phone it in, report what they were observing. And, to ask for the 'rules of engagement.'

A panicked captain, probably younger than Willy, ordered them to fire upon it. He said he was convinced it was a Chinese craft of some sort. His radioman protested that their small arms fire would do very little.

But, his protest fell on deaf ears.

The captain wasn't thinking straight. Not many soldiers were that day.

They aimed their machine rifles to the sky and fired in unison.

The bullets came back almost instantly, popping into the snow piled around their perfect little culvert.

Their very own bullets came right back at them.

They continued to fire until the lights swung around in their direction. They were totally illuminated now and mesmerized by the strange lights. Each of them started yelling out how they couldn't see anything, that it was too bright.

Then, a different light came their way. A large beam that zapped them in one quick burst.

Willy knew they had to run. But, there were few places to run to. He recalled a large flood run-off pipe that was only a few dozen yards to the east. It was their best and only option. He yelled out a command for his men to follow him. They didn't need a second invitation.

Once each of them had crawled into the pipe, and the vomiting began. One after the other, so violent that blood accompanied what little else was in their stomachs.

When that trauma was over, the radioman flicked on a torch. That's when they were treated to the sight of each of them as virtual skeletons. Any parts of their bodies that weren't covered with clothing, which basically meant their faces and hands, were transparent. At first, they thought it was just a trick of the torch light, but it didn't take long for the reality to set in. They were indeed transparent.

After being transported to a MASH unit for examination, treatment, and interrogation, Willy heard reports from the field about a mysterious retreat by the Chinese troops off that particular ridge, right after the strange craft had fired its beam on Willy's unit. In fact, it wasn't just a retreat, it was a stampede. The strange craft obviously wasn't theirs. The Chinese were just as spooked as the Americans.

Willy opened his eyes and looked towards the window. The blinds were down again, and he was still all alone in the room except for the three white-coated attendants. He looked down at his skin—yep, some more improvement since he'd closed his eyes for his trip down memory lane.

He sighed…and suddenly got an irresistible urge for a joint.

CHAPTER 4

"Stick out your tongue, Dad."

Willy gazed curiously at his son, but kept his mouth firmly shut.

Helen was pretending to be busy in the kitchen, but paying close attention.

Wyatt and Willy were sitting across from each other at the dining room table, each with a fresh cup of coffee. They'd been back from the hospital for a couple of hours now, and Wyatt could tell that his dad was relieved to be on familiar ground again. After a three-night stay in the hospital, he had been declared fit as a fiddle. There were no obvious side effects from the weird transition he'd endured.

But, no answers, either.

Being the natural-born detective that he was, Wyatt wanted some answers. And, he wanted them now.

"Well, Dad?"

Willy chuckled, and his professorial features crinkled up into a knowing grin. "You may be the police chief, son, but that doesn't carry much jurisdiction in this house."

"All I asked you to do, Dad, was stick out your tongue."

"Do you want me to raise my hands in the air, too?" He chuckled again. "Am I under arrest or something?"

Wyatt frowned with exasperation. "C'mon, Dad. Quit giving me the gears. I just want to see how you're doing. The tongue is always a good indication of health. If it's white, that usually means some kind of bug."

"Well, just so you know—I've already brushed my teeth since I got back, and my tongue looks fine."

"Prove it. Show me."

Helen walked into the dining room from the kitchen. She took a seat at the head of the table, where she usually sat. Willy always deferred to her on that. While he was undeniably the 'king of the castle,' she was his queen and he always treated her as such.

Wyatt knew that Willy was proud of how Helen had always managed the house. While he'd be out in the garage in his sculptor studio, which was his domain, she kept the house immaculate. Sometimes, she wouldn't see him for several days and nights at a time while he had a project on the go.

The garage was a sight to behold—never once used as an actual garage. The studio occupied the entire ground floor, but it also had a fully functional apartment in the extensive loft area above.

When Willy was in his 'artistic mode,' he'd be out there continuously. Helen never minded in the least—it was his passion and he was indeed an incredible artist. And, Wyatt suspected she was glad not to have him under foot 24/7.

When he wasn't creating, he tended to be quite restless and impatient. Not angry or anything like that, but more just like a little lost soul.

"Oh, for God's sake, Wy, give your dad a break! He just got back from the hospital!"

Wyatt studied his dad closely. He was, unabashedly, wearing a short sleeve shirt, apparently not the least bit concerned about displaying his skin. Skin which had now completely reverted to normal, and Willy seemed to show no concern at all that the phenomenon might suddenly return.

"I just want to make sure, Mom." Wyatt stuck out his own tongue and displayed it to his parents. "See? No big deal. You can see that my tongue is nice and pink, which is healthy. Show me yours, Mom."

She laughed—her hearty laugh that she reserved just for her son, who always loved to tease her so much.

"I'm just so glad to have your dad home, now. And it's so good to have you hanging around with us for a bit, too. Feels like old times."

"You changed the subject, Mom. Stick out your tongue."

"Oh, alright! Just to shut you up!" She slid her tongue out of her mouth, and wiggled it back and forth. "This is just going to get your dad horny—all we need now is for him to have a heart attack!"

Willy laughed and gave his wife a wink. "See you upstairs?"

Helen gave him a playful slap on the shoulder. "Why don't you take your only son out to the studio and show him your latest creation?"

Willy got to his feet. "Good idea. C'mon, 'only son.' Follow me."

Willy led the way out through the back door, and down a little slate pathway to the detached garage at the rear of the house. Wyatt realized that, at least for now, he wasn't going to see his dad's tongue. Okay, he'd play along—for a while. But, Willy's resistance set off alarm bells in his head.

Wyatt hadn't been in Willy's inner sanctum for years—strange, considering that he lived only minutes away. He always saw the finished products, when they were being loaded by crane onto flatbed trucks to be hauled away to some fortunate location for permanent or temporary display.

He had also visited Lake Louise many times to watch his dad compete in the annual ice sculpture competitions. But, it had been at least a decade or more since he'd been in this shrine—where all the creativity happened, where his dad was the most proud and fulfilled.

He glanced around the cavernous room and could see several works in various stages of completion. Willy seldom worked on one piece of art at a time. He always had several on the go. He always explained that it helped keep each work fresh, gave a break to the vision for a day or two, and then when he went back to it after working on another one for a while, he could look at it through new critical eyes.

They just stood inside the door for a couple of minutes. He felt like they were in church together, and there were indeed some similarities to being in a place of worship. Something solemn, something magical. Objects that were lifelike, but silent. Ghostly in some ways, religious in others.

Wyatt whispered, "It's been so long since I've been here. It still gives me such an overwhelming feeling, a feeling I can remember so clearly."

Willy smiled warmly at his son. "Why are you whispering?"

Wyatt chuckled. "I dunno. Seems like the proper thing to do."

"Well, stop whispering. You won't wake any of these characters up, I promise you."

He crooked his finger for Wyatt to follow, as he walked over to a large object in the center of the room covered with a tarpaulin. He grabbed a corner, and yanked it off with a flourish.

Wyatt gasped. Staring back at him was a 60s era hippie, as lifelike as could possibly be imagined by an artist's vision. He was about six feet tall with long hair and a big glorious smile on his boyish face. In one hand, he held a rifle, barrel pointed towards the ground. In the other hand, he held a document, but one that had clearly been torn in half. It had jagged edges, and the figure's hand holding the document was erect and proudly waving it in the air like one would wave a flag.

Wyatt spoke in a whisper again. "Dad…this is brilliant. I'm not an artist, but I know exactly what this is depicting. He's a draft-dodger, isn't he? Defiantly pointing the gun to the ground, and waving a draft notice torn in half?"

Willy smiled. "Very good, son. That's exactly what it is."

Wyatt raised his voice now. "Wow! This is amazing! The expression on his face is so happy, so victorious. And, the detail in his face, his hair, the rifle, the draft notice. God, how on earth do you do this stuff?"

Willy blushed. "A lot of tools…and time."

"Did you have a sketch to work from? As your model?"

Willy tapped the side of his head. "Only up here."

"Amazing. How long?"

"This one has taken me about two years—but I've been working on others, too, of course."

"What material is this?"

"Marble."

"Jesus! That must have cost a fortune!"

"It did, especially since it was one big slab. But, I also charge a fortune for what I do, so the material costs never concern me."

"What will you sell this one for?"

Willy shuffled his feet. "Well, this would normally go for a hundred thousand. But, my intention is to give this one away."

"What? Why?"

"I want to convince the city council to mount this in the Town Square, downtown. As a monument to the brave people who made this city what it is today.

"They deserve a monument, some measure of thanks and a sense of pride for the brave choices they made for peace. And, we're getting short on time. Most of them are getting on in years—they're all younger than me, because they were of the Vietnam years. But, in a couple of decades they'll all be dead. Would be a shame to give them a monument after they're gone, don't you think?"

Wyatt nodded. "Did you get a commission from the city council for this?"

Willy shook his head. "No, they turned down an idea about this in the past. So, I'm just hoping that once they see it, they'll want it."

Wyatt shook his head in astonishment. Then, he leaned in to his dad, wrapped his arms around him and gave him a bear hug. Willy hugged him back, and Wyatt could feel his eyes starting to mist up.

He let go, and stood back. "Okay, show me your tongue now."

Willy laughed. "Hey, an affectionate little moment of bromance sure isn't going to convince me to stick my tongue out!"

"You're amazing, Dad. And, you're doing a phenomenal thing here. I'm very proud of you."

"I'm proud of you, too, Wyatt. Tell you what—when they lay me out in a coffin, you can tell the undertaker to stick my tongue out if it means that much to you."

They both laughed.

"Dad, I really don't want that to be my last memory of you."

Willy chuckled, then turned to lead the way back out to the driveway.

But, before Wyatt followed, he noticed something odd. There was another object, way off in the east corner of the studio, covered with a tarpaulin as well, but surrounded by other finished and half-finished pieces.

He pointed and walked over to it. "What's this, Dad? Another surprise piece that you're going to spring on the world?"

Willy called out. "That one's not worth looking at. I did that a long time ago, and I'm kind of ashamed of it. Not fit for viewing. C'mon, let's get back to your mother."

Wyatt walked around the statues that were blocking it, and pulled off the tarpaulin.

"Wyatt! No!"

Wyatt stood in stunned silence, staring at the ghostly apparition in front of him.

The detail was absolutely brilliant, even more breathtaking than the draft-dodger statue. This one was constructed of a softer material. He guessed soapstone.

It was clearly a soldier in battle, kneeling. Wrinkled and torn uniform, helmet on his head. His face was so alive, so riddled with anguish. The eyes were closed and actually squinting, pinched; as if in pain, in fear, or... maybe blinded?

He was grasping a machine gun in both hands, the index finger of his right hand pulling tightly against the trigger. The gun was pointed towards the sky. And, there was drool of some sort seeping out of the soldier's mouth, draping over his chin.

The only parts of his body that weren't covered in military fatigues were his face and his hands.

The statue was both beautiful and vocal. It was screaming out something, seemingly a message of pain and abject fear.

These things were clear to Wyatt even though he didn't have an artistic bone in his body. It was a credit to the artist to be able to convey such messages to the uninitiated.

But, it was one of the most macabre images he'd ever seen.

The skin on the face was transparent.

The bone structure of the skull displayed itself in full shocking horror.

And the hands gripping the machine gun were the hands of a skeleton.

CHAPTER 5

The Druid Hills, Georgia.

It was an enclave unto itself, but also enjoyed the status of being a suburb of the City of Atlanta. With a median family income of around $250,000, it was the most affluent satellite of the massive city.

Druid Hills was a planned community, conceived by a prominent Georgian and developed with the determined efforts of several leading families, including the Candlers of Coca-Cola fame. It flew in the face of the demographics of Atlanta, with only 6% of the population in the Druid Hills being African/American. In Atlanta, it was over 50%.

About 20,000 people lived there, and a good majority of them worked at the prestigious Emory University along with its affiliated hospitals. Typical of affluent university towns, there was the usual abundance of parks and 'soft' recreational facilities. Generally, a quiet place to live. A studious place to live. It was away from the hustle and bustle of Atlanta.

In addition to the university, it had one other major employer.

The Centers for Disease Control.

The CDC employed 15,000 dedicated people, but only about 5,000 of those at its headquarters in the Druid Hills. The rest were scattered across the country. It was formed in 1946, and was the leading national public health institute in the United States. A federal agency, it was established with the main goal in mind of protecting public health and safety through the control and prevention of disease, injury and disability.

One of its main target areas was the research, understanding, and annihilation of infectious diseases in the United States and around the world. The CDC had performed crucial roles in outbreaks of SARS, Ebola, and virtually every other scary epidemic or potential pandemic that had hit the newswires in the last half-century.

Of particular concern now to the CDC was the emergence of antibiotic-resistant bacterial infections, an ominous trend that put the world on a path towards a drastic change in health management, and perhaps in lifespan expectations.

The CDC maintained extreme vigilance against diseases entering the United States from other countries, so easily accomplished these days with global travel being so prevalent. Infections alien to America could be deadly, due to the lack of natural resistance and known drug preventions or cures.

No doubt, the CDC was one of the world's most crucial organizations, and they had their hands full with challenges that no one anticipated decades ago, when it was established.

Dedicated people, busy at their jobs—too busy perhaps to be aware that another, more obscure organization, was operating right under their noses.

It hadn't always been there. It was an organization that was formed only a year after the CDC, and had headquarters that were fairly fluid up until just a few years ago. It was formed under the orders of the President of the United States, Harry Truman, back in 1947. Formed after a famous event that had left the world scratching their heads in wonder and mystery.

That famous event prompted the formation of this shadowy organization, and 'shadowy' was a good word for it. It operated entirely in the shadows. Literally and figuratively.

Its base of operations was deep in the bowels of CDC headquarters—in a level of the basement structure that most CDC employees probably didn't even know existed. All of the elevators went officially down to basement level one. But, there was one more level; a level that only a select group of people with special magnetic cards could access. A level that could only be reached by one particular elevator. An elevator that, for everyone else in the building, was always 'out of order.'

No one puzzled over that—they were far too busy.

The headquarters for this organization had a suite of plush offices, a large meeting room, a lunchroom, a fully-equipped lounge, a small gym with hot tub and sauna, and a state of the art medical lab and clinic. There were no windows though, because this was, of course, just a basement.

Technology was present as well, in abundance, with capabilities that would rival the Pentagon.

Which was no coincidence, because this organization reported to one senior official at the Pentagon, and no one else. Not even the president had access to what this shadowy outfit did. Its budget was buried within the billions assigned to the Pentagon, and easily filtered beyond prying eyes.

Even though a sitting president had ordered this organization to be established back in 1947, the Executive Office involvement had long since ceased. It was just a rumour now, an urban legend. And, it was best kept that way, for the good of America. Sometimes, secrecy was essential, and sometimes things had to happen without hindrance and political meanderings.

It was a government within a government. It had power beyond belief, and pulled the strings masterfully within its narrow mandate.

It had power, for sure, even in the name of its current head, Chad Powers.

He was an imposing figure, standing six and a half feet tall, and weighing 250 pounds, give or take. His heritage was a long line of defense contractors, going all the way back to WWI.

Chad stood at the head of the granite table in the elegant meeting room. A serious table, with only twelve chairs. It would never ever have more than twelve chairs. Because, for secret societies like this one, tradition was paramount.

Chad took a headcount, and then sat down in his leather chair with its padded armrests. He glanced around the table, nodding at several of his favorites and deliberately ignoring the ones who always tended to annoy him.

All of the people around the table served out of entitlement. And, every single one of them could trace their heritage back to the inaugural twelve who were appointed back in 1947. None of them were outsiders. It was like royalty. They served out of entitlement and birth.

Membership had been passed down over the decades from family member to trusted family member.

They were all princes and princesses in the true sense of the words, and none of them could ever be fired.

The bylaws and traditions of the organization forbade that. And, traditions were important. The United Kingdom and the Netherlands were based on tradition. Ruling families still had more power than most people realized. America may have gained its independence from England back in the 1700s, but, if truth be known, it still believed in those cherished traditions that the country had pretended to cast aside.

The members of the board served until they decided their competency was in question, and then passed their crowns down to the next groomed and designated family member.

No one could be fired. But, they could be killed. happened on many an occasion. When it did, tradition took New 'royalty' had to be introduced, which took a while for eve used to.

But, being pragmatists, they accepted it. It was just reality. There had to be 'escape' clauses, even with royalty. And, each of them around the table knew that 'escape' clauses had been used time and time again in England over the centuries, too. America should be no different.

They all came from crucially patriotic American backgrounds: defense contractors, aircraft manufacturers, chemicals, oil and gas, pharmaceuticals, hotel chains, auto manufacturers, the military elite. The list of backgrounds was extensive, and they were all rich as sin. That was mandatory. It was also mandatory that never, ever, would a politician sit at that table. This was not a political group; the entire purpose of the group was to do what was right without the interference of children playing in sandboxes.

Chad started the meeting with his usual two-finger salute to the group.

Tapping his right temple, he announced, "I'll call this meeting to order. We'll break for lunch at noon and relax in the lounge after we adjourn, for informal discussions. We do have a busy agenda today, so our lounge discussions will be a good way to unwind.

"The first order of business is this disturbing episode in Canada." He directed his stern gaze at a woman named Allison Fisher, the youngish matriarch of one of the world's largest hotel chains.

"Allison, you're our Canadian expert and designate, and you also have some hotels up there. You were supposed to be on top of this loose thread. It's gone rogue on us. Give us your report, and make it concise."

Allison cleared her throat and began to speak, clearly and concisely.

Chad listened carefully as he glanced around the table at the twelve regal members. He smiled inwardly. Chat didn't like some of them, but they all had the 'right stuff,' and that's all he really cared about. And, they all had their own private armies that also worked in the shadows, armies that carried out orders without knowing where those orders came from.

There was nothing they couldn't do.

They all had their separate and diverse personalities, their 'day jobs,' their occupations. And, they all, of course, had their own individual names which carried unrivalled prestige and influence.

But, collectively, they were simply known as 'Majestic 12,' and had been since 1947.

CHAPTER 6

"So, in closing, keep your wits about you. It's tourist season, and there's bound to be trouble here and there. We're a small community and a small police force, but we're known for tolerance and peace. And, I think we've done a great job of keeping the peace, and keeping this great little city safe. It's tempting at times to treat trouble-making transients with a heavy hand, but we have to be careful to make sure the punishment fits the crime."

A young officer raised his hand from the back of the briefing room.

"Yes, Mike?"

"Chief, I think some people passing through here during the summer take our friendly attitudes for granted. They push the envelope with drugs and some of the bar violence. Puts us in a difficult position."

Wyatt nodded. "I understand. It's a fine balance, Mike. Use your best judgement and, if you're not sure, bring me in on it. I'm on call 24/7, you all know that. We're not New York City where the police chief is usually inaccessible. I'm just one of you."

A female officer, Linda Harkins, jumped in. "Are we still expected to look the other way on drugs?"

Wyatt shook his head. "We've never looked the other way, Linda. We just choose not to sweat the small stuff. We always let the violators know that we know what they're doing, and we reserve the right to arrest them if they let it get out of hand, give drugs to kids, or blatantly sell drugs on the street or in public places. And, when I say 'small stuff,' I mean grass and hash. I don't really give a shit if someone's smoking a joint or a pipe, as long as they're not dealing and as long as they don't do it right in our faces. But, for any drugs stronger than that, we have zero tolerance. Clear?"

Linda nodded, but then raised her hand again.

Wyatt sighed. "Linda, Linda, I haven't had my eighth cup of coffee yet. I don't know if I'm up to more interrogation."

Linda laughed. "Chief, just one more question and then I'll pour you a coffee myself. What's our position on the dog ban in downtown for this summer?"

Wyatt shook his head. "One of the stupidest laws ever passed in this city. You have my permission to ignore it, and just give polite warnings. No tickets. I'm still working with city council to try to change that draconian piece of legislation."

He noticed all the heads in the audience nodding. No one liked that law. He added one more point. "Just make sure dog owners pick up the poop, though. You're allowed, and encouraged, to ticket them for not doing that."

Snickers all around.

"Okay, folks, hit the streets. And, as they used to say on *Hill Street Blues*, 'be careful out there.'"

One of the officers laughed. "*Hill Street Blues?* Chief, are you really that old?"

Wyatt made a face. "No, I only heard about that show through the grapevine. Now, get outta here before I throw you in a cell for insubordination and disrespecting your elders!"

The group of almost two dozen police officers and dispatchers laughed and headed out to the parking lot. Wyatt loved them all—he had a great group of officers. Dedicated and motivated. He knew his style as police chief probably helped make them the way they were. They all respected him, enjoyed his laid-back approach to policing, but knew also that he could be as tough as nails when he needed to be.

He became somewhat of a hero around town two years ago during an attempted bank robbery in the downtown area. Violence was rare in Nelson, so when it occurred it was a shock to the city's nerve center.

Wyatt happened to be in the bank at the time, just withdrawing money like a regular customer, dressed in civilian clothes like he usually was.

Two men had rushed in, guns drawn, clearly high on drugs. Wyatt could tell by the craziness in their eyes and the frenetically nervous measure of their movements. He guessed crack cocaine.

He could also tell by the way one of them whirled around in panic and fired twice into the chest of an old woman who'd simply dropped her plastic coffee mug.

Wyatt's pistol was in his hands in an instant, and a second later the gunman was dead. His partner, who'd been standing on the ledge of a teller's counter, fired wildly at Wyatt just as he was diving to the floor. Wyatt rolled several times as the punk kept firing, ceramic dust kicking up from the bank's newly tiled floor. After his third roll, Wyatt aimed upwards and fired, sending the thug to bank robber hell.

That fateful morning, within the span of only one minute, three people were dead. Wyatt knew, as did everyone else on the police force, that shit could happen within an instant. A damn instant. So, no one took his relaxed style for granted—they knew he could kill and they knew he was probably the bravest man in the city. But, he led by example, not by anger or demands.

Everyone also knew his background. He had been living in Nelson out of choice, for ten full years now. Glad to be back in his hometown. Glad to have left his life in the RCMP behind. He'd achieved the rank of Inspector, and had performed a pivotal role heading up the anti-terrorism task force in Toronto for several years. Foiling more plots than the public ever knew. Canada was a bit different than the U.S. in that way—secrecy was maintained, unless the public was still in danger. In America, every silly little plot uncovered was broadcast to the mass media, and Wyatt figured the only reason they did that was to ensure that budgets were maintained or increased, or because they needed to ramp up the fear level.

The RCMP always showed more class...and more modesty. The Mounties were usually just content to be the silent, invisible heroes, keeping Canada safe from behind the scenes.

Wyatt had loved his career with the Mounties, Canada's equivalent of the FBI. But, it had been time to come home, time to live a different lifestyle, one that was more peaceful and fulfilling.

And, while he wasn't one to ever run away from anything, his move back to Nelson was the one exception.

He'd had his heart broken back in Toronto. His fiancé died of complications from brain cancer. She was five months pregnant when she passed away, and the baby was far too premature to be saved. It was a girl.

He had no choice but to leave Toronto behind for his own sanity. Too many memories. Too much sadness.

Ten years now, and no one had re-entered his life. Wyatt wasn't carrying a torch anymore—he just hadn't met anyone who'd captured his heart again. He knew that would be a tall order.

Wyatt wiped away a stubborn tear and headed down the long hallway to his corner office. He seldom cried anymore; he'd done enough of that over the years. But, once in a while one or two tears made their appearance with very little warning.

He smiled and nodded to his secretary before entering his office. Susan smiled back at him.

"How did the meeting go?"

"Good. Typical Monday morning session. Some good questions. Everyone's ready and willing to take on the hordes."

She giggled. "You mean the hordes of shoplifters?"

"Yes, Susan. We should thank our lucky stars, huh?"

"For sure. By the way, your dad called."

"Oh, good. It's about time."

Susan stood up and walked over to the coffee machine. "Why don't you get settled in, and I'll bring you a coffee? You can sip it while talking to your dad."

"I think I'll need a whisky for that conversation."

"Why? What's wrong?"

"Oh, he's been avoiding me for a couple of weeks, that's all."

"Arrest him, then."

Wyatt laughed. "Good idea. I should!"

He walked into his office and sat down behind his massive desk. Piles of files awaited his attention, but Wyatt knew that most of them were crime notices from other police forces across Canada, and some from the FBI. Just alerts, people and things to be on the lookout for. There were also a few files pertaining to budget issues and the usual political stuff that came with being the Chief of Police of a small city. Issues that every police chief had to deal with, but were much more prevalent in a small center where every other municipal official was working only part-time.

Wyatt was one of the few full-time municipal officers. The mayor was busy most of the time running his hardware store, squeezing in only a few hours a week to bang the gavel. All of the city councillors were either real estate agents or restauranteurs. And, the city manager ran a karate studio, and grew a little hemp on the side.

Wyatt picked up the phone and dialed the familiar number.

The stubborn old man answered on the first ring.

"Hello?"

"Dad, it's me. Returning your call."

"Well, I guess I was returning your many calls."

"Yes, glad you acknowledge that. Why have you been ignoring me?"

"Because…well, just because."

"That's not much of a reason, Dad. I was shocked about what I saw in your studio, and you owe me an explanation for that...that thing. I'm your son, for God's sake."

"I know, I know...but I warned you not to lift that tarp. You invaded my privacy."

"Oh, knock it off, Dad. There's no privacy when it comes to family. If you can't trust family, you can't trust anyone."

Susan came in with a steaming hot cup of coffee. Wyatt nodded his thanks, and then asked her to close his door.

"What was that?"

"Nothing, Dad. Just talking to my secretary."

"Oh."

Wyatt took a long sip and then spoke softly into the phone. "Dad, I wouldn't have been so shocked if that sculpture, which you built many years ago, didn't mimic what just happened to you. Surely you understand that."

"Just a coincidence."

"Do you think I'm stupid?"

"No. But, that isn't why I called you back."

"Okay, so why indeed did you call me back?"

"I have good news. I think city council is going to approve the permanent mounting of my draft-dodger sculpture."

"What? That's fantastic news, Dad! How did this happen? I thought it was a dead issue."

"Well, I got a call from the mayor. The city may get a new hotel. One of the biggest luxury resort chains, Diamond Hotels International. They have hotels all over the world, and in Canada they have them in Vancouver, Toronto, and Montreal. But, they're branching out now into exclusive mountain resort locations, building smaller boutique hotels. They've chosen Nelson as one of those locations."

"I hadn't heard about this. That's incredible news for the city. But, what does this have to do with your sculpture?"

"Well, this is the best part. My sculpture got written up in a couple of art digest magazines over the last few months, along with photos and stuff like that. This hotel chain got wind of it. They're based in the U.S. and they think that the sculpture would be a unique addition to their hotel, considering so many years have gone by since the Vietnam war and it's not as sensitive an issue now as it was a few decades ago. They think it would be a great marketing gimmick, recognizing the unique heritage of

Nelson as it relates to the American draft-dodgers. Might attract a lot of U.S. tourists."

Wyatt shook his head in amazement. "Gotta hand it to those yanks, huh? They sure know how to market, and don't hesitate to pounce on opportunities. So, where do things go from here?"

"Their CEO is flying up here next week to scout out sites for the hotel. She also wants to meet with the mayor and me. And, wants to see the sculpture in person."

"I'm so happy for you, Dad. This is going to make you feel so appreciated, and it'll be an incredible tribute to all the ex-pat Americans living here. Such a great sense of pride, eh?"

"It is, it is!"

Wyatt could hear the excitement in his dad's voice. It sent nice goosebumps up his back.

"Maybe you can draw me into the discussions, too, Dad. This is so exciting; I would love to meet her."

He heard the phone at the other end clunk onto a table, then the shuffling of some papers. After a few seconds, Willy was back. "I'll arrange that, Wyatt. I'm sure she'd love to meet the Chief of Police. I found her name in my notes. It's…Allison Fisher."

"Great—let me know a date and time. And…I'm not letting you off the hook on that explanation you owe me, though. So, think about that in the meantime."

CHAPTER 7

He jerked bolt upright in bed.

And, just sat there, staring straight ahead at the bedroom door.

He could hear his wife breathing softly beside him, but he didn't look down at her. Instead, he was held spellbound by a light—a strangely soothing light. It wasn't a table lamp, or a headlight from a car shining through the window. More like a glow. A glow that surrounded his body like a halo...or a shield.

It was a hot night, and Willy was wearing only his underwear. He knew he wasn't dreaming, because he was fully alert. Or, at least if he was indeed dreaming, he was alert within the dream itself.

He reached over to the night table and picked up his watch, the face of it illuminated clearly by the glow emanating from his hands. Three in the morning. He knew he'd gone to bed around 10:00. What woke him? The glow?

Willy rubbed his front teeth—suddenly they hurt like hell. He never had dental problems, so what was this all about?

The glow was getting brighter now, and he was afraid that Helen might wake up. He shoved the sheet aside and eased his feet down to the cool hardwood floor. He walked out onto the landing, down the stairs, and into the kitchen. He splashed some water on his face, and then immediately turned around and headed out the back door, pulling his studio keys off the hook on his way out.

He had no idea why he was doing this in the middle of the night. He just knew that he had to.

Willy opened the door and went into the dark studio. He flicked on the lights and went over to a large block of granite that was sitting in a corner.

Looking down at his half-naked body, he could see that the glow of light had dissipated, but he was mildly surprised to see that his skin was once again transparent. It had come back.

He rationalized that the CAT scan must have triggered something, something that wasn't as simple as just the temporary reaction he'd had at the hospital. Almost like 'muscle memory,' his body itself had a memory—a memory of something that happened sixty-five years ago, and it wasn't going to forget all that easily.

At that moment, in his studio, Willy resembled a skeleton once again. It didn't scare him as much as it had a couple of weeks ago in the hospital. In fact, even that time hadn't frighten him all that much, not like it had when the weird phenomenon happened to him in Korea. He had been warned then that it could happen again, but he'd stupidly ignored the warning.

In the hospital, he'd been more horrified than scared. Horrified that other people had now seen him in that state, particularly Helen and Wyatt.

Back in November, 1950, at the American hospital in Seoul, South Korea, he and his four men had been examined thoroughly. They'd been transferred there by helicopter from the MASH unit in the field. Doctors were puzzled, and with good reason. Medical schools didn't train them for this.

But, after a few days, other doctors arrived—ones that did seem to have some training in this, or at least some understanding. That was the impression that Willy and his comrades had. They were a very serious medical crew—didn't talk very much. Just probed a lot, stuck needles in them, and injected them with some kind of dye. Then, the soldiers were subjected to radiation, as the doctors studiously watched on a monitor as the dye seeped through their veins.

The transparency condition had subsided by the time they'd arrived in Seoul, but it came back again. Willy got the impression that was exactly what the doctors wanted. The low levels of radiation they were being subjected to brought it back.

After several days of tests and observation, the five of them were taken to a conference room. Already seated around the table were three doctors and four senior officers of the United States Marines. One was a general and the other three were colonels.

They asked them how they were feeling and made notes. There was very little compassion or regret for what had happened to them. It was more just clinical—very official, very businesslike, very 'military.'

The general finally spoke, and he was the last person in the room to speak before the five soldiers were dismissed and cleared for action back in the field again.

He told them what to expect. Willy had no idea how he seemed to know what they could expect, but it dawned on him that this had happened before. They'd seen this before, somewhere, sometime. The man knew what he was talking about. There was no hesitation, no doubts, and no 'maybes.'

He spoke slowly and deliberately, looking them in the eyes, moving his gaze from one to the other.

"You have each been subjected to the power of a very unique infiltration weapon. It was from an enemy force that has injected itself into this war, and it's a weapon that we have no defense against.

"Please be assured that you will suffer no ill effects on your quality of life. We can't help you any more than we already have, but you are not in any danger. That's the first thing you need to know. The weapon does not seem to have had the intent of killing, it was more likely designed to warn us, scare us, and intimidate us. Or, perhaps, this enemy didn't really know what effect it would have."

Willy raised his hand respectfully, indicating that he wanted to ask a question. The general raised his hand, too, palm facing forward, indicating that he wanted Willy to shut up.

"No questions will be allowed. You will each just listen and be silent.

"This weapon infiltrated your bodies and changed your genetic structure. It was not radiation that you were subjected to, be rest assured of that. However, radiation seems to be what will set off reactions. The infiltration has a defense mechanism, almost like antibodies.

"As you know, when you get sick, your body produces antibodies to fight off infections. In this case, with what has infiltrated your bodies, radiation poisoning triggers a reaction similar to an antibody reaction. Your body fights off the radiation, and the extremely gruesome reaction it produces is the end result of the defense mechanism. Think of it almost like swelling—when you get swollen glands, that's simply the antibodies that are fighting the infection in your glands. The antibodies cause the swelling, just as they also cause fever when you're sick.

"In your cases, transparency and the glow surrounding your bodies was the symptom of the defense mechanism working. It seems as if this extreme reaction is only triggered by radiation. Other infections in your bodies do not trigger this at all.

"Over the last few days, we have introduced certain bacterial infections to your bodies. You weren't aware of this, because nothing happened to you. You didn't swell, you didn't get fevers, and you didn't vomit. This is because your antibodies weren't

working. They no longer need to work for normal everyday illnesses. You have a silent defense mechanism in your bodies now which kills infections virtually instantaneously.

'The only time this defense system seems to not be so silent is when you are exposed to radiation. That, and only that, triggers an extreme reaction such as what you have seen.

'This may be confusing to you—because I started out by saying that this weapon did not use radiation against you. I assure you, it didn't.

'What happened is similar to what happens when you first get a polio vaccine. You have a slight reaction, maybe a swelling in your arm or a small fever. Then, those symptoms fade, and you are protected for life. This infiltration weapon caused similar symptoms—which have now faded. We triggered them again just to test the radiation theory, but other than that you have no lingering effects from the weapon. Basically, you were 'vaccinated' in that culvert in North Korea.

'We don't know if that was the enemy's intended outcome with this infiltration weapon. As I said, they may not have known what the weapon would do. But, that seems to be the outcome, and you now have it with you for the rest of your lives.

'There are a few other things you should know. We predict that there will be a 'fountain of youth' element with this infiltration. Your bones will remain strong and will resist the normal weakening that comes with age. You won't get arthritis and you won't suffer loss of bone density like the rest of us will.

'More remarkable than that, though, is that your muscular system will undergo incredible strength bolstering. We'll call it 'Hero Syndrome' for lack of a better phrase. You will find that, as the years go by, your strength will increase. But, it won't be the same for each of you. It all depends on your original genetic structure. As I said, it's been altered now, but by how much depends on your baseline when you were born.

'There are some more things that you need to know. Your teeth will be incredibly durable, and you will also never go bald. You may, unfortunately, have already noticed some rawness on your tongues. That will keep getting worse...until it doesn't anymore. But, you will be left with scaly tongues. That is something that will not revert.

'You each may find that certain talents will become noticeable, talents that you never had before and never would have imagined. It could be anything at all—mathematical prowess, or musical skills. Artistic tendencies, or athletic excellence. Or...there may be nothing at all. Again, it very much depends on your original DNA ladder.

'Listen to me carefully, now.

'You must never breathe a word of this to anyone. You must hide these side effects and never, ever, allow yourselves to be exposed to x-rays. You'll never need them anyway, so it would be a moot point for you to even undergo an x-ray.

'Mr. Carson, you're an officer, so we can trust that you'll exercise your obligations in this regard. You other men are not currently officers, but because of what you have

endured, we are elevating the ranks of each of you to lieutenant, effective immediately.

"In addition, in recognition of your brave service and for what you have experienced, we are depositing one hundred thousand dollars, in each of your names, into Swiss bank accounts. You will not be able to draw from these accounts until the turn of the new century; so, the year 2000. Worth waiting for, and worth remaining silent for.

"And, even by then, you will be restricted to no more than ten percent each year until death. Upon death, the funds will be collapsed and credited to your estates. You will be given the numbers to your accounts once you complete your tours of duty here in Korea, and the original principal and interest will be given a special exemption from income tax.

"I must warn you that any disclosure of what has happened and what has been discussed in this room will invalidate the monetary agreement we have made with you. If you respect your obligations, we will honor ours to you. You are each university graduates—I don't have to tell you what a hundred thousand today will be worth after being invested conservatively for fifty years. Do the math yourselves."

Willy did indeed do the math. He gasped—it would be worth about four million by the year 2000.

The general stood, signalling that the meeting was over. Willy and his comrades got to their feet as well, stood at attention, and raised their right hands in salute.

The general saluted them back. "Gentleman, I'm sorry about what has happened to you. But, it isn't all bad, is it? Let me just remind you of one thing. Your genetic makeup has been altered permanently. If you haven't already sired children, I don't have to tell you that your new genes will be passed on in varying degrees once you do propagate. That depends very much on the priority of the mother's genes, compared with yours. Nature is unpredictable."

Willy snapped out of his daze and found himself standing at his workbench, fingering his powerful rock saw. He plugged in the extension cord, pulled on his goggles, hefted the saw over his shoulder, walked over to the chunk of granite sitting on the floor in the corner, and turned on the machine. With the skill of the incredible artist that he was, he began to create. He didn't know what he was creating, his hands just moved the saw in cadence with the signals coming from his brain.

As he worked, he once again thought back to that day sixty-five years ago.

And, to three years later when he'd returned stateside after the war.

A time when he'd discovered he had a talent for art, sculpture in particular. Despite having struggled with silly little paper cut-outs or playdough in grade school, he had suddenly developed the ability to create incredible sculptures of virtually anything—but, particularly, the human body.

He also thought back to one horrific day when there had been an accident on the freeway. Not thinking, he'd pulled his car over onto the soft shoulder and proceeded to lift the rear bumper of a Volkswagen three feet in the air, high enough for other rescuers to drag the mangled body of a little girl out from under the rear left wheel.

Willy glanced at his watch. A couple of hours had gone by, and his skin had now returned to normal. The glow had completely disappeared as well.

All that was left of the night was a beautiful piece of granite now carved into the shape of a perfect sphere. Well, except for the base.

He knelt on the floor and, with both hands, easily rolled the heavy granite onto its side. The saw whirred one more time and he proceeded to shape the bottom of the chunk of granite to complete the effect.

It was now a perfectly shaped ball, and he had no idea why he'd done this or what it was supposed to be. Except…a ball. A massive, heavy ball.

Willy Carson unplugged his saw, removed his goggles, and put them back on the workbench.

His final sobering thought before heading back into the house to rejoin his lovely wife Helen in bed, was to remember back to that romantic night forty-six years ago when their wonderful son, Wyatt, was conceived.

CHAPTER 8

The drive from O'Hare was always frustrating, but more so today than usual. Not only was it raining, but the traffic was horrendous despite being several hours before rush hour would even begin.

She steered her Audi R8 onto an off-ramp, deciding she'd had enough. Side streets would have to suffice until she reached her home in the Trump Tower.

Wabash Avenue seemed worlds away at this point, but she knew that on the back avenues her car would at least be moving, giving her the feeling of accomplishing something. It might take her just as long to get there, but in her mind she wouldn't be so frustrated.

It was bad enough that the flight from Atlanta International was both turbulent and late, but then the landing in Chicago was rough enough to tear the trunk off an elephant. Now, this infernal traffic. Some days everything went wrong—and, if it started out that way, it usually just continued that way.

She zoomed her sleek sports car down a back alley, then onto a street she didn't recognize, but didn't care either. All she knew was that she was heading in the right direction because she could see the iconic Trump Tower off in the distance. It looked like she could almost spit to it.

The powerful engine revved as she beat it through a yellow 'caution' light and sped along the next block.

Then, she heard it.

Just a quick burst of the siren, but enough to let her know that her day was going to suddenly get a lot worse. She'd been going at least twenty miles over the limit, and there would probably be no mercy. Especially considering who she was, and what she was driving.

She pulled off to the side and the police car slid in behind her. Looking in her rear-view mirror, she saw him sitting there, talking on his radio, and punching 'sweet nothings' into his dashboard computer.

Then, he was just there, rapping on her window. She rolled it down and smiled demurely at the young officer.

The smile worked for most things, but she felt silly doing it today. It felt too obvious…and phony, and even kinda cheap. But, she did it anyway.

It wasn't the inevitable fine that bothered her, it was the demerits against her driver's license. She already had a few and couldn't afford any more or she'd be walking or cabbing it everywhere. Or, heaven forbid, public transit.

She could tell that the officer was a bit flustered—her smile usually did that to people.

It wasn't necessarily the smile, but more the eyes. Her eyes were the most piercing blue color anyone could imagine, and it sometimes just caught people totally by surprise. They were so blue, they almost looked fake.

And, with the dress she was wearing, her shoulders were exposed, displaying what she thought was a beautiful greeny-blue rose tattoo. Very tasteful, and very striking. Even though some of her closest friends told her it looked more like a cabbage than a rose, she didn't care. It stood out from the crowd and that was important. Not being 'ordinary' was important in this world full of conformists. At least in her opinion it was important.

"Ma'am, could I see your driver's license and registration, please?"

She already had them out of her purse and handed them to him.

"No problem, officer. I'm so sorry…and so guilty. I've had a hell of a day. Rough flight in, scream-worthy traffic, and I just want to get home."

The young man smiled, and pointed to the east. "Home's not too far away for you, I can see by your address."

"Yes, at least as the crow flies. But, about four more hours at this rate."

His face had a broad grin on it now, a silly *Mad Magazine* kind of grin.

He then looked down at her driver's license. "I have to ask you the official question. Is your name Allison Fisher, and do you still live at Trump Tower, 401 North Wabash Avenue, Chicago?"

"Yes, officer, that's me alright."

The grin came back across his baby face.

"You own Diamond Hotels, don't you?"

Allison nodded slowly, a bit suspicious about his seeming obsession with who she was, more than about what she'd done. He must know already that she had several demerit points against her. Was this going to be a shakedown?

"Yes, officer. If you could just write out the ticket, I'll be on my way. As you could tell, I was in a bit of a hurry and still am."

He handed her documents back to her.

"You're free to go, Ms. Fisher. Just slow it down a bit, okay?"

Allison was shocked. If anyone deserved a ticket, it was her. Speeding along a residential street, and a repeat offender at that.

"Well…thank you. I didn't expect this. You're so kind."

"If I gave you a ticket, ma'am, you'd lose your license for a while. Your record is really bad, you know."

"I know it is. Oh, you're just too kind."

"No, you're the kind one, ma'am. My father is the doorman at Trump Tower. He talks about you all the time. How you're the only one who actually gives him the time of day. And, that night last year when my mom was rushed to the hospital, and you drove my dad there yourself and stayed with him. He never forgot that…and neither did I. I was hoping I'd meet you one day, so this is just one of those nice coincidences."

"George? George Nichols is your father?"

He nodded, still with that goofy smile on his face. But, now his smile meant a lot more to Allison than it had just a few minutes ago.

"What's your name, son?"

"I'm Frank."

She slipped her hand through the window. "Pleased to meet you, Frank. And, your father is one of the kindliest, most gentlemanly men I've ever met."

He shook her slender hand. "Thank you, ma'am. He is a great guy, isn't he?"

"Do you have a girlfriend, or wife, Frank?"

"A girlfriend, ma'am."

"Why don't you take her out for a nice dinner on me at Trump's restaurant in my building? Called '*Sixteen*,' and it's one of the best in Chicago. Just give my name and it will be my pleasure."

Frank shook his head. "Oh, no, ma'am. I couldn't do that. It wouldn't be right. But, thanks."

Allison realized all of a sudden what she'd done. Insulted his integrity as a police officer, an officer who was letting her off from a big fine and possible loss of license. Of course he couldn't accept. She was just so accustomed to thrusting out favors to people, she didn't even think.

"I'm so sorry, Frank. That wasn't the right thing for me to say. I was just so thankful, and overjoyed to hear that you're George's son. Please accept my apology. That was very improper."

He tipped his cap. "No problem at all, Ms. Fisher. It was a pleasure to meet you, a real pleasure. Please drive carefully." Then, he was gone.

Allison waited until the cruiser drove away, then she pulled slowly out from the curb and moved at a responsible speed the rest of the way home.

It took her another hour to get there, but she sighed in relief when she finally pulled up out front, only to be greeted by George himself, who took her keys and tossed them to the valet.

Allison threw her arms around George and gave him a big kiss on the cheek. Then, she pulled back and looked into his grandfatherly eyes.

"I met your son, Frank, today. He let me off on a speeding ticket. Such a wonderful and polite young man, just like his dad. Even the 'young' part."

George smiled. "Well, it is a small world, isn't it? Yes, I'm proud of him and he was probably real thrilled to meet you. I talk about you all the time."

Allison laughed. "He told me that. George, do you have a crush on me?"

"Yes, but don't you dare tell my wife!"

"I wouldn't think of it. She's such a lucky woman."

"Speaking of lucky, when on earth are you going to get lucky?"

"George!" Allison slapped him playfully on the shoulder. "How do you know I'm not getting lucky?"

"Because I'm the doorman. I know everything."

"Maybe I'm sneaking out, instead of sneaking men in. Have you ever considered that?"

"No. You're not a cheap thrills kind of lady. I'm talking about a real romance, Allison, someone for you to fall in love with."

Allison's eyes dropped and she stared at the sidewalk. "Well, it's tough. And, you're right, it's been five years now, so it's about time. But, it's... tough."

George leaned in and planted a gentle kiss on her forehead. "I'm sorry. I've made you sad. It'll happen in good time. Just don't work so much—give yourself time for yourself. And...I reserve the right to interrogate the guy before you marry him, okay? Deal?"

She lifted her eyes and smiled. "For sure, you will definitely be the one I'll turn to. You'll probably scare him away, but I wouldn't trust anyone more than you."

Allison gave George a little wave and headed towards the front door.

She stopped and glanced back. He was still standing on the sidewalk, watching her.

"Well? Aren't you going to do your damn job and open the door for me?"

* * * * *

Trump Tower was a ninety-eight storey behemoth, towering in spectacular fashion over the Chicago skyline. It was the sixteenth tallest building in the world, and fourth tallest in the United States.

But, the tallest building in America was actually the building where Allison worked—the Willis Tower, at 108 stories. The head office of the company she and her brother owned, Diamond Hotels International, took up four floors in that iconic building, which at one time had been famously known as the Sears Tower.

Her apartment in the Trump Tower was on the ninetieth floor, and was a luxurious 3,000 square feet. More space than she needed, but for her it was soothing to have room to wander around.

And, she did a lot of that—she didn't sleep very well, or very often. Many a night would find her wandering back and forth between her three bedrooms, the kitchen, the living room, the study, the gym—and then inevitably just lying down on the floor, head propped up in her hand, looking out at the view.

And the view was magnificent. Floor to ceiling windows, looking down over the Chicago River and the entry to the massive body of water known as Lake Michigan.

Allison knew Donald Trump personally. Well, of course she did. Donald knew everyone who mattered, and with her hotel chain being one of the world's largest, he had made a point of knowing her. And, making sure that everyone in the world knew that he knew her.

She didn't mind. And, she actually didn't even mind Donald. Sure, he had an ego, but that was also part of his persona, his act. He was a showman, and a lot of what he did, he did with his tongue firmly planted in his cheek.

Allison hadn't seen him much lately, though. Ever since he'd launched his presidential bid, he didn't visit Chicago very much any more.

She had to hand it to him though—this Trump Tower was one of the most magnificent structures in the world. Just to look at it from the street was an eye candy experience.

It gave the impression of being solid glass, with three setback features that matched with surrounding buildings. The effect on the eyes was one of pure splendor, and it was a building that was hard to move your eyes from. When Donald did something, he did it right. People may find reasons to criticize him, but they would be hard pressed to deny his sense of creation. And, his power to simply make things happen.

Allison enjoyed living there—it was close to the Willis Tower, so she didn't spend her whole day commuting to work and back. And, it was convenient to everything.

Because of who she was, most people assumed that she was into the typical billionaire lifestyle. But, she wasn't. She had inherited this. It wasn't her choice. It just…happened.

She would have preferred to be running along the Chicago River pathway right now, but was far too tired. She also wanted to cook something nice, but was too tired for that, too.

She'd probably just order a pizza.

Allison Fisher walked over to her telescope and adjusted the view. Closed in on her office in the Willis Tower, glad that for now she wasn't there. Tonight, she'd take a good look at the sky. That's how she liked to spend her evenings, scanning the heavens. Most people would be surprised to learn that she didn't spend her nights in the clubs.

Allison Fisher was an astrophysicist.

Masquerading as an hotelier.

The masquerade had started five years ago. Allison was working as an astronomer at the Jet Propulsion Laboratory, enjoying what she did, but not making very much money at it. The big money was in the family business, the hotel business. But, she'd shunned that in favor of following her heart and her passion at the JPL.

Her younger brother, Robert, had joined their dad and mom, but he wasn't the favored one. Her dad, also named Robert, found him a job on the executive floor, but the one he really wanted to be there was Allison. Robert didn't have the same brainpower, the same 'can do' attitude. A nice guy, but not heavily endowed with gray cells.

Allison had married her high school sweetheart. A graduate of the Wharton School of Business—coincidentally the same school Trump had attended—and an absolute marketing whiz. He joined the family business in her place, and understood why Allison wanted no part of it. Jack was just that kind of guy—understanding, considerate, kind, and she'd loved him with all of her heart.

But, Allison just wanted to be up in the stars. Not hanging around boardrooms.

It happened five years ago…

She was attending a conference in Seattle, and her parents and Jack were attending a hotel opening down in Los Angeles. They had decided to drive up and join her in Seattle, and from there the plan was to cross the border into Canada and do the Rocky Mountain trek.

They never got that far.

On the coastal highway in Oregon, they drove off a cliff. The police suspected that her father had fallen asleep at the wheel. But, there wasn't much left of anything to be able to determine what the cause had really been. It didn't matter. Her father, mother, and beloved hubby were all dead. All gone in the blink of an eye.

Allison and her brother, Robert, became instant owners of one of the most famous and luxurious hotel chains in the world.

She'd lost not only the absolute love of her life, but also her dynamic and caring parents, whom she'd cherished more than life itself.

But, Allison inherited more than just a hotel chain. She also inherited a sacred trust, and by default became a member of a secret society.

The Majestic 12.

Not that she wanted it any more than she wanted the hotel chain. It was an obligation. And, one that she had no choice but to honor, because it was an obligation thrust upon her by her father.

She had been groomed to be his replacement, a post she knew she'd have to assume eventually. If her dad ever developed dementia and was declared unfit, or when he eventually died of old age.

He'd just died earlier than anyone had ever expected.

Allison learned about Majestic 12 at a fairly young age. Her dad had spent weeks with her, explaining how it had started and why it had started. How her grandfather was one of the founding members, one of the original twelve. And, how, when he died, the baton had been passed to her father.

And, now, the baton had passed to her.

Allison was thirty-eight years old now and rich beyond her wildest dreams.

And, privy to secrets that any conspiracy theorist would kill to be privy to.

In one respect, she was honored to be a part of such an elite group. And, the cause, for the most part, was a noble one.

In another respect, it made her feel dirty. Made her feel like she was cheating the world and all its naïve beings who thought that everything was just hunky dory.

That dirty feeling had come to her today, looking into the eyes of Frank, the boyish police officer. Him doing her a favor just because he was a nice guy, and because he thought she was a nice lady.

And, then, she had that feeling again when George kissed her on the forehead. George who cared about everyone else more than himself. Cared that Allison found the right man, wanted her to fall in love again. He had such simple 'wants.'

If only he knew.

She walked over to the window again, peered through her telescope, and focused in on one particular cluster of stars.

Allison sighed with contentment.

And, she thought how ironic it was that up there everything did indeed look hunky dory.

CHAPTER 9

There were plenty of perfect sites in Nelson for a luxury hotel. Especially on the fringes of the small city, where the cluster of old heritage buildings transitioned into more rural living. Kootenay Lake, of course, was the jewel, and any hotel would want to take in that view, and possibly even incorporate a marina if the hotel was situated close to the water.

Wyatt was sitting in the Rockies Café with his father, waiting for the mayor and the hotel lady to arrive. It was an exciting day…for everyone. But, particularly for his dad, who seemingly was on the verge of having his most impactful sculpture displayed right in his own city. Wyatt could tell he was proud—not just for himself, but for every American who'd settled here. Finally, they were going to have a monument erected in their honor.

"So, Dad, what are you thinking?"

Willy grabbed the coffee pot and refilled both of their cups.

"Son, I'm just bursting with joy. You know, I'm an artist and, just like any artist, recognition is important. But, I left that need behind a long time ago—back when I was just struggling. I've made my mark, my works are displayed everywhere and art has made me a somewhat rich man. But, this…this is just so different."

"Yeah, it's personal for you this time, isn't it?"

"Damn right it is." Willy waved his hand, gesturing around the crowded café full of men and women in their sixties, all of them looking a lot younger than they really were. "These people made this town the city that it is today. They chose Canada, chose us for our freedom and peaceful attitudes. And, they stayed—they damn well stayed. Didn't go running back when they were offered amnesty. We need to recognize that and thank them for who they are."

Wyatt nodded and glanced around the café. He knew most of the people who were drinking coffee this morning; it was a daily ritual for some of them. The informal morning coffee club. Nothing organized—these old draft-dodgers didn't believe in schedules or organized events. Everything was spontaneous and spur of the moment for them—maybe it was the era they grew up in, or maybe just because if they hadn't run to Canada they might have lost their lives in a war that no one understood or believed in. Perhaps they realized life was more precious than the average person did.

A couple of men got up from a table in the corner and started walking towards the door. They noticed Wyatt and Willy, and detoured their way.

One of them, who Wyatt knew as Jim Barnes, called out in a bellowing voice, "Hey, Chief, why aren't you out there protecting us from all those obnoxious American tourists?"

Wyatt laughed. "I think I'll leave that to you, Jim. You probably still speak the language, don't you?"

Both men pulled up chairs and sat down.

Jim was a lawyer and ran a small office on Baker Street. But, no one would peg him as a lawyer, not in a million years. He was wearing blue jeans and a Toronto Blue Jays t-shirt, rounded off with an Argonauts ball cap and a short ponytail hanging down the back of his neck. The other guy was Steve Jackson, who was a little less obvious about the aging hippie look. Steve wore a mustard-colored leather jacket and a Tilley hat. Steve ran a sporting goods store.

Both men were immensely successful, and extroverts in the extreme.

Jim's law office was known throughout British Columbia as one of the shrewdest firms for tort cases. He didn't look the part, but opposing lawyers feared him. He never lost, and while tort cases weren't common in a small city like Nelson, that was just where Jim lived.

Every week or so, he flew his private jet out of the Castlegar Airport to Vancouver, to spend time in his second office there and litigate cases that were more common in the bigger cities. Jim's fee was $500 an hour, and he was worth every cent. He always dressed casual, except when he had to preside over a deposition or argue a case in court. Then, he reluctantly wore a suit.

And, Steve, well, he was the ultimate extreme sports guy. His store specialized in ski equipment, both for water and snow. In addition, he owned two helicopters and, like Jim, was a licensed pilot. He and another pilot on his staff, took people up for mountaintop heli-tours, soaring over the peaks of the Selkirk Mountains and occasionally venturing eastward over the Monashees, the Bugaboos, and the Rockies.

In the winter, a big part of Steve's sports equipment and helicopter tour business was flying daredevils up to where the virgin snow was, well away from any ski resorts. Heli-skiing was becoming big business, as skiers were demanding bigger and better hills and thrills.

Both Jim and Steve were draft-dodgers, having escaped to Canada in 1969, about a year before their names would have been called.

They had been best friends back in the States as young twenty-somethings, and were still best friends today. They'd cheerily dashed across the 49th Parallel together forty-six years ago and then helped each other get settled in their new country.

They'd stuck together, bonded forever in the intense experience of being fugitives. They'd both even lived in the same rented house for years before they started seeing the fruits of their labours and were able to buy their own homes.

Jim patted Willy on the back. "Well, old fellow, some pretty exciting rumors going around town about you lately."

"Hey, what do you mean by 'old fellow,' Jimmy-boy? Have you forgotten all the times I've beaten you at arm-wrestling?"

Jim, never one to back down from a challenge, either in a courtroom or a coffee shop, rolled up the right sleeve of his t-shirt and planted his elbow firmly on the table.

"No, I've never forgotten, Willy-boy. And, it's driving me crazy. How the hell can an eighty-seven-year-old man beat someone more than twenty years younger? So, let's give it another go. You're a bit older than the last time we did this, and I had my Cheerios for breakfast."

Willy laughed and sneered at him. "You're still a pussy. Soft from sitting at a desk. Okay, if you insist."

He rolled up his sleeve and they positioned their elbows against each other, hands clasped together.

Jim muttered, "Steve, you're the referee. Be fair—to me!"

Steve chuckled. "Feels like deja-vu. Okay—ready, set, go!"

Willy smiled, and Jim grimaced, as the 'clash of the titans' began. But, the clash didn't last long. Within mere seconds, Jim's arm slammed backwards onto the table.

Rubbing his arm, consternation written across his face, Jim exclaimed, "How the hell do you do that all the time? It's always the same. You don't even play along and make me think I've got a chance!"

Willy took a sip of his coffee. "Jim, I would never tease you like that. Wouldn't be fair to lead you on!"

Jim shook his head, and then looked at Wyatt. "I'm gonna have to start arm-wrestling the Chief of Police. Might have a chance with you."

Wyatt winked. "I don't know about that, Jim. Like father, like son, you know."

Steve jumped in and changed the subject. "Willy, as Jim said before he felt compelled to prove his manhood, we've been hearing rumors about your sculpture. That it might get put on display after all?"

Willy put his finger up to his lips. "Keep that quiet, boys. Try to squelch that rumor. Might jinx it. But, yeah, might hear something more firm today."

Jim finished rubbing his sore arm, and stretched his arms out behind him. "Heard that we might get a new luxury hotel here, too, and that it's tied in to your draft-dodger sculpture."

Wyatt laughed. "God, these small towns never cease to amaze me. When I lived back in Toronto, things like this would stay secret. But, here, Christ, everything gets out."

Steve stole a sip out of Wyatt's cup. "Well, remember, Wyatt, this kind of news wouldn't even get noticed in a city like Toronto. But, for a small city like ours, this is front page stuff."

"Yeah, true, but it's more likely that everyone who lives here is just like a gossipy old lady."

Jim crossed his legs and directed his gaze at Willy. "I heard you were in the hospital for a few days. Are you okay now?"

"Yeah, not a big deal. Just complications from falling off the steps of my porch. Hurt my hip."

"How did that keep you in the hospital for days?"

"Just some complications, but I'm okay now. They just wanted to be safe, considering my age."

"Yeah, right! Those doctors have obviously never arm-wrestled you!"

They all laughed.

Steve pointed at Willy. "I think you've just been working too hard, not getting enough sleep. That's why you fell down the stairs."

"No, really, I get lots of sleep. Don't worry about me."

"I was walking my German shepherd in the wee hours of the morning—must have been three or four days ago—and walked past your house. I could see the lights on in your garage studio, and heard your trusty old saw humming away. That was around 4:00 in the morning. Do you do that a lot?"

Wyatt answered for his dad. "Steve, my dad has been doing that for years. Sometimes, he'll work all the way through, from morning until the next dawn."

Jim scraped his chair back along the tile floor, and stood up. "C'mon, Stevie, we have to get changed into our golfing duds—only an hour till tee-off."

Steve glanced at his watch. "You're right. Okay, gotta run, boys. See you soon—and Willy, good luck with the statue. We're all so excited for you, bud. And, for us, too—you've done us a great honor with that sculpture."

Willy smiled. "The honor was mine, guys."

Jim leaned down and warmly rubbed Willy's back. "I may tease you, but you know I'm just kidding about the 'old man' thing. Take care of yourself—for us, okay?"

"I will."

"You'd better—because I love you like a grandfather!"

Jim ducked out of the way as Willy swung his big hand in his direction. Willy laughed and cracked, "Get outta here, you miserable draft-dodging hippies!"

After they'd left, Wyatt's cell phone rang. He answered it on the first ring. He didn't say much, just listened and muttered, "Okay."

He clicked off and said, "Let's go, Dad. We're gonna meet them at Murray's store. They're afraid they'll attract too much attention if they come in here."

* * * * *

Murray Hinton was Nelson's mayor, but most of the time he was just known as the owner and proprietor of Murray's Hardware. Just down the street from the café, it only took Wyatt and Willy five minutes to get there.

They went inside and were greeted by Murray's wife, Kathy, who was manning the check-out counter. She greeted them with a big smile and pointed to the back of the store.

Murray had a conference room in the rear, one that he used for informal council meetings when no one was in the mood to meet at City Hall.

Wyatt opened the door. Murray was standing at the end of the table with a coffee cup in his hand.

Standing beside the mayor was one of the most stunning women Wyatt had ever seen. Not beautiful in the classic sense; better than that.

Real, alive, with an effervescence that surrounded her like a halo.

Her image hit him in the gut like a ton of bricks. Butterflies were fluttering in his stomach. He silently begged them to stop.

She wasn't too tall, and she wasn't too short.

Long brown hair, a perfect figure…and the face of an angel.

She walked up to both of them and held out her hand. Willy shook it first because Wyatt was too slow to react. He was too busy staring at her, with his mouth slightly open.

"I'm Allison Fisher. You must be the man I've been dying to meet. Willy Carson, right?"

"Yes, pleased to meet you, Allison. And, this is my son, Wyatt, our Chief of Police."

She turned to Wyatt and smiled. It was a smile that made Wyatt melt—he actually felt like he'd shrunk a couple of inches. Her eyes were the most mesmerizing orbs; a piercing blue that seemed almost unreal, like they'd been painted by an artist.

She held out her hand to him, and he took a couple of seconds to react. Then, he did, and the touch of her hand sent what felt like a gentle electric current up his arm.

She was talking now. "Are you okay, Wyatt?"

He snapped out of it. It was weird. *What was that all about?*

Wyatt licked his lips, trying desperately to get some moisture action going.

"Yes…yes, I'm fine. Pleased to meet you, Allison. You just looked… familiar to me. It was a bit of a shock. Have we met somewhere before?"

Her warm smile radiated into his consciousness, and her words left him wanting for more.

"No, I don't think so. I surely would have remembered you."

CHAPTER 10

The four of them strolled leisurely along Baker Street, and then down Hall Street towards the scenic waterfront.

Murray led the way in a manner that mayors tend to do; wearing an authoritative swagger, pointing here and there, smiling and waving at enthusiastic groups of people. Wyatt was surprised the pompous ass wasn't wearing the *Chain of Office* around his neck. The warm temperature today was probably the only thing that had stopped him from donning it.

Murray and Allison walked in front, with Wyatt and Willy pulling up the rear. Wyatt could tell that Murray was totally taken with the billionaire. No surprise, and Wyatt didn't resent that the man was trying to hog all her attention. He was, after all, the mayor, and the official host for Allison while she was in town.

Wyatt really didn't mind walking behind her either.

He had a nice view.

The way she walked was almost musical—he couldn't help but hum in his head the tune to Roy Orbison's *Pretty Woman.*

They had all chatted together back in Murray's store for about half an hour before they headed out on their walking tour. Wyatt was glad that it only took him a few minutes to regain his famous composure. The woman had certainly stirred up a reaction in him—something he hadn't felt in years.

Well, truth be told, he'd never felt like that before, even with his fiancé. It was an instant attraction.

Love at first sight? Or lust at first sight? He didn't know what it was.

It couldn't be love, because he didn't even know her. And, it couldn't be lust because he hadn't been looking at her that way, and certainly hadn't been undressing her in his mind.

So, it must have been that thing called 'chemistry,' something that he had never been sure he even believed in...until now.

What he did know about chemistry between two people, was that it was never singular—that it was a mutual thing. So, on that basis Wyatt deduced that since he had felt it, then she must have felt it, too. It was an electricity between them, that both would have had to have felt.

And, the way she smiled at him, how she had shaken his hand, the way she'd spoken to him, convinced him that she indeed was in the same boat as he was. Throughout the meeting back at Murray's store, she'd directed a lot of her side of the conversation to him.

He could tell, though, that she was adept in a boardroom setting—playing the group, asking all the right questions, using the proper inflections in her voice to convey sincerity. She was indeed a pro. But, still, he had the feeling that a lot of what she was saying had been directed at him.

Or, he was just deluding himself, which was entirely possible.

No matter, that wasn't why they were all meeting today. There were more important things at stake—for the sake of the city, and for the sake of his father.

And, of course, for the sake of Murray Hinton as well—he was coming up for re-election in a year's time, so landing a major hotel project would be a huge feather in his cap and would pretty much guarantee his victory.

Murray was already campaigning. A born politician. He stopped at virtually every store along the way, rapping on the windows, gesturing with well-practised waves, making sure that everyone noticed the splendid specimen of a woman by his side.

And, she was splendid—and also astute enough to dress for the audience.

She clearly was aware that she was visiting a small city, one that still had the personality of a small town. She'd done her research.

Allison was wearing a pair of Levi's jeans, and she wore them better than any of the models Wyatt had seen in the famous brand's ads. She had a very shapely ass, which seemed to move independently of the sculpted legs. Jeans had never looked better.

She also wore a simple pink blouse, hanging casually around her hips. No jewellery, except for a cross necklace. No engagement or wedding rings either, Wyatt was happy to see.

Yes, walking behind Allison Fisher was definitely a nice place to be.

They turned left onto Lakeside Drive and strolled along until coming to a little park beside the lake. Allison suggested they all sit down at one of the picnic tables.

The setting was beautiful; the lake a sparkling jewel and the mountains surrounding it looked almost surreal.

Allison ran her right hand through her long hair, and shook her head in astonishment.

"I didn't know vistas like this even existed in the world. Sure, there are lakes and mountains everywhere, but there's something unreal about this place. Stunning, just stunning."

Willy leaned his elbows on the table and shifted his position on the picnic bench so that he was facing Allison.

"It must be such a contrast to where you live. I've been to Chicago many times and, while I love it there—it's as great a city as any—I couldn't possibly live there."

She nodded. "Oh, how right you are, Willy. But, it's just a different lifestyle completely, isn't it? I mean, for some people, the city is the only place they could possibly be. They would go crazy in a town like this. Too quiet, too laid back. And…sadly, for a lot of people, scenery doesn't mean squat. They couldn't care less about whether or not they're looking out at mountains and lakes, or glass skyscrapers."

Wyatt took off his jacket. Even though there was a nice breeze down by the lake, he was starting to feel the sun burning through his clothes.

He then asked her the question he'd been pondering.

"Allison, this is a controversial place for an American company to build a hotel in. Why are you considering this? Won't it be bad for your reputation?"

She laughed. "Oh, poo to that. Diamond Hotels' reputation is golden. Nothing can touch it. We're an icon in the hotel world; if any company can get away with a controversial decision, it's us. This setting here in Nelson just can't be ignored."

"But, the draft-dodger legacy?"

"Oh, that's just old crap! It's all settled down now. It's part of history and what a colorful history it is. The Vietnam War still stirs up emotions from one extreme to the other, but it is still just history.

"And, one hell of a history—I mean, it doesn't get much better than that from a marketing standpoint. Brave young men and women fleeing from being drafted into a war that proved in the end to be a useless waste of life, and a war without even a victory? History has proven the dodgers right."

Wyatt persisted. "But, there could be a political backlash. America is still fighting useless wars, with seemingly no end in sight."

"Too bad. We have a business to run."

"Politicians here in Canada may be sensitive to this—fear of enraging the Americans, who are still our closest friends and allies."

Murray jumped in. "Hey, I don't have a problem with it at all!"

Wyatt snickered. "Murray, I know you like to think of yourself as a politician, but you're hardly who I'm referring to. You run a hardware store and, for a few hours a week, you wear the mayor's garments. Get over yourself."

"Well…I do have some…influence."

"Who with? The Premier of British Columbia? The Prime Minister of Canada? C'mon, get real."

Allison smacked the palm of her hand down on the table.

"Stop bickering, boys. This political stuff you'll just have to leave to me. My executives and I do have some experience building and managing hotels all over the world. We deal with politics all the time. And, sometimes, some…incentives…are needed to make things happen."

"Bribes?"

"Let's not call them that. You are, after all, the police chief. Let's just say that pots can be sweetened for a country or a community. As the Godfather said, 'offers that can't be refused.'"

"I understand how those things work, Allison. Large corporations do it all the time, and it's certainly legitimate as long as they're not greasing palms. Guarantees of job creation, contributions to city services, parks and recreation. All that jazz is legit. But, this idea of yours sounds so political as to perhaps be beyond even those things. You're throwing the draft-dodger legacy right in America's face, as well as the face of the country that gave them refuge."

Murray frowned at Wyatt. "Jesus, Wyatt, don't you realize how important this would be to our city? Are you trying to scare her away? I don't understand you."

"I just want us all to be realistic here, Murray. Getting excited over 'pie in the sky' is not a good thing."

"It's not 'pie in the sky.' And, this doesn't really have anything to do with you. If it wasn't for Willy, you wouldn't even be at this meeting. You're the police chief. I'm the mayor. Development opportunities are my responsibility to bring to City Council. You don't get a say."

"I do have a say, Murray. The minute you involved my father in this, it became my turf as well."

Allison made a gesture with her hands, spreading them outward. "Peace! Truce! Let's all agree that, yes, it's controversial, okay? But, that's not a deal-breaker. Let me work things out in a professional manner from my end. I'll respect all concerns, and I promise that I won't make any grand announcements exciting people needlessly until it's a done deal from all sides. Fair?"

Wyatt nodded, as did Murray and Willy.

Allison looked around, taking in the panorama. "I see that there's a little airstrip over there on the shores of the lake."

Murray nodded. "Yes, that's the *Norman Stibbs Airfield.* Just charter flights. Small private planes; no jets and no commercial flights."

"And, I see alongside that is a marina."

"That's the private marina operated by the Prestige Resort. Would you want a marina with your hotel?"

"No, that's not my vision. Too commercial, too tacky. Most of our hotels are in the high-rise luxury market; very high-end, very 'resortish.' Our strategic outlook takes us in a different direction for the future. Those hotels are still important to us, but we want to branch out into a different market. Still the discerning traveler, but we want to go after the traveler who wants something with more character. More quiet and serene. Boutique hotels that embrace scenic spots in upscale markets around the world.

"In essence, we're appealing to the baby-boomers, the ones with money to travel and the ones who are sick and tired of the party hotels and casinos. People who just appreciate the finer things that nature offers. Not families with noisy kids who just want to splash around in the pool. We want the quiet, intelligent, classy, and spiritual tourists.

"Think of the irony here—we're going to appeal to the baby -boomers who are exactly the age group the draft-dodgers fall into. I think it's brilliant to have one of our flagship hotels located right here, in baby -boomer country, in draft-dodger country."

Wyatt scratched his chin. "I didn't think of it like that. It is kinda brilliant."

Allison laughed and clapped her hands together. "Good, I'm finally winning you over! Overcoming your cynicism."

Wyatt smiled. He couldn't help it—her exuberance was contagious.

Murray asked, "What do you picture the hotel looking like? What design?"

Allison shielded her eyes with her hand and scanned the townscape.

"No more than four storeys high. I believe you have a six-storey limit here in town, so we would be less than that. More expansive than tall. I see perhaps a maximum of 200 rooms. No pools, no saunas, no gyms—none of that trendy stuff that other hotels build in.

"We don't want phony, trendy clientele who want to show off how active and current they are. It's amazing how many people stay at hotels like that and use all those facilities, but never use them in their communities at home. The gym freaks who pretend they work out regularly and want everyone to know that—we don't want them. We want refined guests who appreciate the real things, the genuine things. The ones who scorn 'trendy.' We want people who read books, appreciate music, photography, museums, and a glass of wine or two."

She winked. "And maybe even the occasional joint."

Wyatt chuckled. "Jesus, you're tough! You don't like your current hotel guests much, do you?"

"I love them, Wyatt. Because the ones we have right now are prepared to pay 500 dollars a night to pretend they're big shots. But, that market won't sustain us. Every time there's a stock market crash or a real estate trough, the fake wealth dries up and our occupancy rates drop down to forty percent.

"We've put too many eggs in one basket. We need more baskets, more sustainable baskets. Clientele who absolutely refuse to pay more than 200 dollars a night, because they're the ones who don't need to show off. Some of these people actually prefer to stay at bed and breakfasts—we're missing out on those people. They're the ones who have real money, and probably even keep some of it under their mattresses. Money that's not subject to being torn apart by market meltdowns."

Willy nodded eagerly. "What you're saying makes sense. A very smart strategic direction, I think."

"Thank you, Willy. Yes, we think it will give us a sustainable competitive advantage over our competitors. And, as far as what you'll see with the hotel we'll build here, I want it to mirror some of these lovely heritage buildings you have. I want it to have an 'old' look, a character look. It will be tasteful, charming, and will be an absolute magnet for the kind of guests we want to attract."

There was silence around the picnic table, as the three of them absorbed all that Allison had said. Wyatt knew that the other two were just as impressed with her as he was—she was clearly an intelligent lady. Allison may have inherited the hotel chain, but she had definite ideas of her own that Wyatt thought bordered on brilliant.

Willy then asked the question that was on all of their lips.

"How does my sculpture fit into this?"

"I've seen your sculpture pictured in a couple of magazines and, of course, I've seen many of your other works in person all over Canada and the United States. But, I think the draft-dodger sculpture is one of the most amazing, most powerful, statues I've ever seen. I want to see it in person while I'm here. Are you okay with that, Willy?"

"Absolutely."

"If my view of it in person matches the enthusiasm I have for it from the pictures I've seen, I propose that it be mounted right in front of the hotel. As guests pull up along a circular driveway, it would be featured in a little park area that the driveway encircles. With water fountains, the whole nine yards. Does that sound good to you?"

"I'd be thrilled."

"Well, I'm hoping something else will thrill you, too. With the marketing campaign I'm thinking of, I'd like you to be the spokesperson for the hotel. TV, print ads, everything. The whole idea of this hotel will be to attract American guests of the type I described—as well as Canadians and those from other countries, too, of course.

"But, I want us to capitalize on Nelson being the center that attracted and retained most of the draft-dodgers. The people who made Nelson the beautiful, peaceful community it is today.

"And, you, Willy, have the good looks and the healthy build that belie your age. You're the symbol of what made this community strong, when the dodgers came here forty-five years ago. You're a marketer's dream for a project like this."

Willy scratched his head and thought in silence for about a minute.

"Well, I'm thrilled. To be an active part of my sculpture's purpose is an opportunity I never would have imagined. But, Allison, you know that I'm not really a draft-dodger, don't you?"

"Of course I do. You were drafted to fight in the Korean War; you were too old to be drafted for Vietnam. But, you snuck into Canada along with the dodgers because you didn't want your son to ever risk being drafted. You came here in sympathy for the Nam dodgers, but also for a safe future for your family.

"It's even more important to us that we have a spokesperson like you. The dodgers themselves never actually fought in a war. They left before they were drafted. But you…you went through a draft. You're someone who was actually drafted and was forced to fight in a war. A war that, like Vietnam, no one could figure out why we were even there."

Willy nodded slowly. "Yes, and like Nam, the Korean War was another one with no victory. We never seem to win wars, but we sure know how to send our kids off to be killed in them."

"So, Willy, what do you say?"

He looked at Wyatt. Wyatt smiled and winked at him.

"Okay, I'm in. For an old bugger like me, kind of an exciting last chapter of my life."

Allison clapped her hands again.

"Oh, I'm so happy! And, I think you have a lot of chapters still left in your life. I mean, just look at you. Most people wouldn't guess your age as being older than around sixty."

Willy laughed. "Just good genes, I guess."

Allison leaned across the picnic table and held out her hand. "Let's shake on it."

Willy shook her hand vigorously. He was more excited than Wyatt had seen him in years.

Murray injected himself back into the conversation. "Allison, it might be helpful to have the mayor of Nelson appear in some of your TV ads. I'll be available anytime you need me."

Wyatt rolled his eyes. Allison smiled respectfully.

She turned her attention back to Willy.

"So, next steps. I'll want to see that wonderful sculpture in person.

"And, since you'll be groomed towards being our spokesperson for this new boutique hotel, I'll need to assure myself of your health before I put you under retainer. I promise that it will be uneventful and, of course, you and I will talk about the financial terms of that retainer once I'm satisfied on the health front."

Wyatt frowned. "I don't understand, Allison. What do you mean?"

"Just a health check—verification that Willy's as healthy as he looks. It's very routine—nothing invasive. Remember, we're making an investment in Willy and we have to know that he's not going to drop dead on us after we've spent a small fortune on advertising."

"Well, my dad can easily get that check-up done. We'll just have our family doctor give him a clean bill of health."

Allison shook her head. "No, it's corporate policy that we use our own doctors. We actually do these check-ups for all of our executives, too."

"Well, okay, just send them up and my dad can schedule it with them."

She shook her head again.

"No, if you don't mind the inconvenience, we have our own clinic that we use. Down in the Atlanta area.

"Don't be scared by what I'm going to say, but the clinic is in the same complex as the *Centers for Disease Control.* That just happens to be where it is. A beautiful complex and there are actually quite a few other clinics that rent space there, too, not just us."

Wyatt just looked at her. He couldn't believe what he was hearing. But, at the same time, he considered that maybe this was just how most big corporations did things these days. It was probably way above his paygrade.

Willy looked at his son and just laughed. "Hey, Wyatt, I've always wanted to visit Atlanta. And, guess what? One of my sculptures is on display at a museum there. It'll be a good opportunity to see if my clients got their money's worth when they paid my exorbitant fee!"

CHAPTER 11

The *Kootenay Palace* was exactly the kind of hotel Allison would never build. Situated along the lake, north of Nelson, it was the antithesis of what she envisioned a hotel should be.

It was nice enough, certainly attractive to look at, and had every facility that the bored traveler could ever want. But, in her view, it was shallow and cold. Why hotels located in a paradise like the Kootenays needed bars and casinos, was beyond her comprehension.

But, that was what the majority of travelers wanted these days—and in fact most of the four hundred hotels in Allison's chain were equipped in exactly that same way.

That had been her father's vision, not hers. She had inherited the results of that vision, but she didn't intend to stay on that path and build just more of the same old, same old.

No, from now on, she would build the hotels she wanted to build, and gradually transform the image of Diamond Hotels into something really special, really unique.

Her brother, who owned forty-nine percent of the shares in the company, would just go along. He pretty much always agreed with whatever Allison wanted to do, and she was convinced he was secretly relieved that their dad's last will and testament had given her fifty-one percent and controlling interest. Robert liked to defer—in fact, he preferred it that way.

She loved her brother dearly, but he could never be counted upon to take the initiative with anything. Decisions were not his strong suit. He leaned on Allison for everything, which in one way was flattering. But, he leaned on everyone that way, so it didn't really make Allison feel all that special. He was just that way. The family genes must have taken an extended vacation when Robert was created.

While Allison didn't respect people who were like that—in fact, she thought it was kind of pathetic—she was inwardly glad that Robert was that way. It gave her total freedom, and an absolute reign over the company that she might not have had otherwise.

People like her brother were indeed good to have as partners if you had no other choice but to have partners. And, in her case, she had no choice. Her father's will had dictated that.

Robert had two children—a boy and a girl. Allison loved her nephew and niece. Both were in their early twenties now, and either one would be great additions to the company. They both had the traditional Fisher brain cells; cells that seemed to have bypassed her brother.

But, only one was suited to being her eventual successor in Majestic 12.

Brother Robert knew nothing about Majestic 12. When Allison's father had decided that she would be his successor in the group, they both agreed that Robert could never be a part of the chain of succession. He just wasn't smart enough, decisive enough, or tough enough. They decided to wait until one of Robert's kids reached an age where they could be assessed.

Allison had finished that assessment now in her mind.

It would be Tim, the eldest. He was the anointed one.

And, one day, after he'd finished university and she got him settled into an executive position with Diamond, she'd orientate him into the secret society. He would be sworn to an oath and her brother would never know a thing.

Tim was smart; he had a mind that was not only logical but forward-thinking. Nothing was an obstacle to Tim—if there was something in his way, he always found a route around it. He had done that all the way through school, and in every sport he'd taken on. He excelled at virtually everything and had the determination of a lion.

To be fair, Tanya was identical in those respects, too. Allison's niece had all those same qualities, so it was close to being a coin toss between the two of them. But, she'd leaned in favor of Tim, because he had a quality that Tanya didn't seem to have. A quality that Allison's dad had possessed, and one that Allison had, too.

Humanity.

Tim cared about people, and always committed himself to doing the right thing. Just like her father had. And, just like Allison always had.

Despite the rigors of the business world and the cutthroat aspects that every successful person had to have the stomach for, Allison believed that retaining your sense of humanity was essential. That quality could never be allowed to get lost in the shuffle of cards.

People always tended to hire and promote in their own likeness—which sometimes wasn't a good thing, because companies could end up being staffed with a bunch of clones of the CEO. But, Allison always accepted that risk. She wanted her executives to be just like her.

And, she wanted her successor on Majestic 12 to be just like her. The one quality she wanted to bring to Majestic 12 was 'humanity.'

With the absolute power possessed by that group, humane considerations had to be maintained as much as possible. Despite the mindboggling secrets the group was privy to, and despite the brutal things they had authorized from time to time, Allison thought that some sense of humanity had always been brought to the table.

By her father…and, for the last five years, by her.

Allison's work on Majestic 12 was probably one of the reasons she didn't sleep very well. Some of the actions she had knowledge of always kept popping back into her head, being replayed over and over.

She had always been well removed from those actions, of course, because none of the members of Majestic 12 ever got their hands dirty. But, knowing about them was enough to cause her to toss and turn in bed at night.

Even though the people who had been killed had been a danger.

Not that they were bad people, they were just…dangerous. Unstable, and insufferably idealistic. Sometimes, otherwise decent people had to die for the greater good. Because they knew too much and weren't realistic, and were reckless enough to want to wreak havoc upon society.

At least that was the way Allison rationalized it all, and she knew that's the way her dad had rationalized it, too. And, his father before him. They'd had no choice. It was a sacred trust thrust upon chosen ones. And, guilt could prey upon a person if there wasn't a way to rationalize things.

The problem was that it wasn't like a normal job. No one could resign from Majestic 12 out of conscience or indignation. They couldn't escape to Canada like the draft-dodgers had. There was no way to escape and, aside from being declared mentally incompetent or demented, there was only one way out. And, that was down…six feet down.

Which was probably why Allison slept so little and sometimes just gave up on her bed and ended up on the floor staring out at the stars. Thinking and wondering, but also knowing that the less people knew, the better.

What was the point of scaring people half to death? It was a burden for those who knew. They almost felt like protectors. At certain moments, though, Allison wondered what gave them the right. If it affected their lives, didn't people have the right to be scared?

Her dad had suffered from the same affliction. She rationalized that things got to him, too, probably because of that humanity quality they shared. Things got really bad for him in the months leading up to his death. He got progressively worse, and far more irritable. Her mom told Allison that he'd started taking Prozac.

Diagnosed with depression.

Allison wasn't supposed to know, and her mom made her promise never to let her dad know that she knew.

He'd be so ashamed. He believed so much in mental strength.

The lack of sleep and the medication he'd been taking must have contributed to the car crash. He must have indeed fallen asleep at the wheel and drove them all off the cliff.

Allison couldn't accept that it might have been suicide, even though there were whispers to that effect. She knew her dad's heart, knew his humanity, and knew that he could never do a selfish thing like take his own life. And, he certainly would never have taken his wife and son-in-law with him. That theory made no sense.

But, the accident still haunted her. The three people she'd loved the most were lost to her in an instant.

She snapped out of her daydream and looked around room 207 at the Kootenay Palace.

Plush pillows, elegant drapes, and grass-cloth wallpaper. Berber carpeting on the floor, and recliner chairs that just begged to be reclined on.

Allison threw herself backwards onto the bed. Yep, even had the obligatory 'heavenly mattress.'

She reluctantly allowed her eyes to wander in the direction of the hotel phone, then glanced at her watch.

Time for that phone call. To a person she never looked forward to talking to.

Chad Powers—the power hungry Napoleon, the current head of Majestic 12. Leadership duties rotated amongst the twelve members, and leaders served terms of seven years and only seven years. Then, they reverted back to being just one of the twelve again once a new leader took over.

Chad Powers had just begun his seventh and final year.

Allison was next in line. The Majestic-elect.

It was a heavy burden to bear for anyone who became the 'Head Majestic.' Except for Chad Powers. He revelled in it.

Allison dialed the number.

"Powers, here."

"Hi Chad. It's me."

"Been waiting to hear from you. How'd it go?"

"Went fine. My pitch went over well, I think. They're all pretty excited here about the prospects of the kind of project I presented to them. I meet with city council tomorrow, and then the next day I'll visit William Carson at his house. To take a look at his sculpture."

"One thing is certain, Allison, you're a masterful presenter. You could sell igloos to Eskimos."

"Well, this is truly 'God's country.' A little gem in a world of jagged rocks. It deserves the kind of hotel I talked to them about."

"So, they bought the charade."

"Hook, line, and sinker."

"Okay, that's good. Next steps?"

"I convinced William about the need to fly him down to Atlanta for some medical tests. He didn't seem at all suspicious. He agreed that I needed the assurance that his health is solid."

"Good. Let me know when he can fly down and I'll have the team here prepared."

"I will. But, you have to promise me one thing, Chad."

"What's that?"

"You have to give me your word that this dear man will not be harmed."

Allison heard an exasperated sigh.

"I don't have to promise you anything. Are you forgetting who I am? You don't take over the helm for another year. Don't get ahead of yourself."

"Chad, I'm recording this conversation. I want your word. If I don't get it, I'm going to tell the city council tomorrow that I've changed my mind on the hotel project. And, then, of course, there will be no need for Carson to visit Atlanta. You'll have to figure out another way to get him there."

She heard him chuckle into the phone. "That's a joke. What are you going to do with that recording? Go to the FBI? You're a paper tiger, Allison. And, you shouldn't ever make the mistake of threatening me."

"Chad, don't you ever make the mistake of underestimating me. You know full well that the other ten in our group would be more than interested in hearing such a recording. No one likes or trusts you, you prick. We all have resources we can discretely call upon, and you know it."

Silence at the other end.

"Well? What's it going to be, Mr. Powers?"

In a soft voice, barely audible, he said, "You have my word."

"What? Louder, please? My recorder needs more volume. And, I want you to state for the recording just exactly what your 'word' is for."

Chad Powers yelled into the phone. "Okay, bitch, you have my fucking word that William Carson will not be harmed!"

CHAPTER 12

This time, he had sleepwalked—out of bed, out of the house, and into the studio.

But, he was awake now, standing in the middle of the vast space, staring at the unfinished ball sitting on the floor.

Well, the 'ball' part itself was finished, but something was telling him he had more to do. It wasn't quite right.

Willy looked down at his half-naked body. Once again, he was wearing only underwear, and once again there was a slight glow surrounding him.

But, what left him aghast every time this goddamned thing happened to him, was being able to see through his skin as if it were cellophane.

His eyes were stinging this time, for some strange reason. Lights would make the stinging worse.

But, he could work by moonlight because it was full tonight, its gentle rays cooperatively beaming through the windows. Yes, that's what he would do. Work by moonlight. Much easier on his stinging eyes.

He was determined to not leave the studio until the damn ball was finished.

He didn't really know what more had to be done, but a little voice inside his head was telling him that his hands would know.

The power saw would move in cadence with his hands, and his hands would be guided by his instinct. Instinct that would only come to him once he started his work.

He stared at the ball a little bit longer. It sure looked finished to him. It was a perfect ball, perfectly round. If someone wanted to buy a sculpture of a round ball for some stupid reason, this was about as good as it could get. Smooth surface, not a blemish anywhere.

Suddenly, though, he knew what the problem was. It was too smooth, too perfect. It wasn't supposed to be like that. Imperfections were needed. He couldn't define them in his head, but something told him that it would all come to him once the trusty saw was in his hands.

Willy glanced quickly out at the moon and then back down at the ball. Then, he rubbed his stinging eyes. Definitely no lights tonight—he would work by moonlight.

Maybe that was a good thing. His snoopy friend, Steve Jackson, might decide to walk his German shepherd in the wee hours of the morning again, and it wouldn't be a good thing if he got extra snoopy this time and peeked in through the window.

It was just pure dumb luck that Steve hadn't done that a few nights ago when he said he'd seen the studio lights on—he would have been shocked at the sight of a transparent Willy. How could Willy possibly explain that?

Might be a good time to finally invest in blinds for the windows, but Willy had always resisted that. He liked to be able to look outside even when it was dark out, and he didn't like the feeling of being closed-in.

Well, he would just finish this task tonight and that would be the end of it. Hopefully, this wouldn't happen to him again. Something was pushing him to finish this, so he had to just get it done.

He'd never been one to believe in the supernatural when he was young, but he'd been enlightened back in Korea.

What had happened to him there was pretty damn freaky, and what was explained to him by the general in Seoul had been bang-on. His life had unfolded just as the general had told him it would.

The 'fountain of youth' element, the incredible strength, the indestructible teeth, the full head of hair. And, the talent for art, which he'd never exhibited as a kid.

The general had been right about all that, and he'd been right also in his warning about x-rays.

What had happened to him since the CT scan had been off the charts. It had awakened an anomaly inside of him and right now he was being driven by something.

It wasn't a coincidence—the transparency of his skin and his body glowing like a dim light bulb were a direct result of that scan.

And, the fact that he was being driven now to do this sculpture of a sphere—a stupid sphere—was a direct result of the CT scan, too. Willy was sure of it. It made no logical sense otherwise. Of course, none of this was logical, but he was trying his best now to just simply 'connect the dots.'

He was sure that the only way to stop this weirdness was to finish this thing that he was being driven to do. Tonight, he would do just that. He wanted this chapter of his life over with, once and for all.

* * * * *

"Gimme nother puff off that!"

"Fuck off! Git your own. Yer fault for usin all yers up."

Brody Finch lashed his hand out and slapped his friend across the face, sending the joint flicking to the ground. Matt Lawson dove to his knees, feeling around in the dark with his hands, while his eyes hunted desperately for the telltale glow of the tip.

"Is gone! Probly over there in the grass somewhere. That was my las one!"

Brody laughed and shook his head, then smoothed both of his hands through his long greasy hair, pressing it back behind his ears. "Good! Now yer in my boat. No drugs lef for any of us."

Matt pushed his woolen toque farther up on his forehead. "What the fuck we gonna do now? Still a whole night lef, and we got nothin."

"Aw, fuck, Matt. Gettin sick a this grass shit anyways. Gotta get us sum heroin. Haven't had a shot of that shit since Vancouver."

"Yeah, but ain't none of that in this fuckin town. Jus seems be nothin but blades here. Bored with blades. But, was better than nothin—that was my las one. Was jus startin to feel it, too."

Brody pointed at his friend's head, and laughed. "Why ya wear that fuckin toque, man? Ya look stupid—look like ya tryin be black or sumpin."

Matt's eyes flared at Brody. "That's a fuckin prejudicial thin to say, Brody!"

"Is not 'prejudicial,' idiot. Is 'prejudiced.' That's the proper use of the word."

"You a fuckin teacher all a sudden? Fuck off—les get sum drugs."

Brody smoothed back his hair again. "There's sum heroin in this town—I heard it today in that bar. We jus half ta go back there an connect."

"We needs money, or sumpin ta trade."

Brody started walking up Baker Street. "Follow me. Will score sumpin."

* * * * *

Willy stood back and admired his work.

Yep, this is good.

Something deep inside his brain told him that this was what the sphere was supposed to look like.

He picked up his power drill and rammed it down for one final touch, one final tunnel. Then, he hefted his saw with both hands and carved out one more mountain range. Then, within seconds, one last canyon.

No, not finished yet.

Willy put the tool down and knelt. Then, with ease, he rolled the solid granite sphere onto a different side, a sphere that must have weighed at least 400 pounds in his estimation. He alternated with the drill and the saw until more tunnels, canyons and mountains appeared out of nowhere. But, he knew that it wasn't really out of nowhere—he seemed to know exactly where these things had to go and how they had to look. He didn't know how he knew, he just knew.

And, he didn't care either. He just wanted this damn thing finished so the weirdness would end.

*****

Brody and Matt staggered along Baker Street, then detoured up several side routes. They were looking for an easy target; some place they knew would have something of value. They didn't want to break into a house—too messy and they were both too stoned to keep their wits about them. They might get hurt.

Instead, they were looking in backyards; looking for lawn mowers, small barbecues, and power tools. Shit like that. Stuff that had value—wouldn't be much value, of course, but maybe enough to buy themselves a hit or two.

So far, nothing worth stealing. They were starting to get discouraged. They tried to peek through the windows of a few garages, but all of the windows were covered except for one. And, all that was in that one was an old car. They didn't want to steal a car—again, too messy. And, too hard to unload. Too traceable.

They turned off Baker Street onto a quiet crescent. Brody held up his hand.

"Shh…hear that?"

"Yeah. What the fuck is it?"

"I dunno. Les check it out."

They walked along the street, following the sound. It was a humming noise. Or whirring. Brody couldn't really distinguish between hummings or whirrings. It was all just noise to him. He crooked his finger, motioning Matt to follow him in through a backyard.

Then, he pointed. "Is comin from that big fuckin grage."

They crouched and approached the building cautiously. It was all dark, not a light on anywhere inside. But, there was still that strange humming or whirring noise, whatever the fuck it was.

Brody got down on his knees and crawled up to a back door. Matt followed his every move. There was a window to the right of the door, and Brody eased himself up carefully and peeked inside.

"Jesus fuckin Christ! There's a fortune of equipments in there!"

"What equipments?"

Brody backed out of the way. "Look for yerself."

Matt got to his feet and peered in through the dirty window. "Holy shit! We gotta get that stuff! Is all power shit, too!"

Brody pulled a Swiss Army knife out of his pocket and flicked open the tool that he wanted. "This'll do it. This lock easy shit fer me."

Matt grabbed his arm. "But, what 'bout that whirring noise thing?"

Brody grunted. "Probly jus air conditionin or sumpin like that."

He fumbled with his tool until the lock popped. Then, Brody turned the handle and opened the door. They both entered slowly, carefully, feeling their way in the dark.

The moon had gone behind a cloud, so it was darker now than it had been a few seconds ago when they were peeking through the window. Brody pulled his trusty BIC lighter out of his pocket and flicked the wheel.

They both gasped in unison. They were in a short corridor which Brody could see led to a larger open area up ahead. The corridor was lined with shelves and mounting hooks. A massive array of power tools hung on the hooks, all shiny and new-looking.

Brody didn't really know what he was looking at, but it all sure looked expensive. His mouth started drooling as he pondered all of the heroin this stuff would buy.

Matt grabbed his belt, and whispered, "Brody, we gotta go back out an steal a pick-up truck ta haul out all this shit. Then we jus sell the shit an dump the truck!"

Brody nodded, and whispered back. "Right. This a fuckin gole mine. But, les check it all out firs."

They walked slowly through the corridor until finally reaching the open area, which curved to their left. They turned the corner and were now in the wide expanse of the garage. The whirring noise got louder the farther in they went.

Brody suddenly held out his right arm, stopping Matt in his tracks. They both stared straight ahead.

At the end of the garage near the front door, was a figure. He had his back to them and hadn't seen them yet. He was a big guy, and seemed to be hunched over some large ball thing on the floor.

Matt whispered. "Goddamn! We can't walk way from this shit. We can take him."

Brody nodded. "Probly an ole bugger. Be easy."

Matt looked questioningly at his partner, who seemed to be hesitating. "Well?"

Brody swallowed hard and replied, "Okay. Now er never. I'll lead. We'll rush the asshole." Brody held up his hand. "Wash my fingers. On three."

The garage was huge. They had a good sixty feet to cover in their dash for the cash. But, Brody wasn't worried. He flicked his fingers up one at a time. Once the third finger made its appearance, he whispered, "Now!"

They ran, their well-worn running shoes squeaking along the cement floor. Both of them had their arms out in front of them, ready to tackle the figure and deal with whatever it was they had to deal with. Nothing would stop them from stealing this stuff. As of now, it was all theirs. The old bugger just didn't know it yet.

When they were within twenty feet, the moon suddenly made its appearance again. Brighter than ever. Harsh on the eyes. For a second, Brody was blinded, until another thin cloud passed over, leaving a kinder glow coming in through the window.

Suddenly, the figure heard them—or more likely, heard their shoes.

He swung around to face them, an ominous-looking power tool in his hands.

Something made Brody stop. He put on the brakes, but the soles of his cheap runners stuck to the cement, causing him to do a face plant. Matt, as usual, followed Brody's every move.

When Brody was finally able to look upwards from the floor, the first thing he saw was Matt.

Half-kneeling beside him, mouth open in horror, eyeballs bulging out of his forehead.

Brody followed Matt's eyes up to the ghostly apparition towering above them.

He couldn't help himself.

Brody Finch screamed like a girl for the first time in his life.

CHAPTER 13

They scurried backwards, as far away as they could get doing the crab walk. The revulsion on their faces made Willy feel sick to his stomach.

His immediate reaction was one of horror at being seen this way by strangers. He'd gotten used to the idea that doctors and nurses had seen him transparent—that was okay, they were accustomed to seeing sickening things. And, he trusted that they'd respect his privacy.

The worst part of that experience at the hospital, though, was knowing that his wife and son had seem him that way. But, he'd reconciled that in his mind, too—they loved him and it didn't matter how hideous he looked. They'd still love him.

But, strangers, now, that was a different story. He actually felt sorry for these two scumbags. They'd obviously broken into his studio to rob him, and judging by how they'd been charging him at full speed, they also intended to cause him harm. Maybe irreparable harm.

Until they got a glimpse of who they were dealing with.

The ear-splitting scream from the one with long greasy hair was enough to wake the dead—which ironically was what Willy knew he looked like right now. The walking dead.

The other character, the one with the toque on his head, just whimpered like a maimed puppy.

He indeed felt sorry for them, despite what they had been intending. He wouldn't have wanted to witness what they'd just witnessed—it would probably scar him for life.

They were sitting on the cement floor, frozen in place. Each of them had their hands up to their mouths and just stared at him.

Willy slowly leaned over and laid the power saw down on the floor.

As he did, he noticed that the transparency in his arms had dissipated since the boys had made their move. For a split second, he wondered if a dramatic change in emotions could cause the effect to disappear.

He'd been startled when he turned around, watching the two of them running at him. They were in shock, too, at what they saw, but he was also in shock from knowing that they'd seen him that way.

He wasn't fearful at all—he knew he could handle himself. He was just more in shock at being seen.

Willy spread his arms out to his side, displaying to the boys that he no longer had something dangerous in his hands. Then, he walked slowly towards them.

"See? Nothing in my hands. I'm not going to hurt you. And, I'm not going to phone the police. Why don't you just leave by the way you came in, and we'll forget about this whole thing."

The boys were silent. Willy figured they were about eighteen or nineteen, very skinny and unhealthy looking. Pock-marked faces, shabby clothes, pale complexions. They looked like they hadn't had a ray of sunshine or a good solid meal in weeks.

"C'mon. Get up and be on your way."

The greasy-haired kid slid back on his bum a few more feet, then cautiously rose to stand, feigning defiance. The toque-headed guy watched his friend and followed his move. They were both standing now, unsteady, but at least they were standing.

Greasy kid spoke first. "We wan moneys."

"You can't have any money. You're lucky I'm letting you leave."

Toque kid got brave and found his tongue. "You gots lots a tools here. We gonna take sum with us." He glanced at his friend. "Right, Brody?"

The one called Brody, and clearly the one in charge, smiled. "Better we get money stead, now we got this old bugger trapped. Take us to the house, man, and git us sum cash."

Willy shook his head.

Brody took a knife out of his pocket and wielded it in the air. "Matt, grab that rope thin off the bench over there." He pointed.

Matt scurried over to the workbench and brought back a long length of heavy rope.

"Okay, you won take us to the house, we'll go ourselves. Tie him up, Matt."

Willy spread his arms out again. "Guys, don't make this mistake. You can leave here and nobody gets hurt, and neither of you gets arrested. Take the deal."

Brody shook his head. "We in charge here. And, what the fuck were you wearing? Sum kinda costume? Glow in the dark shit? You some kinda twisted perv, man? Maybe you enjoy being tied up."

Willy didn't like the direction this was heading. The kids were starting to feel empowered now after their initial shock. He wished he was still in his transparent state—they would have just crab-walked out of here without any of their drug-fueled courage returning.

He leveled his gaze at the one called Matt. "Don't come near me with that rope, son."

Matt laughed, and pushed his toque higher up on his forehead. "You not sum tuff guy, man. You jus an ole man. Put yer hans behind yer back."

Willy shook his head. "I know you just want drug money, boys. I feel sorry for you, but I don't keep money around. Please, just leave."

Brody was starting to get impatient now. "Do what Matt said! Put yer hans behind yer back. I sure there's money in that big house. And maybe a pretty ole wife we can have funs with, too. We'll find out. But, you be out here, listenin to her scream."

Willy sensed a rage building inside his gut now. He no longer felt sad for these kids. The implied threat against his wife had pushed his emotions in a different direction. He wished to God they'd taken his offer, but now they'd just have to deal with the consequences. For an instant, he pictured himself back in that trench in Korea, firing his rifle wildly into the air, aiming at a relentless enemy that seemed to be showing no mercy to five soldiers who were clearly no match.

Well, he was a match for these scum and they were going to find that out fast.

Brody thrust his hand out at his buddy. "Go git him! Wrap that fuckin rope round his neck stead. That teach him."

Matt sneered and rushed at Willy, both hands extending the rope out, intending to snare his neck.

Willy's hands moved in a blur. He grabbed the outer edges of the rope and twirled it around Matt's neck.

The little coward's face lost its sneer—replaced instead by a look of panic as Willy pulled tight on the ends of the rope, squeezing the boy's scrawny throat into a choking, hacking tube. He was struggling now, swinging his fist wildly at Willy's head. Willy let go of the rope and grabbed Matt under his armpits.

Then, he simply thrust him upwards with a force propelled by rage, totally devoid of any restraint that he might have felt a few seconds before.

The ceiling of the studio was ten feet high. Matt took the full impact on the top of his head, grunted, and crumpled harmlessly to the floor.

Brody gasped, swore, and rushed Willy at full speed, knife slicing the air. He was met by an open palm to the nose. Willy's arm was straight as an arrow, locked at the elbow, and didn't recoil even an inch. Brody fell backwards. It was as if he'd run into a brick wall.

He wiped the blood from his nose, crawled to his feet and took a swing at Willy's head with the pocket knife. Willy ducked, then grabbed Brody under the chin with one hand and thrust him backwards, sending him airborne a full twenty feet into the workbench.

Both thugs were out for the count.

Willy looked down at them, relieved that the situation was now under control, but sad that he'd had to do this. Despondent that they hadn't heeded his warnings.

He rushed out the door, along the driveway, and into his house through the back.

He went into the kitchen and pulled his cordless phone off the wall mount. He punched in the numbers.

A groggy voice answered on the third ring.

"Hello?"

"Wyatt, it's me. I need your help."

In a voice that seemed even groggier than when he'd first answered, Wyatt said, "Dad, can't this wait until morning?"

"No. I've hurt a couple of kids. I need you to come over here."

Suddenly, the voice was wide awake. "I'll be right there."

CHAPTER 14

"I've always thought that the Jet Propulsion Laboratory was part of NASA."

"No, not at all—although, we did work closely together on a lot of projects."

Wyatt leaned over the kitchen counter and refilled Allison's wine glass. "So, who's behind the JPL?"

She raised her glass. "What shall we toast to?"

"Well, how about new opportunities and new horizons?"

Allison laughed. "Sounds good—also kind of a coincidence."

Wyatt motioned with his glass towards the door to his deck. "Let's go outside and you can tell me why that's a coincidence."

She followed him outside and they stood side by side at the railing, looking out over Kootenay Lake 150 feet below. She sighed, and Wyatt stole a glance. She was wearing a New York Yankees baseball cap today, and her long brown hair was tied into a ponytail sticking out of the back of the cap.

She looked adorable, and he marveled to himself once again how adept she was at 'dressing down.' Here she was, this billionaire, standing with him on his deck dressed like she'd come right off the farm. He loved that about her already, and this was only the second time they'd been together.

She gushed, "Oh, Wyatt, this is just stunning."

"Yeah, it is, isn't it? It's a very long lake, actually just an extension of the Kootenay River, which eventually merges with the mighty Columbia River and then they head off together on a rough and tumble journey to the Pacific Ocean."

"Do you have a boat?"

"No, but I want to get one. Well, that's not entirely true—we have a police boat." Wyatt pointed. "Moored at the marina down there."

"That's kinda sexy. A Miami Vice cigar boat?"

Wyatt laughed. "No, far from it—a Sea Ray, but very fast. The bad guys can't get away from us on this lake."

Allison nudged his arm. "What bad guys? Spitters, litterers?"

"Ha, ha. Think you're smart, don't you, big city woman? Well, we get some action once in a while. Dognapping is very popular here. When we put out dragnets, we have to include 'kibbles and bits' in order to flush out the location of our victims!"

Allison smiled and took a sip of her wine. "You love it here, don't you?"

Wyatt nodded as he gazed out over the lake. "Yeah, I do, Allison. I did the big city police stuff and, while I enjoyed it, I think it prepared me for this. I was ready for a lifestyle change."

"I can understand that. I envy you."

"Hey, you haven't answered my question yet. Do I have to sit you down in the interrogation room and shine bright lights in your eyes?"

Allison rested her wine glass down on the ledge of the railing. "I forgot what you asked me. This gorgeous view has a way of numbing the mind. What was your question again?"

"I was asking about the JPL."

"Oh, yes. Well, the Jet Propulsion Laboratory is actually a part of the California Institute of Technology. We did a lot of testing of new technologies and helped build components that NASA needed in its space program.

"NASA never did much building or innovating themselves. A lot of people would be surprised to hear that. Their main role was, and still is, to envision and set goals and objectives—then just operate the missions. Just like most large companies these days, they outsourced a lot of what was needed to make those missions happen.

"For example, we at JPL designed and built the Mars Pathfinder spacecraft. Then, we worked with NASA to direct that mission. With the space shuttle program, the Canadian aerospace industry actually designed and built major structural components for the shuttles, including the space-arm, nicknamed Canadarm. That was what was used to do repair work, retrieve cargo, load cargo, et cetera. So, Canada can be proud to have been a big part of NASA's history."

"I didn't know that. You're just a little wealth of information, Allison."

"Not really—that was just my life before the hotel business." She suddenly snapped her fingers. "Oh, I remember there was something else I was going to tell you. You said that we should toast to 'new horizons,' and I said that was a coincidence, remember?"

Wyatt lit a cigarette. "Yeah, what did you mean?"

"Well, the JPL also had a big part to play in that New Horizons Space Probe—you know, the one that's sending back pictures right now of Pluto?"

"Really? Those pictures are amazing—we're learning so much more about that little planet now. Or…is it still a planet?"

"I'll always consider it a planet, and I'm an astrophysicist. So, you should pay attention to me." Allison giggled.

Wyatt couldn't help but smile at this powerful woman who was a paradox. Brilliant, educated, a wealthy businesswoman—but also a silly little girl when she wanted to be, or more likely when she just wanted to let her guard down.

"I find it easy to pay attention to you. Maybe it's that Yankees baseball cap."

She shook her head, flinging her ponytail in his face. "I think you just like my ponytail. Makes you think I'm a country girl."

"You do seem like a country girl. Honestly, you don't seem like a hotel tycoon. And, I mean that as a compliment. You don't seem like an astrophysicist either."

"What's an astrophysicist supposed to be like?"

"I dunno—perhaps someone kind of geeky. You're far from 'geeky.'"

Allison picked up her wine glass and walked over to one of the chaise lounges. She sat down and stretched her legs out. "Oh, I'll bet you sit in one of these chairs with your coffee and cigarette every morning."

Wyatt stretched out on the chaise next to her. "Good guess. Part of my morning routine, for sure."

"Well, I guess I am a bit of a geek, Wyatt. I love anything to do with outer space. It's my passion."

"What are you doing running a hotel chain, then?"

"I inherited it. My dad, mom…and my husband, died in a car crash five years ago."

"Oh…I'm sorry. I didn't know."

"That's okay. My brother and I took over the company and I left the JPL. I try to put the best enthusiasm I can muster into the hotel business, and I'm darn good at it. But…it's not my first love and not what I'd choose to do. It is my dad's legacy, though, and before him, my grandfather's. I can't ignore it—I'm sure they'd be looking down and cursing me if I didn't keep it in the family."

"I understand. Must have been a shock to lose them all at once like that. Bad enough to lose your parents, but your husband…"

"I really loved him. And, my parents, too, of course. My mom was still so healthy and vibrant. And, my dad was really young for his age. And strong. A former Navy guy."

"Did he serve in one of the wars?"

"No, he was too young for WWII or Korea. But, he did some tours around different parts of the world, and was actually seconded to the British Navy for a couple of years. The U.S. and Britain did a lot of cross-training back in those days. My dad was a hot-shot weapons specialist, so he was in big demand."

"When was that?"

"He was assigned to the HMS Diana from '55 to '57."

Wyatt frowned. "The Diana? There's something I remember about that ship. Rings a bell."

Allison lowered her voice. "Yes, it was 1956. The ship was ordered to sail through a radioactive fallout zone in the Indian Ocean. The Brits had done a nuclear test and wanted to find out the effects on sailors and the ship itself. An atrocious thing to do. Two-thirds of the 300 or so sailors have now died from radiation sickness. Lawsuits have been denied to the families due to the 'statute of limitations' expiring. Definitely a controversial part of England's history, and long-forgotten by most."

"I'll bet your dad never forgot."

She shook her head. "No, he certainly didn't. It made him angry just to talk about it."

"Was he affected by the radiation?"

"No, he was one of the lucky ones. There were a few like him who suffered no ill effects."

"That's strange, eh? You'd think all of them would have suffered the same way."

Allison sipped her wine and didn't reply.

She looked sad all of a sudden—Wyatt decided to change the subject. "So, did you work on the Mars Pathfinder mission that you were telling me about?"

"No, I was too young for that one. I did do work on the New Horizons Pluto project, though. That was launched ten years ago, so it was a long-term assignment. Now it's finished—the space probe moves out into the dark reaches of outer space now, never to be seen again and never to take another photo."

"Kinda sad, eh? When you worked on something so important, for so long, and then it just comes to an end."

Allison grimaced. "Yeah, but the information the probe gathered will live on. Just like with the Mars Pathfinder. It landed on Mars in July, 1997, but it had a roving probe that wandered around taking pictures—in fact 550 of them.

"I was too young to be involved in the design of the Pathfinder, but one of the jobs I had when I was at JPL was to analyse all of those photos when they came in. Well, not just me—there were several of us physicists doing it. I was still doing some of that work when I left in 2010. Fascinating. So, it does all live on. Nothing is ever really finished, know what I mean?"

"Yeah, I think I do. I can definitely see where your passions lie, because we've hardly talked about the hotel industry at all so far."

She laughed. "It shows, does it? Well don't you worry—I'll do a marvelous job at building our hotel here. So, tell me about your history. Any wife in your past?"

Wyatt got up from his chaise and stood at the railing.

"My fiancé died of cancer ten years ago. She was pregnant. Baby couldn't be saved. That's why I resigned from the RCMP and moved back here. Too many memories back in Toronto, and I needed to have a different kind of life. More meaningful.

"I know that sounds kind of 'new age,' but it's the way I felt at the time. And, I'm glad I did it. Life's too short to be constantly barraged by some of the horrible stuff I used to see with the Mounties. You can take those memories to bed with you only so often, until they start to eat away at your soul. So, now, I prefer the spitters, shoplifters and dog nappers in Nelson instead."

Allison joined him at the railing, and rubbed his shoulder. "I'm so sorry about your fiancé and child. Sounds like we've both had to deal with some major heartbreaks in our lives."

Wyatt gazed into her mesmerizing blue eyes and, for just that moment, he could see that this powerful businesswoman was letting her guard down a wee bit more. There was genuine compassion in those eyes—that wasn't something even the most manipulative power broker could fake.

"Let's change the subject. It sounds like your meeting yesterday with city council went well."

"Yes, it did. They're all very excited and so am I. The next step is to choose the site and file a plan with council. Then, after we get the approvals, we'll break ground. I move very fast—you'll be impressed, I promise."

Wyatt blushed. "I'm already impressed."

She rubbed his shoulder again. "Wyatt, I don't think your dad was too impressed though. He seemed really nervous and unsettled this morning, back there in his studio."

Wyatt's mouth went dry. He was hoping she hadn't noticed Willy's mood.

"I think he just has a tough time letting people see where he works, see his unfinished creations. That studio is kind of his sanctuary."

"Are you sure he's okay?"

"Yeah, he's fine. He's thrilled about his draft-dodger sculpture finally getting center stage."

"Okay. But, he seemed a little upset when I noticed that other thing he'd been working on."

"The sphere? I'd never even seen that one myself. I'm surprised he didn't have it covered—he usually does that with the new things he's working on."

"I loved the draft-dodger sculpture. It's really special and we'll give it prominence at our new hotel, for sure. But, he never talked to you about that sphere project before? Never explained it to you?"

"No, and he didn't seem to have much of an explanation this morning either when you asked him about it. Remember, though, he's an artist. Sometimes I think those types are just possessed, and don't really know why they do things. I've seen a couple of other weird sculptures that he never had any explanations for."

"That sphere is beautiful though—and such a perfect ball. And those canyons and mountains are so precise. He even drilled in tunnels. Seemed like he was working off some kind of model."

"He is good, isn't he?"

*****

Back in her room at the Kootenay Palace, Allison reflected on the lovely afternoon she'd spent with Wyatt. She turned on the radio and tuned in to a classical music station. Then flopped back onto the 'heavenly' bed and closed her eyes.

She really liked Wyatt. Such a gentleman, but at the same time so confident and curious. A man who was easy to talk to, and actually interested in things she had to say. Men like that were rare. In fact, she hadn't met a man like that since her wonderful husband.

She enjoyed her job as the CEO of Diamond Hotels, but at times really resented her role with Majestic 12. There were so many lovely people she met who she couldn't be totally honest with. She hated being deceptive, especially to a special man like Wyatt Carson.

She couldn't tell him that in their analysis of the Mars Pathfinder photos they had discovered something utterly shocking on the surface of Mars. Some of the photos had been leaked and some conspiracy sites had already put two and two together. But, no one paid attention to those sites, and the photos were deliberately made 'grainy' by the JPL, so the conspirators couldn't really tell what they were looking at—at least not with any certainty.

But, Allison and others had seen the full resolution photos.

On the surface of Mars was an exact full-size replica of the same Sphinx that sat mysteriously in Egypt's Giza Plateau. The tourist attraction that everyone thought was just, well, 'one of those things.' A once in a lifetime sight, if you were lucky enough to travel to Egypt.

Or…to Mars.

Allison also couldn't tell Wyatt that her elderly father, before he died, had incredible strength, a full head of hair, and still had every single one of his original teeth.

That he had acquired a strange musical talent after returning from the HMS Diana. That he, just like Wyatt's dad, could never have any x-rays done or he'd be all aglow and turn transparent.

And, that there was a reason why he and two other shipmates on the Diana never experienced any radiation sickness—or any other sickness for that matter—for the rest of their lives.

That it had something to do with the aft gun turret of the HMS Diana, a turret that contained a 4.5-inch radar-controlled surface-to-air gun that had activated itself and aimed towards the sky as the ship sailed through that radioactive cloud.

Her dad and two others were in that turret, trying to ascertain why the gun had reacted automatically.

Then, they looked up and saw it.

And felt it.

The powerful beam that blinded them for a few seconds. The beam that caused them to vomit blood within minutes of being exposed.

She couldn't tell Wyatt that these objects in the sky with the powerful beams had been spotted at every single military conflict in the last 100 years.

At every war, every nuclear test, every serious conflict.

And, she couldn't tell Wyatt that the New Horizons probe that had just sent back photos of Pluto wasn't really designed for Pluto at all.

Pluto was just a fly-by.

The stated purpose of the mission, and the photos of Pluto, were just smokescreens for the real purpose of New Horizons.

The naïve public thought that this was all just for their entertainment. Just to further their knowledge of Pluto.

Like, who really gives a shit about Pluto?

Did they really think that their precious tax dollars went towards financing a horrendously expensive ten-year mission to a planet that probably wasn't even really a planet?

The probe had just finished a 3.5-billion-mile journey to show the world what Pluto looked like.

But, the world couldn't handle the knowledge of what the probe was really intended to do.

It would now keep on flying, off to the outer universe into the Kuiper Belt, onward to its real destination. This probe, the size of a grand piano, had a most serious mission—much more serious than sending silly photos of Pluto back for the masses to enjoy.

And, she definitely couldn't tell Wyatt that the sphere that she'd seen in Willy's studio this morning—the perfectly carved piece of granite with the mountains, canyons and tunnels—was a familiar object to her. Every single mountain, canyon and tunnel seemed to be exactly where they should be.

Because she'd already seen renditions from the Hubble Space Telescope. A long time ago. Not clear photo images, more just computer imagery. But, enough to scare the shit out of those fortunate enough—or unfortunate enough—to see them.

Yes, Wyatt would indeed be alarmed to know that the real purpose of the New Horizons probe was to seek out and photograph up close and personal, the exact sphere that his very own father had sculpted a copy of in his studio.

CHAPTER 15

"No reports at the hospital, and none of my officers have seen anyone looking like those two guys. They're either laying low, or they've left town. I'm guessing the latter. It's been three days now, and no sign of them. So, don't worry, Dad—I don't think they'll be back."

Willy paced back and forth in the studio, while Wyatt sat calmly on a stool near the window.

"I can't believe they were able to walk out of here, Wyatt. They were out cold and I was only away from the studio for a few minutes, phoning you."

"Dad, I know from experience that unconsciousness sometimes doesn't last very long. We've had prisoners that looked half-dead, then they suddenly bounced back to life ready to take on the world. These two punks probably woke up and just got the hell out of here as fast as they could. You scared them—they probably didn't think you'd be able to fight back."

Willy nodded.

"Don't worry about it. They just wanted to steal some stuff, and now they're gone. They won't be back."

"Yeah, you're probably right."

"So, what did you hit them with? One of your tools?"

Wyatt noticed a bit of hesitation before his dad answered. And, being trained in observing and interrogating, he noticed his eyes make a quick involuntary movement. A nervous movement that was totally out of context with the conversation.

His father's eyes glanced up at the wood plank ceiling.

"No, I just used my fists. Lucky for me they were in pretty weak shape. An old guy like me wouldn't have had a chance otherwise."

Wyatt nodded, got up from his chair and walked to the center of the room. He stared up at the ceiling, right at the spot where his dad's eyes had flicked to.

There was something.

He went over to the workbench and grabbed a flashlight, then walked back to the same spot and flashed the torch at the ceiling.

"Wyatt, what are you doing?"

He could see it clearly now. A splatter of blood with some green woolen material stuck to it.

Wyatt lowered the flashlight and directed his attention back to his father.

"Dad, that's blood up there. And, didn't you say one of the guys wore a toque?"

Willy nodded.

"A green toque?"

Willy nodded again.

"You'd better come clean with me—now. How did the guy's head get way up there?"

Willy stood motionless. His mouth started to move, but no words came.

Wyatt walked back to the workbench and was just about to put the flashlight down when he noticed something else. He shone the torch along the edge of the counter. More blood, and this time there was a clump of hair stuck in the mess.

"Dad, tell me what went on here!"

Willy walked over to him and put his hand on his shoulder. "I had a burst of strength, probably from the anger I felt about their threat against your mother."

Wyatt pushed his hand away.

"Dad, you're eighty-seven years old! Are you telling me you took on both these guys by throwing one of them up into a ten-foot-high ceiling and the other one across the floor into this workbench?"

Willy nodded, sadness covering his face like a mask. "As I said, a burst of strength."

Wyatt pointed. "You were standing over there, in the center of the room?"

"Yeah."

"So, you threw one upward, and the other one over here?"

Another solemn nod.

"Dad, from over there to this workbench is a good twenty feet. At my age, I couldn't even do that, let alone muster the strength to throw a human body straight up into a ceiling."

A look of resignation came over his dad's face. He grimaced and leaned his head sideways.

"I guess it's about time I told you some things."

*****

Listening to his father for the last hour had left Wyatt spellbound. It sounded like a movie script—for a horror film.

It was almost impossible to believe, but here was his dad sitting right in front of him, telling him this tale—and, because it was his father, he believed every word of it.

The story ended with Willy asking, "Well, what do you have to say?"

Wyatt let out a long breath—a breath that he was sure he'd been holding for the last sixty minutes or so.

"I knew that transparency thing was a weird reaction, but I never could have imagined this. When I saw you like that in the hospital, I was horrified. And, I did kinda wonder why you seemed so calm. Now I know why. This happened before, and you were told that x-rays would set it off again."

"That's right. I wasn't really concerned—but I was alarmed that you and your mom saw me like that. I'd gone for so long keeping it all a secret, and I'd done a pretty good job of it. Until that day."

"Now I understand that other sculpture I found over there in the corner—the skeletal-looking soldier. The one you'd covered up with a tarp."

Willy just sighed and lowered his eyes.

"Was it the Chinese? Or the Koreans? A secret weapon they had?"

His father looked up again and shook his head.

"I don't know. The general just said it was an enemy—he didn't say who. But, I heard afterwards that just the sight of that thing in the sky sent the Chinese and Koreans into retreat. So, I don't think it was their craft."

"Well, aside from little green men, who else could it have been? They were the only two enemies we were fighting in that war. And, we wouldn't use a secret weapon against ourselves. Unless…"

"Unless what?"

Wyatt was thinking about what Allison had told him about her own father and the crew of the HMS Diana. The British had indeed used a weapon that infected their own sailors—just to test the effects of radiation. Luckily, her dad had escaped any consequences, but most of those sailors had died of radiation sicknesses years afterwards.

"Well, I guess there have been incidences where countries have tested weapons against their own people—so maybe that was it. There was Agent Orange here in the U.S. and the HMS Diana nuclear incident in 1956—Allison told me her father had been on that ship."

"I've thought about that over the years, Wyatt, wondering if they'd tested something on us. That general didn't seem surprised by any of the side effects—he seemed to know a lot about it, as if he'd seen it happen before. And, the doctors in Seoul appeared to know what they were testing for."

Wyatt scratched his chin. "That could be it then. Stick out your tongue now, Dad. I want to see it. No need to hide it from me anymore."

Willy leaned forward and stuck it out as far as he could.

Wyatt recoiled. Shocked at the sight, he couldn't control the involuntary reaction. His hands flew to his mouth and he felt the hairs rise on the back of his neck.

"Shit, Dad! That's horrible! Looks like fish scales! Does it hurt?"

"Sorry about that, son. Now you know why I didn't want you to see it. And, no, it never hurts—in fact, it always feels just kind of numb."

"Mom must know about that tongue. I mean, you do still kiss, don't you?"

"Yeah, she knows—but that's all she knows. I gave her some bullshit story about how some of us drank water contaminated with traces of acid during the war. Kinda lame, but she bought it."

"After hearing this story, no wonder you're so youthful for your age. I just thought it was good family genes."

"Well, I guess it is, really. I told you the general said that my DNA was permanently changed. And—keep this in mind, Wyatt—you were conceived after the Korean War, so part of the 'new me' is in you. Have you noticed anything strange about yourself?"

Wyatt shook his head, and then chuckled. "Aside from my devilishly handsome looks, no, nothing at all."

Willy smiled. "Now, remember I was sworn to secrecy on this. You can't repeat anything to anyone."

"Christ, what can they do to you now, Dad? That was almost seven decades ago!"

"I get visits every three years or so, Wyatt. From people who never give their names. They check on me, ask questions, then they leave. They know where I am and I have the feeling they'll always know where I am, no matter where I go."

"I want to meet these people the next time they come around, Dad. I won't let on I know anything, but I want to check them out. Okay?"

"Okay, son. There's another reason why we have to keep this between us. Money was deposited into a Swiss bank account for me back in 1950. I had to wait until the year 2000 before I could access it, and even then I was restricted to only ten percent a year until death. But, once I die, the account gets collapsed and the full amount gets credited to my estate. I haven't drawn one cent from it yet. The money's been invested, and has now reached over five million."

"Christ!"

"Yes, indeed. But, here's the kicker—if they discover that I let the 'cat out of the bag' on any of this, I lose the money."

"We'll keep it quiet, Dad. Just between us—don't worry. But, we have to make up some kind of excuse to Allison to make sure that they don't give you any x-rays when you're down at the CDC clinic for your checkup. If they give you x-rays that would certainly let the 'cat out of the bag.'"

"Yeah, we'll think of something that will convince her. Might just say I get reactions to radiation—like rashes, things like that."

Wyatt nodded. "God, no wonder those boys took off faster than antelopes. You must have scared the shit out of them, seeing you glowing and looking like a skeleton, then experiencing your strength—they must have thought you were some kind of creature from Mars. Or a superhero."

Willy laughed. "I do feel sorry for them, have to be honest. Sure, they were scum, but no one deserves to be scared like that."

Wyatt stood and walked over to the sphere in the corner. "Dad, what the hell is this all about? What is it you've made here? Looks like a planet with mountains, canyons, tunnels—is this supposed to be Earth?"

Willy shook his head. "I haven't got a clue what it is, son. It can't be Earth—I've already double-checked the topographical maps and none of those features match. I don't know what made me create it—as I told you, I just woke up in the middle of the night, in a daze, and felt compelled to do it. I had no control at all—was like I was on auto-pilot, hypnotized maybe. It's a real mystery."

Wyatt knelt down and tried to roll the sphere. It wouldn't budge no matter how much of his strength he put into it.

"Somehow, Dad, you've kept this incredible strength a secret from me and Mom your whole adult life. So, now I want to see it firsthand. Roll this sucker. Show me."

Willy sighed. "See, even with my own son I'm becoming a circus freak. Okay, I'll oblige you. But, I can do much better than just roll it."

Wyatt watched in stunned silence as his dear old father crouched, wrapped his arms around the solid granite sphere, and lifted it into the air.

Clutching it tightly against his chest like a newborn infant, he stood with ease to his full and youthful six foot, three-inch height.

CHAPTER 16

"How yer head doin?"

Matt Lawson gently rubbed the bandage plastered to the top of his skull.

"Is kay, I think. Still gettin headaches, but not as bad. How yers?"

Brody Finch tilted the bottle and sucked back the remainder of his beer. Snapped his fingers at the waitress on the other side of the bar, pointed to both empty bottles, and held up two fingers.

"I dunno, Matt. The low part of my head hit that bench thin. Was bleedin, but seems to haf stopped now. Neck aches, though."

"Freaky night, huh? Ya think that was a costume he was wearin?"

Brody shook his head. "No, he looked normal after few minutes. Sumthin wrong with that guy. And gotta axe myself why he dint want to phone the police. Dint you wonder bout that?"

Matt nodded. "Yep, thought that was strange. And…what kind of man can t'row people round like rag dolls? Even karate guys can't do that. I weigh a buck-sixty and he shoved me straight up in d'air."

"Well, he tossed me bout twenty er thirty feet into that bench. And, he's an old dude. He got sum lab in that place, maybe? Making sum super drug or sumpin?"

Brody turned his head at the sudden loud chatter up at the bar. He noticed they were all watching the TV mounted on the wall behind the counter. Some were laughing and pointing at the monitor, and there was some applause.

Then, he saw a familiar face on the TV screen. He grabbed Matt by the arm and pulled him up from his chair. He pointed at the screen. "Look! Is him!"

They both stared with their mouths open in astonishment at the image of the handsome old man who'd scared the shit out of them several nights ago. Then, the image disappeared and the news feature was over. Everyone at the bar applauded and clapped each other on the back.

Brody rushed up to the bar with Matt in tow. They sat down on stools and ordered more beers. Then, Brody turned to the middle-aged guy next to him.

He motioned his head in the direction of the TV. "What wuz that all bout?"

The man smiled at him. "Oh, just something on the local news about one of our local celebrities. Willy Carson. He's a renowned sculptor, and news just broke that he's going to be the spokesperson for a new luxury hotel to be built here. We haven't had a new hotel here in about a decade, and this is going to be part of that big chain, Diamond Hotels. And…his sculpture in honor of draft-dodgers is going to be a monument in front of the hotel. We're kind of excited!"

"His name Willy Carson, you said?"

"Yeah, he lives just off Baker Street. Big beautiful house. He's quite wealthy from all his artwork. Well-loved guy, we're all so happy for him."

"Thas good news fer yer town, eh?"

"Oh, it's big news, son! Big news!"

Brody nodded.

"You boys just passing through?"

"Yup."

"Where from?"

"Vancouver, on way ta Calgary."

The man stood up and held out his hand. "Nice chatting with you. Safe travels."

Brody shook his hand. "Thanks, man."

After the man had moved off, Brody grabbed Matt by the collar of his shirt and tugged him back towards their table.

"We gotta talk bout this."

*****

"We never need to intervene until things become weird. These people have always been allowed to go about their daily lives until something happened that would be too hard to explain."

Allison nodded agreement. "I understand that, Chad, but he's an old man."

"They're all old now, Allison. That's the problem. Most of them will outlive all of us, so we need to continue to keep an eye on them—and, after we die, our successors will need to carry on watching them in our place. Who the hell knows how long they'll live?"

"C'mon, Chad. They're not going to live forever."

"That's the problem. We just don't know. Look how healthy they are! The only ones left now are those who weren't killed in accidents. And, they're all kind of prominent, so they attract attention. Maybe they became prominent because of the special talents they acquired? I don't know, but because they're famous in their communities, anything weird that happens with them will attract attention. We can't ignore that, and we just don't know how long they'll live."

The other ten sitting around the boardroom table remained silent as the exchange between Allison and Chad ran its course. They were accustomed to seeing the two of them spar—Chad being the 'lame duck' leader, and Allison being the 'heir apparent.'

Chad didn't want to give up the reins, and Allison was reluctant to take them. A bit of a dilemma for each of them. But, succession was mandatory, and they both knew they had no choice in the matter.

It was indeed just like royal heritage. There were age-old traditions that couldn't be ignored. Not in England and not in the boardroom of Majestic 12.

Allison pointed her index finger at Chad. "William Carson better walk out of here under his own steam, or I'll hold you personally responsible, Chad."

Chad Powers glared at her, then flipped open the file in front of him.

"We have a more serious problem to deal with today. You each have a folder in front of you with a photo and a brief synopsis of the subject matter. Those folders cannot leave the room, by the way, so commit everything to memory.

"We've all been following the preliminary debates and campaigning for the presidential election—which is still over a year away. The man whose face you see in the photo is a familiar one to all of us—indeed to every citizen in America."

Phillip Stang, a prominent defense contractor, interrupted. "Why are we discussing him? He's not a candidate."

Chad held up his hand. "Let me continue. You haven't had a chance to read the synopsis yet, so I'll give you all an executive summary. As you know, we never get involved in politics unless we have to. And, for good reason, no politicians are ever allowed to sit around this table. Majestic 12 is non-political.

"However, some disturbing intelligence has come to our attention. This man is close to announcing his candidacy for the presidency. In fact, he's very close. And, he intends to run as an Independent, even though at one time or another he's been both a Republican and a Democrat."

Allison looked up from the folder and noticed one gentleman, who she despised, squirming nervously in his seat as Chad talked.

She'd already scanned the contents of the folder—Allison was a speed reader, a talent which none of her colleagues knew she possessed. After what she'd just read, she was feeling a tightening in her stomach, that terrible feeling you get just before having to make a speech.

The squirming man across the table from her was Charles Farmington, the CEO and major shareholder of one of the nation's largest energy companies. He was probably the sleaziest businessman she knew, and a well-known drunk.

And, unbeknownst to almost every citizen of the United States, Charles Farmington was America's biggest contributor to the slow, but sure, death of the Gulf of Mexico. The BP-owned and operated Deepwater Horizon oil rig explosion grabbed all the headlines back in 2010, resulting in not only the loss of eleven lives, but also the unstoppable leak of 5 million barrels of oil into the precious waters of the Gulf.

'Unstoppable' because it has never been stopped, to this day, even though the government declared that the crisis had ended six months after the explosion.

But, fifty other abandoned wells were leaking, too; wells that had never been capped properly by Farmington's company, Tempest Energy Corp. Some of them had been leaking for two decades, yet BP was blamed for most of the pollution that now existed in the Gulf. The Deepwater Horizon had been a convenient tragedy for Farmington's company. With his connections in Washington, they were willing to look the other way at his transgressions and agreed that recouping costs from the United Kingdom-based BP was the best solution.

Allison despised the man, and her imagination began spinning as to why Charles Farmington was squirming in his seat right now. She concentrated on his eyes, and then stuck her two index fingers quickly into her ears. So quickly that no one noticed.

She only needed a second. A quick pop of her fingers back out again, and that was all that was needed to trigger the unique engine in her brain.

Suddenly, Charles's thoughts were in her head and almost immediately she knew why he was so nervous. This power she had only lasted a few seconds at a time, and only worked with one person at a time. But, sometimes a few seconds were all she needed to learn something important—or salaciously gossipy.

She had channeled Charles' brain into hers for just an instant.

It was a power she'd inherited from her dad's altered DNA. It wasn't a power her father had ever exhibited, but she was told by him that different aspects of the DNA might be passed along to her that he had never displayed.

She could thank the HMS Diana for the little gift. Or, rather, thank the strange flying object that had fired that beam at her father and two others on the HMS Diana back in 1956.

The moment ended and Allison was paying attention once again to what Chad was saying.

"...and someone in this room has unfortunately passed along information to this man that he intends to use in his campaign. This is an unusual campaign this year, as we've all noticed. For the first time in history, we have an up swell of real serious anger amongst the electorate, and certain candidates from both parties are tapping into that anger.

"They're challenging the status quo, the corporate donors, threatening to disclose wrongs and untruths. This is happening in both major parties, and the people love it. And, with a couple of the more bellicose ones grabbing all the headlines, the others are frantically trying to catch up—trying to soak up some of those headlines for themselves.

"Well, this man whose face is in your folder, is planning to blow everything wide open about certain secrets. That will be the platform for grabbing his share of voter attention. And, the public will eat it up.

"Truths that are sworn to be protected at all costs by the charter of Majestic 12, are going to be splashed all over the mainstream news. He is such a prominent and well-loved figure in the Senate that the major networks will have no choice but to cover his assertions.

"This is very serious, ladies and gentleman. We have to deal with it as we are obligated to do."

Allison's sad eyes gazed down at the photo in her folder. Senator John Hartford. She'd met him before—he'd stayed in the royal suite at one of her hotels in Honolulu. They'd even had dinner together.

She knew what he stood for...and what he stood against. For years, she'd watched his performance in the Senate. Always on the right side of the equation, always standing up for principle and opposing every stupid war that America had managed to dupe itself into.

He'd called for a new investigation into 9/11, had demanded to know why twenty-eight pages had been redacted from the 9/11 Commission Report. Demanded answers on the rumored involvement of Saudi Arabia in the tragedy. He never got anywhere. No one listened to him. Senator Hartford had been a lone voice in a wilderness of liars and cowards.

Allison always hoped…and prayed…that John Hartford would run for president one day. The country needed someone like him.

Chad was talking again.

"The last politician who threatened to expose the secrets protected by Majestic 12 was John Fitzgerald Kennedy. Now, we have another one. Someone who thinks it's time America knows what it doesn't know. Now, it's even more serious than it was back in 1963—because a lot of time has passed and things are a lot more imminent now than they were back then."

Allison had heard Charles Farmington's thoughts. In fact, in her mind she'd even seen him sitting in a bar with Senator Hartford. She'd heard his mind cursing his own drunken stupidity. Charles had told the senator everything. And, she saw him pass a thick file to him on their way out of the bar. She could only guess what was in that file. And, she couldn't help herself thinking, "*Go, Senator, go.*"

"I'm calling for a show of hands. Senator Hartford has to be neutralized, and it's our duty to vote on the sanction. As usual, a simple majority is all that's required, and no explanations are needed if you vote against this action."

Allison leaned forward and glared down the table at Chad.

Allison knew she had to be very careful how she expressed herself right at this moment, because all eyes were on her and she knew she probably stood alone. She also couldn't completely hide the fire in her eyes—a fire that came easily to her every time she looked into the evil face of Chad Powers.

"Before we vote, Chad, can we discuss alternatives? Senator Hartford is a reasonable man, and we could take the unusual step of bringing him into our confidence. I'm sure he would appreciate the chaos it would cause if certain information was made public. We can try to convince him—it's worth a try. He's one of the country's best and brightest. Hartford should be president—we'd be better off with him at the helm than any of the other candidates. He's a good man, they don't come any better."

Chad shook his head. "No, Allison, that's not up to us. Our mandate is clear and you know that. We are not charged with making judgements like that. Our job is to protect the truth, first and foremost." He scanned his eyes around the table. "Alright, a show of hands, please?"

Ten hands flew up, including from the little sleaze, Charles Farmington. Allison kept her hands firmly in her lap. Chad glared at her for a moment, then declared, "It's affirmative, then. Meeting adjourned."

As they all got up to leave, Allison noticed out of the corner of her eye, the crooked finger of Chad Powers gesturing in Charles Farmington's direction. That gesture meant that Charles had to stay behind for a few minutes for a private chat with the head of Majestic 12.

Allison knew that, after today, she'd never see Charles Farmington again.

She'd seen the entire succession plan of all the members. Charles' successor was his eldest son, Kevin. Allison hadn't met him yet, but knew that she and the others would get that honor at the next meeting, if history proved to be a predictor.

She didn't feel anything at all about the pending demise of Charles Farmington. But, she did feel pangs of anxiety in her gut over Senator John Hartford. The pangs were literally eating out her insides as she rode the elevator up to the main lobby of the Centers for Disease Control.

As Allison Fisher walked out to the relative calm of her car, she thought back, way back.

Images in her head of talent lost to her country in the last few years, even the images of those who were lost before she had assumed her seat five years ago.

All of the members of Majestic 12 knew the history.

A history of scientists, astronomers, meteorologists, engineers, astrophysicists—all dead before their time.

And, she thought of that brave President of the United States who had dared to ask what he never should have asked.

John Fitzgerald Kennedy.

But, she had the feeling that even if JFK had known what was going to happen to him, he still would have had the courage to ask. He was just that type of man, much like Senator John Hartford. Two peas in a pod. And, soon to be side by side in heaven, looking down, shaking their heads in disgust.

CHAPTER 17

Allison hadn't been to her parents' house in several months. Those were visits that were hard to commit to. It was the home she and her brother had grown up in, and it held so many memories for both of them that it seemed almost haunted every time she walked the halls.

But, she had to make an appearance once in a while just to make sure everything was okay. Her brother couldn't be bothered, but that was just the way he was. He liked the investment that the house represented for both of them, but didn't really revel in the sentimentality of it.

Allison was different. She was very sentimental and, after their parents' deaths, she'd convinced Robert that they should hang on to the house for a few years. With the housing crash, it had fallen in value from five million to around three, and Allison felt that they should wait until it had regained its value again.

It was now safe to sell it, for probably around six million, but she was still resisting her brother on putting it up for sale. Neither of them needed the money, so it was kind of a moot point. But, she felt that her brother just wanted it gone, wanted the memory of it erased. For Allison, selling it felt almost like chopping off one of her limbs.

She guided her Audi down West Fullerton, then headed north on Lakeview Avenue. After a couple of minutes, she turned left onto the familiar street, the setting for most of her tomboy mischief when she was a kid.

Twenty-eight West St. James Place was one of the more exclusive addresses in Lincoln Park, which was itself one of the most exclusive neighborhoods in all of Chicago. The area was bordered to the west by the Chicago River, and to the east by Lake Michigan. Chockfull of upscale restaurants and coffee shops, art and antique galleries, and even the oldest nightclub in Chicago, called Neo. While Chicago was known worldwide as a cultural center for some of the best jazz and blues music imaginable, Neo featured any kind of music your little heart desired. The famous acts that had hung out there included David Bowie, Iggy Pop, The Clash, and U2.

Allison had met Bono there one time with her dad—they visited him backstage after an impromptu show he'd put on. While he was nice enough, she was put off by how full of himself he was, and how quickly he launched into bragging about his personal influence on solving the world's environmental problems. Influence that Allison knew for a fact was exaggerated—Bono was a 'legend in his own mind.' He went on *ad nauseum* about how society was oblivious to how much carbon they were spewing into the atmosphere. Allison was too polite to ask him if the private jet he'd flown over in from London was being powered by apple juice.

She'd so wished that her dad could have arranged a 'meet and greet' with Bowie instead.

Lincoln Park was mainly a white neighborhood and had more than its share of expensive private schools, which Allison and Robert had attended all the way up until their entrance to university. The education at those schools had been superb, but Allison had wished that the socialization had been better. They'd rubbed shoulders with primarily rich kids, which didn't exactly give any kid a realistic look at what the real world was like. Being born rich had its drawbacks and, in Allison's opinion, the wealthy children had a much harder struggle on the social side once they were out in the jungle. That was one of the reasons she'd resisted joining the family's hotel empire, choosing instead to study physics in university. After graduation, her joining the Jet Propulsion Laboratory had shocked her parents—they thought she was just going through a phase; that she would shed her rebellious energy after college and join the family business. But, Allison had surprised them all and took a relatively low-paying job as an astrophysicist at the JPL and stayed there until the tragic car accident.

Money had never mattered very much to Allison—being her own person was what was important, which was hard to do in a dominant, rich family. Now, she had more money than she knew what to do with and, ironically, wasn't half as fulfilled as she'd been when she was making just a tiny fraction at the JPL.

But, she was running the hotel empire as a family obligation, and serving as a member of Majestic 12 as another obligation. She regretted that her life was now consumed with obligations. She'd never envisioned that it would be that way.

She turned into the circular drive of the deserted mansion at Twenty-eight West St. James Place, and turned off the powerful engine of her Audi R8.

Every couple of months or so, Allison came by to pay her respects to the family abode. They had housekeeping and gardening staff there on a regular basis, to make sure the home's appearance was kept up and that it looked lived in. So, there was no real work for her to do when she visited. She just came to soak up the atmosphere…and to remember.

There were two other vehicles parked in the driveway. One she recognized as belonging to Mark, the caretaker. He'd been with the family for forty years, and Allison kept him on after her parents died. Mark was like family to her.

The other vehicle was a van, with the lettering *Lincoln Pest Control* along the side. She'd seen this van here many times before. Being an old house, they'd had problems with wasp nests in the rafters and mice multiplying behind the walls. She guessed it was one of those two problems once again.

Allison opened the front door and entered into the massive 'Tara-style' foyer, with its mandatory winding staircase. That staircase alone brought back memories—she could still picture her and her brother sliding all the way down and falling onto their asses at the bottom. When there was no one else in the house, she still indulged herself once in a while.

Mark came out of the study, which was just off a small hallway to the left of the foyer. Behind him came the pest guy, trudging along with his equipment in tow.

Allison rushed up to Mark and embraced him with a big hug. "So good to see you! How have you been? How's the family?"

He smiled warmly at her, probably remembering back to when she was just a little girl. "Hello, dear. Family's fine—grandchildren total six now and they're all growing up way too fast. But, more importantly, how are you?"

"Aw, I'm fine, Mark. Kind of busy lately, but that's okay. My brother's still nagging me about selling the house, but I don't think I'm ready yet. Plus, I'd still like to see your smiling face for a few more years."

"That's sweet of you. But, I understand that you're going to have to sell it eventually. I'll settle for a cup of coffee with you once in a while after that happens. I won't let you forget about me."

Mark chuckled. "You're probably too embarrassed to remember that I even changed your diapers once in a while. We formed quite the bond, you and I. Diapers will do that."

Allison giggled. "I don't remember, of course, but I do remember you telling me. I think you say that just to keep me off balance, having me know that you've seen me naked!"

"Well, I guess I have—and I have to say, your butt doesn't look much bigger than it did back then!"

Allison kissed him on the forehead. "I love that you're still the old flirt you always were. So, I assume that gentleman standing behind you is the pest guy?"

"Yeah, this is Chuck. Chuck, meet Allison Fisher, the owner."

Chuck mumbled something that Allison thought was 'pleased to meet you,' but she wasn't quite sure.

Mark wisely decided to do the talking for him. "Had to call Chuck in—as you know, his company's been here many times before. This time, for mice again. Need to get rid of these little buggers in case you do decide to sell. Chuck thinks we may have the problem licked now—their droppings were only seen in the study area of the house, so we're probably down to the last room. As usual, we had to pull out some of the wall panels to set the traps up inside. We put the panels back in place again, don't worry. Once we allow enough time for the traps to work, we'll come back again and take them out. So, everything looks normal in there for now."

"That's great, Mark. I can always count on you."

Mark leaned forward and gave her a warm hug. "Take care of yourself, dear. I'll see you soon."

He and Chuck headed for the door, but then Mark suddenly snapped his fingers and turned back to face her.

"Oh, I forgot something. Getting old, Allison. Losing my memory. Your dad had kind of a secret panel in the wall behind his desk. We discovered it when pulling the panels off—that one just came off real easy. It was installed with a clasp, designed to pop on and off. I've found that a lot of successful businesspeople had things like that—their safes were like decoys, because they seemed to like to keep some other important stuff behind secret panels. So, there you have it. All we found in there was a locked briefcase. I put the case on his desk for you. Okay?"

Allison frowned. "That's strange. Okay, Mark, I'll check it out. Thanks very much for that."

CHAPTER 18

Allison's father had a study that most people could only imagine in their wildest dreams. Three of the walls were solid oak paneling, dark stained, giving the room a seriously intimidating ambience. The fourth wall was a bookcase, lined with all the old classics.

A massive chandelier hung from the middle of the ceiling, controlled by a dimmer switch that could change the mood of the room with just a twist of the fingers. A wet bar sat invitingly in one corner, and small antique end tables were situated at strategic spots throughout the office, each adorned with study lamps.

Another corner of the room was graced by a baby grand piano. Music was one of the skills her dad brought back with him from the HMS Diana. And, once he'd bought this house, he made sure to purchase a piano as well. He'd never had a lesson in his life, but could play the instrument like a maestro.

Allison had always loved coming into the study as a little girl—it was her favorite room in the house. Her dad would put his work aside when she popped in, and immediately accede to her girlish demands that he play a tune for her. She'd then curl up in his leather chair, the same one she was sitting in right now, and listen to the beautiful melodies that flowed from his fingers, from his brain…and from his soul. Not once could she recall ever seeing sheet music in front of him. The music had just come from… somewhere else.

She looked away from the piano and spun around in the leather chair. Facing the huge ornate desk now, she slid her hands across the smooth oak with hand-carved images of ancient explorers. She slipped off her shoes, and braced her bare feet against the lion-paw legs and ran her toes down along the detailed indentations.

Then she sat back in the chair, sighed, and looked down once again at the pile of papers that she'd pulled out of the briefcase after breaking the flimsy lock with a pocket knife.

Allison had spent the last two hours reading the material, and was still in a state of shock.

She decided a drink was in order.

She walked over to the bar, poured herself a scotch neat, and then headed to the piano. She tapped out a few notes to the Carpenters song, *Close to You*, and then drained half her glass.

Allison couldn't sit still, but she didn't want to leave the room yet either. She went, glass in hand, over to the couch against the wall closest to the door, and stretched out.

She just closed her eyes and thought. Back to that day about fifteen years ago when her dad had sat her down in this very room and told her everything. Everything.

That day she had learned about the HMS Diana, that her dad had suffered side effects from some strange 'enemy.' Glowing body, transparency, superhuman strength, teeth that would last forever, a full head of hair that women would swoon over well into his old age. And the musical talent, of course.

He'd suffered similar side effects that Willy Carson had suffered, except that in her dad's case, his father had already been one of the original members of Majestic 12 when it happened to him. So, her dad knew a hell of a lot more than Willy Carson did. He knew for a fact who the 'enemy' was.

When her grandfather died, her dad assumed his spot on the Majestic 12 panel. And, that day when her dad had told her all of this, he also told her she was his designated replacement once he died.

She'd learned so much that day.

Majestic 12 was formed in 1947 after a very specific incident. President Harry Truman ordered it put into place after the furor that surrounded the Roswell, New Mexico UFO crash. Of course, the world was told it was a weather balloon. Hardly anyone believed that flimsy story, not even to this day. But, despite that, the government had managed for decades to keep a lid on it.

Keeping lids on things started with Roswell, and with the formation of Majestic 12. President Truman was so worried that the population couldn't handle the knowledge about extra-terrestrial intelligence, that he wanted an elite group vested with the absolute authority and unlimited power to keep those secrets.

He believed that no one should hear that these 'enemies' had visited us in 1947. And, that they'd visited us again in the fifties during the Korean War. And, that there were reports of them visiting the scenes of battles all the way back to WWI. But, Korea was when they actually started intervening in our battles. When he retired from office in 1953, Truman was satisfied that Majestic 12 had been the right thing to do. They were efficiently smothering events and he thus set in motion the mandate that they would continue as a group until the end of time. With total autonomy, reporting to only one high-placed general in the Pentagon, a role that would of course also have to be replaced as the decades wore on and generals died or retired.

The 'enemy' appeared again in 1956 above the HMS Diana. Truman wouldn't know that it made its presence visible once again during the Vietnam War, actually sinking two ships—American and Australian destroyers, by turning their own weapons back against them, utilizing some kind of defensive shield. Even fighter jets had no success against these things, having their own missiles deflected right back at them.

Every nuclear test, anywhere in the world, had seen their presence. Observing, watching, hovering, beaming.

By the time the conflicts in Iraq had arrived before and after the turn of the new century, the American military had decided they couldn't fight these things and that it would be dangerous to even try. While orders like that had been issued in the fifties and sixties as well, they weren't rigidly enforced because it was hard for any military professional to believe that their advanced weaponry couldn't fight back against any conceivable enemy.

In the Iraq conflicts, there were numerous accounts of confused troops on the ground reporting entire fleets of this strange 'enemy' hovering over the desert horizon—and calling in their fighter jets to deal with the things, only to see their own planes turn around and scoot off back in the direction they'd come from. It was hard for them to watch their own air support abandoning them and leaving an enemy hovering over captured territory. But, orders from on high told the pilots to not engage—in fact to *never* engage if they saw these things.

The very first head of Majestic 12 was Truman's Secretary of Defense, James Forrestal. But, according to what Allison's father told her, Forrestal was removed from his post as Defense Secretary in 1949, only two years after assuming office. And, only two years after being appointed head of Majestic 12.

Something strange happened to Forrestal in 1948.

Under heavy guard, he visited the secure area where the bodies of the alien creatures recovered from Roswell were being kept preserved. He insisted on seeing for himself what only he, the president, the Pentagon, certain scientists, and the members of Majestic 12 knew about.

He was told to just observe, not to touch, as he wasn't wearing any protective gear. He ignored that advice because, as far as he was concerned, he was the Secretary of Defense and no one was going to tell him what he could or couldn't do.

He touched one of the naked little bodies. Almost immediately, he felt sick. Dizzy, unsteady on his feet, mumbling incoherently. Forrestal was rushed back to Washington, put through rigorous tests, and eventually declared healthy.

But, over the next few months, he reportedly became erratic and irrational. He confronted Truman on virtually everything as it related to aliens, UFOs, and the mandate of Majestic 12. He objected strenuously to the purpose of the group, and opposed the oath of secrecy. He wanted the information that only Majestic 12 was privy to, to be made public. But, Truman was adamant that the mandate remain as it was originally established.

Then, all of a sudden, one mysterious day in 1949, Forrestal was removed by Truman from his post as Defense Secretary and from his role as head of Majestic 12. He was committed to a military-affiliated hospital and kept under guard day and night.

Two months later, just after his family had filed a petition to have him moved to a different facility, he was dead. Suicide. Jumped from the sixteenth floor corridor window of the hospital that he'd been committed to.

From the window in the hallway, not the window in his room.

Despite the presence of guards who were on duty 24/7.

And the medical examiner's reports ignored the strange appearance of a bathrobe sash tied around his neck.

James Forrestal, the very first Secretary of Defense the U.S. had ever had, and the very first head of Majestic 12, was dead by suicide in 1949.

And, not that it was relevant at all, but Allison reflected that Forrestal's death was just a few months before William Carson experienced his terrifying ordeal with the 'enemy' in Korea.

She opened her eyes and stared at the chandelier. She squinted her eyes and let the diamonds of light blur in her vision, as she pondered what had caused her father to plan to blow the lid off Majestic 12.

The piles of papers she had pulled out of the briefcase contained detailed correspondence with an investigative reporter named Darren Sheppard. She'd never heard of him, but the correspondence referred to articles he'd written for the *Chicago Tribune*, *Los Angeles Times*, and the *Washington Post*. So, the man was obviously well-connected.

Her dad had told him everything. Even obscure facts like the Sphinx that was situated on Mars, and the small alien bases that existed on the dark side of the moon rumored to be 'scout' installations. He'd given Sheppard the entire history of Majestic 12, detailed all the murders that had happened over the years to silence scientists and astronomers. He told him about the visits the 'enemy' had made to every military conflict and nuclear test.

In his last letter to Sheppard, he even provided him with background information on why there had been such an increase in UFO sightings over the last two decades, and why they were getting progressively more frequent every year.

Allison's dear father had told Sheppard the real reason why Earth was seeing an alarming change in its climate, why the summer heatwaves and winter storms were getting more brutal, and why there was such an increase in earthquake and volcanic activity.

And, why there was now such a tolerance, and indeed encouragement, of the degradation of society through social media and brain-dead entertainment. Why there seemed to be so many distractions and technology addictions taking the public's attention away from the horrors that were mysteriously creeping up on their lives every single year. Permissiveness had a purpose, and it was by design.

Allison was a member of Majestic 12 because it had been an honor bestowed upon her, and her dad had convinced her that it was a sacred trust. That she was obligated to serve.

Now, all that was shot to hell with what she'd just read. What kind of an honor was this when her own father had been trying to betray it? She was conflicted now; she had only agreed to serve because she adored her father and had trusted him with her very life. If he'd lost faith, what did that mean for her? Majestic 12 suddenly seemed like a farce. It had always been insidious, but she'd ignored that reality for the greater good. But, her dad seemed to have given up on the greater good concept. He'd wanted everyone to know. To know everything.

She got up from the couch, walked back to the desk, pulled her iPad out of her purse, and fired it up.

Her dad had been dead for over five years, but none of this information had ever appeared under a Darren Sheppard byline. If it had, it would have been earth-shattering news.

Allison decided she wanted to meet this Darren Sheppard.

She googled his name and several articles popped up.

The one that jumped out at her right away, the one that made her stomach flip and the blood pulse through her veins in a feverish rush, was the Wikipedia summary.

Darren Sheppard was dead. He'd killed himself with a gunshot to the head on June 30th, 2010.

Which was the very same day that Allison's parents and husband were killed when their car went over a cliff along the Oregon coast.

CHAPTER 19

He recognized them right away. Even though it had been dark that awful night in the studio, he still recognized them. Hard to forget scummy-looking druggies.

They'd rung the bell twice, and Helen opened the door and greeted them in her usual courteous way, despite how they looked.

Then, she beckoned Willy to come out of the back living room.

Helen turned away from the boys, and frowned at him questioningly. In front of her husband, she couldn't hide her concern. "These lads say they need to talk with you. Do you know them, Willy?"

Willy took one look and tried hard to suppress his shock at seeing them again. He patted Helen on the shoulder. "It's okay, hon. I talked to them before about doing some odd jobs around the house. There's some old junk in the studio that I may want to have hauled away."

She looked relieved. "Okay, dear, I'll leave you to it, then." Helen then hurried back to the kitchen, where she had some apple pies ready to slide into the oven.

Willy went out onto the porch, then crooked his finger, motioning the boys to follow him. They rounded the side of the house, down the driveway, and into the unlocked studio. Once the boys were inside, Willy closed the door behind him, folded his arms across his chest and glared at them.

"What the hell do you two want? Why are you back here?"

The leader, who Willy recalled went by the name of Brody, spoke first.

"You dun hurt us good few nights go, Mister Willy Carson. Went to a doc's office an got all stitched up."

Willy nodded. "Well, that's what you get for breaking in. And, trying to attack me. What did you expect?"

"I don think anyone would expec an ole dude like you to do what you done ta us. Or look like the way you done look. You were a skeleton, man! What's the deal with that? An how you get that strong?"

Willy chuckled. "You were probably high on drugs and delusional. Suffering hallucinations. Go home, or to whatever hole you crawled out of. Leave me alone and don't come back here."

The one called Matt started shifting nervously from foot to foot, probably in desperate need of a fix. He pointed at Willy. "Don you be tellin us what to do! We be tellin you!"

Willy put his hand on the doorknob. "I'll ask you boys once again. Leave, please."

Before he had a chance to open the door, Brody took a courageous step forward. Willy could tell by his body language that he was armed with new bravado. Not exactly the scared kid who had screamed at the top of his lungs a few nights ago while slithering backwards on his ass along the floor of the studio.

"Do yer hotel people know what a freak you is?"

Willy took his hand off the door handle. "What are you talking about?"

"We hear you sum big shot sculptor. That you gonna be the main man fer a new hotel. Do they know you sum kind a freak?"

Willy couldn't find the words. But, he knew this was a shakedown, and he could feel a pain developing in the pit of his stomach as that realization set in. These two little punks were going to squeeze him. And, he couldn't afford to have bad publicity, not just because of the hotel deal, but mainly because of the five million dollars that had been promised to his estate if he kept his condition a secret. He wanted Helen and Wyatt to have that money.

"An how they feel if they knew you beat up two young guys like us?"

Willy found his voice. "It's your word against mine. And, it was self-defence."

"You some superhuman, dude? No one do what you done. Or look like you looked. How you do that?"

"Again, your word against mine, so give it up and get out of here."

Brody sneered. "We went ta doctor in a town close ta here. He stitched us up and we tole what happened. He has a record of that."

Willy tried not to show any concern on his face. "So what? That's not proof."

Matt spoke up again, giggling as he did. "They know you deal drugs?"

"Drugs? Get lost."

"We lef a lil stash here fore we ran out that night."

Willy's eyes involuntarily darted around the cavernous room, wondering where they could have possibly left something.

The first thought that came into his head was that they were bluffing. These punks had been desperate for drug money that night, so it was highly unlikely they'd already had drugs on them. But, his second, more paranoid thought, was whether or not he could afford to take the chance.

"Who cares? Everyone in this town has grass."

"T'aint grass, man. Sumpin mush more serious than that. You do jail time fer what we planted."

Willy stared into their eyes, from one to the other. Assessing them.

Both had steely gazes; no nervousness, no hesitation. He believed them. The little buggers perhaps weren't as dumb as they looked or sounded. Maybe they'd indeed been astute enough to stash something before they ran, something that they could use against him either for vengeance or for money. They could have hidden the stuff anywhere—it was a huge studio, with lots of equipment and cubbyholes. It would take him forever to search everything.

"That TV station that had you on the news—they probly love ta hear our story bout you, how you look, how you threw us, and how much drugs you got."

Willy sighed, and asked the question he didn't want to ask. Hadn't wanted to show a weakness. Once they sensed that, these scum would probably pounce on the opportunity like rabid dogs. But, thinking fast, he realized that he had no choice. They had him over a barrel and he couldn't afford the publicity. The ramifications would be too great. He needed to make this go away.

"What do you want?"

"Five thousan dollars be mighty nice—morrow afternoon, round 4:00. Side the bench in front of the yout hostel on Baker Street, there be a garbage can. Put the moneys in a bag and drop the bag in the can. We be watchin."

Willy nodded. "Okay, but that's all you're going to get. I want you to leave town right afterwards."

Then, he decided to try to put some fear of God—or of Superman—into them.

"If I see your ugly mugs still hanging around I can't promise that I won't become Superman again. Get my drift? But, I won't drop the bag into that can unless I see an envelope sitting on top with my name on it, with a note inside telling me where I can find your stash. We'll do an exchange. One of you should guard the can to make sure no one picks up the envelope by mistake until I get there."

Brody nodded. "Souns fair. See you morrow, an don be fuckin late."

CHAPTER 20

Allison was sitting in Chad Powers' lavish office, waiting for the egomaniac to arrive. His secretary knew her, so there was no problem with letting her wait for him inside.

She glanced around the cold, massive room. It suited Chad's personality. Not one photo of a smiling family member, and she really never expected to see any.

No, instead, the walls were plastered with pictures of missiles—big ones, small ones, pointy ones, cigar-shaped ones. All menacing looking. Weapons of mass destruction that the U.S. was always so adept at accusing everyone else of having.

Chad's business was munitions manufacturing; specifically, deadly missiles that could be launched from submarines, destroyers, F15s, F16s, F18s, and any other fucking F-type plane in existence. She knew that his company also manufactured the monster minute-man missiles that lay in wait in the underground silos of Wyoming and the Dakotas, programmed to launch at a moment's notice at Russia, China, or North Korea.

Before Chad had taken the helm, his father and grandfather had guided the company through the turbulent years of the 20th Century, including being front and center in the design of the outer shell structures for *Fat Man* and *Little Boy* before they were dropped mercilessly on Hiroshima and Nagasaki in 1945.

Chad was proud of his company's history. Allison thought his sense of pride was pathetic.

She noticed that his desk was solid chrome, including the table top itself. No papers or files anywhere in sight. There wasn't even a computer terminal. She surmised that a man like Chad probably spent more time barking orders than actually doing anything.

Allison had flown into Atlanta for this one day only. Normally, she just flew commercial in the executive class cabin, but since today was to be a quick 'there and back,' she took her company's private jet—a Gulfstream that allowed her to sneak in and out of private executive terminals when she was in a hurry.

And, today, she was in a hurry. She didn't want to spend any more time in this foul city than was necessary. She resented just having to be in Atlanta for the monthly Majestic 12 meetings, so she really didn't enjoy this extra unplanned one.

But, it was necessary. She had to know for sure. And, she couldn't know unless she was here in person, staring into Chad's evil eyes.

Since this wasn't an official Majestic 12 gathering, she wasn't meeting with Chad at the CDC offices. Instead, she was in downtown Atlanta on the fortieth floor of the headquarters for Chad's company.

Suddenly, the door opened and the despicable hulk entered, his wide shoulders barely clearing the door frames.

No hello, no pleasantries.

"Got your message this morning that you were flying in. This better be important—I have a busy day ahead of me."

"Well, good morning to you, too, Chad. Do I at least get a smile with my cup of coffee?"

"No smile, but you can help yourself to the coffee over there." He pointed to the Keurig machine in the corner of the room.

Allison walked over to the machine, inserted a strong K-Cup from Jamaica, and pushed the buttons.

"Do you want one, Chad?"

He shook his head, and gave her an annoyed look. He was already sitting at his desk, twiddling his thumbs. Waiting patiently to hear what it was that was so important to cause Allison Fisher to fly in on her private jet.

Allison thought wryly that if the egotist would at least allow some paper or a computer to reside on his desk he wouldn't have to sit there idly playing with his thumbs.

She walked back to the guest chair with her coffee, sat down and took a long sip of the fragrant java.

"So, what is it you want to talk about, Allison?"

She crossed her legs and couldn't help but notice Chad's black eyes flick downwards for just an instant, capturing for himself a quick glimpse of the sexy curve of her thighs.

"Have you set things up for William Carson's visit next week?"

Chad nodded. "Yes, don't worry. He'll go to our clinic at the CDC and be in and out in less than three hours."

"Please, I want your word that he'll be okay."

Chad sighed. "God, Allison, is he some kind of father figure to you? Don't get your knickers all twisted up. He's far too prominent for us to let anything happen to him. Could open a can of worms. And, you already recorded my promise to you, so leave me the fuck alone."

"So, what exactly are you going to do?"

"I told you already—we're going to try to help him, to make sure this doesn't happen to him again. I'm sure he doesn't want it to happen again, either, and we can't afford to have these incidents being made public. Up until now, we've been lucky. If he hadn't had that damn x-ray, we wouldn't have this problem right now."

Allison placed her cup down on the chrome desktop. Chad quickly slipped a coaster underneath it.

"Well, he and the rest of the 'Korean Five' have been pretty instrumental to us. Because of them and many others, we learned a long time ago how dangerous these…things…are. If we didn't have those relatively innocent encounters to warn us off, it could have been a lot worse."

"I agree. Again, all we're going to do is conduct some non-invasive tests and if we have a solution for him, we'll use it. Totally safe, I can assure you."

Allison nodded. "Okay. Remember, he thinks it's just a routine check-up for the hotel spokesperson role, so be careful not to alarm him in any way with things that aren't routine."

"Agreed."

She moved on to her next concern. "Chad, I know the vote won over at our meeting the other day, against my wishes, but I wanted to appeal to you once again for us to take a different tack with Senator Hartford. I know John personally. I can convince him to shelve his plan to expose us. I'll come clean with him, and show him the error of his ways."

Chad shook his head emphatically. "No, Allison. The vote was taken and the majority ruled. I'm sorry."

"I take over the helm from you in a year's time. Why don't you give me just this one, in deference to me as your successor?"

"I don't owe you a damn thing—in fact, I think you'll be dangerous for Majestic 12 when you take over. You think far too much, care far too much. We can't have that. I wish the charter allowed me to stay on for another seven years, that would be far more secure for the group and for the country."

Allison leaned forward, and rested her elbows defiantly on the edge of the ugly chrome desk.

"Well, from my standpoint—and from that of many others—you don't think hardly as much as you should. You're reckless and ruthless. A good man is going to die because of you, and I could prevent that if you'd just let me talk to him. Senator Hartford should be the next President of the United States, and you're going to rob the American people of that."

Chad starting twiddling his thumbs again. "Well, it won't be the first time that's had to happen. Need I remind you of history? Of Texas in 1963, and California in 1968?"

He sighed in exasperation. "I'm getting bored with this discussion. Are you finished yet?"

Allison suddenly inserted her index fingers inside her ears and then quickly pulled them back out again, popping her ear drums as she did. Chad didn't notice a thing.

She wanted to hit him between the eyes with a direct question, and let him ponder afterwards why she was asking. Allison knew it might be a dangerous question, but something inside was driving her to ask this arrogant prick what needed to be asked.

"No, I'm not finished. I have a question for you. Were you familiar with an investigative journalist by the name of Darren Sheppard?"

Chad swallowed hard as she stared almost hypnotically into his cold dark eyes. He hesitated, then shook his head. "No, should I be?"

A scene suddenly flashed in front of Allison's eyes—and she knew that it was coming directly from Chad's brain. His memory of an incident; either his interpretation of what he had been told had transpired, or...

The terrified face of Darren Sheppard—a face she recognized from the Wikipedia article—eyelids clenched shut as another man's gloved hand held a pistol to his temple. The trigger finger pulled, and a shower of Sheppard's blood and brain matter blew out through the other side of his head.

She now had the real story behind the Darren Sheppard "suicide."

Allison wanted to mind-fuck Chad Powers one more time before she flew back to Chicago. And, she had to do it quickly before this strange telepathic power used up its usually short few seconds of fuel. "Do you miss my father, Chad? Did you enjoy working with him?"

He nodded. "I had a lot of respect for your father, Allison. I miss him dearly. I wish you were more like him. And, of course, your dad, having served on the HMS Diana, suffered the same effects from the 'enemy' that William Carson got hit with in Korea. He had to live with that and keep it secret right up until that tragic car accident took his life."

Chad's vivid memory suddenly transmitted itself into Allison's brain one more time.

The image of a powerful Ranger Rover flashed across the essence of Allison's mind. Very clear, very graphic. The car was silver and racing at breakneck speed.

Allison's question had triggered Chad's imagination, giving her the answer she needed. He was playing the highlight reel in his head—his own recollection of what had happened—and Allison was seeing it as clear as if she were watching TV.

She could see her father's distinctive red Mercedes rounding the corner going north. In the same frame, she saw the Ranger Rover heading south on the opposite side of the bend.

Suddenly, for no apparent reason, the Range Rover moved over into her father's lane. As they both rounded the corner heading towards each other, it was apparent that the Range Rover's nerves were steelier than the Mercedes'.

The sinister driver never wavered out of the lane, not even by a fraction of an inch. It was a dangerous game of 'chicken,' and only one driver was playing it.

At the very last second, the Mercedes swerved into the left lane to avoid a head-on collision.

And the car's momentum, unforgivingly, carried it over the cliff, plummeting two hundred terrifying feet to the rocky shore of the Pacific Ocean below.

The last thing Allison saw in the video playing in her brain was a massive fireball.

CHAPTER 21

It was 3:00 in the afternoon. The Sun was shining, the air was hot and muggy, and relaxing on the porch was what Willy preferred to continue doing right into the early hours of the evening.

But…he had someplace else to be at 4:00.

"Do you want some more lemonade?"

He turned and smiled at his wife—still pretty in her mid-sixties, a relative 'spring chicken' compared to him. She was holding out the lemonade pitcher.

Of course, she'd made the lemonade herself—none of that store-bought crap for her. It had to be authentic; real lemons squeezed by real hands, mixed with natural British Columbia spring water, topped off with just a touch of sugar.

She always threw in a pinch of cinnamon as well—Willy wasn't too crazy about that part of her recipe, but he humored her. All in all, it was still delicious.

"Sure, Helen, fill me up." He held out his glass and she poured. Then, he reached for the remote control unit on the table and punched a button, causing the ceiling fan on the porch to move itself to top speed.

"Thank God we have this covered porch and that fan. I don't know what it is, Willy, but every summer just seems to get hotter and hotter."

Willy wiped his sleeve across his forehead. "I know. Warm weather is nice and we'll sure miss it once winter rolls around again and we're out there shoveling snow, but this incessant heat is getting a bit ridiculous."

"Well, my tomatoes in the back are doing really well. They seem to like the heat."

"No, Helen, I think they like you. Everything thrives under your touch…even me."

Helen stood up and very quickly sat back down again—this time in Willy's lap. Then, she cupped his face in her hands and kissed him. She pulled back and looked into his kind eyes.

"What a nice thing to say! I sure am lucky to have you—we've been together a long time, but it seems like just yesterday when we were sneaking across the border like a couple of rebellious kids."

"Well, *you* were still just a kid when we did that—only twenty for God's sake. But, me—I was already a dirty old man at forty-two! That was a long time ago, wasn't it?"

Helen smiled. "And Wyatt was just growing inside of me when we made our dash to Canada."

"Your parents sure hated my guts, though. I don't think they ever forgave me for stealing you away from them—which is too bad, because I liked your folks a lot."

Helen shook her head. "We've talked about this before, dear. They did like you very much. My dad and mom were Republicans though—it was in their blood. Patriotic to a fault. It wasn't that they didn't like you, it was that they didn't like what you stood for and what you stood against. Their generation had been brainwashed to salute, obey, rally round the flag, and to serve country first. They were too blind to see what our generation saw."

Willy gave his wife a kiss on the tip of her nose. "You're right—I guess I just took it personally."

"They did come around eventually, dear—not to agree with what we did, of course, but they did accept our right to do it. We had some great visits with them when they came up here during those early years before they died—got to spend some quality time with their new grandson, and with us of course."

Helen shifted her butt a bit, and Willy pulled her right leg over on top of his.

"I kinda like you sitting on my lap. Feels like old times."

"Well, I'll just have to do it more often, then."

Willy smirked. "But, what will the neighbors think?"

"Who cares?"

"Helen, darling, I love your attitude. Still the hippie I fell in love with!"

He glanced at his watch. "Oh, I have to get going."

Willy eased himself forward on the chair, and stood while lifting Helen into the air at the same time.

She shook her head in amazement. "How on earth can you still be so strong at your age? And, your looks, too—you don't seem to age at all. In fact, you look more my age. You're the miracle man—and I'm proud to say you're *my* man."

Willy laughed. "I think I've just got 'Dick Clark' syndrome."

"Don't say that, he's dead now!"

He gently eased her down into her own chair again, then went back and retrieved the plastic pouch that had been lying on the floor underneath his.

"Where are you off to, Willy?"

"Oh, just popping down to see the lawyer—some legal stuff to document for the spokesperson role for that new hotel."

Helen clapped her hands. "Oh, Willy—I'm so excited for you! You're going to be a celebrity. Well, you already are, but you'll be an even bigger one! You deserve it, darling."

"We deserve it, Helen. You've always been my biggest supporter and my biggest fan. Couldn't have accomplished all we have if we weren't in it together."

"Aw…that's so nice. But, just think—that amazing sculpture of yours is going to be on display for the whole world to see. It'll bring tears to the eyes of all the old draft-dodgers."

Willy thrust a triumphant fist into the air. "Yes! Some accolades for standing up for peace. Finally."

He turned and started down the stairs of the verandah.

"Oh, Willy, what happened with those two boys who came by the other day? Did you pay them to haul that stuff away?"

He stopped halfway down the stairs and turned back to face her. "Haven't paid them yet. They'll be back to take the stuff away, though. I already showed them what I want hauled out of there."

Helen smiled. "Okay, make sure they don't take away that sculpture!"

She pointed down at his hand. "What's in that pouch you're carrying?"

"Just some documents I need to give to the lawyer, hon—legal stuff."

"Do you want me to come with you?"

"No, no. You stay here on the verandah and have a fresh pitcher of lemonade waiting for me when I get back. I'll need if after a hot walk there and back."

"Why don't you take the car? At least you'll have a few moments of air conditioning."

Willy shook his head. "No, his office is just down there on Baker Street. No big deal. I can handle the heat, especially knowing I have your lemonade to look forward to."

"Okay, I'll have it ready. Do you feel like barbecuing steak tonight?"

"Yum—sounds good to me. Could you do me one little favor, though?"

"Anything, darling."

"Could you leave the cinnamon out of the next batch of lemonade?"

CHAPTER 22

They were watching from inside an air-conditioned Jeep Cherokee. It was a 2015 model, shiny black, equipped with every possible option. The SUV's engine was running as the three of them watched Willy Carson walk down the street.

Brody pointed. "There he go. Only a few minutes ta go now. We'll wait till he close ta the hostel."

Matt giggled. "This gonna be good!"

The third man, a guy named Aaron, grunted. "He doesn't look that tough."

"Oh, you ain't seen nothin. He mus be able ta turn it on an off. It wuz amazin."

Aaron grumbled. "I'll take your word for it. But—one thing is certain, that big house of his is worth a fortune. The man is rich, you were right about that."

Brody was sitting in the passenger seat, and Matt was bouncing up and down in the back. Brody turned to face Aaron, the owner of the shiny black Cherokee.

"You foun that news broadcast thin on yer computer—so you know how famous he is round here. He not a normal target."

"No, Brody, you're right. I think we have a good mark here—an opportunity we can't miss. I'm glad you boys agreed that we needed to think a bit bigger. Opportunities like this don't come along too often."

Brody stared at his new friend in admiration. He loved the way Aaron talked. Very articulate—he'd clearly received the type of education that Brody could have only dreamt of. And, he didn't come from a violent drug addicted family the way Brody had, either. He could tell that it made a big difference.

But, he was no doubt a bad dude, more because he chose to be bad instead of having it chosen for him. He'd done some time in Kingston Penitentiary for manslaughter—was released ten years ago for good behaviour. Since then, he'd been dealing in drugs and had participated in several lucrative armed robberies, home invasions, and two kidnappings.

Every one of his capers had gone well, except for the kidnappings. He hadn't been caught, but hadn't collected anything either. The victims were released unharmed—well, Aaron had said something about 'unharmed' being a relative term, but Brody didn't know what the fuck that meant.

Everything they knew about Aaron had come from Aaron's mouth, but Brody believed him. Didn't think he was bullshitting. He seemed sincere and actually quite brilliant. Brody admired smart people—wished he'd had more education, because he thought of himself as smart. Just hadn't reached his potential yet.

Brody and Matt had met Aaron at a bar in Castlegar several nights ago. Brody had lost count how many nights ago that was, as well as how many beers he'd consumed. But, what else was new?

Aaron owned an old farmhouse on twenty acres of land, off highway 3A between Castlegar and Nelson. Brody and Matt had stayed with him ever since that night at the bar. And, they'd talked. Talked a lot.

Aaron told them the history of the area he was living in. He'd bought his farmhouse from a Doukhobor couple a few years ago for half a million dollars. Brody whistled when he heard that dollar amount. He couldn't even dream that big, let alone count that high.

Brody hadn't wanted to sound stupid, but he forced himself anyway to ask Aaron, "*What da fuck is a Doukhobor?*"

Apparently, as Brody remembered it, they originated in Russia back in the 1600s. They were a kind of Christian religious sect that believed in some shit about a peaceful life, communal living, and hard work. Brody remembered that their motto was '*Toil and a Peaceful Life.*'

Aaron said that they were being persecuted in Russia for their beliefs, and for not agreeing to pledge allegiance or some shit like that. So, they got into trouble with some Tsar called Nicholas. By the late 1800s, they began moving out of Russia, and most of them migrated to the West Kootenay area of British Columbia, Canada.

They became important contributors to the B.C. economy, particularly with agriculture, and they were quiet and peaceful little nerds. Brody laughed when he heard all this—reminded him of the Jim Jones cult mass suicide down in Guyana years ago.

Aaron had patiently corrected him on that—saying that it wasn't that kind of cult. They were good people who believed in peace and living a simple life. The food in their restaurants was to die for, and they protected each other to their deaths. Aaron liked that.

Brody was surprised that a tough dude like Aaron seemed to appreciate these kinds of people. So, Brody decided he could appreciate them, too.

He remembered that Aaron's farmhouse was in an area called *Shoreacres*, and the dirt road to his house was off a drag called Doukhobor Road. So, the area was obviously affected in a big way by their influence if they could have a major road named after them.

Brody was jarred out of his little daydream by Matt pounding on the back of his seat. "Is worked, is worked! He headin fer the yout hostel!"

Aaron turned to Brody. "Tell your friend in the back to shut the fuck up. He's getting on my nerves."

Brody swiveled his head to the rear and held up a fist. "Matt, you heard him. Shut up. If you don calm down, you gonna blow this fer us all."

Matt pouted and lowered his head. Brody turned back and stared out through the front windshield, and watched Willy Carson make his way up Baker Street.

In a soft, calm voice, Aaron said, "Okay, it's working to plan. He's well away from the house. Time for you and Matt to do your thing. I'll pull around into the back alley."

* * * * *

Willy wished he'd accepted Helen's advice and taken the car.

God, it was hot.

It felt as if someone was pointing a hairdryer at his face. A sweaty breeze that did nothing at all to relieve the swelter—in fact, it made it worse.

As he walked along Baker Street, he was barraged with greetings. People were coming up and shaking his hand, clapping him on the back, shouting their congratulations. He knew he was a popular figure in town, but that TV news broadcast had propelled him to new heights.

Willy figured that, at this point of his fame, he could probably easily run for mayor and win the damn job. Beat that sleazy little wimp, Murray Hinton, hands down. He smiled to himself.

Maybe I'll do that—what the hell. Just to piss him off.

The farther he walked up Baker Street, the fewer people he knew. By the time he reached the youth hostel, he was in foreign territory. The street was practically empty, except for a few grungy-looking characters hanging around the front of the hostel.

Transients just passing through—looking for some peace and inspiration in the mountains for a few nights. Not really troublemakers; just kids that probably looked dirtier than they really were.

Most of the teens and young adults who passed through Nelson in the summer were from the big cities—and they hitchhiked and backpacked their way from town to town. Smoked a few joints along the way, drank a few beers, and partied with some of the locals in each town they visited. All frivolous, harmless fun.

Willy looked inside the garbage can, then took a seat on the bench in front of the hostel. The two scum had told him to put the five thousand dollars in a bag, but Willy decided to use a pouch instead. Figured he would have looked kind of strange walking up Baker Street with a brown paper bag. Also, Helen would never have believed he was taking documents to the lawyer in a bag.

He looked at his watch. It was already five minutes after four o'clock. The boys were late. He got up, walked over to the garbage can, and stole another glance inside—hoping no one he knew noticed him doing that. He felt like a homeless bum.

Nope—definitely no envelope in there.

Maybe the boys got scared and abandoned the extortion? He hoped.

Willy decided he'd give it fifteen more minutes, then just head home for a nice glass of lemonade; hopefully without the cinnamon.

*****

Helen was busy stirring a fresh pitcher of lemonade when she heard the doorbell. She ran from the kitchen, thinking that her dear forgetful husband had left his keys behind as he usually did.

She opened the door and was shocked to see the two disheveled figures standing on the porch. Not as shocked as she was the first time she saw them, but shocked instead because she wasn't expecting them.

"Oh, hello, boys. I thought you were my husband. Are you looking for Willy? He's out right now."

The taller boy smiled. "No, Miz Carson. We jus here ta haul way sum stuff your husban show us in the grage."

Helen smiled back. He seemed pleasant enough, despite looking rough. She felt kind of sorry for the poor lad. He obviously couldn't speak very well, but he was trying. His friend standing behind him looked a bit frantic—bouncing from one foot to the other. He couldn't seem to stand still. Helen had seen this before—drugs. She shrugged.

"Okay, I didn't know you were coming by. But, if Willy has shown you what he wants you to take, then it's fine with me. You'll have to come back again for payment though. I don't have any money in the house."

The tall boy nodded. "Thas no problum, Miz Carson. We cum back."

"Come on in, then. I'll get the keys to the studio and we'll go out through the back."

"Studio?"

"Oh, that's what Willy calls it. He's an artist. It's never been used as a garage."

"I see."

Helen led the boys to the back of the house and pulled the keys off the hanger. She opened the back door and headed out to the studio. She could hear the footsteps of the boys behind her.

She opened the door and ushered them inside.

"Okay, there you have it. You know which stuff he wants you to take, so go ahead and do your work. Do you have a truck?"

"Yeah, Miz Carson. In the back alley."

Helen felt a bit uncomfortable with all of this, but she trusted her husband. If he had hired these boys for this job, then he must know what he's doing.

She turned and started to head back to the house. "Once you finish, you'll probably be thirsty. Come up to the verandah and you can have some lemonade. I've just made a fresh…"

Helen was cut off mid-sentence by an arm that wrapped roughly around her throat. She tried to muster a scream, but that was smothered by some kind of material that was shoved into her mouth. Then, a gunny sack went over her head and she could sense them tying it tight with drawstrings.

Next, her hands were pulled behind her back and bound together with something. It was tight. Too tight.

Suddenly, Helen was spun around and shoved roughly toward the back of the studio. Then, out the door and onto the gravel alleyway. She could feel the stones kicking up underneath her feet.

She heard a car door open and another voice, a more articulate one.

"Throw her in the back. We have to get out of here fast."

They dragged her along the gravel. The sound of a tailgate opening. Then, she was lifted into the air and tossed inside the vehicle like a sack of garbage, her head banging against the roofline as she went flying in.

Suddenly, Helen heard something else. A gate squeaking open and a dog barking.

Then a young woman's voice, one she recognized. "Hey, what's going on there?"

The tall one's voice. "Aaron!"

Then, another voice she recognized. A man's. "Sharon! What's wrong?"

Helen now heard two sets of footsteps along the gravel, along with the distinctive sound of a dog straining and panting against a leash.

The man she presumed was Aaron yelled out. "Forget them! Let's get out of here! Get in the car, both of you!"

"But…"

"No buts! Get the fuck in the car!"

The last sounds Helen heard were the tailgate slamming shut, two of the car doors opening and closing, then the wheels of the vehicle spinning on the loose gravel as it began its escape down the alley.

CHAPTER 23

It made him want to cry. But, he couldn't—he had to be strong for his dad right now.

Willy was doing enough crying for the both of them, anyway.

To Wyatt, it felt as if someone had reached inside his chest and ripped out his heart.

He watched silently as his father sat sobbing on the sofa in the living room, a room that seemed emptier now than it ever had before.

Wyatt's eyes wandered around the room, taking in all of the little treasures that his mother loved. The ornamental book-ends, the dried flower arrangements that she'd made herself, the Tiffany lamps sitting on each of the end tables, and the old phonograph cabinet standing on display in a corner of the room as a remembrance of simpler days past.

He glanced up at their wedding photo on the mantle—the handsome couple who looked happier than any two people could ever hope to be. Happy and confident, ready to take on the world, looking forward to their new peaceful life in Canada. Embracing a life that didn't involve non-stop news headlines of the war in Vietnam. A life that didn't threaten that young men and women could once again be drafted into sacrificing their lives for the pursuit of geo-political chess moves in a faraway land. A land that no one understood, or even gave a shit about.

They didn't want a life like that for their child, for anyone's child. They'd participated in protests at home to no avail. Had attended rallies to no avail. No one in government listened, no one cared—all they wanted was that the protestors don uniforms, pick up rifles, and get over to the humid jungles of the Far East and kill people for reasons they didn't understand. There was no need to understand, no need to ask questions; the only need was that they obey. And, be prepared to die for whatever cause they were told was honorable.

Wyatt admired his parents for what they did—and for what all the draft-dodgers did. They were braver than the ones who stayed behind and accepted the indignity of being told their lives weren't important; in actual fact, not much more important than the Asians they were being told they had to kill.

Wyatt knew his parents had to endure being ostracized by friends and family back in the States. They were branded as cowards, un-Christian, and unpatriotic. It was as if they weren't even entitled to have a say in how they lived the only life that God had given them.

Eventually, people came around to their way of thinking, but that didn't happen until many years after the war; when everyone realized that they'd been lied to on so many fronts, that elaborate deceptions had been engineered to garner support for an unpopular war.

And, the final nail in the coffin came when the "peace" that was negotiated wasn't really a peace after all. It was just a ruse so America could leave Vietnam and save face. Peace with honor.

Right after they left, the Communists from the north overran the south, and all the American lives that had been sacrificed for years to prevent exactly that from happening were deemed in vain. It was a war that, sadly, was never intended to be won.

Eventually, after having to endure years of shame and virtual banishment from their own country, they were invited home again. A nation in pain had forgiven and forgotten. Wyatt's parents, all the protesters, and all the draft-dodgers, were exonerated. And forgiven—sort of.

Until the next war. Luckily, the draft had never been reconstituted again since the Vietnam war. Maybe that was one lesson a nation had finally learned, and the American ex-pats living in Nelson were proud that they might have had something to do with that.

But, very few wanted to go home again. The definition of "home" had changed for them. Home for them was the refuge that had supported them, the refuge that had given them a feeling of safety and security.

Wyatt glanced down at his dad. Right now, he knew that he wasn't feeling too safe and secure. He was worried sick, and with good reason.

Willy was slumped over, elbows on his knees, head in his hands. Sobbing, and moving his head slowly from side to side.

It was 6:00 in the evening, and Willy had been too distraught so far to answer many questions. He'd been vague about why he was out at the time.

All indications were that the kidnapping had occurred between 3:45 and 4:30. The times when Willy had left the house and arrived back.

The living room was full of officers, all looking for evidence of someone having been in the house. So far, they'd found nothing. Wyatt had assigned several others to scour the studio and the alleyway, and knock on the doors of neighbors.

Wyatt pondered the pouch sitting on the coffee table. A pouch he hadn't seen before, and he could tell that there was something bulky inside. He hadn't asked his dad about it yet, but it was now that time. Something told him that he needed to ask him in private, though.

Wyatt stood and called out to all of the officers. "Please clear the room for a few minutes. I need to ask my dad some things in private. Go help the others with the neighbor interviews."

They all nodded and obeyed. They knew that when Wyatt asked something of them, he had good reasons for doing so.

Once they'd left, he sat down on the couch beside Willy and put his arm around his shoulders. He leaned in and kissed him on the cheek.

"I love you, Dad. But, it's time for you to tell me what you were doing. You've been saying things for the last two hours about how you're to blame for all this. So, tell me about that."

Silence.

Wyatt picked the pouch up off the table, snapped open the clasp, and pulled out the contents.

He whistled.

"Dad! There has to be a few thousand dollars here. What's this all about?"

Willy took his hands away from his face and looked into his son's eyes.

Then, he sighed and spoke slowly in a monotone. "It was those punks, Wyatt. They were blackmailing me. Said they were going to tell their story about what a freak I am to the media. And, they said they'd planted some hard drugs in my studio. I was paying them off and they were supposed to tell me where the drugs were stashed. I know now that was just a ruse to get me out of the house. They wanted Helen. They wanted much more than just that pile of money."

Wyatt rubbed his shoulders. "That means they're going to call with some demands, Dad. Calm down. They turned down all this money for a bigger score. They're not going to hurt Mom."

Willy shook his head. "They're crazy, Wyatt. Druggies—not thinking with a full deck."

"They want money, Dad. Lots of it. We have two choices—when they call, we can either pay them or try to trap them. My suggestion is that we arrange for a drop-off. We won't take any chances with Mom's life. I promise you that."

Willy nodded and licked his dry lips. Then, he said, almost in a whisper, "Spoken like a good son. But, what would you be suggesting to me if she was somebody else's mom and wife?"

Wyatt stared back, speechless. His dad had just asked one of the toughest questions any police officer could ever be asked. He opened his mouth to answer, thought he knew exactly what he was going to say, but then just slowly closed his mouth again without uttering one word.

Willy grimaced. "I thought so. You need to assign someone else to make this decision, Wyatt. You can't be objective, for the very same reason why doctors go to see other doctors when they get sick. They can't safely diagnose themselves. We need to do the right things to get Helen back, and if that means paying money, fine. If that means planning a trap instead, fine. But…we have to get her back alive."

Wyatt's wise father had once again taught him a life lesson.

Wyatt wrung his hands together. "Okay, Dad. You're right, as you usually are. Once they contact us and we have all the facts we need, I'll hand this off to one of the detectives to make the safest recommendation."

"I have lots of money, Wyatt. You know that. If money will get her back alive, we'll pay. But, if there's a strong likelihood that they'll just kill her even if we pay, then we have to go for their throats. And, she may already be…"

Wyatt grabbed onto both of his hands and squeezed hard. "No, don't even think that! They want money, Dad. Remember that. Their best chance of getting money is to show us 'proof of life.'"

Willy nodded. "Yes, I know you're right." Then, he lowered his head, hands covering his eyes. Wyatt could tell he was sobbing again. "Christ Almighty. My weird condition has brought this down on my wife. I feel like I just want to die, Wyatt."

Wyatt was experiencing a different feeling entirely than what his dad was feeling right now. He tried hard not to let his imagination run wild—tried not to picture her in any kind of position of restraint. Tried not to envision the twisted criminals who had stolen her freedom. Didn't want to think about what they might be doing to her. Refused to let the image of her face—tear-stained, fretful—creep into his brain. Didn't want to imagine her fears about whether she'd get out alive or not.

His mother, the caring and selfless person that she was, was probably worrying more about how her son and husband were coping with this.

But, Wyatt couldn't help it—all those thoughts crept into his head anyway, and he started feeling a strange tingling in his hands and feet.

He wanted to kill someone; whoever had done harm to his mother deserved to die a horrible death. And, he wanted to be the one to carry it out.

The tingling in his hands was getting worse. His feet had actually gone numb now, but his hands seemed to be on fire. It was strange—he'd never had these sensations before. Must be the stress, and the fact that he was so close to this horror story.

Wyatt got up and went into the kitchen. He turned the tap on and let the cold water rush over his hands. It seemed to help, but as soon as he took his hands out from under the tap, the fiery tingling came back. He put them back under again.

Suddenly, he heard his name being called.

He ran back into the living room. One of his officers, Clark Wilson, was standing there with a young couple beside him.

"Chief, I think you know these folks, Sharon and Bob Hunter from the house behind the alleyway?"

"Yes, yes, we've met before at one of my parents' parties." Wyatt noticed, out of the corner of his eye, his dad getting up from the couch and walking over.

"Well, they saw them take your mom."

Wyatt let out a deep breath, and rubbed his hands together. They were tingling even worse now. "Why did you wait, folks?"

Willy jumped in. "What did you see?"

Sharon spoke first. "I'm sorry, we were scared that they were going to come back for us. We locked all the doors, set the alarm, and went down into the basement. We only came out when we saw the police at our front door."

Wyatt shook his head. "Okay, doesn't matter. I understand. Just tell us what you know, quickly."

Clark jumped in. "Sharon gave us a description of the vehicle, Chief. A black Jeep Cherokee, late model. And a plate number."

"Fantastic! Who owns it?"

Clark shook his head. "Didn't check out. The plate was for a 2006 Chevy Malibu, stolen off a car in Vancouver a couple of months ago. Car registered to a Stuart Barkley. We've already talked to him in Vancouver.

He's solid."

Wyatt's heart sunk, but he quickly bounced back. "Okay, we can probably assume the Jeep is a stolen vehicle, too. Check on reports for stolen vehicles of that type over the last six months."

"Already in the process, Chief."

"Good. Okay, Sharon, Bob, what did you see?"

Sharon swallowed hard. "I was coming out the back gate with Rusty—our dog—and I saw them throwing who I thought was Helen into the back of the Jeep. She had something over her head, so I couldn't see her face. But, I recognized her outfit—pink slacks, red blouse—she wears that outfit a lot in the summer. Anyway, Bob was right behind me and heard me yell out. We started walking towards them, but one of them shouted and the other two jumped into the car. Then they took off fast."

Willy took a step towards Sharon. "The other two? So, there were three of them?"

Sharon stammered, 'Y…Yes, Willy. Two…younger guys, guess around twenty? Skinny, greasy, jean jackets, one had a green toque. And…the d…driver…we didn't see him. But, he sounded…older."

Willy glanced over at Wyatt with a question in his eyes.

Wyatt just nodded. No one else in the room knew about what the two of them knew. They didn't know that Willy had already encountered the two young guys a couple of times, and that on this very day he'd planned to meet them in an extortion pay-off. For now, Wyatt intended to keep that knowledge between the two of them.

"Okay, Sharon and Bob—you did good."

Bob hadn't said a word yet, and Wyatt suspected his male pride was suffering a bit. Their decision to hide in fear in the basement and not even phone the police after the kidnapping, was probably something he was regretting right now.

It was a stupid thing for them to do—time was so precious in kidnappings and it could make a difference between life and death. But…unfortunately, Wyatt was seeing more and more of this lately, especially with the younger generation. More concern for 'self' than anything else.

He addressed them again. "You're free to go. And, you don't have to be afraid. These guys know you saw them, and they're probably quite certain that you've talked to us by now. There would be no point in them coming back for you."

Sharon shivered. Bob wrapped his arm around her shoulder and squeezed her tight.

They turned and began to leave by the back of the house. Wyatt called out to them. "Actually, show me where you were standing out in the alley when all this happened, and where the SUV was."

As he and Willy followed them out to the back alleyway, Wyatt shoved his hands in his pockets. They felt like they were actually burning, but he knew they weren't. There was no rash on his hands, no loss of movement—just a constant hot, tingly sensation he couldn't understand. His feet were still completely numb, but, luckily, like his hands, they had suffered no loss of movement.

Sharon and Bob came to a stop in the middle of the laneway. "We were right here, and the SUV was there." She pointed. "Right behind the back door to Willy's studio."

Wyatt scanned the gravel of the lane, looking for anything that the kidnappers might have dropped. Nothing.

There were no noticeable tire tracks. This lane was well-traveled, so it would be impossible to discern anything from an individual vehicle.

"I can't believe they did this in broad daylight, Chief."

Wyatt nodded. "I think they were pretty stupid, Sharon. And, because of you, we might have a chance of catching them. Thank you."

He pulled his hands out of his pockets, reached out, and took hold of Sharon's hand.

At that moment, a shock reverberated through his body. Like an electrical shock, a little stronger than the shock you would sometimes get by touching a door handle on a dry winter day.

Then, something else happened. It was as if he was standing in the alleyway when it happened, standing exactly in the spot where Sharon showed him she was standing.

He saw the two young guys throw his mother into the back of the Jeep. Winced as he saw her head bang on the roof as she went in. Saw the hatch door slam shut.

One of the thugs looked back, then whirled around and yelled out, "*Aaron!*"

Then, Wyatt heard Bob's timid voice from behind. "Sharon! What's wrong?"

The driver was shouting now. "*Forget them! Let's get out of here! Get in the car, both of you!*"

One of the young guys now. "*But…*"

The driver again. "*No buts! Get the fuck in the car!*"

The Jeep sped off, kicking up gravel as it did. Wyatt raised his tingly hands up to shield his eyes from the stones that were flying back at him.

Then, he seemed to be in the air. Soaring above the vehicle as it made its way quickly out of Nelson.

Wyatt floated above it, watching it weave its way along several side roads until it finally reached Highway 3A, going southwest towards Castlegar. The wind was blowing through Wyatt's hair as he soared along above the Jeep.

It was a calm feeling, almost peaceful. The sky was blue and the Sun was blazing, but he couldn't feel any heat from its rays. The only heat he felt was in his hands and feet.

The Jeep turned off onto a secondary road. Wyatt saw a sign that said, '*Shoreacres.*'

He aimed his consciousness down, closer to the pavement and saw the sign, 'Doukhobor Road.' They went northwest about two miles, then turned off onto a dirt road.

Wyatt was there, right above them, right there when they turned off the dirt road onto the long driveway for an old farmhouse. Old, but in good shape. Quite a large house—wood frame exterior walls, stained dark brown. A roof constructed of pine shingles, marred in spots with growths of moss.

Wyatt hovered above the house and watched while they dragged his mother out of the back. She had a gunny sack over her head, and her hands were tied behind her back.

They shoved her roughly towards the front of the house. She stumbled and fell to her knees and the two young guys grabbed her under the arms, yanked her to her feet, and practically dragged her through the front door. The driver of the Jeep was the one who had the keys to the house.

Suddenly, Wyatt was back on the ground again, back in the alley behind his dad's house.

He heard Sharon's voice. "Chief, are you okay?"

He found his own voice. "Yes, I'm fine, Sharon."

"It looked like you were off in a daydream for a few seconds there."

A few seconds. That's all it had taken.

The tingling and burning in his hands and feet had disappeared.

All that was left was Wyatt's body trembling as if it were a cold winter day.

His brain moved into overdrive.

This entire weird experience reminded him of a seminar he'd attended about fifteen years ago. He and several other RCMP inspectors had flown to Quantico, Virginia. While Quantico was primarily a military installation, it also housed the Behavioral Analysis Unit of the FBI. The BAU. The subject matter of TV's hit series, *Criminal Minds*.

The RCMP and the FBI did joint training quite often, and sometimes just shared special tools each of them had that could be called upon once in a while, to solve challenging crimes. The two institutions worked closely together and had a great relationship.

The seminar topic was something called 'Remote Viewing,' and the session was merely a sharing of top secret information about something spooky that the FBI, C.I.A., and Naval Intelligence had been experimenting with for decades.

Not always successful, but sometimes it had succeeded beyond their wildest dreams. It had been used to track down missing persons, hideouts of some of America's Most Wanted, and terrorist cells. In fact, it had been used to "see" certain events before they happened, allowing intelligence agencies to prevent them.

It was a team of people who possessed a special skill.

A skill that allowed them to transfer their consciousness to different times and different places. With the inherent talent that these people had, they only needed to focus their energies on a time and place. They were then able to see it just as if they were there.

They generally operated in dark rooms, totally alone with just their own thoughts. They'd be given a time, place, and sometimes an event to focus on.

Remote Viewing was an aspect of ESP that most people did not understand, nor even believe.

The FBI never explained how these people were chosen, or how they had even developed the skill. They only wanted the RCMP to know that the service was available to them if they ever needed it.

Wyatt remembered asking if they could meet some of their 'Remote Viewers.' The answer was an emphatic "*No.*" Their identities were protected. Someone else asked if these people were actual agents.

They answered that none of the 'Remote Viewers' were active agents. They were simply a team of…assets.

He remembered the FBI telling them that very few people in the world possessed this special 'gift,' and that, almost without exception, the gift was awakened inside of them by a traumatic event in their personal lives.

Something personally traumatic almost always triggered it the first time.

As Wyatt stood perplexed in the alleyway with Sharon and Bob looking at him with genuine concern, he remembered one other thing.

About his dad telling him that his altered DNA from the horrific incident in Korea would have, without a doubt, been transferred down to Wyatt when he was conceived.

In one form or another.

In one manifestation or another.

CHAPTER 24

Allison's stomach was doing flip-flops as her private jet circled for a landing over Burlington, Vermont.

She knew that it was going to happen soon. Very soon.

It had to be stopped. All of this had to stop.

Knowing now without a shadow of a doubt that her parents and husband had been killed on the orders of Chad Powers and Majestic 12, she felt empty inside.

For the last five years, she had reconciled their deaths in her mind as just being a tragic accident. One of those fluke things that happened once in a while—wrong place, wrong time. Wrong curve in the road along the Oregon coastal highway. A moment of inattention.

But, after reading the thoughts in Chad's brain for just those few shocking seconds, she knew that he'd had the journalist her dad had been talking to, Darren Sheppard, shot in the head. Disguised as a suicide.

Then, when she'd asked him about her dad, the images of the car accident came through to her loud and clear. Her dad's red Mercedes careening off the cliff while trying desperately to avoid a head-on collision with an assassin disguised as a Range Rover.

And, the deaths of Sheppard and Allison's family had occurred on the exact same day. Chad Powers hadn't taken any chances—didn't want any time to pass between the killings. It would have been too obvious a warning if he'd waited. Someone could have been spooked.

Allison pictured in her mind the hands raised around the Majestic 12 boardroom table; that table made of solid granite symbolizing the cold and determined solidity of the group.

Hands raised, voting in favour of killing her father and the journalist.

Of course, it would have been a special meeting of the group, a meeting with only eleven members in attendance instead of twelve. Chad would have stated the murderous intention, and then asked for a show of hands.

Allison wondered if it had been unanimous. Wondered if anyone had spoken up in her father's defence, just as she had done on behalf of Senator John Hartford.

Her father had never seen it coming. He must have thought that he'd covered his tracks in his conversations with Sheppard. But, somehow, they had found out.

Maybe Sheppard had told someone, or perhaps communications between the two of them over the internet had been monitored?

But, judging from the file Allison had read that was in that briefcase hidden in the wall of her dad's study, it seemed as if all contact had been through written reports, or over the phone. She didn't see any evidence that the internet had ever been used and, knowing her dad, he would have avoided that like the plague. He hated technology. But, surely they must have met on the sly once in a while, so maybe they'd been under surveillance?

Right after the deaths of her three family members, Allison had taken over her dad's seat on Majestic 12. She remembered all the condolences and expressions of grief and compassion from the other members at the very first meeting she'd attended. Even from Chad Powers.

All fake.

They all knew they'd killed her family vicariously.

Killing was an easy thing to do when you were sitting around a boardroom table simply raising your hand in a vote. It reminded Allison of the 'thumbs up' or 'thumbs down' gestures from Caesar at the Coliseum from the movie *Gladiator*.

That was really, in fact, what they were on Majestic 12—all little Caesars.

The dilemma in Allison's mind was tugging at her—she had given the 'thumbs up' herself to numerous murders over the past five years. Killings that she had been convinced were justified, in line with their mandate. Protecting Americans from the painful truth demanded hard decisions, and she'd been entrusted to participate in those decisions. She'd taken that responsibility seriously, all for the common good. For the greater cause. A few individual deaths to prevent chaos.

And, she had to admit, it was easy to do when you were just sitting around a table talking like businesspeople, talking as if it was just like a simple merger or acquisition discussion.

There was a certain detachment to it all.

They never even had to get their hands dirty. All they had to do was raise their hands and vote. No personal contact with the victims, no consideration of how decent those people might be, what good fathers or mothers they might be. None of that mattered. Not having to consider those things made the decisions relatively easy.

The people who'd died were generally unknown to the 'deciders.'

Most of them were scientists and astronomers, along with a few journalists. People who'd had a conscience attack, and were preparing to blow things wide open. Each of the Majestic 12 members knew that would be dangerous, if they allowed it to happen, so they'd had no choice. That was their job—their sacred trust.

But, it was a different story when it hit close to home.

Knowing her own family had been killed due to the 'deciders' voting on their fate, was more than Allison could handle. Suddenly, she started seeing the faces of the people she'd voted to kill, imagining the families they'd had, and the heartbreak all of them would have endured. She could feel their pain, because it was a pain she herself had endured.

A pain made only worse now that she knew it hadn't been an accident after all.

And, here she was, serving out her father's wishes on the Majestic 12 cabal, doing her duty. When, in fact, her own father had been preparing to blow the lid off the secretive and murderous society. He'd had a pang of conscience. He'd had regrets over the deaths he'd voted in favour of.

Or, quite simply, he may have decided instead that the American people—indeed everyone in the entire world—deserved to know the truth.

The plane landed smoothly and began its taxi toward the executive terminal. Allison turned on her iPhone and read once again the article that she'd saved in her 'favorites.'

The article that announced the mysterious disappearance of oil executive, Charles Farmington. He'd vanished into thin air.

There was background information in the article concerning details that had just surfaced in the last few days about Farmington being under threat of indictment for his company's reckless endangerment of the environment. That at least fifty percent of the damages to the Gulf of Mexico that British Petroleum had been held responsible for were actually caused by the leaking wells of Farmington's Tempest Energy Corporation.

Allison knew that for years the prick had avoided prosecution for his company's negligence, due to the influence-peddling he'd been doing in

Washington. Washington had repaid his monetary favours by holding BP totally responsible, instead of Tempest.

Something must have happened to cause Farmington to start sharing information about Majestic 12 with Senator Hartford. And, something must have happened to cause Washington to suddenly leak information to the press about Tempest's negligence and that Farmington was facing indictment.

And, coincidentally, he'd just disappeared into thin air. Majestic 12 now had one less member, a seat soon to be filled by Farmington's son, Kevin.

The article surmised that Farmington may have fled the country to a safe non-extraditable haven, to avoid the massive fines and decades in prison.

Allison knew that wasn't true. The evil Farmington would never be seen again. And, neither would his dead body.

At the very end of the article was one paragraph that gave Allison the chills—convinced her that the assassination of Senator John Hartford was imminent.

Chad Powers, as usual, was moving fast. Just as he'd done with the bullet in the head of Darren Sheppard, followed later that same day by her father's car being chased over a cliff.

The very last paragraph in the article dropped the subtlest of hints. It stated that Senator Hartford was a close friend of Charles Farmington, and that there were unsubstantiated rumors in Washington that Hartford had paved the way over the last few years for Farmington to avoid liability for his transgressions in the Gulf of Mexico. The article even went so far as to hint that possibly money had changed hands between the oil executive and the good senator from Vermont.

Yes, the backstory had now been created. The character assassination had already commenced, to be followed soon by a real assassination.

Allison knew in her gut that the promising presidential candidate, the respected senator from Vermont, would never be allowed the opportunity to go out on the campaign trail.

In fact, Senator John Hartford might not even see another Vermont sunrise.

CHAPTER 25

Willy watched as his son swung into action. Wyatt ordered several of his officers to conduct grid searches of the areas north, south, and east of the city.

To check out abandoned farmhouses and summer cottages.

To check them all. No exceptions.

The officers didn't question why Wyatt hadn't asked them to cover the areas west of Nelson.

Willy had seen the look on Wyatt's face in the alley when he'd shaken his neighbor Sharon's hand, thanking her for the information about the vehicle.

Sharon had seen it, too, and was clearly concerned that something was wrong with him. It was impossible to miss—the blank look in his eyes, the seizure-like posture of his head and body.

Willy knew for sure that something was wrong.

He'd been accustomed to weird things about himself for most of his adult life, ever since that horrifying incident in Korea.

Willy had acquired powers that were beyond belief. And, he knew how it felt to go into trances when he was possessed by the need to create sculptures.

That power had come to him from above, that awful night way back in 1950.

When he went into his trances, he knew his face was devoid of expression—he could sense that. His eyes glazed over and his hands moved of their own accord. He had little control over what he was doing. Everything seemed to be automatic, beyond his comprehension.

When a sculpture was finished and his trance had ended, he would always look at his creation and wonder how the hell he'd done that. And, why.

A few minutes ago, he'd seen in his son what he knew he himself always experienced. Wyatt's eyes had glazed over and the blank expression on his face was exactly as Willy always pictured he looked when those weird things happened to him.

Willy knew without a doubt that the intense experience of his mom's disappearance had caused something to happen to his son. In his gut, he knew it. Something had been triggered.

For all of Wyatt's life so far, Willy had been waiting for something to appear. Wondering when that would be and what it would be.

Willy's DNA had undergone a dramatic transformation twenty years before the idea of conceiving Wyatt had even been a topic of conversation.

Helen had wanted children, but Willy had never been as enthusiastic about it as she'd been. For one very good reason. He'd been afraid of what a next generation of the altered DNA would look like and be like.

But, after a while, he relented. He'd loved Helen so much and she'd been so excited about the two of them raising a family together. It was her fondest dream. So, he let her have it, despite his misgivings. He couldn't live his entire life in fear, and having a child was one of those wonderful experiences that he didn't want to miss out on. Worth taking a chance.

So, Wyatt was born, and Willy was so relieved at first that everything looked normal.

Wyatt grew up as a normal child, with no apparent abnormalities. He didn't have the extreme strength that Willy possessed and no special talents such as art or music. He seemed…normal.

He'd had several x-rays done during his childhood—the usual broken bones acquired from falling out of trees or from fights in the schoolyard. And, those hadn't generated anything freaky. So, he'd been lulled into a kind of panacea, with his only child exhibiting nothing but normal behaviours. A panacea that he'd allowed himself to get used to.

Until today.

Deep down inside, he always knew in his gut that one day he'd see it. Didn't know when, but he knew that it was inevitable. The DNA was real, and it obviously had its own plan and timetable.

Willy was sitting in the living room while Wyatt barked out final instructions to his officers.

Suddenly, the house was empty—the bustle of activity was over. They all had their jobs to do, and sped off in their police cruisers to carry out their assigned duties.

Wyatt came back into the living room from the front porch and sat down in the chair opposite Willy.

"Dad, everything's going to be okay. My officers will find her. Don't worry."

"Are you going to stay here with me?"

Wyatt shook his head quickly.

"No, I have some patrolling of my own to do. I'm going to call Jan, my sergeant back at the station, to come over here and be with you. You've met her—a lovely lady. She's very efficient—will be a big help to you if the kidnappers phone with any ransom demands."

Willy frowned. "I can't just sit here waiting, Wyatt. I need to be doing something."

"You will be. They will no doubt call with demands. You need to be here for that."

Willy looked up into his son's eyes; eyes that he could tell were on fire with anger and determination.

"You have something specific to do, don't you?"

"I don't know what you mean, Dad."

"I can see it in your eyes right now. And, I saw it out in the alley, too. Something happened to you, didn't it?"

Wyatt hesitated, then shook his head.

"I'm curious. Why didn't you assign anyone to search the area west of the city?"

Wyatt fidgeted with his fingers. "I intend to patrol that area myself."

"Why? You're the police chief."

"I know that area well. I'm the best one to cover it."

"I'm going with you."

Wyatt raised his voice. "No. You have to stay here for the ransom call."

"There won't be a ransom call, will there? Because you'll get there before they have a chance to make the call. Am I right?"

Wyatt stood up. "This is getting silly, Dad. I have to go."

Willy stood as well.

"She's west of the city, isn't she? You saw it, didn't you? Out in the alley. You had some kind of vision, didn't you? I could see it in your eyes, on your face. You blanked out for a few seconds. You left us. Went somewhere else."

Wyatt didn't reply. Just stared down at the floor and sighed.

"I'm your father, Wyatt. You can't fool me. We're too close. And, don't forget, I know things about you that no one else knows. I've always known that certain gifts would show themselves one day. I've been watching for them your entire life. I'm guessing that one of those gifts just made its first appearance today, out in that alley."

Wyatt stared back, unblinking. Then, he nodded.

"Yes, Dad, it did. I saw the whole thing. I know exactly where they are. But, no one else can know how I know. I'd be a freak. You'd be a freak. I have to just deal with this, end it, get Mom back."

"Yes, you do. And, I'm going with you. I won't let you go alone. We'll do this together, just like we always have."

"Dad, it could be dangerous as hell. And…I'm afraid you might not like what you see when we get there."

Willy nodded, tears forming in his eyes. "I'm prepared for that. And, that's okay—what will be, will be. But, I have to be a part of this. You're not going to do this alone. She may be your mother, but she's my wife. The love of my life."

Willy then stepped forward and gave his son a big hug. Wyatt hugged him back and kissed him gently on the cheek. Then, he rested his hands on Willy's shoulders and stared into his teary eyes.

"I'm gonna use this freaky gift, or whatever the hell it is, to make this right. I can't explain what happened out in that alley, but I'm going to use it tonight for all its worth."

Willy wiped away a tear from his eye.

"Let's go get your mom."

CHAPTER 26

Allison drove slowly and contemplatively along the highway south of the city of Burlington, heading towards the wooded area where Senator Hartford lived.

John Hartford was a lifelong resident of Vermont, and had served in the U.S. Senate for a decade. The former Chairman of the Armed Services Committee was one of the most respected Republicans in Congress. He was one of two senators representing the state of Vermont in Washington, and was known for being one of the most outspoken elected officials.

He was known also for his integrity. He'd bucked the party many times by voting with the Democrats. He didn't believe in stonewalling for partisan politics reasons. John simply believed in good government and took his responsibility seriously.

It was a well-known fact that he was preparing to run for president, and the rumors were so strong that he was already getting media attention. Particularly for the fact that he was planning to run as a third party candidate.

An Independent.

Which was tantamount to heresy for the old guard of the Republican party.

Already being branded a traitor, attempts to sully his record in the Senate had also begun—because the Republican party was afraid that he was so popular amongst Americans that he would draw votes away from whoever the Republican party nominee ended up being. No one thought he actually had a chance of winning, but he would certainly cause enough disruption to allow the Democratic party nominee to win in the general election.

Senator John Hartford was a major conundrum for the Republican party.

The latest implications in the press about his relationship with the missing Charles Farmington, hinting that he might have received some payoff from the oil executive to keep the man immune from prosecution for the Gulf of Mexico environmental nightmare, was, to Allison's mind, perfect timing. It not only set Hartford up for some kind of reasoning if he happened to disappear just like Farmington, but it also discredited him in case the assassination failed. Any hint of payola and corruption was poison to a presidential candidate.

According to Chad Powers, Senator Hartford was planning to use the information Farmington had leaked to him about Majestic 12 as a launch pad for his campaign. But, Allison knew Hartford well enough to appreciate that if he was going to use that information, it was because of his strong sense of right and wrong. He was a man with more integrity in his little finger than in the entire two houses of Congress.

He just didn't know how dangerous it was for him to bring that information to light.

Allison couldn't help but wonder if Chad Powers, the leader of Majestic 12, had allowed a political connection to creep into the group's decision-making. Did they really vote in favor of killing the senator because of his plan to whistle-blow the group, or instead was this an assassination to eliminate a strong presidential contender that no one in the back rooms of power wanted to see in the race?

Her mind was whirling as she drove south of the pretty city of Burlington. It was the largest city in Vermont, but that wasn't saying much. A scant 45,000 people lived there, but the state itself had only 600,000 folks. It was one of the least populated states in the Union. No wonder, though, since beautiful forests covered more than 75% of its territory. Not much room left for people.

It was bordered on three sides by Massachusetts, New Hampshire, and New York. Quebec, Canada was directly to the north.

The state was famous for being a haven for skiers—in fact, the good senator was a skier himself, living fairly close to Sugarbush, one of the more popular ski resorts.

As Allison drove south of Burlington, she couldn't help but drool over the scenery—Vermont was indeed a special place and, as a city, Burlington itself seemed to have the best of both worlds. At its doorstep was the massive Lake Champlain, and in its rear-view mirror were the gorgeous

Adirondack Mountains.

She thought that maybe John had been inspired to run for president since the state of Vermont had actually birthed two of them already: Chester Arthur and Calvin Coolidge. But, no, Allison was pretty certain John would want to be his own man and put his own stamp on things.

She looked off to the west as she drove and could see the huge body of water that was Lake Champlain. It was 125 miles long tip to tip—actually flowed right into Canada and the boat ride to the 49th Parallel from Burlington was only about forty miles.

John lived in a heavily forested area south of the city, kind of remote even by Vermont standards. The area was laced with paved single-lane country roads, and even a few dirt and gravel ones.

John's house sat on twenty acres of land—he liked the privacy. Allison knew he wrote novels as a hobby—hadn't published any yet, but she knew that one day after he retired from politics that would become his next passion. And, being a famous senator, he wouldn't have any trouble attracting hordes of publishers.

If he lived that long.

John was expecting her. She'd called him yesterday from Chicago, and told him she wanted to pop by. First, she'd phoned his Washington office, but his assistant said that he was relaxing at home in Vermont this week.

He was happy to hear from her, but curious as to why she was making a special trip to Vermont. Allison gave him the cover story of wanting to get his support for a new hotel she wanted to build in the Sugarbush resort area, right on the edge of the ski slopes. He seemed excited about that, and gave her the directions to his house.

Allison could tell, though, that he seemed subdued over the phone. No doubt because of the allegations being waged in the media against him and his connections with Farmington. That sort of thing always haunted politicians, but especially in this case, when he couldn't really defend himself with Farmington missing.

And, little did he know that Farmington would never be seen again.

Allison knew that time was of the essence. Ever since she'd read the thoughts in Chad Powers' head—discovered that he'd had the journalist and her own family killed on the very same day—she knew he wouldn't take a chance on too much time passing between Farmington's disappearance and Hartford's fate.

Farmington's death didn't need a vote—it was understood as implicit by the Majestic 12 group that the betrayer in their group was going to die.

Chad hadn't said at the last meeting who that betrayer was, but Allison saw it when she picked up Farmington's thoughts across the table from him.

But, a vote indeed had been taken on Hartford's fate and he was condemned to die, despite Allison's pleas at the meeting and her vote against the plot. No one had listened to her. So, his fate was sealed. It was going to happen and she knew it could be any day, or hour, now.

Her thoughts caused her right foot to increase its pressure on the accelerator—in her paranoid imagination, she could see that it may even be happening at this very moment.

She sped down the highway until the elevated countryside hid the massive lake from view. She saw a road coming up and glanced at her notes.

Yep, Pinetree Lane.

She hung a left, and drove down that lane for about a mile until she came to a dirt road with the sign County Road #1. Allison turned right and drove along for about a mile until she finally saw his house. A beautiful Cape Cod style, with three dormer windows and a massive porch. It was red brick with a black tile roof, and it looked magnificent. Fitting indeed for a United States senator.

She knew that John had been a divorced man for the last eight years and, while the tabloids had tried to connect him to many ladies over that time, he'd told her that it was all bullshit and that there was no one important in his life. Neither did he want there to be. He didn't have time, nor the inclination.

His first marriage had been ruined by his busy life, and that life wasn't going to change any time soon. He didn't want to put another wife through that torture—the torture of campaigning, and then the constant bullshit just to stay in office. He didn't have any children, so, aside from his Senate work, John's life was uncomplicated. He maintained offices and homes in both Vermont and D.C., but Allison knew Vermont was where he most preferred to be.

Allison pulled around his circular drive, came to a stop and hopped out of her rental car.

He was standing on the porch waiting for her. A martini in each hand, and Allison knew that they'd both be very dry, straight up, Bombay Sapphire, with three olives. They'd indulged together in Hawaii and several times after that. Always just as friends though—it had never developed beyond that.

John Hartford was the ultimate presidential candidate. Tall and handsome, with slightly graying hair and a confident air about him. He was quick on his feet—possessed one of the most adept minds in Washington, and had that reassuring voice reminiscent of how news broadcasters used to sound. Now, all of the news anchors seemed to be women, and most were brain-dead bimbos chosen presumably for their looks alone.

John always reminded her of a beardless Donald Sutherland.

His voice boomed. "Allison, such a treat to have you visit me. It gets kinda lonely out here in the sticks; a rare pleasure to have a beautiful woman pop by."

She laughed as she bounded up the stairs to the porch. "Oh, John, you're still the charmer. Easy to see why you became a politician."

He slipped the martini glass into Allison's eager hand. "Ha, ha…come on inside. I have some snacky things laid out for us."

She followed him into the living room—surprisingly well decorated, considering that a bachelor lived there. The house was absolutely charming, and everything was in its place. Neat as a pin. Allison thought that maybe he'd cleaned up a bit after he found out she was coming, but knowing how detailed and efficient the man was, that was probably unlikely. He just liked things to be in their proper place, all the time.

She sat down on the plush couch and John plopped onto the love seat opposite her. Cheese, crackers, and pickles were on the table between them, and Allison helped herself.

John took a small sip of his martini, then cut to the chase. "So, you're thinking of building a hotel in our beautiful state and you need me to stickhandle things for you? Sneaky girl!"

Allison grimaced. "No, John, that's not why I'm here at all. I'm here to warn you that your life's in danger."

His hand shook slightly, spilling some of the vintage martini in his lap. He glared at her.

"What are you talking about?"

"I'm afraid we haven't much time. I know you've received some bad press over this Farmington guy's disappearance. That must be stressing you out. They're trying to tie you to influence-peddling on his behalf."

"Well, that's just politics, Allison. They know I'm planning to launch my campaign for president as an Independent, so they're trying to destroy me. If truth be told, my colleagues in the Senate know that I've been pushing for years to have that little sleaze investigated for his leaky wells in the Gulf. BP should never have been held responsible for all of those damages and fines. They ran into the billions, for Christ's sake!"

Allison nodded. "I know that, John. But, you're still in danger."

Hartford looked at his watch. "Sorry, I'm a bit distracted. My bodyguard is due here any minute now. He's bringing some papers over for me to sign—declarations and financial disclosures for the presidential launch."

Allison sighed with relief. "Oh, I'm so glad you have a bodyguard."

"Yes, well, anyone running for president needs these guys. I have one in Washington and one here in Vermont. Necessary evils." He took another, much longer, sip of his martini. "But, why do you say I'm in danger? It can't be any more perilous for me than other politicians."

Allison took a deep breath. "John, I know you met with Farmington. I know he gave you some secret information that you intend to use in your campaign."

Senator Hartford stared at her. "How do you know that?"

Allison shook her head. "Doesn't matter how I know. I just know. He told you some things, didn't he? About a group called Majestic 12? And, of certain information that's been kept from the American people for decades?"

John nodded slowly. "Yes, he did. But, again, how do you know about this?"

Allison sighed. "I'm one of Majestic 12, John. Farmington's been killed. His body will never be found. And, you're next."

John's face went as white as a ghost's. He jumped to his feet and walked to the window. He glanced at his watch again. "Where the hell is Clint?"

"John, did you hear me?"

He turned around to face her. "Yes, I did. And, I don't know what to say. You're one of them? I'm shocked. And…wondering why I'm still talking to you."

"Did Farmington tell you all about the history of Majestic 12? Back when it was established by Truman in 1947?"

"Yes, he did. And I'm horrified by what I was told. The American people have a right to know about these things."

"Do you recall from history that JFK demanded, unsuccessfully, to know the same kind of information that you now have?"

"Yes."

"And, you still think that Lee Harvey Oswald killed him?"

John's eyes went cold. "Are you saying...?"

Allison nodded. "Yes, I am. I don't know how much Farmington told you, but you're a bright man and you can connect the dots. The mandate of Majestic 12 was to protect all of the information related to that subject… the one that Kennedy was interested in…at all costs. You can guess what that means."

John shook his head. "Charles never told me things like that. Only about the truths, the secrets, things that have been lied about, hidden from our people. Don't you think they deserve to know, Allison?"

"Well, that's an argument for another day. You're an idealist, John. There are risks in knowing, but I can't say that I totally disagree with you, even though I'm a member of the group that was sworn to protect those secrets."

"And, you're saying that Charles Farmington was murdered by you guys?"

Alison lowered her voice to a whisper. "A vote was taken, John. You're to be killed as well. And, it will happen quickly, if history is a predictor. John, you're well aware of all of the scientists and astronomers who have died over the last few decades. Abnormal statistical death rates. The odds of even half of those deaths being from natural causes are astronomical—excuse the pun."

John leaned over and placed both hands on the coffee table. His voice was now a growl. "Why the fuck are you telling me this? You're one of them, for Christ's sake! How can I trust you? For all I know, you could be the assassin!"

Allison answered softly. "I just discovered that they arranged to have my own family killed five years ago—that car crash was no accident, John. I guess I've had a rude reality check. I discovered that the reason my family was killed was because my father was planning to blow the whistle, just like you're planning. I don't want this to happen again to a good person. And, you're a good person, John. You should be our next president."

Suddenly, the sound of a car pulling up along the gravel driveway.

John cocked his head. "Good, he's here. I feel like I need him now more than ever. He's planning to stay for several days, too, so I guess that's a good thing right now."

The front door opened and in walked a jovial-looking man carrying a duffel bag and a briefcase.

John walked over and gave him a bear hug. "Great to see you, Clint." Then, he gestured at Allison. "This is Allison Fisher, owner of Diamond Hotels. She wants our help in getting a resort built here in Vermont."

Clint dropped his duffle bag and walked over to Allison. He gave her a warm handshake and one of the biggest smiles Allison had ever seen.

"Great to meet you. From my standpoint, there's no other place in America better suited for one of your hotels. If I can be of any help, let me know. I'm not just the senator's bodyguard, I'm also his close advisor on all things 'Vermonty.'"

Allison was getting good vibes from Clint. His jovial face was a paradox against the rock-solid frame he carried. Probably ex-military and, as with most high-level bodyguards, had probably been a Seal, Ranger, or Delta. She was glad he was there. She would leave it to John to decide whether or not to disclose to Clint what she had just warned him about.

The three of them sat down in the living room after John brought Clint a beer from the kitchen.

Clint raised his bottle in a toast. His voice was as jovial as his face. "To new friends! And new hotels!"

They all toasted and laughed.

Then, Allison saw his eyes wander. Not in a lazy careless way, but in an investigative way. Like someone trained in the powers of observation would do. He tried his best to keep it subtle, but it was out of place enough for Allison's antenna to go up.

She put her drink down on the table and quickly inserted both fingers into her ears. Then, withdrew them in a millisecond, popping her ear drums as she did.

Allison stared into Clint's friendly howdy-doody eyes.

She had to fight hard to keep her head from jerking backwards with the horrifying words and images that suddenly invaded her brain:

A voice, no longer jovial. "This is a complication I didn't fucking need."

An image of her and John being dumped into the trunk of a car.

Then, lying on the deck of a boat, bound and gagged.

Thick sacks positioned beside their bodies.

Yellow plastic rope wrapped around both the sacks and their bodies, uniting them as one.

The sacks imprinted with the word, 'Cement.'

The two of them struggling in vain against their restraints.

And, the once jovial voice, speaking to no one in particular.

"Yeah, they'll sink."

CHAPTER 27

Helen Carson tried to just concentrate on controlling her heart rate. She'd had problems with blood pressure before, and on and off over the years she'd taken medication for it. During the last few months, she'd noticed a marked improvement—but tonight she was in decline.

She could feel that her face was flushed, although that might have been just due to the burlap sack that was still over her head.

It was hot, darn hot—and the sack just made things worse. Thankfully, one of them had reached under the sack and removed that stinky old rag from her mouth. She figured they must be in an isolated place now for them to have done that. If so, screaming wouldn't do her a damn bit of good.

Helen was sitting, her arms tied behind the chair back. She knew the house had solid wood floors, because she could hear the squeak of running shoes as the three of them paced back and forth, discussing their plans. The air in the house smelled fresh and clean—whoever lived here took good care of it. Their voices echoed a bit when they talked, so she figured the room she was in was a good size, and probably didn't have a lot of furniture or paintings on the walls.

Helen concentrated on breathing evenly, through her nose, exhaling through her mouth. Once in a while, she took an extra deep breath and held it for about ten seconds, then slowly exhaled. This helped to calm her down and she noticed that her heart didn't race as much. But, she didn't want to do it too often or too deeply, for fear of fainting from hyperventilation.

The older one they called Aaron seemed to be the one in charge. The other two, Brody and Matt, seemed rather stupid and jumpy. Those were probably the two she had to worry about the most, as they'd more than likely be reckless. Although, Aaron, she guessed, was the hardened criminal who might have more to lose. She knew, from the way they talked, that this was his plan and that he'd done it before.

"So, what de fuck we gonna ass for? How mush? We hant disgust that yet."

"Well, I figure, based on how their house looks, we should demand 100,000 dollars."

Some shuffling of feet. "Think we could ass more an that."

"No, if we ask for too much it will take longer. We don't know how much cash they keep on hand, and she's not telling us anything. We already asked her that. He might have to mortgage his house, which will take time. The longer we have her, the more risk there is to us."

The sound of feet pounding on the floor, almost like someone jumping up and down. Helen figured it was the drugged-up Matt.

"Kay, guess thas the smart thin to do. I jus wan some drugs, man."

"Shut up, Matt. I'm strategicking wif Aaron here."

Then, Aaron once again. "Okay, we phone and demand 100,000 by tomorrow afternoon. Since we used my truck and my house, my share will be half of that and you two can split the rest. Then, we need to separate and never be seen together again."

"Thas not fair. We tole you bout him."

"I don't care—that's the deal. Take it or leave it."

"Brody, is kay. Thas 25,000 fer eash of us. Les do it."

Silence for a few seconds. "Kay, I agree, les get on wif it."

"Alright, then. We have their home phone number, so I'll phone from here. I'll only stay on for a minute or so."

"Won their call display thin show yer number?"

"No, mine's a satellite phone. Can't be traced."

Brody again. "Wait a sec. How we gonna get de moneys?"

"I've already thought it out. I'll reserve a boat at the Christina Lake Marina in William Carson's name. He can pay for it with his own credit card. I'll tell him to take the boat out of the marina and cruise slowly south.

"I'll be in a boat a friend of mine owns. I can just take it whenever I want. He keeps it at his cottage dock. I'll be out in the middle of the lake and will watch Carson with binoculars. Once he's out and well away from anyone else, I'll speed up and cruise alongside. He can throw the bag of money into my boat and then I'll order him to keep cruising around for another forty-five minutes. I'll tell him he's being watched. That will give me time to speed back to my friend's cottage, dock the boat, and get back here to you guys.

"We'll split the money and then I'll drop you off wherever you want. We'll leave her out on the highway somewhere. She hasn't seen me or the way into this property, so I'm safe."

Helen heard Brody cough, and then sputter, "Well, she seen us! She dint have a sack on her head when she saw us! What you think bout that?"

Matt yelled, "Yeah, whaddaya think bout that, Aaron?"

She heard Aaron laugh. "Settle down. You guys look like all the other drugged-out losers on the street. Sorry, guys, but it's the truth. You'll blend in any big city."

"I should punch yer face in fer that."

"Try it, Brody, and I'll kill you without batting an eye. As you know, I've killed before."

"Yeah, big man. How I know you kill fore? You jus pumpin yerself."

Helen heard the sound of a fist hitting flesh, then a thud on the floor.

Then, Matt gasping. "Why you do that? He jus kiddin you."

"I'll do it to you, too, Matt, if you question me. In fact, I'll do worse to you just for the fun of it."

She heard the rustling of a package, and then the flick of a lighter.

Aaron again, his tone impatient. "Matt, you can't fuckin light that butt up in my house. Go outside. Around the side of the house there's an old milk can you can use as an ashtray."

Footsteps, then the sound of a screen door opening and closing.

Helen heard Brody's voice coming from down on the floor. "Hey, she know yer name, too, Aaron. Can't be too many Aarons in these parts. You own this house—they track you."

"No, Brody. I'm smarter than that. My real name isn't Aaron—that was just for you boys to call me something."

"Oh."

She heard footsteps tracing to the other end of the room. "I'm gonna call him now. Be quiet in the background. He'll ask to speak to his wife, so I'll put her on for a second or two."

Then, Helen heard him yelling over to her. "Lady, you be careful what you say when I put you on!"

Except for the beeping of the phone as the keys were being punched in, there was only the shallow breathing of Brody. Helen took another deep, soothing breath and held it for a few seconds.

Then, the sound of the phone being dropped roughly back into its cradle. Followed by a piece of furniture crashing into the wall.

"Christ! A fucking voice message! No one home! His wife has just been kidnapped, and there's no one to answer the phone, not even the police!"

"Jus our luck."

Helen heard footsteps coming towards her. Then, she felt a slap across the sack covering her face. It was hard and, because she didn't see it coming, she wasn't braced for it. She felt her neck stiffen up from the jolt, and tears began rolling down her cheeks from the stinging pain.

"What kind of husband you got, lady? Aren't you important enough for him to stay home and wait for our call? What kind of bullshit is this?"

She felt another slap—but this time she was ready and her head rolled with it.

Suddenly, she felt fingers against her chest, examining the beautiful cross pendant that Willy had given her on their first anniversary, decades ago. It was her favorite piece of jewelry and she hardly ever took it off.

Aaron started laughing. "Are you a Jesus freak or something, lady?"

He yanked on it, causing the chain to break. The force of his hand pulling downward caused the buttons of her pretty red blouse to pop off, exposing her, right down to her waist. Even though it was a hot night, Helen could feel a cool draft against her bare skin. Or…perhaps it was just the sudden feeling of vulnerability that caused her to shiver.

He laughed again. "Well, you better pray to Jesus that your husband answers the goddamned phone next time I call."

He cursed and threw the pendant onto the floor. Helen could hear its tell-tale tinkle as it skittered along the hardwood.

Helen started worrying about what might happen next. Aaron, while sounding intelligent and under control most of the time, was clearly a psycho who could be set off by the slightest provocation. First it was Brody, then Matt, and finally a simple voice message. Helen feared that she was now going to be the outlet for his psychopathic anger, especially since he'd already hit her twice and ripped open her blouse.

Brody's voice. "Hey, man, we try ta phone gan in a few minutes. Best leave her lone, so she talk kay on the phone."

Helen could feel Aaron's warm moist breath as he brought his face down close to her chest. She felt helpless, but she knew there was nothing she could do, except…as Aaron had suggested…pray.

Then, the breath was gone and she heard him take a couple of steps away from her.

Perhaps, if she was lucky, his moment of explosive anger had passed.

For now.

Helen took another slow, deep breath through her nose and held it for as long as she could this time. She slowly exhaled through her mouth and welcomed the lightheaded feeling that came with the mild hyperventilation.

She decided that perhaps she should do this a few more times, and do them more rapidly. Fainting into unconsciousness might be her best escape right now.

Her only escape.

CHAPTER 28

Wyatt steered his police cruiser off Highway 3A, and went north along Doukhobor Road. He was following the exact route he'd seen them drive along when he was 'remote viewing' from above. He'd floated right along with them in his vision, the detail so definite that he'd actually been able to see the odd puff of exhaust from the tailpipe of the Jeep.

He sensed that he was being watched. He turned his head towards his dad in the passenger seat. He was indeed staring at him, a look of both compassion and concern on his face.

"What's wrong, Dad?"

"Considering what we're doing, that's a funny question to ask me."

"Yeah, but you're staring at me. What are you thinking about?"

Willy turned his eyes back to the road. "Are you sure we're doing the right thing? You've left your entire police force behind back there. You haven't told them where you're going. There's no back-up, nothing. Just you and me."

"There's an old expression, Dad. '*Less is more.*' Sometimes more can be accomplished by just a few."

"I don't know if two people can be described as 'a few,' Wyatt."

He went silent for a couple of minutes. "You're right, I'm not sure at all. I'm not sure about anything anymore. I discovered that my own dad has freaky powers and that his DNA was changed by some surreal experience during the war. Then, the awareness that some of that change would eventually appear in me because I inherited your DNA.

"Then, lo and behold, it showed itself with some weird 'remote viewing' power that I didn't even know I had. And, now, I've used it for the first time to track down my mother's kidnappers.

"So, yeah, right now I'm not too sure about anything. Is that surprising?"

Willy rubbed Wyatt's shoulder.

"Fate has a funny way of working sometimes. None of this would have happened if I hadn't been in the studio the night those boys showed up; if I hadn't been exhibiting that weird transparency when they were there.

"Once they discovered I was a local celebrity, they saw me as a gold mine. Ripe for the picking. The perfect mark to extort. Then, they happened to meet someone else who had more grandiose plans than just a mere five thousand dollars. He somehow convinced them that kidnapping was more lucrative."

Wyatt lit a cigarette. "Yeah, fate may be the only way to explain this weird turn of events. But, we have to look at it this way—fate is actually helping us now. This newfound power I inherited from your genes is leading us to Mom. So, that seems like it was almost planned. It made its appearance at the right time, didn't it?"

Willy nodded. "But, back to my first question—will the two of us be enough?"

"It's going to have to be, Dad. We'll do this ourselves. A half dozen police officers out here could only make things worse, anyway. The more people there are, the more mistakes. The kidnappers could panic and hurt Mom…or worse."

"They may have already hurt her."

Wyatt shook his head, and whispered, "Don't think that."

Wyatt turned off onto a dirt road—the same road he had seen in his vision. It was already dark outside, but he couldn't take the chance any longer of leaving his headlights on. He flicked them off and followed the road by the light of the moon. He wouldn't have far to go, from his recollection.

Suddenly, he applied the brakes and pointed. "There, through those trees. You can see the lights of the farmhouse."

"Yes, I can see them. Are you sure that's the house?"

"Absolutely. I've followed the route in my mind exactly."

Wyatt pulled the car off into a clearing in the trees.

Then, he faced Willy. "I want you to stay here for now, Dad. Let me do some reconnaissance and determine the lay of the land. Then, I'll come back to get you and we'll formulate a plan."

"Do you promise?"

"Yes, I promise."

"Then, I'll abide your wish. I'll wait."

Wyatt squeezed his dad's shoulder, then quietly slipped out of the car and gently eased the door closed.

He followed the lights of the house and the light of the moon. Keeping low to the ground, he edged closer and closer to the large farmhouse.

Creeping from tree to tree for cover, he finally reached the front portion of the house. It appeared as if all of the blinds were closed, the light from inside glowing through the slats.

He scanned the area—no sign of anyone outside. Then, he saw the vehicle parked off to one side of the house and, if he hadn't known before that moment, he sure knew now that this was the right house. The black Jeep Cherokee that he'd watched from above.

He snuck over to the car and peeked inside to make sure one of the drug freaks wasn't curled up in there in a stoned stupor. All clear. He laid his hand on the hood. Warm.

Wyatt then advanced on the house. He reached under his jacket and pulled out his Smith and Wesson 357 Magnum. He released the safety and held it aloft as he carefully mounted the steps to the front porch, cursing himself that in his rush he hadn't remembered to change out of his Oxford shoes and don some soft, silent joggers.

Crouching low, he moved to the first window and examined all of the slats. Drawn tight. He moved across to the next one and noticed that there was one slat which hadn't drawn tight. He put his eyes up against the glass and peered through the small opening.

During his years with the Mounties, Wyatt had observed more than he cared to remember.

Scenes a lot worse than this one.

But, seeing his wonderful mother sitting in a chair, head covered with a burlap sack, chin resting on her chest, hands tied behind the chair back, blouse ripped open, shook Wyatt to his core.

He blinked several times to clear his eyes of the tears that were welling up.

And, he fought back against the overwhelming urge to vomit.

Seeing victims of crime was one thing, but seeing his own mother in such a degrading and submissive condition was almost too much to bear.

Wyatt shook his head and forced himself to recover.

He looked away.

Then, he moved away, down the porch stairs and onto the front grass again. He had to find out how many more doors there were. Coming in through the front door probably wouldn't be too smart. He had no idea if there were any weapons inside. It could be a suicide mission.

He crept along towards the southeast section of the house. He was just getting ready to round the corner when his nose caught a familiar scent.

Cigarette smoke. Faint, but distinct.

He lowered his Magnum, held it in both hands, and pointed it straight ahead of him at chest level as he slowly rounded the corner of the house.

Then everything went black.

But, before it did, he was aware of something heavy and metallic connecting with his forehead.

The last sound he heard before the darkness engulfed him was the deafening gunshot from his unforgiving Magnum.

CHAPTER 29

Allison watched Clint closely as he guzzled a good half of his beer. She looked at him differently now—now that she knew what was going through his head. Suddenly, he didn't appear so jovial, so friendly. She knew that was just the façade of a killer.

Clearly, Hartford trusted him. They appeared to be very comfortable with each other. Little did John know that the papers his bodyguard had brought along for him to sign were just a Trojan horse.

"So, what's going on back at the office, Clint?"

"Well, John, everyone's running around like chickens with their heads cut off. This Farmington story is developing a life of its own. The press are sitting on our doorstep, and the phones are ringing off the hook. Luckily, you own this house under a corporate name, so you can't be found. Your apartment in Burlington, however, is on their radar. They've camped out there, too."

Allison jumped in. "I wasn't aware you had a place in town, John."

"Yes, I keep it just to have a home close to the office. And, at times like this, it acts as a great decoy."

Clint snapped open his briefcase, and pulled out a pile of documents.

"As they say, the best defence is an offense. So, our suggestion to you, Johnny-boy, is to sign these registration papers, and then just get on with announcing your candidacy. That shows confidence and that you have nothing to hide. We can set up a public event for your announcement speech—we'll do it right in the town square in Burlington. Hometown boy and all that crap. I've taken the liberty of instructing Stephen to get your speech drafted."

Hartford glanced over at Allison, then back at Clint. "Any security concerns?"

"No, none that I'm aware of. We'll maintain the usual tight ring around you—I'll get my usual crew to back me up." Clint smiled reassuringly. "Hey, you've known me for over a decade, John—you know I'd take a bullet for you."

John nodded. "Yes, I know you would. I hope it will never come to that."

"Well, when you're president, you'll have the Secret Service protecting your precious ass. You won't need me anymore."

"I'd still rather have you, Clint. I'll find a spot for you."

Allison wondered if maybe her telepathy had been wrong. These two seemed so close, and Clint seemed so sincere. She popped her ears again and waited for the words or images to appear.

No images this time. Only thoughts: "*I've already got a spot for you, old friend—down at the bottom of Lake Champlain.*"

No, the telepathy was accurate. No mistake. She wondered how he was planning to do it, and how much time they had. The wheels in her head were spinning fast—she had to get John away from Clint, so she could talk to him and convince him to find a reason to leave the house—either with her, or by himself.

But, would he listen to her? He'd already been skeptical of the story she told him, and expressed the worry that Allison herself may be the assassin. He'd known Clint a lot longer than he'd known Allison. Would she be able to convince him that Clint was about to betray him, to kill him? And, about to kill her, too, just for being in the wrong place at the wrong time.

Why would he listen to her? How could she explain it? That she'd popped her ears and Clint's thoughts came into her head? That she'd inherited this power from her dad's DNA being downloaded to her? And, that her father had become a superhuman from being zapped by a strange craft while cruising on a British Navy vessel?

Sure, all that was believable. Right. Hartford's first phone call would be to the local mental hospital to come and pick her up.

As John was signing the documents, Clint went to the kitchen and got himself another beer out of the fridge. "Allison, John? Do you guys want anything?"

They both shook their heads.

John kept signing and Allison kept thinking. What were her best options?

As she saw it, there were three.

The first was to get John alone and try to convince him to run for it. That seemed the best option, but also the least likely one to succeed. John wouldn't buy it.

The second option was for her to just run for it herself. Get herself out of danger. Find an excuse to leave and then just leave. And, hope against hope that after Hartford was killed, they wouldn't bother tracking her down. But, that seemed weak—she was a loose thread, and the last one to see John alive with Clint. Allison was convinced that she was stuck here now—that Clint wouldn't let her leave under any circumstance.

So, that left only the third option…

Clint came back and sat down, this time in the wing chair facing the fireplace.

He said, to no one in particular, "You know, I wish it were winter—it must be darn pretty out here with all the snow. With this massive fireplace on, it would be nice and cozy."

John looked up from his papers. "It is, Clint. I've invited you out here before for some snowmobiling, but you've never been able to swing it. Let's do it this winter, for sure."

"Yeah, and let's get a couple of nice loose women out here with us!" He glanced at Allison. "Oops, sorry Allison. That doesn't make me sound too good, does it?"

She smiled at him. "That's okay—boys will be boys."

Now or never.

Allison got up and went into the kitchen. Her eyes scanned the room, and landed on a large cast iron frying pan sitting on the stove.

It would have to do.

Keeping her back to the men, she picked up the pan and held it down low. Then, she turned and walked slowly into the living room, holding it in her right hand behind her back.

She came up behind Clint and took a deep breath. Then, she carefully brought her right hand out from behind her back. Just as she was raising the heavy pan up into the air, readying it for a tennis-like forehand, John started talking again.

He was looking down at his papers. "Clint, could I get you to witness a couple of…."

John must have sensed something was different, because he suddenly looked up. Straight into Allison's eyes. "What on earth…?"

In reaction, Clint turned his head slightly towards John just as Allison was swinging.

She ignored John and focused all of her strength on the swing. Allison was a great tennis player, but no racquet she'd ever held had the weight this frying pan did. But, her arms were strong and her swing was solid.

With Clint having turned his head at the last second, the pan hit him in the back of the head instead of along the side as Allison had planned. It connected viciously with the base of his skull and the sound of cast iron against human bone was sickening.

Even though the swing was fast, to Allison everything seemed to move in slow motion.

Out of the corner of her eye, she saw John Hartford holding up his hand in a feeble attempt at signalling her to stop.

Clint's first reaction was a slight motion forward. He was a big man, so the strike of the pan wasn't enough to send his body flying. No, instead he went slumping forward for just an instant, then his head and neck stiffened and moved slightly backward. Then he crumpled onto the coffee table and his body immediately began twitching.

Allison dropped the frying pan and stared in stunned silence at the convulsing body.

Hartford was in shock. His eyes were wide and his hands were shaking.

"What have you done? Are you insane?"

He leaped to the floor and held his hands out towards his friend. But, he didn't know where to put them, seemed almost afraid to touch him. His hands hovered in the air, non-committal.

Clint's body was still twitching and shaking in nightmare-inducing fashion, from his head all the way down to his feet.

Then, suddenly, the twitching and shaking stopped.

It seemed as if that was the signal John needed to touch him. While sobbing, he put his fingers up to Clint's throat and held them there for a few seconds. He grabbed one limp wrist. Then, the other wrist.

He raised his eyes and glared at Allison, shaking his head sadly.

John's right hand moved quickly. It reached underneath Clint's jacket, and pulled out a pistol.

He released the safety and pointed it at Allison's head.

CHAPTER 30

"Keep your hands where I can see them! You're here to kill me, aren't you?!"

Allison slowly raised her hands into the air. She realized they were shaking and feeling tingly—kind of a burning sensation, almost as if an electric current were running through them.

She'd never killed anyone before—at least not by her own hand.

She'd of course participated in decisions to have countless people killed over the last five years. Judge, jury and executioner—performing her duties on the board of Majestic 12. But, all that had seemed so remote—she'd never known those people, had never seen them up close and personal.

They'd each been no more real than file folders—just mere dossiers with photos and bios.

Not like this.

Actually performing the act of taking someone's life was totally different.

She hadn't even intended to kill Clint. She'd just wanted to incapacitate him so she and John could escape safely. If he hadn't turned his head at the last second, he'd probably just be unconscious. Instead of the frying pan hitting him on the side of the head, it connected directly with the back of his head.

At a spot that Allison knew was very dangerous, very vulnerable.

The Medulla Oblongata.

Otherwise known as the brainstem area of the spinal column. Soft and susceptible. The slightest injury to that area could cause instant death. Or, even worse, life in a vegetative state. It was an area of the body that Allison was always surprised had such little protection, as if God forgot about that part.

She'd had a close friend in high school who died from a brainstem injury during a gymnastics routine. That's when she'd learned all about that essential part of the body, and she'd learned it the hard way.

A terrible coincidence that she'd now caused someone's death in that exact same way.

"How many more are coming for me, Allison? Hard to believe you're it."

She found her voice. "John, I didn't intend to kill Clint. I only wanted to knock him out. He was planning to kill us—I saw it in his head. I have… an ability. I can read thoughts."

Hartford stood up and held the gun steady in his hand—now pointed at the middle of Allison's chest. He used his left sleeve to wipe the tears away from his eyes. He glanced down once more at his limp friend.

Then, he directed his attention back to Allison.

"You sure had me fooled. Smart lady—in order to kill me, you had to first take out my bodyguard. I'm going to phone the police, Allison. You've just killed one of my most loyal aides, but you're not going to get me. Not today, at least."

He walked over to the coat rack, reached inside the pocket of his jacket, and took out his cell phone. The entire time, he kept the gun levelled at Allison.

He looked down at his phone and started punching in the numbers. She took advantage of that moment—slid her arms down slowly and poked her fingers into her ears. Then, she quickly popped them back out again.

She talked slowly and softly. "John, right now you're thinking about what you're going to tie me up with. You're thinking of some duct tape you have in the garage. You're picturing it hanging on the wall, fourth hook to the left of the door. For a second, you were actually thinking of shooting me, out of fear that I'd find a way to still get you. But, you quickly changed your mind because of the publicity. You thought that you'd get better political capital out of holding me for the police, and being celebrated as a brave hero in honor of your dead friend. Then, I could hear you thinking that an announcement to run for president would be timed very well after this. The sympathy and bravery angles. Am I right?"

John stared at her in shock. He turned off his phone and walked slowly towards her, still warily holding the pistol at chest height.

"What the fuck?"

"I'm right, aren't I, John?"

He nodded slowly. "Okay, so what am I thinking right now?"

"You're thinking that I must be some kind of freak."

Hartford nodded and blinked his eyes several times in rapid succession. "One more time—what's on my mind at this moment?"

Allison held her gaze steady, staring straight into John's misty eyes. "You're thinking that at a different time, a different place, you'd like to fuck me."

"Jesus…" He lowered the gun and Allison lowered her hands.

"How are you able to do that?"

"Doesn't matter right now—I promise I'll tell you everything later. Right now, we have to get out of here."

"What did you see with Clint?"

"You and I bound and gagged, in a boat, with bags of cement lashed to our bodies. He planned to dump us overboard."

"Christ..."

"They got to him, John. Either that or he's always been an operative. I can tell you this much—when orders are given, they're usually given to a network of assassins. Those killers never know who's giving them the orders, nor do they care. And, they never know why. They're very well paid, and they couldn't care less who's paying them."

"I don't know what to say. I guess…thanks."

"Good. Right now, we have to go. I don't know where yet, but we need to get away from this house. We'll take my rental car—they don't know to watch for that, because clearly Clint didn't know I was going to be here. I picked that out of his head as well."

John shook his head. "No, I never told anyone you were coming."

Allison picked up her purse and slung it over her shoulder. "Go get your wallet and any other identification you might need, just in case."

John walked to his office and was back a couple of minutes later, briefcase in hand.

He cocked his head towards the door. "Okay, let's go. You can tell me more as we're driving."

Allison took a quick peek out the window before opening the front door. She raised her hand up to shield her eyes from the setting sun, and she knew in an instant her eyes weren't playing tricks on her.

"John, we have another problem. Take a look."

He walked to the window and followed her gaze.

"Do you see it?"

Allison heard his frantic breathing. This was a nightmare that was getting worse for him by the minute.

John nodded slowly. "Yes..."

Allison took another peek, being careful to stay off to the side of the window frame so as not to be seen. Out on the road past the driveway, partially shielded by a clump of trees, was a small truck parked on the side of the road. Attached to the truck was a trailer with a boat.

"Those are the guys with our transportation to the lake."

Suddenly, the sound of a cell phone buzzing.

Allison could tell where it was coming from.

Clint's pocket.

She ran over and pulled it out of the dead killer's jacket. The screen lit up with a text. It read: '*Is it done yet? Should we advance?*

Allison dashed back to John, holding the phone out for him to see the message. John read it and gasped.

"We can't get out the front door with those guys sitting there."

"Worse than that, John. They need an answer. Otherwise, they'll suspect something is wrong. We have to make them think that Clint succeeded. We need them to have their guards down."

Confusion was in his eyes. "What…"

"John, we're trapped. We can't leave because they're out there. And, we can't stay here either. So, we have to clear the path for ourselves."

He nodded in understanding. Allison could tell that his brain was working slowly right now—he was having trouble thinking ahead. Probably still in shock over Clint, and now this latest scary surprise. Killers waiting outside in a truck, pulling the boat that was supposed to dump them at the bottom of Lake Champlain.

"Senator, pull that gun out of your waistband and cock it. I'm going to text them back."

And, she did. With the words, '*It's done.*"

CHAPTER 31

The cracking sound reverberated through the still forest, and Willy knew in his gut that it was a gunshot. He was already on the edge of frantic while sitting in the car waiting for his son to return, and the sudden violent noise caused his heart to skip a beat.

He flipped the handle on the door and flew out of the car as if with wings. Despite how anxious he was feeling, Willy had the presence of mind to shut the door quietly. While breathing a silent prayer that Wyatt and Helen were okay, he reminded himself that the kidnappers at this point didn't know whether or not Wyatt had come alone.

He was sure his son had been discovered—he just hoped and prayed that the gun had been fired by Wyatt and not by someone else.

Willy crouched low and made his way through the thick foliage towards the dim lights of the farmhouse. He cursed under his breath as low-lying branches scraped against his arms and legs. His heart felt like it stopped for a second or two when there was a rustle in the bushes ahead—then he breathed a sigh of relief as he watched a racoon scurry out of his way.

The adrenaline was pumping through his veins and he could feel his lungs straining—it was a hot, muggy night and breathing was difficult, made worse by the anxiety he was feeling. Willy had no idea what to expect when he got to the house, but, whatever it was, he knew he would have no choice but to just deal with it as best he could.

* * * * *

Wyatt opened his eyes slowly. His vision was blurry, but he could see that he was inside a house. It took a few seconds for him to get his bearings, and his head hurt like hell.

Then, he remembered. He'd been hit by something metallic, and his gun had gone off.

He glanced up and saw a skinny kid with a green toque brandishing his 357 Magnum, swinging it around in the air as if it were a toy. The kid was breathing heavily and shifting his weight from one foot to the other and back again.

A slightly older man suddenly appeared in his vision, coming from behind the chair that Wyatt was sitting on. He tried to move his arms, but realized that he wasn't just sitting on the chair, but tied to it as well.

He glanced to his left and saw another kid sitting on the floor beside the chair that his mother was tied to. The sack was still attached around her head, a head which was now erect. When he'd peeked through the window, her chin had been drooped onto her chest. Wyatt was relieved to know that his mother was now conscious.

The kid with the pistol in his hand looked like he was high on drugs. Wyatt was worried about him.

The punk looked at the older man and then pointed at Wyatt. "He wake now. I thought I might have kilt him wif that shovel. What we gonna do now?"

The older man knelt down in front of Wyatt. "Who the fuck are you?"

Wyatt shook his head. He didn't want to say anything and alert his mother that he was there. It wouldn't be good for these guys to know they were mother and son.

The man reached down and unbuttoned Wyatt's jacket. He reached into the inside pocket looking for identification. Wyatt was relieved that he'd left his badge and wallet in the glove compartment.

The guy reached behind Wyatt and patted his ass, searching again for some means of identification.

"Are you a cop, man?"

Wyatt just stared at him.

The toque kid screamed, and waved the gun in the air. "Of course he a cop! Looka this fuckin gun! Is a monster!"

The kid on the floor shouted, "Shut up, Matt!"

"No, you shut up, Brody!"

The older man sneered, "Very smart, boys. Now he knows your names."

Matt laughed. "Big deal. He seen us now, too. You shoulda cover his head like the ole lady."

Brody stood and pulled the sack off Helen's head. "I guess this sack don matter no more. Aaron, why don you make nother phone call to the ole man, and she can talk to him."

Wyatt glanced at his mother and pursed his lips, silently telling her to shush. But, it was too late. Her eyes widened in recognition and she opened her mouth in astonishment.

Aaron noticed it. Snatched the gun out of Matt's hand and shoved it roughly up against Wyatt's forehead.

"Okay, lady, you know this man. Tell me who he is—I'll count to three."

He cocked the gun. "One…two…"

"No! Stop! That's my son, Wyatt!"

"Okay, now we're getting somewhere. Is he a cop?"

"Yes! He's the police chief! There are probably more outside, so you better let us go and just make a run for it!"

Aaron glared at Wyatt. "Tell me, or I'll shoot your mother. Are there more outside?"

Wyatt shook his head. "No, I came alone."

Aaron motioned to Brody to get up off the floor. Then he un-cocked the pistol and handed it to him.

"Go outside and check. If there's anyone out there, shoot them."

Brody's hand shook as he frowned at Aaron.

"You s'posed to be in charge here. Why don you go? Why me?"

"Because I'm telling you to go."

Matt lurched forward. "He chicken. Gimme the gun—I'll go."

Aaron yanked the Magnum out of Brody's hand and flipped it to Matt. "You've just earned an extra ten percent share of the ransom, Matt. Go… and be quick."

* * * * *

Willy crept silently up the stairs to the front porch. Crouching low, he moved along the edge of a window to a spot where the blinds hadn't completely closed. He squinted his eyes and peeked inside.

He caught his breath at the sight. His wife tied to a chair with her blouse split down the middle. His son sitting helplessly next to her, tied up on another chair. He saw the kid named Brody standing off to the side, and an older man was pacing back and forth in front of the two captives.

Willy couldn't see the crazed druggie, Matt, though. Maybe he was in the bathroom.

He didn't see Wyatt's gun anywhere, either, and he wondered what had happened to it. Then, he remembered the gunshot. Maybe Wyatt had shot Matt?

Suddenly, there were footsteps.

Off to the side of the house, moving down along the path towards the forest that Willy had just come out of a few minutes before.

Willy got down on his knees and moved slowly along the porch floor. He had to get away from the illumination of the window. He crawled to the steps and went down, one knee at a time.

There must be a side door. The kid must have come out of the house that way. He still couldn't see Matt, but he could hear him, shuffling carelessly along through the forest.

He moved slowly to the side of the house, and saw the door.

He chose the perfect tree.

And, then, the perfect rock.

He stood behind the tree and waited.

For a few minutes, there was silence in the forest, as Matt moved out of range. But, then, he started back, and the shuffling of his feet through the underbrush got louder as he got closer.

As he passed the tree, Willy could see the skinny little drug freak holding Wyatt's pistol out in front of him.

Willy lunged out with the rock and slammed it down hard against Matt's wrist.

The kid squealed in pain, and the gun went flying out of his hand. Willy spun him around and wrapped one arm around his neck and a hand over his mouth.

"Shut up. We're going to walk into that house nice and quiet, okay?"

The kid nodded, then quickly chomped his teeth down hard around Willy's index finger. Reacting on instinct Willy pulled his hand away, and in that one split second Matt wriggled free of his grasp. He dove to the ground and felt around for the gun.

Willy had no idea where the gun was and he certainly couldn't see it in the dark.

Matt suddenly stopped groping.

The kid flipped from his stomach to his back, while raising his right arm upwards. The gleam of the gun's shiny metal flashed in his hand.

Willy brought his left foot down hard on Matt's wrist, pinning his gun hand to the ground. Then, he rammed his right knee down into the kid's gut. He heard the air expel from his lungs.

Willy was done with this kid now. He'd tried to salvage him, but the risk was obviously too great. Two wonderful lives were at stake—the only people he loved in the entire world—and he decided in that instant that he couldn't take the chance. This scum's life wasn't worth the risk.

He clenched both fists as tightly as he could and raised them out to each side of Matt's head. Then, he rammed them inward at lightning speed.

Willy winced in horror as he watched Matt's skull collapse under the force. The drug addict's ugly pockmarked face scrunched together and his ears disappeared from view as the skull imploded under the force of Willy's powerful, angry fists.

*****

Wyatt's stomach was doing flips as he watched the nervous Aaron pacing back and forth.

And, Brody just looked scared—this had gone far beyond what he had probably expected.

Matt had been gone for about five or ten minutes, and Wyatt was relieved that he hadn't heard any gunshots yet.

He pictured his dad sitting out in his police cruiser—a sitting duck. He prayed that Willy had heard the earlier shot and left the car for a safer hiding place.

He shifted in his chair, moving his shoulders as much as the rope would allow, trying his best to loosen the knot that was tied around the back.

Wyatt glanced over at his mother—tears were running down her cheeks as she watched him trying fruitlessly to get free.

Suddenly, Aaron stopped pacing. He stomped over to Helen and slapped her across the face. Then, he reached underneath her chair, picked her up, and threw her and the chair back against the wall. Helen screamed as she collapsed helplessly to the floor with the chair on top of her.

Wyatt felt a sudden fire burn inside his chest, and he yelled, "You fucking bastard!"

He leaned forward in his chair until his feet were planted firmly on the floor. Then he dove into the air as far as his feet could possibly take him with a damn chair burdened to his back.

Aaron turned at the last second, but not fast enough to get out of the way. Wyatt found his target, head-butting Aaron with as much force as he could muster.

They both collapsed to the floor, Wyatt on top. Aaron thrust his hands up against Wyatt's chest, desperately trying to get him off, but not before

Wyatt was able to slam his head downward once again.

Aaron cursed and managed to shove his way out from under. Blood was dripping from his forehead, and he swore once again while wiping his eyes with a shirt sleeve.

Now, both Wyatt and Helen were on the floor, lying on their sides with their chairs still attached.

The thug stood and slammed his fist into the wall. "I'm going to kill both of you!"

Brody yelled. "What the fuck you talkin bout? We wanna ransom!"

"Plans change. We'll just go grab the old man and force him to withdraw the money from the bank. I want to kill these two now. It'll be fun."

"We not killin anyone! You crazy? These two done nothing ta us."

"You're a pussy, Brody. Matt will help me."

"Matt's crazy like you."

"Hey, I'll let you fuck the lady first, before I do her."

"You a sick man."

Wyatt struggled with the rope. The force of his dive at Aaron had caused it to loosen, and he twisted his body as he lay on the floor, trying frantically to get it loose enough to get the chair off his back.

The dialogue between the two kidnappers had taken a turn for the worse. Brody was trying his best to stop the direction it was going in, but he wouldn't be strong enough to fend off Aaron, who was about twice his size.

And, Aaron sounded just crazy enough to do exactly what he said he wanted to do. Clearly, he wasn't just a normal thug—he talked like a psychopath. The type of bad seed that seemed normal and intelligent when he was at his best, but explosive and out of control when things didn't go his way.

Aaron walked over to Helen, who was still lying on the floor with the chair attached to her back.

He pointed down at her. "She's a good looking woman, for an old bag. She's my gift to you, Brody. But, if you don't want her, I'll have her."

Suddenly, a new voice invaded the room. "Get away from my wife!"

Wyatt turned his head in the direction of the voice, a voice he'd cherished his entire life.

No one had heard the side door open.

There stood his dad, with Wyatt's Magnum in his hand. He was standing with his legs spread apart and a look on his face that Wyatt had never seen before.

Aaron dove to the ground and wrapped an arm around Helen's neck. He placed his other hand on her forehead. "Drop the gun, old man, or I'll break her neck!"

Willy hesitated for just a second, but then he dropped the gun. "Leave her alone. Just go away and we'll forget this ever happened."

Aaron laughed. "You're not in a strong bargaining position. You owe us some money, and we're going to get it."

He nodded at Brody. "Pick up the gun, Brody, and hold it on him."

Brody walked forlornly over to where Willy stood, bent over and picked up the gun. Then, he held it straight out and pointed it at Willy's chest.

Aaron sighed and let go of Helen. He stood up and stretched his long arms.

"Now, isn't this nice and cozy? All of us in the same room together. Well, except for Matt. I'm guessing you took care of him, old man. That's okay—more money for Brody and I to split. Now, we'll have a little chat about how you're gonna make us rich."

He walked up to Brody and held out his hand. "Give me the gun, Brody."

Brody turned. But, he didn't hand it to him. Instead, with a shaky hand, he pointed it at his head.

Aaron sputtered, "What the fuck are you doing? Give me the gun!"

Brody shook his head. "Don move, Aaron. This shit over."

"Don't be stupid, Brody. I was just kidding about killing them. I wouldn't do that. We're gonna get rich. Don't blow this."

Brody shook his head again, and then turned slightly towards Willy. "Untie them."

That one moment of inattention was all Aaron needed. He lunged at Brody and knocked the gun out of his hand. Then, he levelled a fist at Brody's head that sent him flying backwards against the wall.

Aaron dove for the gun.

But, Willy was faster. He covered the width of the room in a split second, kicking the gun off into a corner.

Aaron jumped to his feet. "Okay, old man. Let's see what you got."

He went into a boxing stance and began circling Willy. Willy just stood there with his hands at his sides…and waited. He turned his body in the same circle as Aaron; waited patiently for him to make his move. Confidence oozed from his eyes.

The move came, and it was the last one Aaron would ever make.

His fist came in hard and fast at Willy's head. Willy stopped it with his open hand and squeezed, crushing the fingers in his grasp. Wyatt could hear the sound of the bones breaking from way over on the other side of the room; a sickening sound only slightly challenged by Aaron's agonized scream.

With his other massive hand, Willy grasped Aaron under the chin. He ran forward a few steps to get some momentum and then simply shoved the thug into the air, across the room, right through the plate glass window. Wyatt estimated that Aaron weighed at least 250 pounds, but his father threw him just as easily as if he were a mere ragdoll.

Willy opened the front door and walked calmly out onto the porch. Wyatt heard another loud thump, followed by an unearthly gasp.

Then, just eerie silence.

Willy came back into the house and, without a single word, proceeded to untie his wife and son.

Brody was still sitting on the floor in the same spot where Aaron's punch had sent him.

Wyatt shed the chair from his back, picked up his gun, and watched as his dad cradled his sobbing wife in his arms. He then walked over to Brody, offered his hand, and lifted him up off the floor.

The kid looked down. "I so sorry, Mister. I really stupid."

Wyatt put his hand on Brody's shoulder, and squeezed it gently. "You're not that stupid, Brody. You finally did the right thing, and that took some real courage. You made a bad situation right."

Brody looked up and grimaced. "How long I be in jail for?"

Wyatt shook his head.

"No jail for you, son. Just leave town, get off the drugs, and don't come back. I don't think prison would teach you anything more than what you've already learned here tonight. I have a very strong feeling that your life from now on will be a lot different."

CHAPTER 32

Wyatt smiled as he watched his parents cuddling on the couch like a couple of love-sick teenagers. He'd made dinner for them tonight—not that he was that great a cook, but they both were still too distraught from the ordeal at the farmhouse to bother making meals for themselves. In their current state, Wyatt was pretty sure they wouldn't criticize his skills, and it was more than likely that their taste buds weren't even registering anything anyway.

Willy had his arm around Helen's shoulder; she had her eyes closed and was resting her head on his chest. Wyatt knew she was awake though—her fingers were gently stroking Willy's leg.

"I have to head back to my place. Early day tomorrow. Anything you guys need before I go?"

Willy shook his head. "No, I think we're fine. Thanks for dinner, son."

Helen opened her eyes. "Yes, thanks. But, there is something I need before you go."

"What's that, mom?"

"Tell me again why you two kept me in the dark about Willy's condition?"

Wyatt sighed. "Mom, I only found out a few weeks ago myself. And, Dad already explained why he didn't tell us. He didn't want you and me to worry and treat him differently."

Helen lifted her head off Willy's chest and sat up straight on the couch. "I'm sorry, but I can't stop thinking about this. It's been two days now since…it happened…and this is all I think about. Watching your dad throw that man through the window as easily as if he were a rolled up newspaper was the freakiest thing I've ever seen. It was like a bad dream."

Willy rubbed her knee. "It's okay, dear. It's all over with now."

Helen jumped to her feet. "No, it's not! That's the trouble, here. I knew nothing about this, yet I've been married to you for decades!"

She started pacing the room.

Her voice jumped an octave. "There are things that I've never told you—how I felt about you. It made me feel insecure, so I never told you, but I've always admired how good you've looked through the ages. You're twenty-two years older, yet you've always looked younger than me. You don't have any age lines, your hair is thicker than a teenager's, and your body is incredibly muscular. You're eighty-seven years old, and you don't have one wrinkle…or even a saggy ass. You've aged, of course, but you've aged so slowly. I wondered secretly how that was possible—I wasn't going to complain, of course, because it was wonderful. I just considered myself one lucky lady.

"I've always admired your strength, too, but little did I know how strong you really were. At parties, I got jealous at how all the young women flirted with you—I was proud, too, but mainly jealous. You had too much respect for me to ever flirt back at them, but it still made me feel a bit insecure. I never wanted to admit that to you, but I'm admitting it to you now."

Willy just stared at her, speechless.

Wyatt got up and wrapped his arms around her. "It's okay, Mom. Good for you to get this off your chest. Now you know as much as we know, so we're all on the same level playing field."

She pushed herself away from him.

"Don't try to soothe me, Wyatt. We've all just been through an absolute horror because of this. If those boys hadn't seen Willy in the state he was in, they never would have tried to extort money from him. And, then, they met this Aaron monster, and the plan was kicked up an even more dangerous notch. If you two hadn't found me, God only knows what might have happened."

"But, we did find you, Mom. Don't fret about what might have happened."

She put her hands on her hips, and cocked her head. "Wait just one minute. You haven't explained that to me, yet. How did you find me out there in the middle of nowhere? And why was it just you and Willy? Why not a team of officers?"

Wyatt guided his mother back to the couch. "Sit down, Mom."

She sat. "I'm waiting."

Wyatt sighed. "The stress of this incident triggered something in me.

It's a phenomenon called 'Remote Viewing.' I have it, but I didn't know I had it. It's a form of ESP that allows a person to focus in on an event, a time, or a place—past, present, or future—and see it in living technicolor. I basically floated above the vehicle that took you, and followed it all the way out to that farmhouse. We decided that it was best if just Dad and I went to get you. Too hard to explain, and it would have just drawn harmful attention our way."

Wyatt could tell that a light bulb had gone off in his mom's brain. She turned her attention to Willy. "Do you have this skill, too?"

Willy shook his head.

"So, when Willy was told his DNA was permanently changed by that incident in Korea, some of that change passed down to you, Wyatt. Didn't it?"

Wyatt nodded.

"I guess there was no way they could predict what changes would take place in you, but some of the new and improved Willy is definitely in you."

"That's what Dad was warned would happen—and it looks like it did. It can't be just a coincidence that I have this freaky skill."

"Do a lot of other people have it, too?"

"We learned about it down in Quantico when I was with the RCMP, Mom. A few people have it, but not many. It's a skill that's utilized in intelligence circles—all in secret, of course."

"This thing that beamed into your father, could that have happened to a lot of other people over the last few decades as well? Changing their DNA, too? And passing it down to new generations? Is that where these 'Remote Viewers' come from, do you think?"

Wyatt scratched his head. "It's possible, I guess. What happened to Dad was never publicized, and he was ordered to keep it under wraps. So, if it happened to others at other times, I guess they would have been given the same orders."

"Is our government experimenting on us? Or, do other countries really have weapons like this that we can't defend against?"

"You know as much as we do. It's all just speculation beyond that."

Helen stood up and started pacing again. "We can't forget that this kidnapping happened as a direct result of Willy's condition. That shows how dangerous this could be if the wrong people find out. We have to be so careful."

Willy jumped into the conversation. "That's why I've been so secretive, dear. That's why I didn't tell you."

"Oh, you hush up! You should have told your own wife! I could have helped you, protected you. And, by the way, is that why your tongue looks like fish skin? It wasn't due to that lame reason you gave me, was it?"

"No, I made that up. Yes, the beam caused that, too."

"I feel like such an idiot."

Willy stood now, too. "Okay, that's enough, Helen. You're starting to sound like a whiner. It is what it is. Let's just move forward and put this behind us."

"Don't you dare call me a whiner! After the secrets you've kept from me, you have one hell of a nerve!"

Willy nodded sheepishly. "You're right. That was insensitive of me. But, I just don't want to talk about it anymore. For now, at least. Okay?"

"Alright. For now."

Wyatt decided it was time to leave. "I'm gonna go now. Are you guys okay?"

Willy shook his head. "No. Now that we're being open about everything, we need to talk about the mess we left behind two days ago. We've avoided talking about it. What are we going to do about that? There are two dead men out there, and I killed them both."

"Dad, nothing to worry about. I'm the only one whose fingerprints are in databases, and I wiped down everything I touched in there before we left."

"But...what about the bodies?"

"You've lived here most of your life. Do you really think those bodies would have survived more than a day in the open like that? This is cougar and wolf country—they would have been devoured in no time flat. And, whatever was left over after the feast would have been stashed in dens for the winter. So, no point worrying about it."

Helen started gagging, and put her hands up to her mouth.

"Sorry, Mom. Dad and I should have talked about this in private."

She shook her head and swallowed hard. "No...it's...okay. It's a fact, of course. I actually feel better after what you just said. But, it's the image I have a tough time with."

Wyatt nodded and headed towards the door.

Willy called after him. "Oh, one more thing. They emailed the airline tickets to me today. I fly to Atlanta next Tuesday, back on Thursday. I'll be at that lab that Allison uses for her company medicals—remember, she said it was located in the Centers for Disease Control in Atlanta?"

"Right. Okay, Dad. Don't forget—no x-rays."

"For sure. But, can you stay with your mother while I'm gone?"

"Yes, Tuesday to Thursday—no problem."

"The email told me who will meet me when I arrive at the CDC. I tried to contact Allison to see if she'd be there, but her voice message said that she was out of town conducting hotel tours for the next two weeks and couldn't be reached unless it was an emergency."

"Yeah, well, I'm sure she's set everything up properly for you, Dad. She doesn't need to be there—she's a busy lady. Hey, this is the first step towards you becoming the spokesman for our new luxury hotel. And, with your draft-dodger statue front and center, too. We could all use a bit of good news like that right about now."

CHAPTER 33

They approached the house like robots—side by side, arms swinging in cadence.

Two men who could only be described as 'hulks;' barrel-chested, square-headed, both donned in leather bomber jackets.

Their appearance screamed ex-military, as did their erect postures, expressionless eyes, and predator-like swaggers.

Allison gulped as she noticed something else. Their left arms were the only ones that were swinging. Their right arms were down by their sides, slightly behind their hips. Even though they tried to hide them, the long pistol barrels were unmistakable.

They were about fifty yards or so from the front door; only a few precious seconds remained for her and John to find a way to stay alive.

A whispered voice from behind her broke the silence.

"What are we going to do? Should I shoot them as soon as they enter?"

Allison turned, and whispered back, "No, Senator. We have a problem now. They know something's wrong. They're coming, pistols drawn. Our element of surprise is gone. We won't win a shoot-out with these guys."

Hartford swore.

"Okay, let's head upstairs. From there we can get out onto the roof."

Allison was finding it hard to breathe.

In an instant, it occurred to her that perhaps her text message back to these guys on Clint's phone gave them away. Maybe there was a code word that Clint would have used to provide assurance that it was him on the other end. These spooks lived in code.

"The roof's no good, John. That will just delay things. If you had neighbors it would be different—but you're so isolated out here, no one will see us. They'll just come out and get us."

John peeked out the window himself, then nodded in agreement. "Okay, c'mon, Allison. We're just gonna make a run for it, then. We can't go out the front, but we sure as hell can scoot out the back."

He stuffed the gun back into his waistband, tucked his briefcase under his arm, and dashed down the hall towards the back of the house.

Allison followed close behind. "And, then what?"

"You'll see. But, we have to hurry."

As John was unlocking the back door, there was the unmistakable sound of heavy boot-clad footsteps on the front porch.

"We're out of time—let's go!"

Once outside, John slid the pistol out of his belt and looked to each side of the house.

"All clear!"

They ran into the yard, John leading the way to a large wooden shed. He flipped the padlock and opened the double doors.

Sitting in the middle of the shed was the darnedest car Allison had ever seen.

Not really a car—an Arctic Cat recreational vehicle, but it had obviously been modified. It was far from 'street legal,' but that didn't really matter too much right now.

It was brilliant red, with large patches of chrome around where the doors and windows would have been if there were any.

The lower regions of the beast were protected by heavy black plastic rims, and the entire monstrosity sat on four humungous wheels with deep-tread off-road tires.

The frame of the vehicle was raised, exposing the suspension and, even though she didn't know too much about cars, Allison could tell that the suspension on this beast would rival a Jeep Wrangler.

It was just a two seater, but there was a small cargo area in the back.

John threw his briefcase into the rear. "Jump in!"

Allison ran around to the passenger side and, holding onto the rim of the upper frame, hefted herself up into the leather bucket seat. Above her, and beside her, was nothing but open air. No roof, no side windows, no doors. On a normal day, she would have enjoyed this.

The only glass in existence was the front windshield, which, from what Allison knew of these trail explorers, was an absolute necessity to protect exposed faces from rocks, dirt and distressed birds—not to mention the occasional four-legged animal caught in the crosshairs.

John cranked the starter motor and it hesitated. "Hold on. When I get this started, we're gonna fly. It's four-wheel drive and upgraded with 200 horses."

"I don't give a shit, John! Just get us the hell out of here!"

He handed her the pistol. "Here, take this. I need two hands to drive this thing."

John cranked the engine again, but it still refused to turn over.

He juggled the stick shift.

"Damn, it wasn't in neutral!"

He turned the key once more and this time the powerful engine growled to life. The noise within the confined space of the shed was deafening.

Suddenly, through the open shed doors, they saw the back door of the house fling open. The two killers ran out into the yard, guns raised.

"Shit!"

The men dropped to the ground and leveled their pistols at the RV.

John yelled, "Duck!"

They both crouched behind the dashboard milliseconds before the windshield fragmented into a thousand pieces.

With his head down, John used his left foot to manipulate the clutch and slipped the gear shift into reverse.

"Hold on!"

The Arctic Cat leaped from its inert position and raced toward the back of the shed. John slammed his foot down on the accelerator and the Cat felt to Allison as if it were flying.

She knew the rear wall was coming up fast so she braced herself.

Even though she was ready for it, the impact was a shock. The wooden slat wall splintered and the Cat slipped sideways as it rammed its way through.

For a split second, the vehicle was riding on only its two right wheels and Allison held on tight as it threatened to throw her out through the unprotected side.

John spun the wheel at the last moment and it righted itself as they broke through into the open field behind the shed. The interior of the Cat was filled with broken slats of wood and Allison started choking on some small particles that found their way into her throat.

"Here we go!"

John slammed the gear shift into neutral and then rammed his fist forward, forcing it into first gear, expertly synchronizing the gas pedal with the clutch.

The little RV lurched forward with its front wheels in the air for just an instant—then its monster tires dug into the grass and they raced off towards the forest edge.

Allison heard the sound of bullets pinging off the undercarriage and, with her head still low, she peeked to the rear. The two thugs were positioned at the side of the house now.

"They're trying to shoot out your tires!"

John laughed. "That won't do them any good. Those are modified tires—solid rubber."

As they reached the edge of the forest, she noticed them running back towards the front of the house.

"They're going to give chase now, John! Heading back to their car!"

The RV burst through the trees at the forest perimeter and began racing along a primitive dirt trail. The trees were just a blur as the little vehicle tore its way through the underbrush.

Broken branches and potholes were no problem—it was the roughest ride Allison had ever had in her life, but the little beast handled everything in its path.

"Well, they can't follow us in a pickup truck along this path. And, they'll have to detach that boat trailer or they'll never get any speed at all."

"Does that road back there pass parallel to this dirt path?"

The senator nodded. "Yes, not as direct a route, but they'll probably gain on us a bit. They can go faster on that road than we can here."

"Where does this come out?"

"We'll burst out close to the city. It hits that same road they'll be on. Then, it's a quick jaunt for us down to the lake."

"What good will that do us?"

"I've got a speedboat at the marina. We can hit the safety of the water and decide what to do when we're out there."

Allison glanced over at him. John's sharp brain seemed to be back—he'd lost it for a bit after the shock of Clint's death, but now he seemed energized.

She couldn't avoid smiling as she watched the intensity on his face—the determined clenching of his strong jaws and the fire in his eyes. If Allison didn't know better, she would swear that he was actually enjoying this.

At that moment, the good senator from Vermont looked more like Donald Sutherland than he ever had before.

John expertly manipulated the vehicle over ditches, then down into a ravine and back up again. Dodged two deer that were grazing along the path.

The forest was thick and the path was narrow. Allison held on for dear life as the Arctic Cat careened over one obstacle after another. John clearly knew what he was doing, though.

He rammed the gear shift into fourth, and sent the vehicle flying over a small pond, then rammed it down into second as they mounted an intimidating hill.

They were making good time. John estimated that they'd break out to the main road in about five minutes' time. From there, it was a quick jog along a path to the marina.

Suddenly, the path turned relatively smooth, a combination of gravel and dirt. Allison knew that was a sign that they were approaching the road.

John touched her hand to get her attention over the growl of the motor. "Did you fly up in your jet?"

"Yes. It's parked at the Burlington Airport, waiting for me."

"Well, when we're on the water, we can think about how to get out of here."

Allison yelled over the sound of the engine. "Doesn't Lake Champlain flow all the way north into Canada?"

"Yes, it does. About forty miles or so, give or take."

"Enough gas in your tank?"

"Yep, I always keep the boat full."

"That's where we're going to go, then, John. That part of Canada would be Quebec. There will be a border checkpoint at a government wharf when we cross the Quebec portion of the lake. We'll show our creds and then dock on the Canadian side. From there, we'll make our way to Montreal—take a cab or rent a car. Once on the boat, I'll phone my pilots and ask them to fly to Montreal's Dorval Airport and meet up with us there. Sound like a plan?"

John stared at her, astonished. "Jesus, have you ever thought of going into politics? I like how your mind works—quick, concise."

Allison smiled. "That's just the astrophysicist in me, John. We're conditioned to coming up with 'out of this world' scenarios."

"Well, it sounds workable to me. The main thing is we have to get to safety. Who knows how many others are out there looking for us, or who they might call. They'll definitely be watching the airport and the major highways. I don't think they'll consider the water, though. It's our best bet."

Allison frowned as she thought of what they'd left behind them. "John, we made a bit of a mess back there with Clint."

"Well, let's be clear here—*you* left the mess, I didn't."

Allison nodded. "Yes, but I'm sure you agree now that it was a necessary mess."

"I do. I can take care of it, though. I have a…how do I say this… clandestine contact back in Burlington. Most senators have someone like him. He's handled touchy things for me before—not as bad as this, but he owes me his life from our military days. I'm comfortable calling him in on this. He'll clean it up. I can get him to dump that rental car of yours, too, to make sure you can't be traced."

"They can't trace me to that car. Since I was coming to see you, I didn't want certain people at Majestic 12 to be able to track that. I used a separate ID and credit card."

The senator shook his head. "You do think of everything."

Allison smiled. "I have to. My superior at Majestic knows that I have a soft spot for you. If he connects the dots from this bungled assassination to me, I'll be a dead woman walking."

They cruised along for a few more minutes and the road kept getting wider the closer they got to the clearing ahead. Through the trees, they could now see punctuated views of the pavement of the main highway.

Suddenly there was something else in their vision.

A truck had pulled off the highway and was heading straight towards them on the gravel road. A head-on confrontation was seconds away.

The pickup truck skidded to a stop and two figures jumped out. They knelt down in front of the truck and aimed their long-barrelled pistols straight at the looming Arctic Cat.

"Shit! Hold on tight and duck, Allison!"

Allison ducked her head below the dashboard as John swerved the Cat off the path. Suddenly, there was a jolt—it felt as if the little vehicle hit a large boulder. She heard John curse again as the RV went airborne.

It rolled more times than Allison could count.

The Cat didn't have a roof, but it did have a sturdy roll bar which, along with the seatbelts, were probably the only things that saved them.

She said a silent prayer as the Cat made its final roll, right up against the side of a creek bed. Allison's side of the vehicle was in the creek and she gasped as the shockingly cold water babbled against her face and chest.

John was stirring in the driver's seat that was now above her, moaning about his head. He'd probably hit it against the steering wheel.

Then, different voices. One of the thugs was standing in the creek bed, and the other one had climbed up onto John's side. She heard the distinctive sound of a seatbelt being unclipped and was then aware of the struggle to pull John up out of his seat.

Allison heard the thump and splash of John's body as it was thrown rudely down into the creek bed.

"Okay, Senator, time to take you for a boat ride."

A second voice—gruff, cold. "What about her?"

"Just leave her. She must be his floozy. Not worth worrying about."

Allison then heard heavy footsteps splashing out of the creek and moving up the hill away from the Cat. Her right arm was trapped by her own weight, so she manoeuvred her left arm down and snapped off the seatbelt.

She was able to get her face out of the creek and right herself just enough that she could see over the side of the overturned vehicle. They were trudging up the hill, one on each side of the dazed senator.

One thing she was certain of—these killers hadn't checked Clint's body to see if his gun was still there. Otherwise, they would have killed her, or, at the very least, searched both of them. They had no idea that John and Allison were armed.

She flicked the handle of the glove compartment. After they'd made their mad dash into the forest, she'd stashed it in there for safekeeping.

It was stuck.

She tried it again. No movement. The accident must have jammed it.

Allison hadn't wanted to make any unnecessary sounds, but she had no choice now. She smashed her fist against the glove compartment. Then, again…and again.

Suddenly, it popped open and the gun fell out. She reached down into the cold water and, after a few seconds of searching, her fingers found the handgrip of the pistol. Then, she raised her head back up again and peeked over the edge of the driver's side frame.

They'd heard her.

Both had now turned back towards the overturned vehicle, still propping the senator up between them.

An image popped into Allison's brain—a happy carefree day back when she was just a wee girl, out with her wonderful father in a farmer's field, playing target practice with a pistol. Shooting pop cans off stumps.

Allison was a good shot—in fact, she was a crack shot.

She pictured coke cans across the left chest areas of the two coldblooded assassins. Then, Allison held her breath, flicked off the safety, cocked the hammer, and pulled the trigger in two quick bursts.

CHAPTER 34

Willy Carson worked his way through the crowded terminal of Atlanta's Hartsfield International Airport. He only had a duffle bag with him, so he was lucky that he didn't have wait for the damn carousel.

He breezed through Customs and Immigration—having dual citizenship made it a lot faster for him than for a lot of his fellow passengers. He chuckled as he watched them grumbling their way through the turnstiles trying hard not to make eye contact with the officers, doing their best to make their visit to America sound as innocent as possible.

Many of them were tourists from Canada, looking forward to enjoying a bit of the American deep south before winter set in. The south was indeed a beautiful part of the country, not just in the endless varieties of foliage, but also for the architecture and 'buzz.'

Atlanta was one of America's biggest hub cities, with connecting flights available to almost anywhere in the world, and great highways that allowed sightseers to meander to all the old Civil War sites in Georgia and the adjoining states.

He'd boarded in Calgary and had the extreme pleasure of sitting beside a lovely young lady—well, not that young, but to Willy everyone seemed young now compared to his eighty-seven years.

They'd talked a lot during the five-hour flight. Mainly about her work, which Willy had found fascinating due to her obvious passion and commitment. Willy loved meeting people who had a zest for what they did.

She was an orthopedic surgeon with a private practice in Atlanta, but had been up in Calgary for a few days attending a medical convention. Her name was Nancy, and she spoke with an unusually distinctive southern drawl—a linguistic style that Willy always thought made southerners sound dumb and inarticulate. But, with Nancy, he found it charming. The way she pronounced the words and allowed them to hang for an extra beat or two, it carried a unique twang that enriched her sweet tenor voice.

She was fascinated with his story about leaving the United States decades ago out of his opposition to war and the draft.

Willy had been a little reluctant to tell her about that because southerners tended to be the most patriotic of all Americans. Conservative as hell, and hawkish as a person could get. But, Nancy was different—she seemed more worldly than most southerners he'd met, more open-minded. Maybe it was her high level of education, or perhaps even because of the extent she'd traveled around the world, that made her more in touch with alternative attitudes. From what he could tell, she seemed to agree with what he and others had done way back in 1970.

Willy walked through the bustling terminal for about fifteen minutes until he finally reached the rental car wing. He was just about to walk up to the Alamo counter when he saw Nancy sitting on a bench against the far wall.

She looked up as he approached, and smiled.

"Well, fancy seeing you again!"

Willy sat down on the bench beside her. "It's a small world, seat-mate, even here in Atlanta."

"Are you picking up a rental?"

"Yep. You, too?"

Nancy frowned. "I didn't intend to, but the wait for a cab is at least an hour long. Apparently, a dozen flights came in at the same time. Very busy day here. Now, I'm waiting for a rental."

"You didn't drive here?"

"No, I left my car at work. And, I just phoned my husband and he's tied up for a couple of hours—so, a rental it will be. But, no cars available right now, so I'll have to be patient."

"I reserved a car. Why don't you let me drop you off?"

"Oh, I wouldn't want to take you out of your way."

Willy shook his head. "It's no problem. I don't really have a set time today for where I have to be, so it would be my pleasure."

Nancy smiled. "We were so busy talking about other things on the plane, I forgot to ask what you're here for."

"I'm going to a clinic at the CDC for a medical check-up."

Nancy's eyes widened in surprise. "Well, isn't that a coincidence? The hospital I work out of is almost right next door. Emory University

Hospital—only about ten minutes away from there."

"Great, so it's not out of my way at all."

She turned sideways to face him. "Willy, a personal question, if you don't mind—why are you going there? Do you have a unique illness of some sort? Forgive me, but I'm a doctor as you know, and my curiosity can get the better of me sometimes."

Willy laughed. "No, don't worry. You can breathe freely around me. There's some clinic in there that a hotel chain that I'm working with uses for medical checks. They want to look me over before I become a spokesperson for a new hotel up in Canada."

Nancy looked puzzled. "That place is locked up like Fort Knox. I'm not aware of any general health clinics there for the public to visit."

Willy reached into his pocket and pulled out a piece of paper. "It says here that I'm to go to the……and that someone will meet me in the lobby."

She nodded. "That's the only part of the CDC that the public can visit. The CDC is a huge complex—a campus actually—and that museum is in a separate building. But, I'm still not aware of a clinic in there."

Willy shrugged. "That's where I've been told to go. I guess I'll find out when I get there."

"Well, if it's a bust, you can take a tour of the museum. I've been there—it's actually quite fascinating. Gives the entire history of the CDC and the many virulent strains that they've discovered and prevented from spreading. You'll garner new respect for the U.S. medical system once you finish the tour. And, that museum isn't just a part of the Centers for Disease Control, it's also associated with the Smithsonian."

Willy stood. "Interesting. Well, I'll get the car. How far a drive is it to your hospital?"

"Not far—about half an hour, then ten minutes more for you to the CDC. We just go north on I-85, then northeast along US-278. It's a breeze, even with Atlanta traffic. I'll talk you through it."

Willy bent down and picked up both of their duffle bags. "Let's go, Doctor. I feel better about Atlanta traffic now that I have you with me!"

*****

Chad Powers was sitting at the head of the boardroom table on the fortieth floor of his Atlanta office building. The headquarters for *American Armaments Inc.*, the company that his family had held a controlling interest in for about 100 years or so. Famous for manufacturing some of the evillest weapons ever concocted by human creativity. Hiroshima and Nagasaki never knew what hit them and they still didn't know, more than half a century later.

Sitting around the table were the ten members of his executive team. All capable people. And, all as mean as hell.

You had to be mean to be in the munitions business—because every business goal accomplished resulted in mayhem and mass deaths. Balance sheets had a deathly halo surrounding them and income statements were driven by how much conflict existed around the world. And, if it didn't exist, that's where the marketing department had to step in—to help create the conflicts, lobby the politicians who were solidly in their pockets. Remind them about who really buttered their bread. Campaign donations and bribes were done for a reason, and payback was expected.

Without enemies, *American Armaments Inc.* would cease to exist. Executive bonuses depended totally on how much paranoia could be created around the world, how much fear could be instilled in politicians and the American people. Because, without fear, there would be no need for bombs, missiles, and rocket launchers.

Chad glared at his Vice President of Marketing, Vince Tomlinson. "So, what you're saying is that orders are going to start drying up?"

Vince raised his hands in frustration. "What else can I tell you, Chad? You read the papers, too. The Russians are involved now. America is starting to back out of Syria, and rescinding on their promises to arm the terrorists. This year-long conflict has provided a good forty percent of our revenue in this fiscal year. We're pretty vulnerable."

"Well, we still have the Saudis. They're bombing the shit out of Yemen."

"Yes, we'll still be supplying them, but that war doesn't have the staying power that we predicted Syria would have. With the Saudis having shot themselves in the foot by driving down oil prices, their precious royal reserves are starting to run dry. One of two things will happen—they'll have to allow oil prices to rise on world markets again, or they'll have to retreat from their Yemen adventure. There's no margin in it for them, and the Saudis don't have the fortitude to continue a stupid war if they can no longer afford their Mercedes limos. God forbid they'd have to get real jobs—they have no idea what those are."

Chad jotted down some notes on a pad. "We still supply the Israelis."

Vince nodded. "Absolutely, thank God for them. But, they'll just maintain their same level of orders. Nothing extraordinary going on there that will increase our plant activity."

"They might still attack Iran."

Vince shook his head. "All that bluster was just to help scuttle the Iran nuclear deal. None of it had any weight behind it. And, they sure won't attack Iran now, not with them helping Russia in Syria. They're bona fide allies now, and the Israelis won't want to piss Russia off. In fact, they've been talking together in back channels. In a bizarre way, we may be seeing an unholy alliance between Israel, Russia, and Iran.

"Publicly, the Israelis will continue to bluster and demonize Iran, but, privately, I think they see that Russia is a better source for their security now than the U.S. is. They hate us for entering into that nuclear deal, letting Iran off the hook and all that bullshit.

"So, now, I think they'd like to stick it to us—begin cozying up to Russia if Russia can guarantee that Iran won't attack them. What we're seeing is a power shift in the Middle East, from America to Russia, and a lot of countries may start jumping off our bandwagon and follow the new leader. Everyone loves a leader, and right now that's Russia."

Chad started tapping his pen on the table.

"So, what we are seeing is a real danger to our future revenue growth. If the power shifts, we're out in the cold. All of the clients we could count on in the past, we won't be able to count on anymore. And, if America gets cold feet and backs off from starting these pesky little wars, our revenue dries up from that, too. Peace could be a real killer for our balance sheet."

"Yep, that's the strategic outlook, boss. We will have to re-forecast our five-year revenue plan and get the board to sign off on it. It won't be a pretty picture, and it won't be a pleasant board meeting."

Chad slammed his pen down hard on the table, causing all of the executives around the table to jerk to attention.

"No, not yet! You're the marketing guy. There are things you can do. If the landscape is changing, we can change with it. We'll *have* to change with it. We can sell our missiles to the Russians, the Iranians, and the Syrians. If this conflict is going to continue on without America, they will still need weapons. With Russia's economy in such sad shape from the sanctions and oil prices, their plants won't be able to keep up with demand."

Vince Tomlinson stared at him, mouth hanging open in astonishment.

Chad stared back. "What? Why are you looking at me like that?"

"Chad, we can't sell weapons to the Russians. It's illegal. There are sanctions in place, and even before that it was taboo for us to even consider, what with the Cold War being still fresh on everyone's minds."

Chad dropped the pen and smashed his massive fist down on the boardroom table.

"We have a business to run, and it's your job as our Marketing VP to find new markets for us! They're a new market!"

"But, how could we get away with it?"

"Easy, peasy. We've always sold to the Israelis, so with their new cozy relationship with Russia we can broker the sales through them. Russia bankrolls them, we sell to the Israelis, and they simply transfer the weapons to Russia. And, Russia can use those to re-supply Iran and Syria. We can easily re-tool our plants in Europe and Israel to comply with Russian specifications. No one in Congress will be the wiser. We'll just be supplying the Israelis as we've always done, and, let's face it, that's one of the reasons we opened a plant in Israel a decade ago. Hides it quite nicely. We'll kick back a commission on the sales to the Israelis for their trouble."

Vince wiped beads of sweat off his brow. The other members of the executive team just listened to the exchange without interjecting. Chad knew they'd keep their mouths shut. This was Vince's turn to be on the carpet; from time to time they all had their turns. There was no margin in jumping in to defend a colleague.

Vince took a long sip of water, then he stood. "Okay, I'd better get started. I have a few phone calls to make."

Chad stood as well, his sudden movement signalling that the meeting was over.

"Yes, do that—and with our usual utmost discretion. Use the standard cryptics."

He looked around the table at the other executives, who were also now standing. "I don't have to say to any of you that this is all very confidential and stays in this room—but I've said it anyway. You've all been warned."

He turned back to Vince. "Be the hero, Vince. Find us some new markets. The bonuses will be substantial for all of us, needless to say."

Chad walked over to the coffee machine as the executives quietly filed out of the room. Poured himself a cup and then resumed his seat again.

As he sat in the cavernous room all by his lonesome, staring out the window at the gleaming glass skyscrapers of downtown Atlanta, he subliminally changed hats. Now, he was going to be the head of Majestic 12 for the next few minutes.

He had problems and, right now, no solutions. Charles Farmington's death went off without a hitch, but somehow Senator Hartford had escaped his snare. The three assassins who had been sent had disappeared.

Into thin air.

And, so had Hartford.

He must have had help, and the first name that popped into his mind was Allison Fisher. Had she warned him off? Had Hartford then hired extra bodyguards to protect his precious ass?

Hartford was in possession of the explosive material Farmington had slipped to him and, if the opportunistic politician used that material to launch his presidential campaign, all hell would break loose. Which would mean that Majestic 12, under Chad's leadership, would have failed in its one and only mandate—'to keep a lid on things.'

It was a simple mandate in principle, but had always been so difficult in execution. Chad had lost count of how many scientists and astronomers he and his team had ordered killed over the years he'd been in charge. Yet, now, the most important execution had failed. And, he had to rectify that before it was too late.

The administration was working hard to justify confiscating guns from the population, but even that was moving too slowly. The damn Republicans insisted on their 2nd Amendment rights, even with the horrific slaughters that had occurred at schools and theaters. The NRA was stronger than anyone had ever given them credit for.

But, that was a different problem entirely and not his concern. The White House would have to deal with that. Chad's responsibility was the control of information.

He opened his briefcase and pulled out several files. He studied the oldest file first—the one that contained the very first images of something that was terribly wrong. This file went back to the 1980s—the images had come from the Hubble Space Telescope, and were grainy, abstract, and hard to decipher. But, they all knew what they were looking at.

Then, he opened up the other files, one by one.

First, from the 1990s.

Then, from the turn of the new century.

And, finally, from the last decade.

He absorbed the general progression of the thing. The larger it got, the clearer it got. The more distinct it became decade after decade. Unmistakable. Still not much detail in these images, but enough evidence to tell them it wasn't going away. In fact, it was getting closer.

Then, he opened the most recent file, which he'd already studied at length. It was so morbidly fascinating he was compelled to look through it again.

These were the images sent back from the New Horizons spacecraft, the Trojan horse that had sent useless photos of Pluto to justify the craft being up there. Now, it was well past Pluto, out in the Kuiper Belt, finally doing what it was really meant to do in the first place.

Its 3.5-billion-mile journey to Pluto was just the tip of the iceberg, and simply a clever diversion.

Even though Chad had already seen these photos, he couldn't help but gasp once again. The photos were much clearer now, with the New Horizons being much closer to the thing than the Hubble Space Telescope.

The thing was a sight to behold, and it was massive. The vague details that had been seen on previous images weren't so vague anymore. The canyons, mountains, and tunnels were now more distinguishable.

The size of the thing was what astonished Chad the most. It was beyond comprehension.

He knew that Earth's heatwaves were going to get worse as the thing got closer.

The magnetic pressure was scientifically undeniable; it would begin pulling the Earth apart at its seams.

Earthquakes and volcanos would become more severe, and winters more brutal. Tornados and hurricanes would pop up in areas that had never seen them before.

Sinkholes that were now common around the world would spread, causing entire neighborhoods to disappear.

New havoc was also being triggered on the Sun by this thing, and that fact was being kept from the general public. Majestic 12 had done a great job downplaying it, while at the same time giving orders to increase chemtrail activity in the sky.

The public didn't know that the Earth's precious magnetosphere was no longer protecting them the way it had in the past. It was weaker, because the solar energy from the Sun had been stimulated by this…thing.

Radiation was getting through to Earth at rates never seen before. Sunburns today meant something a lot more serious than sunburns had decades ago.

Radiation. The invisible killer.

Citizens were complaining about artificial clouds being formed by special planes in the sky, ruining their beautiful clear days. But, there had been absolute silence from governments in response. Complaints were ignored, because they just couldn't be answered.

These artificial clouds, called chemtrails, contained substances—metallic pollutants, really—that actually protected people a wee bit more from the radiation they had no idea they were being exposed to.

One of Majestic 12's jobs was to continue to make sure the public didn't know they were being unsafely exposed. Because, if they knew they were being slowly radiated to death, who the hell would do essential work in the great outdoors or spend gobs of money on vacations?

The economy would collapse from frightened people cocooning

themselves.

All of this was just the start.

It would get worse.

But, they still had some time.

Time to still enjoy the fruits of labor and riches. For some, anyway.

And, maybe some time to just figure it all out.

Maybe there was a solution.

For now, the only solution was control of information.

One incident at a time, one person at a time.

Chad picked up the phone and called his chief physician, Doctor Phillip Lansing, at the Majestic 12 clinic in the CDC museum building.

"Lansing, here."

"Phil, is Willy Carson there yet?"

"No, we're expecting him any minute now."

"Okay. Any questions at all?"

"No, Chad. We're good here."

"To be clear, Doctor, you will do exactly the same as we did to the other problem cases."

"I'm clear on that. They've all been successful…so far."

Chad played with the lock on his briefcase while gazing pensively out the window—up at what would otherwise have been a blue sky, but was now instead a sky laced with a weird spider web of chemtrail clouds.

"Alright, then. I've had enough problems this week, Phil. Don't create any more for me."

CHAPTER 35

Visitors venturing into the David J. Spencer CDC Museum were usually unprepared for the unique experience they would have within those hallowed halls.

It was one of the most iconic museums in the world, not just for the fact that it was associated with both the Centers for Disease Control and the Smithsonian Institute, but also because it provided an indelible learning experience that would not soon be forgotten.

The museum was named after the CDC's most influential director, who served from 1966 until 1977.

Doctor Spencer was a vibrant public health giant, and a firm believer in the need to preserve the CDC's colorful history. Under his leadership, the CDC saw dramatic expansion, adding numerous global and domestic health programs—ranging from malaria and disaster relief, to reproductive health and tobacco restraint. His drive and vision also led to the first and only worldwide eradication of one specific disease—Smallpox.

Inevitably, at least half of the people who visited the museum were dragged in there by curious and enthusiastic friends or relatives—those with a science bent who couldn't contain their enthusiasm.

But, by the time the tour was finished, the reluctant ones almost always wanted to return for another visit—to try to soak up for a second time what had probably gone over their heads the first time around.

The museum had that effect on people. Those who came in yawning, determined that they were going to be bored out of their minds, came back out again with their eyes wide in wonder—brains infused with a weird combination of horror and fascination.

The museum used a brilliant combination of award-winning exhibits and innovative programming to educate visitors about the value of public health, and boasted quite rightfully about the vast accomplishments of the CDC over its storied history.

About 90,000 people each year endured the strict security to get through the turnstiles. This was not an easy place to get into. The museum was actually the only building on the entire CDC campus that allowed visitors, but, even with that, the security was tight. Two separate searches were conducted on every single visitor—one while entering the parking lot, and the other one inside the front doors.

But, once in, the trip was worth it.

Who wouldn't be fascinated to learn about scary things like Ebola, Anthrax, Smallpox, and Malaria? Diseases made famous in countless medical horror movies, let alone the front pages of newspapers. Afflictions that to most people were foreign and unimaginable. But, the museum made them seem very imaginable indeed—and created an appreciation for the fact that without an organization like the CDC, these horrifying and very alive "creatures" would destroy everyday lives. In fact, lives would be very short indeed.

So, at the very least, the museum forced people to think about things they normally wouldn't think of. They came away with an awareness of the organization's mission of preventing disease, injuries and disabilities, and encouraging healthy lifestyles.

The powerful long-term impact of a visit to the CDC's museum was, quite simply, that a healthy life wasn't to be taken for granted any longer. And that, indeed, was a good thing.

One amazing feature of the museum was the CDC Disease Detective Camp. A fun and interactive program that was open to high school juniors and seniors.

Through hands-on activities and seminars over a five-day period, "campers" took on the roles of disease detectives and learned firsthand how the organization safeguarded the nation's health…and indeed the world's. Teams of kids probed a simulated disease outbreak, using some basic epidemiology and laboratory skills, and then reported their findings to a cabal of CDC scientists. Additional activities included lecture hall sessions, mock press conferences, and behind the scenes looks at the CDC nerve center.

Generally, students went home from these "camps" breathless. Follow-up surveys showed that a good number of "campers" pursued medical or scientific careers as a direct result of participating in this unique experience.

Doctor Phillip Lansing had participated in these Disease Detective Camps during the early part of his career as an Endocrinologist. He was also trained in epidemiology and internal medicine, but his main area of practice and interest was endocrinology. He was thrilled to know that several of his students who had attended "camp" over a decade ago were now practising medicine. It was nice to know that he and others had had some impact on the life choices of these intelligent young people.

He was no longer associated with the program, and he missed it. He was now confined primarily to the second basement level of the CDC Museum building, to an area that most people had no idea existed. And, those who had to know just for building maintenance purposes, didn't have a clue as to what went on down there.

The only ones who knew everything that went on were the members of Majestic 12. And, of course, himself as the chief physician. Even though Phil didn't participate in any Majestic 12 meetings, and wasn't allowed to vote or have any input into what went on, he knew pretty much everything. He had to know, because a big part of his job was 'containment,' and he was paid over two million dollars a year to "contain," as well as to keep his mouth shut.

He had enjoyed his work in the educational areas of the CDC much more than he enjoyed his work now. But, ten years ago he'd sold his soul to the devil. The money he earned now was ten times what he'd earned before and it easily financed his lavish lifestyle.

An existence he knew—from *what* he knew—that in all probability had a relatively short shelf-life. So, he'd decided a decade ago to simply grab the brass ring while he could, because if he waited too long there wouldn't be enough time left to grab it.

Phil had a small and specialized staff of doctors and nurses who worked with him down in the well-equipped and lush dungeon of Majestic 12. All they knew was that they were dealing with human examples of health management, humans who required special treatment and diagnosis. All within the confines of the sworn secrecy of the CDC.

They were forbidden to discuss any of the procedures that took place inside the dungeon clinic. They didn't know what the penalty would be if they did, but Phil was pretty sure that Chad Powers had used enough of his naturally intimidating personality to get the message across that the repercussions for loose lips wouldn't be pleasant.

In the ten years that Phil had worked for Majestic 12, there hadn't been one incident of medical personnel breathing a single word of what went on down there. So, 'containment' was working in more ways than one.

He'd just hung up the phone.

Talking with Chad Powers always gave him the shivers.

The man was the devil incarnate, as far Phil was concerned.

But, he figured that Chad was probably the best person to do the job that he had to do. Anyone weak, or with even one ounce of compassion, wouldn't be capable of making the kinds of decisions that Chad had to make.

Phil also knew that Chad constantly violated the protocols of Majestic 12. The other eleven members didn't know the half of it.

They didn't know that 'keeping the lid on things' involved the kind of medical tampering that Phil and his team did. That was totally outside their 'need to know,' as far as Chad was concerned. Phil never disagreed with him—he understood the reasons, and his job was to execute decisions, not to question them.

And, he was paid well for it. He just tried not to think of the cruelty and inhumanity of it all, because, if he thought too much, his own compassion would rise to the surface. And, that would be dangerous.

So, Doctor Phillip Lansing resolved his internal conflicts by utilizing self-hypnosis. It helped him focus and guaranteed that he was able to function most of the time as just a brilliantly-tuned machine.

As he waited for Willy Carson to arrive, he studied his medical charts and notes. He'd done this procedure so many times now he could do it with his eyes closed. It was simple, although complex in its outcome.

When he first started doing these procedures on the problem cases Chad sent to him, he wondered why Chad just didn't have these people killed. God knew Majestic 12 had eliminated hundreds of others in their quest to contain information. But, Chad had outlined to him what they'd discovered about these special people over the last few decades. And, Phil understood.

While Phil's job was to suppress the side effects, that suppression wouldn't change one very important fact. Each of the people who had been affected irreparably by those strange beams from above had undergone a DNA change. That could never be reversed and, in fact, would be passed on to their offspring. Nothing Phil could do would change that. All his procedure could do was suppress the side effects that were drawing unwanted attention to their weirdness.

But, what he did learn from Chad was that each of these people were needed and couldn't be killed.

Because they were walking talking receptors, almost like lightning rods.

They were living across all four corners of the planet, and some had never had to have their side effects suppressed. Because they'd followed orders and avoided x-rays. Those who had made the mistake and underwent x-rays had to be tricked into visiting the Majestic 12 clinic in Atlanta.

But, they couldn't be killed.

It would be insane to kill people who were receptors, no doubt an unintended side effect of the beam weapon used on them. They were picking up signals, clues, intelligence—all information that could be used if it came to that. If the worst possible outcome looked like it was indeed coming to pass, there was nothing better than having advance knowledge—these people were equivalent to tapping into Nazi cryptic codes during WWII.

Willy Carson would leave the clinic a different man today.

But, not totally different.

He most definitely couldn't be killed because he was far too valuable.

Phil knew that was why each of these special people received visits every couple of years or so from Majestic 12 operatives. Just to "keep in touch." In case there was something to learn.

Those visits would continue, and probably increase in frequency, as the thing got closer.

Phil was an endocrinologist. An expert in his field, but a field that in his opinion was easier than a lot of specialties.

It was the study of hormones and the glands that secreted those hormones. Hormones helped control the activities of the body and had major impacts on metabolism, reproduction, food absorption, growth, development, energy, temperament, and aging.

Hormones also controlled the way an organism responded to its surroundings, and went a long way towards providing adequate energy for crucial functions. Sometimes too much energy; sometimes too little.

The glands that comprised the endocrine system included the pineal, thyroid, parathyroid, thymus, adrenals, pancreas, ovaries, testes, hypothalamus, and pituitary.

While Phil felt that his specialty was actually quite simple, he knew that was probably because he was actually quite brilliant. To the lay person, the endocrine system was complex as hell, held together by delicate balances of activity and sometimes precise levels of medication.

Diabetes was a perfect example, as was erectile dysfunction and thyroid hyperactivity.

In addition, the most important factors in aging could be connected directly to the endocrine system. As aging occurred, the endocrine system of glands becomes less efficient, leading to the obvious changes in the body that most people in their seventies and eighties were painfully aware of.

Phil remembered back to a famous experiment that had been conducted a few years ago, that demonstrated this principle quite vividly. Researchers removed the pituitary glands of mice. Then, they injected all of the hormones that were known to be produced by the pituitary gland.

Much to their scientific glee, they observed that the mice that had the gland removed lived longer than a control group of mice who still had the gland.

The conclusion was that, even though the scientists had tried to replicate the known hormones of the pituitary gland, there was obviously at least one other mysterious hormone coming from that gland that they didn't know about. This was why the mice without the gland lived longer, and the mice that still had the gland died at their normal expected ages.

Something else was being emitted from the pituitary gland—some kind of aging hormone.

The pituitary gland was a curious one—powerful as hell, and only about the size of a pea. Just a tiny protrusion off the bottom of the hypothalamus at the base of the brain, but it controlled more functions of the human body than most people realized.

The most common method of treating pituitary tumors was for a neurosurgeon to go in through the patient's nose due to the pituitary gland's location. The nose was the easiest and most direct route, and there was also the benefit of leaving behind no visible disfigurements.

The procedure was called an endonasal endoscopy.

Phil would take that same route in—but the major difference was that he would be leaving something behind instead of taking something out.

Suddenly, Phil's thoughts were jarred by the ring of his office phone.

After only a couple of seconds, he hung up. Willy Carson had just arrived at the lobby security desk.

He took one last look at his charts, then headed out into the hallway to take the elevator up to the lobby from the second level basement clinic.

Willy Carson thought he was just getting a medical checkup today, in order to qualify for his new role as spokesperson for Diamond Hotels. And, Willy hoped and expected that he'd be leaving there with a clean bill of health.

He would, of course, but he'd also be leaving with an annoying nosebleed that would hopefully dissipate nicely in a couple of days or so.

CHAPTER 36

Allison glanced out the window of her Gulfstream jet, as it winged its way across the prairies of Alberta and over the tips of the Rocky Mountains. She'd made this spectacular trip many times before and never tired of it.

Just the contrast of the golden wheat fields of the vast prairies, suddenly punctuated by massive and wealthy cattle ranches that provided the most succulent beef in the entire world, was candy to the eyes.

Then, another contrast—the vast open spaces transformed into the gleaming glass and steel office towers of Calgary, a city that was one of the planet's most influential energy capitals. From sublime open spaces to instant metropolis; which was an apt word for Calgary, considering it was the city used as the location for the early *Superman* movies, becoming the fictional 'Metropolis' on the silver screen.

After the cityscape came the most amazing transformation of all. Within just a few minutes of passing over Calgary the view from the plane would change again. The foothills, this time—rolling terrain that gave a strong hint as to what was to come next.

The snow-capped Rocky Mountains—breathtaking and snow-capped, even in the heat of the summer, because they were just so damn gigantic.

As Allison looked down, the crests of the towering, angry peaks seemed to be so close as to be almost scraping the belly of the jet. For just a second or two, the thought crossed her mind that if a plane went down here there would be little chance of survival, let alone a chance of rescue.

"Where are we right now?"

She glanced across the aisle at the only other passenger on the plane.

"Well, Senator Hartford, we're just passing over the Rockies and headed towards the next groups of mountain ranges—the Monashees, Bugaboos, and Selkirks."

She glanced out the window again. "If you look out your window right now, you'll see Lake Windermere, then follow the river to the south and that next body of water is Columbia Lake. Soon, you'll see Kootenay Lake, and then shortly after that we'll be soaring down the southeast side of the massive Okanagan Lake."

"How long till we land?"

Allison glanced at her watch. "About thirty minutes."

John checked his own watch. "What's that place called again where we're landing?"

"Penticton."

"And what's its claim to fame?"

"Mainly tourism—it's in the Okanagan Valley, which is British Columbia's wine country, so, it gets very hot and stays quite dry. It's one of Canada's most popular vacation areas due to its lakes, as well as some great ski resorts."

John leaned sideways in his chair. "Ever since your pilots whisked us out of Montreal, you've been very secretive about why we're going to this place."

"We're going there to keep you safe, Senator."

"Allison, don't keep me in the dark. How am I going to be safer in this...Penticon place?"

Allison laughed. "For a famous senator, you don't pay attention too well, do you? It's 'Penticton.'"

John sighed. "Okay, Penticton, then. How will that place be safer for me?"

"It won't. But, after that we're going to another place that will be. We'll rent a car and drive about half an hour down to a town called Osoyoos. It's only about three miles from the U.S. border at Washington State. It's actually Canada's only desert."

John unbuckled his seatbelt, stood up in the aisle and stared down at Allison. "Forgive me, but I'm accustomed to being in control of my own destiny. You're teasing me. I don't care whether this Osoyoos place is a desert or a rain forest. What's there?"

"It's better if I just show you when we get there. It's hard to describe, and I don't want you forming impressions in advance and voicing your usual senatorial objections.

"And, yes, John, you're used to being in control. But, right now, you're not, and it's going to have to be that way if you want to have any hope of surviving another attempt on your life."

John reached up into the overhead bin and pulled down his briefcase. He flicked it open and brought out his cell phone.

Allison reached up and grabbed his hand. "What are you doing?"

"I feel isolated from everything. Have to find out what's going on in the news."

She ripped the phone out of his hand. "I assumed you were more tech-savvy, John. From now on, until I say otherwise, no cell phones. Aren't you aware how easy it is to track these damn things? Don't even turn the stupid thing on."

John looked sheepish for a second, then he recovered. "Okay, you're right. I forgot. But, I feel really vulnerable right now. I'm used to being in touch with people 24/7. The real danger is largely over now, isn't it? They won't try again."

"Sit down and enjoy the rest of the flight, Senator. The scenery out that window is spectacular."

John grunted and put his cell phone back in his case. Then, he threw the case onto the seat beside him and reluctantly sat down.

"You do trust me, don't you, John?"

He looked at her, eyes glistening all of a sudden. After a few seconds of silence, he said, in a soft tone, "Yes, I do. After what you did for me back in Vermont, risking your own life to save me—and killing three men to do it—how could I not trust you? I owe you my life."

"Good, then just let me do what I do."

He smiled. "Yes, you seem quite capable. If I get to be president, maybe I can convince you to join my cabinet? How does Secretary of Homeland Security sound?"

Allison laughed. "If you had a spot for a Secretary of Astronomy I might take you up on that offer. Otherwise, I'll continue to run Diamond Hotels."

"Maybe I can create that position."

"You'll be president—you can do anything you want. Well…almost."

"Does the President know about Majestic 12?"

She shook her head. "No, not as far as I know, anyway. After Truman formed the group in 1947, he mandated that the Executive Branch would never have the chance to interfere. And, to my knowledge, it never has."

John was silent for a few minutes. "Okay, I'll ask again. What's in this Osoyoos place?"

"My company owns a vineyard and winery there, called *Diamond Vintage Wines*. We actually supply most of our hotels in North America with the wines we produce from that winery. Wonderful blends, award winners all."

"Good. I could use a glass of wine—or maybe something stronger. Then what?"

Allison chuckled. "That's it for now. You'll find out when we get there."

* * * * *

The rented Hyundai Sonata Limited, trimmed in a sleek arctic white color, weaved its way south along scenic Highway 97, passing along the entire length of Skaha Lake until it transformed itself seamlessly into Vaseux Lake. The entire drive to Osoyoos was lined with lush vineyards, snaking from the rolling hills right down to the edge of the highway.

John's eyes were wandering from one side of the highway to the other, taking in the constantly changing landscape.

"God, it's gorgeous here. If I wasn't running for my life, I might actually enjoy this."

Allison turned her eyes from the road for just a second—it was a curvy one, so a second was all she could risk.

"Yes, it is beautiful. My dad bought the vineyard about thirty years ago, made some much needed improvements, and now it's world class. I always enjoy coming here. The people who work for us are marvelous. We pay them very well, of course, but they have incredible loyalty to us for more reasons than money. Our wine master, Derik, is from Germany. And, his wife, Gerndle, is a real charmer. Very intelligent folks and very committed.

"About fifteen years ago, their young son was diagnosed with a brain tumor. Inoperable. My dad wouldn't accept the diagnosis, so he arranged for young Kurt to be flown down to the Mayo Clinic for an operation and a series of follow-up treatments. Dad paid for everything. Kurt was only ten years old—it took a year, but he was completely cured. He's twenty-five now, and studying medicine at the University of Calgary. He told me he wants to be an oncologist. Amazing how some gestures can make such a permanent impact on people's lives, huh?"

"That's quite the story. I can understand why they're so loyal to you."

"It's more than that. I don't think they feel they owe me or my family anything. They just had a chemistry with my dad right from the beginning. They would have done anything for him, too, if they had the resources. Anyway, my dad bequeathed that they always be taken care of, and I'm honored to uphold that promise. And, they know that I will. They're like family to me."

"Amazing. And, humbling. I'm not as rich as your dad was, or as you are, but with whatever wealth I've had I have to admit that I've never done anything for anyone."

Allison reached over and rubbed his arm. "That's not true, John. As one of the two senators from Vermont, you've done an awful lot for your constituents. You're just not giving yourself enough credit. Take stock—you'll be surprised. And, if you become president, just think of the difference you'll make then."

John snorted. "Maybe not. Sounds like the president role is more of a puppet existence than I ever realized. And, hell, I may not even live that long. Look at me now—a possible presidential candidate driving around with a murderer in a part of Canada with names of towns I can't even pronounce!"

Allison choked on her Dentyne gum. "The way you said that, it does sound kind of strange. But, remember, all three of those killings were self-defence."

"C'mon, Allison. Are you forgetting about all the deaths you said you voted in favor of in your Majestic 12 meetings?"

She swallowed hard, then spoke in almost a whisper. "No, I'm not forgetting—although I'm *trying* to. I guess swinging that frying pan at Clint's head, and firing into the chests of those other two killers, made it more real to me. But, voting in favor of protecting secrets seemed nobler, more honorable. It doesn't seem that way to the same extent any more, but, for my five years of serving on that board, it was just a remote function.

"We didn't know the targets, we were just convinced that we were doing the right thing to protect the American people from things that would scare them to death at the very least, and cause unbelievable chaos at the very worst. So, there was a kind of…rationale behind it."

"I think I understand. But, don't you think people deserve to know?"

"I'm not sure what I think anymore. You're a seasoned politician. How do you feel about what you now know, the things that Farmington shared with you?"

"There is intelligent life out there in the universe, and they've been visiting us for a very long time. You people at Majestic 12 have convinced the world that most of those visits were hoaxes, that they weren't real. They were real, and they're probably coming for us. If I had a family, I'd want them to know."

"Why, John? So you could quit your job and just enjoy life? On what? On what money? How would life continue? Would we have any police forces, or fire departments? Would governments survive? Would society act in a decent manner, or would it just decide to take what it wants, when it wants?

"What quality of life would exist during those many years before an event happened? Think about that. What would normal people do? How would they live? Would they turn into animals?"

"Well, now I know about it, and I still want to be president."

Allison shook her head. "You're stronger than the average person. But, think about this. What would it be like being president of a country in absolute anarchy, where no one obeyed the laws, no one observed common decency anymore?

"Forget about anyone paying their taxes, and good luck arresting them and throwing them in prison. You'd be lucky to have anyone working at enforcement any longer, let alone enough room in the prisons. It's a real dilemma, John. You haven't thought it through. You want to blow the lid on this, but is that the right thing to do? Really?"

John was silent for a few minutes. "You told me your dad was getting ready to blow the lid, too. That's why he was killed."

"Yes, and that knowledge is what's causing the conflict I'm feeling now. It's too close to home now. I'm giving you all the reasons for Majestic 12, the rationale behind the decisions we made—and I don't even know if I believe them anymore. What we've done is barbaric. It's twisting my brain and soul around in knots."

"You saved my life."

"Yes, I did. You're the first example of the conflict I'm feeling, after discovering the truth about my father. I also happen to think you'd make one fine President of the United States. We still need a strong leader until the end comes, and so do all the other countries who don't have the technology to know what we know. We also need strong leaders afterwards, for those who survive."

"The Russians and the Chinese must know."

"I don't know how much they know—our respective governments don't do a great job of talking to each other, do they? But, maybe they do know, and maybe they have their own versions of Majestic 12. Anyway, that's way above my pay grade."

John scratched his head. "I'm puzzled, though. All you know so far is about a bunch of UFO sightings, landings, and beams being shot down to Earth. There's no timeline here. Not yet, anyway. What's the harm in warning people, disclosing what we know, putting plans of action in place and getting the public's support for those plans?"

Allison glanced over at him, puzzled. "Is that all that Farmington shared with you?"

"Yes."

"He must have been holding out on you, keeping back a trump card."

"What do you mean?"

"He didn't tell you about *Gargantuan?*"

"What the fuck is that?"

Allison turned the car off the highway onto a secondary road. "We're only about ten minutes away now."

"Answer me! What the fuck is *Gargantuan?*"

Allison sighed. "I promise I'll tell you more later. Right now, we need to get you settled."

They drove in silence until the winery finally came into sight. Allison always loved this place—very isolated from the tourist traffic, and the concrete and glass structure looked like it was right out of a Star Trek movie.

She pulled up in front of the building and parked the car. "Don't forget your briefcase, John."

"What am I going to do for a change of clothes?"

"Don't worry—there's plenty here for you to choose from. We'll take care of you."

Allison led the way up the stairs and into the front lobby. An attractive middle-aged blonde woman ran out to greet her from a glass enclosed office.

"Allison! What a surprise!"

Allison wrapped her arms around her and gave her a big hug. "It's been a while, Gerndle. You're looking wonderful. How's Derik?"

Gerndle waved her hand. "Oh, he's the same. Out in the oak room testing some samples. He'll be so happy to know you're here."

"And Kurt?"

Gerndle held up her hand with her fingers crossed. "So far, top of his class. Hoping that continues."

"I'm sure it will. Gerndle, this is John Hartford, a friend of mine and an esteemed guest. He'll be staying with us for a while in the 'Treehouse.' Has to be a secret. He's a very important man, and his life is in danger. Lips need to be sealed. Understand?"

Gerndle reached her hand out and John shook it. She squinted her eyes. "You do look familiar, but I won't ask anything more. If Allison wants you safe, we'll keep you safe."

John nodded. "Thanks, Gerndle. I'm honored."

Gerndle nodded back. Then, she spun around. "Follow me. I'll get you settled."

After a quick detour to her office to retrieve something from her desk drawer, she waved her hand and said, "Let's go. We can chat later."

They walked down a long corridor, and then out through a back door and along a small stone pathway, which led to a small building. Allison always thought it resembled the outer shell building of a cemetery crypt. It stood alone, amongst lush grapevines and dense fruit trees. Black, solid stone, twelve inches thick, and only about 200 square feet.

Gerndle thrust out the remote device she'd taken from her office, and pressed on it with her thumb. They heard the click of the lock and she opened the door wide.

While motioning them inside, Gerndle flicked on a light switch and then shut the door behind them.

Allison looked down at the familiar sight in the center of the floor. The room had nothing at all inside it except for this one hatch—round, about six feet in diameter, and with a metal handle in the center.

Gerndle pointed the remote down at the floor and pushed a button. There was a loud click. She reached down and pulled up on the hatch by the handle. Once it had opened completely, it swung back on its hinge and rested on the floor.

She then punched another button on the remote. The sinister aperture revealed by the open hatch suddenly lit up like a Christmas tree—all the way down.

Allison always thought it resembled a submarine's conning tower, right down to the steep metal ladder. Which was its only way in or out—except, of course, for the hidden escape tunnel.

Senator John Hartford turned and stared at her, pale face and wide eyes betraying his shock.

He positioned himself closer to the opening and reluctantly gazed down into the brightly-lit abyss.

Barely heard, he muttered under his breath, "What the fuck?"

CHAPTER 37

"Go ahead, John. I'll be right behind you…or should I say…above you. About 30 feet down, you'll reach a catwalk. Step onto it and wait for me."

John shook his head in disbelief.

Slowly and carefully, he made his way down, glancing up once to make sure Allison was following him. He trusted her, but still wasn't completely sure about everything.

This woman was full of surprises—first, she'd warned him about his life being in danger, then admitted to being a member of Majestic 12, and finally killed three men and engineered his escape to Canada.

And, to top things off, after the horror they'd gone through in Vermont, they'd flown together in the lap of luxury on her private jet to what seemed to him like hillbilly country in the mountains of Canada's West.

Now, here he was climbing down into the bowels of the earth in a vineyard that was obviously more than just a vineyard.

Step by careful step, John made it to the catwalk—basically just a metal gangway attached to the wall of a structure. It reminded him of a fire escape walkway.

He stepped onto the catwalk and the first thing he noticed was a thick metal door with a keypad lock. He looked down along the length of the steel structure he was standing on and saw three more doors identical to the one in front of him. Each of the four doors were separated by about forty feet. He estimated that, considering the distance on each side of the outermost doors, the entire structure was about 200 feet across.

Allison sidled past him onto the catwalk and keyed in a combination. He heard a beep, and the sound of the lock's tumblers releasing.

"Okay, John, this is it. Your new home for a while."

Allison pushed open the heavy door and flicked a light switch on the wall.

John just stood on the threshold for a few moments, stunned at the welcoming sight in front of him.

The ceiling was a good ten feet high, graced by a chandelier in the front foyer. A long hall led past several doorways, right to the very end, which opened into a large lounge area.

He whistled. "God Almighty, Allison. What the hell do you have here?"

She ignored his question and walked on ahead. She pointed to her right. "That's the kitchen, and it leads into a large dining area." She pointed to her left as she walked. "These three doors are bedrooms. You can take your pick."

Allison led the way down to the lounge area, with John following in stunned silence. She stopped at the entrance and made a flourish with her hand. "Everything you need for relaxing."

John's eyes wandered around the massive room. It was adorned with a couple of sectional sofas in the corners, facing towards a big screen TV mounted on the wall. One wall of the room opened into a small office alcove, complete with a desk and computer. Another wall was graced with a wet bar, the glass shelves on the wall decorated with a countless selection of spirits and liqueurs. Built into the lower section of the wall was a wine cooler, filled to the brim.

He looked over at Allison, his mouth open—but he forgot what he was going to say.

She laughed. "I know. A little bit overwhelming, isn't it?"

John pointed to a far wall. "Those two sets of drapes. How can you have windows way down here?"

Allison walked over to it and pulled aside one of the drapes, revealing a blank wall behind. "Just an illusion. Trick of the mind. Helps relieve claustrophobia if the mind thinks there's a window behind. Just like on a cruise ship when you're unlucky enough to have an inside cabin."

"And, you have TV and internet reception down here?"

"Yep, cable and WIFI. Can't promise they'll still work if there's a major cataclysm, but in a minor one they should be operational."

"Jesus. Of course, I've heard about these things, but I've never seen inside of one. It's just as luxurious as a high-end condo."

Allison nodded. "The idea being that if we're going to be cooped up for a while, we might as well be comfortable. You may have noticed when you were out on the gangway, that there are three more units side by side. All four are identical. They can be kept separate and distinct, or connect through blast doors in the storage area."

Allison pointed to a door at the end of the hallway. "That's the storage room. Stocked with everything a family of four would need for three years. Each unit has a storage room like that, and that's where all the units connect if we wish to connect." She chuckled. "All depends on how well we're getting along."

"Water?"

"We have our own well. Drilled down 250 feet, so it's very pure and protected from any contaminants from the surface. We also have filters and water purifiers installed on the automatic pump mechanism, just in case anything gets into the water.

"We're well protected in here as well—several feet of dirt on top of us is a great insulator from all sorts of dangerous elements, including radioactive fallout. These units are made of solid sheets of steel with protective sleeves on the corners. And, the steel shells are encased in two feet of poured concrete, just for extra measure."

John shook his head in disbelief. "Sanitation?"

"The toilets are the composting type, ventilated. Leftover refuse would be emptied every few days and added to the soil of our garden."

"Garden?"

Allison nodded. "Yes, that steel ladder that connects to the catwalk goes down another sixty feet, to three additional levels.

"The first level down is a composting area for our garbage and recyclables, ventilated sideways and then up to the outside. The second level down is our vegetable garden, where some refuse from the composting area and the toilets would be added from time to time. It's completely enclosed and already equipped with rich soil. Organized into separate fields that can be rotated from season to season; one being left empty each year for regeneration. The garden is equipped with fluorescent lighting for growth and photosynthesis, and with an automatic sprinkler system as well.

"The last level down is our mausoleum. Again, completely enclosed, and equipped with a dozen or so concrete coffins."

John felt his throat getting dry. He figured it must have been the mausoleum part that choked him up. He walked over to the bar, opened a small fridge, grabbed two bottles of water, and passed one to Allison. He twisted the cap off his, and sucked back the entire contents in one long swallow.

He put the bottle down and wiped the sleeve of his shirt across his mouth. "How do you get your power?"

"Cooking is by either alcohol fuel, or electricity. Our electricity source is solar. We have a farm of solar panels installed in an open area about a quarter mile away from the compound. Underground wires connect the panels to our battery compartments. We have a huge supply of fully charged batteries to last us for many years in case the sun source dies on us for a while."

John sat down on one of the sectional couches, took off his shoes and stretched out. Allison curled up in one of the corners.

"Well, what do you think?"

John let out a long breath. "I'm amazed. Astounded is probably a better word. I find myself breathing hard, probably just subliminal, knowing where I am. I'm not convinced that the air is good—all in my head, I guess."

"I understand. Let me assure you the air is top quality. The air system we have is referred to as an NBC module. Outside air is sucked into the ventilation duct and enters the first filter, a ULP—Ultra Low Penetration—filter. This thing removes about ninety-nine percent of airborne particles that are 120 nanometers or larger, including nuclear particles, molds, and spores. After that, the air enters an AC filter—Activated Charcoal—which is a military-grade filter designed to protect against chemical and nerve agents. From there, the air enters the unit, fully cleansed and ready to breathe."

"What if all this stuff stops working? Geez, we know how often things break down up in the real world."

"We have replacement filters and parts. As well, my brother and I are fully trained in basic maintenance; as are Derik and Gerndle, who stock and maintain the units and have guarantees from me of permanent refuge here for them if a catastrophe happens."

"That still isn't a guarantee that everything will work and that you'll be able to fix what needs to be fixed."

Allison cocked her head. "Really, John, what guarantees exist up above? This is the best chance to survive whatever happens. But, no, there are no guarantees. You and I just found out over the last few days that there are no guarantees we could even live to see the next day."

John scratched his head. "Good point. You're right, but I just feel so damn vulnerable down here."

"That's because you're used to being in control. Some of that tendency has to be sacrificed in a place like this if the worst happens. But, it's darn safe down here. All of the doors to the outside of the units and between the units are blast resistant to a very high pressure rating. We also have blast valves on all of the outside air vents, designed to close shut if there is a change in outside pressure, and designed to re-open again when air pressure returns to normal. So, if there's an external explosion, we're totally impervious to it down here. Even the hatch at the top of the ladder is a blast door."

"But, if something happens, we're trapped down here! That hatch up above opens up into a concrete structure. If that thing comes down, the hatch ain't gonna open—no way."

"First of all, if something happens, we might not mind being trapped down here for a few weeks, months, or even years. We do have air sensors that we can elevate through the vents to test the air quality. But, yes, if that housing up above comes down in a blast, our hatch won't open.

"We do, however, have another way out of here. An emergency escape hatch. In the storage rooms for each of the units is another blast door. It connects to a tunnel, and the tunnels from all four of the units connect to a single tunnel which leads along underneath the surface for about 100 feet. Then, it goes up on a gradual slope to a blast hatch. The hatch opens from the inside, but not from the outside. If there's debris on top of it, jamming the hatch from opening, there's an explosive charge that can be activated—almost like the ejection mechanism in a fighter jet."

John slowly shook his head from side to side. "Sounds like you've thought of everything."

"Well, my dad did, not me. I simply carried on with some improvements here and there, but he made sure this was state of the art at the time it was built, and gave it the ability to be added onto and improved."

John stretched his arms out behind his head, starting to feel more comfortable the more he listened to Allison. "When did he build this?"

"He oversaw it, but had a specialized crew that actually constructed it. It was finished about fifteen years ago. I think he got a bit paranoid from all that he knew. Decided he needed something for his family and close friends, just in case."

"But, it's so far away from your home in Chicago."

Allison grimaced. "That's the one disadvantage. If something sudden happens, we wouldn't be able to get to it in time. But, Dad figured that was a risk he would take. With his position on Majestic 12, he was in the know. He would have plenty of notice for anything major that was going to happen.

"He didn't want to build a bunker in the States—was afraid of the militancy and chaos that would exist if something even minor happened. Especially with the number of Americans who own guns. No, he figured it would be safer here in Canada, and here in a more rural area—an area that is really just an innocuous vineyard. Not a logical place for anyone to look for a bunker. But...just in case...we do have gun lockers."

John slid his feet onto the floor and sat forward, resting his elbows on his knees. "Allison, I know a lot of people who told me they built these things. I never thought much of it, never had an urge to build one of my own. Even after that Farmington sleaze shared the stuff about Majestic 12 with me, I didn't consider building one. I was more obsessed with just blowing the whistle, using it as a cornerstone of my campaign, and then concentrating on solutions—actions to prevent or fight back against what might be coming."

"John, you're not unlike most people. And, let's face it, most people couldn't even afford one of these, let alone the land they'd need to install it in. But, bunkers have been around a long time—this is nothing new. The Cold War caused a rash of them to be built right across North America and Europe. Most of them are primitive, more just bomb shelters than anything else. Not intended to be lived in for long periods of time.

"Some fairly rich people have built new ones over the last few decades, not because they knew of anything specific, but more as a status symbol—and having more money than they knew what to do with. A lot of former missile silos have been bought from the government and converted as well. I don't think most people ever expect to use them.

"We own a separate company that builds these. It's hidden through a shell organization, because we don't want it associated with Diamond Hotels—that'd be kind of negative synergy. Anyway, it's doing extremely well. The company is called *Survival Structures*, and its revenue growth has been off the charts. Just goes to show how paranoid some people are these days, even when they don't know they actually have reason to be. But, they are afraid of some things—not the things that people were scared of during the Cold War. Nuclear war is the least of their concerns now.

"My managers at *Survival Structures* tell me that the most common reason for people plunking down tens and hundreds of thousands of dollars for these bunkers is economic collapse. They fear that when the shit hits the fan, the common folk will take out their anger on anyone with wealth. There is a definite fear of total social breakdown and anarchy.

Armed gangs roaming downtown streets, looting, and killing. Then, when the shelves are empty, they would head out to the suburbs—to the rich neighborhoods where these desperate swarms would feel entitled to take, by force, whatever they want.

"There is a feeling that the police would be overwhelmed so the military would be called in. And, even then, because of fears of other countries taking advantage of our total collapse, the military would have their hands full keeping the borders safe. How far could they be spread to protect neighborhoods?

"No, at the very best, they'd be protecting the nation's corporate and institutional assets, downtown areas, government buildings. It would be every man for himself. So, that's the main reason rich people are building bunkers—to protect themselves from their fellow citizens."

John shook his head. "My God, what have we come to? If we think that society would become like rabid dogs, we've either ruined the way people think with our stupid governing decisions, or over the generations we have indeed been bred down to the animal level."

Allison laughed. "C'mon, John, don't be so naïve. Technology is turning people into self-obsessed narcissists. The entertainment industry puts celebrities up on pedestals, so-called role models like Miley Cyrus; singers and dancers who are showing kids that they can be as decadent as they want and not have to apologize for it. And, the media, well, that's another story. One lie after another and, when they get caught at it, people just shrug and accept it. I've been part of those lies—we plant them all the time to explain away anomalies.

"The middle class is disappearing, the poor can't get jobs, and the rich get richer. There's a powder keg of anger building in the country and it won't take much to set it off. A manmade or natural catastrophe will have a lingering after-taste in this day and age that never would have been seen even during the horrors of the World Wars. Civilization just isn't that civilized, or kind, anymore. You say we're like animals—we're worse than animals. We can only blame ourselves—we've let it happen. And, one day, we'll pay for it."

John looked into Allison's beautiful, intelligent eyes. Even though the topic they were discussing was a serious one, he could still see the optimistic sparkle that had always been there through all the years he'd known her.

"Do you fear economic collapse the most, Allison? Is that why you have this…bunker?"

She shook her head.

"What do you fear the most, then?"

In an instant, the sparkle left her eyes.

"Gargantuan."

CHAPTER 38

"Allison, that's the second time you've mentioned that word. So, I think you need to finally just come clean with me. What the hell is 'Gargantuan'?"

Allison sighed. "I intended to tell you, Senator. Maybe this is as good a time as any."

"It is. I'm ready…I think."

"Alright, here we go, then. Brace yourself…"

*****

John laid his head back against the sofa and closed his eyes. Allison had adjourned to one of the bedrooms for a well-earned nap. But, John didn't have the energy to move even one muscle. He always found that mental activities tired him much more than physical ones. And, for the last three hours, his brain had been put through its paces—mental gymnastics in the extreme.

Not that he'd said very much. He asked the odd question for clarification, but there wasn't a hell of a lot to say. Allison's explanation had been exhaustive and detailed, even though a lot of what she told him was still just speculation, rather than fact.

It had been three hours of listening and absorbing. John was used to that, of course. In the Senate, the debates sometimes went on well into the night. And, in his spare time, he had to prepare himself for votes by reading new bills, some of which were mind-numbing and several hundred pages long. So, exercise of the brain was something the good senator from Vermont was accustomed to, for sure.

But, he wasn't accustomed to hearing tales such as he'd just heard, and that was what had exhausted him now more than ever before in his life.

It was the subject matter, tainted with the seeming futility of it all, which was now causing him to drift off into dreamland.

John knew full well how he dreamed. Perhaps it was the analytical life he led, or maybe it was just the way his subconscious was. But, John didn't dream in the abstract the way most people did.

In fact, his dreams tended to be factual, reflecting what took place during his day, or what was on his mind.

Most people dreamed in symbolism—if they were worried about something, a snake or some other fearful creature would be slithering across the floor. But, not John—if he was worried about something, that actual thing he was worried about would be in his dream.

If deadlines were piling up on people, creating incredible stress, they'd dream of being chased or having the walls of a room closing in on them. John, however, would dream of the actual projects that had the deadlines attached to them.

He'd always wished he could dream like normal people did. He loved hearing about the wonderful fantastical adventures people would experience, and wished that he could have those flights of fancy himself.

But...he never did. His dreams were just darn boring, and John sometimes feared that meant he was a boring person.

He figured that lingering thought preying on his mind throughout most of his life perhaps was what had propelled him to be in politics— forcing himself to become an exciting, dynamic politician. And, lately, maybe that was what had been propelling him to want to become President of the United States.

Maybe he was overcompensating?

He rested his head into the soft leather of the sectional sofa and closed his eyes. He knew he'd be asleep within minutes, and he also had a pretty good idea of what his focused, organized brain would be dreaming about.

*****

The Great Flood—Noah's very own flood—was supposed to have devastated the planet 4,400 years ago.

But, did it really happen? No one knew for sure, although it was the stuff of religious teachings and even motion pictures. And, because no one knew for sure, there was no way of knowing the timeline.

All that the world's population thought they knew was that it happened an awful long time ago and, if it was caused by the hand of God, He must have had a good reason.

But, if it did indeed happen, could it have been caused by something else? Something more believable perhaps than the hand of God? And perhaps 3,600 years ago instead of 4,400?

That particular something was big, and dark, and mostly hidden from view. Telescopes had been challenged indeed trying to find this thing. But, the Hubble telescope did. Now, the little probe that had recently passed Pluto was sending back some interesting photos.

As far back as 1983, The Washington Post reported that a heavenly body, possibly as large as the giant Jupiter, had been found in the direction of the Orion constellation by an orbiting telescope aboard the U.S. Infrared Astronomical Satellite.

It was reported as being a mysterious object indeed, and possibly so close to Earth that it could actually be part of our solar system. So little was known just from that orbiting telescope that astronomers weren't really sure what it was. The image wasn't clear, more just a blob in the lens. Some theorized that, instead of a planet, it might actually be a giant comet, a protostar, or even a distant galaxy that was intruding on our solar system.

No follow-up article ever came from The Washington Post. Their reporting of this discovery in 1983 was followed by utter silence.

But, in 1991, a man named Doctor Robert Harrington, the chief astronomer at Washington's Naval Observatory, wrote a paper.

He was in charge of NASA's search for a large planet at the edge of our solar system. His method concentrated on examining the orbits of the two outer large planets, Neptune and Uranus.

He was stunned to discover that these two massive planets were being pulled down in their orbits. Something that had obviously never been there before was now exerting extreme pressure—magnetic pressure. He knew that the only thing that could cause such an effect was a large object, and that it had to exist down in the direction of this unexplainable motion of these giant planets. He also knew it had to be big and below the plane of the planets, known as the ecliptic.

That led to several trips by Harrington to New Zealand, because he knew that was his best bet to spot this monster if it really existed.

Because of what he observed with Uranus and Neptune being pulled down, he calculated that the Southern Hemisphere was the logical place to be to have any hope of a sighting. He was also pretty sure of its location in the celestial world, so he went down to New Zealand in the spring, knowing that it could only be seen around that time of the year.

Even then, it would be tough, because it was a very dark object. In his determination, he thought the thing could possibly be a Brown Dwarf—a failed star that had never really reached its potential.

But, it could also actually be the tenth planet in our solar system. It just never came around to visit all that often. Its calculated orbit was a mindboggling 3,600 years, and quite possibly could have made its last visit around the time of Noah's flood.

In fact, if it did, the flood was more due to the power of Gargantuan than the hand of God.

Gargantuan had been absent for an awful long time, but it was coming around once again on its long elliptical orbit.

It had been known by other names over the years.

NASA's affectionate name for it had always been 'Planet X'—not too creative, but it did the trick.

Conspiracy theorists loved to call it 'Nibiru.'

But, Majestic 12 called it 'Gargantuan.'

Doctor Robert Harrington made those trips to New Zealand with nothing more elaborate than an eight-inch telescope and a camera.

His last trip was in 1992, when he reportedly provided NASA with the successful results of his investigation. Friends and family reported that Harrington was ecstatic about what he'd discovered—excited that his calculations and determination had paid off.

He died shortly thereafter of apparent esophageal cancer.

His memory was honored by having an asteroid named after him: 3216 Harrington.

The results of his last trip to New Zealand were never made public.

When Gargantuan comes, it will pass Earth twice—on the way in, and again on the way out. After it swings away to go out past the Sun once again, it won't be seen for another 3,600 years.

The closest it will ever come to Planet Earth will be fourteen million miles. Most people would shake their heads at hearing that distance and wonder what all the fuss was about.

What most wouldn't think about is the magnetic pull that every single object in the solar system has on all the others.

A delicate balance exists that keeps everything in its proper place. Just the mere fact that an object so far away could have had an effect on the orbits of Uranus and Neptune, showed the power of magnetics and gravity.

And, that wobble effect wasn't just noticed for the first time in the 1990s—there were written observations from early astronomers way back in the mid-1800s about how the orbits of those two planets were out of whack, wobbling.

Astronomers also acknowledged that any object coming up from the southern hemisphere would probably just sneak up on Earth. Coming up from a desolate area made it almost impossible for a professional astronomer to see it, let alone an amateur.

Even comets coming from that direction would probably only be seen with enough time to give a measly couple of weeks' notice of impact.

Gargantuan wasn't a comet and it wasn't going to hit the Earth—there was no danger of that. But, fourteen million miles was just a hair-breadth away in astronomical terms. Nothing as big as Jupiter would be able to swing past us at that distance without causing absolute havoc.

And, the havoc had already started a long time ago.

Each year that Gargantuan had drawn closer to the Earth on its 3,600 mile round trip had brought changes to the climate. A little bit here, a little bit there—but slow and sure.

And, accelerating in the last two decades as its massive size exerted more influence.

All of the changes in the climate had been blamed on humanity's excess. The ultimate distraction, and an opportunity to raise tax revenue to build underground bunkers for the elite.

Manmade greenhouse gases, in reality, have had a miniscule effect on the climate, although the general public had been convinced otherwise.

Everyone knew intuitively that something was happening. Something was wrong. But, they'd been convinced all along that they were the cause.

The planet was simply being ripped apart at its seams.

The Earth's core was now hotter than the surface of the Sun, and that change had only occurred within the last twenty years.

Massive crevices had formed in Mexico and the mid-western United States. Sinkholes were popping up everywhere, yet no one seemed to notice that this was unusual. No one had clued in that phenomena like that couldn't possibly be caused by greenhouse gases.

The polar ice caps were melting at record rates, and summers were getting hotter to the point that some sections of the planet would eventually become uninhabitable. Where would the people go?

Winter storms were establishing new records every year.

Fish, dolphins, and whales were dying in record numbers as the ocean temperatures and currents were deviating far from the norm.

Dozens of volcanos were erupting at the same time now, all across the globe. Earthquakes were much more frequent and the warnings about mega-quakes and tsunamis were dominating the airwaves.

In 2008, NASA announced that the THEMIS spacecraft had discovered a breach in the Earth's magnetic field ten times larger than anything previously thought. The opening was huge—four times bigger than the width of the Earth itself. That breach was allowing twenty times the normal amount of solar particles to enter Earth's atmosphere.

The only thing protecting Earth's inhabitants from the dangerous radiation of the Sun was the magnetosphere, which was now seriously depleted.

Radiation—the silent killer.

This danger had not been announced to the people—the only innovations that had happened over the years were more aggressive attempts to convince people to use higher-numbered sunscreens. And, despite those sunscreens, there were reports from across the globe of people suffering from unusual sun blisters that would eventually turn into skin cancer. This was despite the extensive use of sunscreens.

Folks had no doubt noticed the specially-equipped planes that crisscrossed the skies on most clear days, spewing out chemicals that mysteriously expanded into cloud formations within mere minutes. No government would admit that they were creating an artificial barrier to block out the most dangerous rays of the Sun. But, those rays still got through, despite that clandestine effort.

Neither would governments admit that chemtrails had a dual purpose—one for protection from the Sun, and the other to hide what else was up there.

The estimated time of arrival of Gargantuan was somewhere between 2015 and 2020. No one knew for sure when it would make its closest approach.

But, Earth was now seeing four times the number of natural disasters each year than had occurred two decades ago. And this figure would get larger—much larger.

The magnetic pressure from Gargantuan could cause a pole flip—Africa might become the new North Pole, with the Arctic sitting at the Equator. The entire appearance of Earth could change, with the likelihood of only ten percent of its inhabitants surviving.

Astronomy being an inexact science, it might be better, or it might be worse. No one knew for sure.

One thing was for certain, though, Gargantuan was incoming.

It had already been seen by the little Pluto probe. And, it had been seen before by both the Hubble and space-borne telescopes.

Even Doctor Robert Harrington was unaware that it had already been viewed prior to his big discovery.

He'd stumbled upon something that others had known about for quite some time. No one foresaw that he would find it, nor expect that he'd want to tell the world about it. But, the man was persistent—a serious, dedicated astronomer, who cared about what he did for a living. Right up until the day he died.

He did, however, have the honor of having an asteroid named after him. An honor that very few got to enjoy, even posthumously.

Recent images, however, showed something that no one could have predicted.

It was certainly shocking enough that an unknown planet was invading our solar system.

But, worse than that, Gargantuan also had its own atmosphere.

Artificially created from within.

It had mountains and canyons—just like Earth.

It was so gigantic that over 1,000 Earths could fit within its spherical mass.

And…it had life.

* * * * *

John awoke with a start and, for a brief moment, forgot where he was.

He wiped a sleeve across his sweaty forehead and cursed his decision to take a nap.

As he gradually regained his alertness, he heard a gentle snoring sound coming from one of the bedrooms.

The senator was surprised—he hadn't known that women snored.

CHAPTER 39

Wyatt glanced at his watch as he pulled into the visitor parking lot of the Castlegar Airport.

Just in time, he hoped.

Knowing Allison Fisher for even the short time he had, she seemed to be the type of person who made sure she was either bang on schedule or well ahead of it. That was a quality he really admired in her, although one that was hard to measure up to.

Since leaving his RCMP post in Toronto and moving out to the relaxed lifestyle in the west, he'd become a bit lazy about deadlines and schedules. That was more of a big city thing, and he was glad to have left it behind.

While the airport was only half an hour from Nelson, he'd been delayed a bit leaving the house.

Not his house. His parents' house.

He'd spent all morning with them, even though work was piling up on his desk back at the station, and there were plenty of nationwide cases that needed local alerts authorized. All of that would have to wait. The stress his mom and dad were going through right now was more important and far more worthy of his time.

It was understandable that they'd be stressed—the changes that his dad had undergone in just the last few days were not only weird, but had thrown their lives upside down.

He walked towards the terminal building and glanced upwards at the sound of an approaching plane. It was a sleek executive jet, and he guessed that it was probably Allison's. Not too many jets as expensive as that one normally graced the tarmac at Castlegar.

Wyatt was glad she was here. They had some serious things to talk about, all related to his dad. He'd sent her a text message yesterday—wasn't sure where in the world she was, but was hoping she'd text him back fast.

She did even better than that—replied that she was flying out of Penticton and would meet him in Castlegar.

He had expected that they'd just be talking on the phone, but this was much better. Not just because the matter he wanted to talk to her about was so serious, but also because he was really looking forward to seeing her again.

Yes, he knew full well he had kind of a schoolboy crush going on—the fluttering in his stomach was a dead giveaway.

He stood inside the terminal and waited patiently, but unfortunately the butterflies weren't being so patient.

Wyatt watched a band of merry fishermen pick up their rods at the over-sized luggage carousel. He smiled as he saw four young men claiming their golf clubs at the same carousel—trash-talking each other as they started making their way down to the rental car counter.

Then, she was just there. Standing right in front of him, hands braced confidently on her hips.

While he'd been gazing around, daydreaming, trying hard to calm his stomach, Allison had playfully snuck up on him, as quiet as a mouse.

"Well, aren't you going to be a gentleman and carry my bag?"

He couldn't hide the silly smile that instantly spread across his face. "I would if it didn't have wheels. But, you look perfectly capable of pulling it yourself."

She slapped him playfully on the shoulder. "Chivalry is surely dead in this section of Canada."

Wyatt grabbed the extended handle of her case and led the way towards the parking lot. He flashed her his most devilish grin.

"Good to see you, Allison. And, for you, I'll pretend to be a gentleman. Just this once, though—can't take a chance on ruining my aloof reputation."

She slipped her arm inside his free one and walked along beside him.

"You're anything but aloof, Mr. Chief of Police. But, I do love the subtle hint of danger that lies just beneath your surface. Adds an air of mystery about you."

Wyatt stole a quick glance at her face as they walked. Those blue eyes of hers always took his breath away. Unusual for someone with such dark hair to have the bluest of blue eyes.

"Is that your natural hair color?"

Pretending to be insulted, she exclaimed, "What kind of question is that to ask a lady? Of course it's my color. Is yours natural?"

Wyatt laughed, and ran his fingers through his hair. "What's left of it, yes. But, I was thinking of dyeing it ginger—whaddaya think?"

"Don't you dare! I was thinking of offering to cook dinner for you tonight, but I don't know if I want to have dinner with someone who one day might have red hair."

"Dinner sounds great—so forget about the ginger idea. I'll stroke that off my bucket list. But, you'll definitely love the appliances at my house—all high end. They'll be glad to get some use, because I usually just pick up food on the way home."

"Okay, it's a date. So, what made you ask about my hair color?"

"Your eyes are just so darn blue for someone with dark hair. I've never seen such blue eyes before, even on fair-haired people."

Allison giggled.

"That's a nice compliment. You're forgiven. Yes, they are unusual eyes—I got them from my dad. Everyone always comments on them, and some say they're even hypnotic. Spooky, huh?"

They reached the police cruiser and Wyatt popped the trunk.

"Do you want to sit in the back seat behind the 'bad dude' screen, or up front with me?"

She squeezed his arm, and lowered her voice to a husky Lauren Bacall tone.

"Well, I've always had this fantasy about being the prisoner of a handsome police officer."

While soaking up another long stare into her mesmerizing eyes, Wyatt noticed she was blushing.

He wasn't oblivious to the fact that she'd been flirting with him.

He was enjoying it immensely. But, he knew that the conversation he was going to have with her in a few minutes would totally ruin her mood.

"Funny, I've had the same fantasy my whole life."

She frowned. "Really? Being the prisoner of a handsome police officer?"

"Yeah, but only if he looked as good as me!"

They both laughed as they jumped into the car.

Wyatt steered his way out of the airport parking lot and headed northeast along Highway #3A towards Nelson.

Then, he took a couple of deep breaths and allowed the tone of his voice to change.

"Willy has aged about ten years in just over a week, Allison. What the hell did your doctors do to my dad?"

CHAPTER 40

Willy was sitting hunched over the kitchen table; Helen beside him, rubbing his arm, trying hard to soothe him. It wasn't working.

"Allison's here, Dad. Remember her?"

Willy squinted, and then slipped on some specs.

"I never had to wear these darn things before, but now I do. Picked them up at the pharmacy today. Might need prescription glasses, though."

He gazed up at her, and Allison was relieved to see the recognition suddenly appear in his eyes.

"Yes, you're the hotel lady. You're building one here, and you wanted me to…I'm sorry, I can't remember exactly what you wanted me to do. But…look at me. I don't think you'll want me now."

Allison walked over to him and rubbed his back. Then, she leaned down and held out her hand. He shook it, and she was shocked at how much weaker his handshake felt than the last time she'd seen him just a few short weeks ago. He was robust then, and as vibrant as a man twenty years younger. Now, he just seemed…old.

She looked up at Wyatt. The puzzled look on his face reflected how she felt.

Allison could sense the tears welling up in her eyes. Willy had indeed aged at least ten years since he'd been down to the clinic in Atlanta. He didn't look his full eighty-seven years yet, but he did look mid-seventies. And, at the pace he'd aged already, in another week he would indeed be eighty-seven.

Helen whispered. "This has been happening ever since he got back from Atlanta. I can see the changes every single day. What have you people done to my husband?"

Allison shook her head. “I have no idea, but I’m going to find out. I’m so sorry.”

Wyatt sat down on one of the kitchen chairs and glared at her. He was looking at her now in a way Allison had never seen in the short time she’d known him. At this moment, he looked like…a police officer.

“My dad has always seemed young for his age. That was presumably one of the things that appealed to you about him being a spokesperson for your new hotel here. He agreed to a medical check-up at your clinic, to qualify him.”

Wyatt gestured his hand in Willy’s direction. “And, this is how he comes back? He’s aged virtually overnight. What did they do to cause this? They weren’t really supposed to do anything at all—just some blood tests, EKG, stress tests—things like that. It was supposed to have been just a goddamned physical.”

Allison lowered her eyes to the floor, and then just as quickly raised them again. In an instant, she knew what she had to do. Decisiveness had never been a problem for her, and that skill roared to the surface now in front of these three wonderful, innocent people.

“Can I borrow Willy’s car?”

Helen jumped up and pulled the keys off a hook on the wall. She handed them to her.

“It’s the Cadillac on the rear driveway.”

“Thank you, Helen. Now, where’s the nearest phone booth, if you still have any left?”

“Three blocks south along Baker Street, in the parking lot of the Mountain Mall.”

Wyatt stood. “Why do that? Just use our landline here, or your cell phone.”

Allison shook her head. “No, I can’t—not for the conversation I’ll be having. Be back soon.”

“I’ll go with you.”

“No, Wyatt, this isn’t a conversation for someone in your position to listen to. I won’t be long.”

*****

After three long rings, he picked up. The distinctive southern accent that she knew so well—Doctor Phillip Lansing, chief physician for the Majestic 12 clinic in Atlanta.

"Lansing, here."

"Hello, Phil. It's Allison Fisher."

"Oh, hi there, Allison. Long time no talk."

"I need to speak with you off the grid. Go to the phone booth in the lobby of the CDC, and phone me back at this number." She read out the phone number from the sticker on the phone.

"I'm in Canada, so punch in the international access code."

Silence at the other end.

"Phil? Did you hear me?"

"What's this about, Allison?"

"Just call me back within ten minutes, Phil. I'll be waiting."

She strummed her fingers against the glass of the booth while she waited. Allison knew it would be tough to get information out of Phil, because it was apparent by the appearance of Willy Carson that more was being done at that clinic than even she was aware of. But, she had no doubts whatsoever that Chad Powers was fully aware of the procedures that were being performed there.

At the seven-minute mark, the phone rang.

She didn't waste time on small talk. "Willy Carson was supposed to get an injection of some sort that would offset the terrible side-effects he was getting from x-rays. But, he's aged ten years in just over a week. What the hell did you do to him?"

"That's something I can't talk about, Allison. We did nothing that would cause him any real harm. He's…just…returning to normal now."

"He's one of the 'receptors.' We weren't supposed to do anything to those people."

She heard an exasperated sigh at the other end. "Relax. His ability to receive messages is still intact. He's just lost some of his special talents, and his youth. And, indeed, he won't have any more reactions to x-rays. That's guaranteed."

"Does Chad know about this?"

"Yes, he does. And, he does run the show, Allison. He doesn't have to tell you or the others everything."

"Do you know everything, Phil?"

A few seconds of silence. Then, "Yes, Chad brought me up to date on what's out there and the estimated timelines. He trusted me and, of course, he needed to, with what he was asking me to do here at the clinic. I haven't told anyone else."

"These people here in Canada have become friends of mine, Phil. It's personal for me now. I want to know what you did to Willy."

"I can't tell you that, Allison."

"Phil, I'll make this very clear and I won't repeat myself. Since you say you know everything, you must know about all the doctors, scientists, astronomers, and journalists who have died or disappeared over the last decade."

Allison could hear his heavy breathing. He was starting to get the message.

"Did you hear me?"

Softly, "Yes, I heard you, Allison."

"Tell me, Phil."

"I…can't."

"No one will know that it came from you. You have my word on that, and my word is a hell of a lot better than that bastard's, Powers. But, you also have my word that if you don't tell me right now, I have resources available to me as a member of Majestic 12 that can make you disappear almost as fast as it will take me to hang up this phone."

Under his breath, Phil muttered, "Oh, God."

"God can't help you now—in fact, He probably can't help any of us. Whatever short time you have left, Phil, do the right thing to make sure you're alive to enjoy it."

Another long silence. Rapid breathing was the only sound coming through the phone.

He finally talked, so slowly and softly that Allison had to strain to hear him.

"I inserted a chip in through his nasal passage and attached it to the external skin of the pituitary gland.

"It has a long-life battery, and emits signals that trigger the aging hormones of the gland. The alien beams seem to have had the effect of deactivating that aspect in all of the victims.

"While their DNA did indeed change, and they all became living 'receptors,' there was the unexpected suppression of the pituitary gland that not only slowed down aging and somehow gave them incredible strength, but also made each of the victims subject to transparency from exposure to radiation."

Alison sighed. "You've done this procedure to others as well, I presume."

"Yes. Only the few who were careless about the x-ray instructions. About a dozen or so."

"Can this chip be easily removed?"

"Yes, through the nose again. The chip is on the left side of the gland—*his* left."

"Side effects?"

"After it's removed, the aging process will slow down again. He'll get his strength and vitality back, and unfortunately will once again be subject to transparency. But, that's about it. Well, maybe a bit of a nose bleed, too."

"Okay, you have my word, Phil, that this will stay between you and me. And, you won't be harmed unless you decide to run to Chad and blab that I threatened you into telling me. I'll know if you do, and I can promise you it will be one of the last things you'll do."

*****

Wyatt was leaning against the door frame of his parents' room, watching the two of them cuddled up together on the bed.

Helen was holding a handkerchief up under Willy's nose, catching the streams of blood that came rushing out sporadically. He was trying his best to keep his head tilted back, but every once in a while he'd get careless and the blood would stream out again.

"The doctor said this would only continue for a few hours or so, Dad, so be a good patient."

"I know. I had one of these when I came back from Atlanta, too. I'll put up with it."

Allison was sitting on the edge of the bed, watching them. Wyatt hadn't said very much to her since they'd returned from the hospital.

He'd been blown away by how accurate her assessment was about what needed to be done. So was the doctor. That phone call she'd made from the booth must have been a real doozy.

After they x-rayed Willy and saw that insidious little chip perched on the nether regions of his brain, it was clear that Allison knew what she was talking about.

Wyatt had protested when the doctor insisted on doing an x-ray on his dad, but Allison had calmly pulled him off to the side and whispered, "*Don't worry. He won't go transparent this time. But, once that chip comes out, it's back to the old story.*"

How had she known that? How could she have possibly known that x-rays made his dad go transparent?

A million questions were running through his head.

And, he was impatient now—he wanted answers. But, he didn't know where to start. Why had that Atlanta clinic inserted a chip up his dad's nose? He'd gone down there just for a simple check-up. What the hell was that chip all about? And why had he aged so much since he returned from Atlanta?

Wyatt decided to start his barrage of questions with that one.

"Allison, why did that chip cause aging?"

She looked up at him, unmistakable sadness in her beautiful blue eyes.

"It was designed to trigger the aging hormones of the pituitary gland, and to eliminate the side effect of transparency from x-rays. When your dad was beamed during the Korean War, his DNA changed and his pituitary gland slowed down its production of aging hormones."

Wyatt felt his heart racing, and a rush of blood to his face. It seemed as if the world he'd been living in had just been an illusion. First, the revelation that his dad had shared with him a few weeks ago about his powers, and about the weird thing that happened during the Korean War. And, now, this beautiful hotel executive seemed to know more about his dad's life than even he had known until just recently. Was he losing his mind—or living in some bizarre alternate universe?

"How did you know about that beam incident during the war, Allison? And, I never told you about his reaction to x-rays. How do you know this stuff?"

"We know all about your dad. We've been watching him for an awful long time, and have had unfettered access to his medical history his entire adult life."

"Who's 'we?'"

"It's about time we all had a long chat."

Wyatt took a step towards her. "He was supposed to get a simple medical check-up at your clinic for the hotel spokesperson position. Was that just a ruse?"

Allison lowered her pretty blue eyes and let out a long sigh.

"I won't be building a hotel here in Nelson, Wyatt. Not now, not ever."

CHAPTER 41

John Hartford paced the floor of his prison. Well, not exactly a prison, but it felt like it. Right now, it was a safe sanctuary, and he thanked his lucky stars that Allison had known exactly what to do when they were running for their lives.

He never could have imagined that his career as a U.S. senator would lead to this—hiding out in a luxury condominium underneath a vineyard in Canada.

It had only been a day and a night so far, but it felt like a month. Allison had left him alone, telling him she was flying to a place called Nelson. Some other backwater town, John assumed—he didn't really care. He just wanted her to hurry back, so they could figure out what to do next.

John tried imagining what it would be like having to live down in a place like this for weeks, months or—God forbid—years. It was too bizarre a thought. Maybe for some people it would be okay, but, for a person like John, who was accustomed to using his brain constantly, it would be mind torture.

The absence of windows was one of the worst things—the inability to look outside just to see what the weather was like, made John realize how important the simple things in life were. In his busy public life, he took little luxuries like that for granted. But, no longer—he would now treasure every chance he got to enjoy the great outdoors, to breathe in the fresh air.

He continued to pace aimlessly, from the living room, down the hall to the main entrance, and then back again.

Suddenly, he remembered the bar—walked over and pulled a bottle of cognac off the top shelf. Poured himself a straight shot and sucked it back. The strong liquid took his breath away, but he welcomed the feeling.

Made him feel alive.

He had no doubt that down here, after a long period of time, it would begin to feel like death—or at least make one wish for the arrival of death.

What would be the point of living if this was all there was? And at his age, what would be the point of wasting years down in this luxury dungeon? Then, to go back out again to what? Desolation? A barren landscape? Or—the most horrific thought of all—a world ruled by alien beings? If that was the way life would be, there would no point ever leaving this underground sanctuary.

He shuddered, and poured himself another glass. After he downed that one, he poured another.

John walked over to the couch and sat down—figured it was the smart thing to do before the cognac kicked in.

He picked up the remote control, turned on the TV, and surfed through the channels—only Canadian shows and news. Not even one American channel, even though he knew this little town called Osoyoos was close to the U.S. border.

Damn Allison—she'd probably done something to limit the cable input to Canadian content only. For his benefit and safety, of course.

He'd suspected the same thing about the WIFI. There was a desktop computer in the office area and John had already played around with it. While he was able to get internet connectivity, he could only surf sites on a Canadian browser. It was almost more like an *intranet* rather than an internet. A local area network in place of broad band. Very little else was available. Email applications were blocked, as were Skype, Twitter, and Facebook. All of them refused to open in the browser. And, it wouldn't respond to his attempts to download the apps.

He smiled. Allison Fisher was not only drop-dead gorgeous, but she was also very sly, very sharp. That darn woman was incredibly capable—could look several steps ahead and plan for every outcome.

Well, she was an astronomer by education, so visualizing beyond the obvious was second nature to her.

And…she had that strange ability to read minds. What was that all about? She'd shoved her fingers into her ears, and popped them right back out again. Then, for a short period of time, she could read and see his thoughts.

While that skill was unsettling, her demonstration of it during those tense moments back at his house helped convince him to trust her. And, thank God he had, because Clint and those other two goons had come there to kill him. If it wasn't for Allison and her weird skill, he wouldn't be alive right now.

For the entire duration of their mad dash to freedom—trail-riding through the forest, racing by boat up Lake Champlain into Quebec, flying from Montreal to Penticton—John had concentrated hard on trying not to think about how attracted he was to her.

He was scared to death that she might be able to read his mind if she stuck those fingers in her ears again. But, the more he tried not to think of her—especially when they were relaxing on the plane—the more she crept into his mind.

It was really hard to try not to think of something; it just seemed to make it worse.

He thought back over all the years he'd known her and wondered if she'd always had that power. On more than one occasion, he'd undressed her in his mind. Did she know? Was she horrified? Did she think he was some kind of perv?

A shiver shot up his back as he thought about some of the fantasies that popped into his mind when he'd been with her at conferences, dinners, or out for drinks. Just quick little thoughts at certain moments. Had she picked up on them?

It wasn't that she was just a gorgeous woman—that was the least of what made her attractive. There were plenty of gorgeous women around, each one usually more gorgeous than the last one. They were a dime a dozen, and John never had any problems with having to choose. But, most were forgettable.

What made Allison so attractive was her brain—at least to John, anyway. A lot of men wouldn't like that too much, but John found that quality irresistible. Her ability to argue and debate, being able to take charge of any situation, her uncanny ability to foresee and instantly calculate solutions in her head.

She was a woman with an abundance of energy and completely adept and comfortable with taking action.

John found all of these things irresistible. Coupled with the way she looked, Allison was the kind of lady who was hard to push out of his mind.

Which made his efforts to keep her from reading his mind even more challenging than it would be for just the garden-variety beauty.

It wasn't that he was a dirty old man or anything—he just didn't like the fact that she could see him literally drooling over her. It gave her an edge he didn't have—she knew how he felt, but he had no idea how she felt.

He was vulnerable, which wasn't something the Senior Senator from Vermont was accustomed to at all. John was used to being in control and, aside from Allison's weird talent, this situation he was in right now was making him feel very restless. And useless.

There had to be something he could do.

He walked over to the bar and poured another cognac. Just one more. Might help him take a nap.

It was only 3:00 in the afternoon, but time seemed to lose all meaning underground. It really didn't matter whether it was morning, afternoon, or night. It was all the same. Just a dreary existence. An existence without purpose. No reason to get up, but every reason in the world to just go back to bed.

John finished his drink and stretched out on the couch. He thought about all the things Allison had told him. He was astonished that as a United States senator he had known so little. Until Farmington had passed along that documentation to him, he'd had no idea that this secret organization existed. How was that possible? He was a senator, for God's sake! Part of the government!

Of course, he'd participated in discussions over the years with other members of Congress about how some things seemed to happen that were a surprise to them all, things that put them at loggerheads with whoever the president was at the time. Upon reflection, John now realized that a lot of the times the presidents themselves had seemed puzzled, at a loss for words, scrambling for explanations.

He remembered Allison's mention of JFK and how he had demanded to know everything there was to know about the UFO files. The C.I.A. had turned him down, ignored every single request he'd made. And, then, eventually, he was killed.

The C.I.A. probably knew a lot more than anyone knew, as well as every single detail about Majestic 12.

Allison seemed to think it was still ultra-secret, and maybe that was true insofar as how it started back in Truman's days. But, a lot of time had passed since then, and secrets generally didn't stay secret too long. John was convinced that Majestic 12 was just the tip of the iceberg on command and control.

But, either way, regardless of how many other agencies were in on it, Majestic 12 was clearly a 'government within a government.' Which was a horrible realization for a dedicated and idealistic politician like John Hartford.

John knew he was an idealist—which was both a negative and a positive. A negative because he could become easily disillusioned and disappointed. A positive because he was convinced that he could actually make a difference. He truly believed that good government was essential to America's survival and prosperity. And, just like the Founding Fathers, a few good people could make an impact.

Now, with the world getting ready to crash down around them, he was stuck underground, hiding like a scared rabbit.

Deep down inside, he always knew that the natural catastrophes and climate changes that had been accelerating over the years had deeper, more logical reasons than just carbon emissions and greenhouse gases. He'd always felt that there was something more powerful at work—the changes had been far too severe and had been coming far too fast, faster than scientists had estimated.

Now, his inner suspicions had been confirmed—he wished they hadn't been, but at least it was a known quantity for him now. The doubts that had been nagging his mind for so long were gone.

A planet named Gargantuan was on its way. Its magnetic pull was tearing the Earth apart, and its effects had been slowly but surely increasing for decades. To the point now that, because it was so relatively close, the effects were getting more severe by the day. It had been just a gradual thing in the 70s, 80s, and 90s, so gradual that people just wrote it off with the comment, "*Well, that's the weather for you. If you don't like it, wait a minute.*"

No one had a clue that something sinister was sneaking up on their peaceful little world. That their world would never be the same again, and that most wouldn't even survive to realize that horror.

If the magnetic attraction didn't destroy Earth, the damn interloper had colonies of beings living in it. Underground, just like him.

No one knew what they looked like, telescopes hadn't picked up any living beings on the surface, but there was plenty of evidence that colonies existed underground. There were tunnels, the openings large enough for small spaceships to enter and exit. And, on the backside of Gargantuan, there were probably larger tunnels for the larger ships.

Or, perhaps those ships were always just hovering…somewhere. There had been enough UFO sightings over the last 100 years to indicate that they were possibly everywhere. There had even been alien bodies discovered, according to Allison. Little beings that looked like bizarre deformed human toddlers.

But, were they the same beings that inhabited Gargantuan? Or, were they from a different source entirely? What indeed was the Earth up against—an assault from several different worlds perhaps?

She had told him that the dark side of the Moon had what Majestic 12 and NASA determined as being 'scout bases.' What the hell? Scout bases?

No wonder these UFOs were being seen everywhere if they could easily zoom in from a planetary body as close as the Moon. Had they been inhabiting the Moon, underground perhaps, just like Gargantuan? Surveying Earth for the big year when Gargantuan was close enough for a mass invasion by the major forces? Were those scout bases picking the spots, the vulnerable spots? Was it their job over the last century to intervene and disrupt our wars, to make certain we didn't harm the planet too much before Gargantuan arrived?

Did the living beings on Gargantuan plan on taking over Earth and moving out of their dark barren planet? Would they even be able to survive in our atmosphere? Right now, they lived underground and had some kind of artificial atmosphere, but had they adapted? Or did they have the technology to adapt?

Or, was it possible that these scout bases on the Moon had already sent inhabitants to live amongst us…or under us? Had they been here for longer than we would want to know? Did they move amongst us? Had they tested everything to the point that they already knew the Gargantuan residents would survive just fine?

The aliens would only have one shot at it—to be able to extricate mass numbers of living beings from Gargantuan and move them down to Earth.

There would be a relatively short window of about a year or two, as Gargantuan rounded the Earth in its elliptical orbit. Back around the Sun again, for the beginning of its next 3,600-year orbit.

If they waited too long to migrate down to Earth, it would be too late. They would be too far away for a mass evacuation and would have to wait another 3,600 years before their next chance at it.

Maybe it was now or never?

John's brain wouldn't stop spinning. The questions kept coming and the paranoia was getting worse by the minute, not the least bit helped by the four shots of cognac.

It was either the booze or his idealistic nature, maybe a bit of both, but John was convinced that he had a role to play right now. Not later, but right now.

He wanted to be the next president, regardless of whether the country was in a mess or not.

The country…indeed the world…needed him.

So did the current sitting president. He had to have already been brought into the loop on all this, and he would need a few good men around him, rather than those paid hacks that made up his Cabinet.

The president would need someone from Congress beside him on this crisis, someone who truly represented the people. Someone he could trust.

He needed Senator John Hartford.

There had to be solutions: military, chemical, biological. They just had to pick the best ones; hell, maybe all of them would be needed.

But, they couldn't all just hide underground and let this happen without a fight.

It was entirely possible that Allison's fears could be wrong, too. Maybe Gargantuan had already done its worst damage to the Earth and nothing more of any note would happen.

John needed to talk to some scientists.

Maybe the little creatures who inhabited Gargantuan would just leave them the hell alone? Maybe they didn't want Earth at all. That fear might have been misplaced. The worst case scenario may not happen.

John got up and walked over to the phone on the kitchen counter. Like everything else, it too had limited scope. And, no buttons to push. It automatically rang through to one destination as soon as the receiver was picked up.

The winery office.

"Hello?"

"Hi, Gerndle. It's John Hartford."

He heard her giggle. "Well, of course it is, John. You're the only one down there!"

"Yes…yes, of course. Listen, Allison said I could come up and take short walks outside if the coast was clear. That I should check with you first."

"That sounds lovely—it's a beautiful day up here. I'll make a pot of tea for us. Derik is here, too; you haven't met him yet. It would be nice. And, yes, the coast is clear—no strange people around."

"Great. I'll be right up. And…could you make that a pot of coffee instead of tea? I think I need a jolt of caffeine."

"No problem, John. See you soon." She giggled again. "Can you find your way without directions?"

"Not funny, Gerndle, not funny at all."

John hung up the phone. Before heading to the main door for his climb up the shaft, he stuffed his iPhone into his front pocket. No cell reception down in this place—he'd tried already.

He'd find some private time outside, a spot with a strong signal, to make a phone call or two and check for messages.

Today, he was going to take charge of his life again. There were things he could do.

His mission in life was public service, and he felt like a useless little coward hiding underground. He wasn't doing the duty he'd been elected to do—in fact, he was abandoning it.

Allison was only doing what she thought was best. She was just trying to keep him safe and he loved her for that.

But, he was a long way from home now. A long way from danger.

And, he was a United States Senator, for God's sake!

That had meaning.

Real meaning.

CHAPTER 42

It was a bright morning, one of the most brilliant of any morning he could remember over the last few glorious summer months.

Or, maybe it just felt that way—maybe he appreciated it more today.

Wyatt took his steaming cup of coffee out onto the deck and gazed westward over the lake. The water was already starting its daily dance of sparkling diamonds, even though the Sun had just started peeking up over the mountains to the east.

He walked around the corner point of the deck and rested his cup on the railing. Then, he raised his hand up to shield his eyes as he stared in the other direction, east towards the sunrise.

Wyatt put his sunglasses on and stole a longer glance. The Sun's glare was strong and, despite his concentrated stare, he couldn't see anything else in the vicinity of the big yellow ball. But, as Allison had forewarned, there were indeed cloudy streaks in the sky across where the Sun was rising. They crisscrossed each other and as he watched he could see them slowly spreading out, creating a cloudy eastern sky out of what had started out as a lovely shade of Robin's egg blue.

Chemtrails, she'd called them. On certain days—when, due to atmospheric changes, it was easier for people to see the "thing"—specially-equipped planes would go up and paint the canvas. Shrouding from view any possible sight of the intruder.

Then, late in the day when the Sun was setting, the planes would do it all over again in the western sky.

Oftentimes, during the middle of the day, the chemtrails would appear again, but their main purpose then wasn't to hide anything. Due to the position of the Earth and the sheer strength and brightness of the Sun at that time of day, it was impossible to see the "thing" anyway.

No, in the middle of the day, chemtrails were intended to shield humans from the extreme radiation that was getting through due to the weakening of the Earth's magnetosphere—or at least this was how Wyatt had understood it.

Allison had said that the best times to see the "thing" were at early sunrise and late sunset, when the rays of the Sun weren't as bright and the Sun itself was more distinguishable as just a round ball, instead of being a burning sphere. The glare of that sphere during the day made it impossible for people to look up.

But, sunrise and sunset were different. At those times, with the weaker rays of the Sun being not only diffused by Earth's atmosphere, but also bouncing off its horizon, Gargantuan would sometimes make its appearance.

Not always, just sometimes.

It all depended on the air quality that day, degree of cloud cover, and the richness of the ozone layer. When those measurements were taken by meteorologists and astronomers, the alarm would go out…or not.

If the alarm went out, then so did the planes.

At various places across the planet, this scenario played out, day in, day out—morning, noon and night. It was an expensive undertaking and one of the reasons why government deficits were climbing faster than could ever be explained to taxpayers. Balanced budgets were a thing of the past; deficits were the 'new normal.'

But, it sounded as if deficits were now the least of the world's worries.

The chemtrail spraying was not an equal opportunity undertaking. It was selective, designed for those areas of the world where people would be most likely to notice or ask questions about alarming sights in the sky.

So, for cost reasons, cities were the first priority. They had the most educated humans, ones not so easily fooled. If they saw the ghostly image of a strange ball in the sky that wasn't supposed to be there, they were the ones most likely to ask.

Next on the list were areas that were vacation or retirement getaways. These places tended to have the clearest of skies, well away from the city pollution. As well, their residents tended to be the types who weren't working, or at least weren't working all that hard. Because their lifestyles were more relaxed, they also tended to be the types of people who would take the time to gaze at the sky, even set up a telescope.

Other than that, even the cities themselves were prioritized—right down to education and income levels. At the low end, chemtrailing was ignored—the people were too ignorant, poor, stoned, or drunk to understand anything as complex as the sky and what it was supposed to look like.

And, neither would those people even care—in those inner city areas, crime was their most cherished pastime and running around with their heads down was more common than gazing up at the sky.

So, countries and cities were able to keep costs under control by labelling every area under their jurisdiction, and prioritizing their spraying accordingly.

Some countries chose to opt out completely, because the people being governed were too primitive or were already living under varying degrees of martial law, dictatorship, or communism.

North Korea was a perfect example—they hadn't yet had even one day of chemtrailing. Myanmar and Bangladesh were two others who chose to opt out. According to Allison, the list of opt-outs was actually quite long.

But, generally, in the developed world, there was 100 percent compliance.

Wyatt had asked her about the risk of people enquiring about the chemtrailing activity itself.

She replied to that with a really good question. "*How many times have you asked about it?*"

He gulped. "*Not once.*"

"*And, you're actually a branch of government yourself, highly educated, and you used to hold a senior position in Canada's national investigative police force. If anyone would ask, it would be you, don't you think?*"

Wyatt felt sheepish. "*You're right. I feel kind of stupid now. I never really took much notice of them before. Sure, I'd see the streaks up there, and always noticed that they eventually just expanded into clouds. And, I'd read something about them once in a while in the newspaper, but that would usually just make my eyes glaze over. It would just be one more 'conspiracy theory' in my view, people looking under their beds for monsters.*"

Allison smiled at that remark. "*Don't feel stupid. That's what we've counted on with the chemtrailing program. They do indeed look just like weird little skinny clouds, and they're designed to expand into authentic-looking clouds within just a matter of an hour or so after spraying.*

"*And, we also counted on the 'conspiracy-theory' eye-rolling. We've done a superb job of making every conspiracy theorist sound like a whack-job. They have no credibility, due to our propaganda against them. So, only the smartest people listen to them and research these things—but those people are in such few numbers that they're easily ignored...or managed.*

"*We count on the fact that the average person doesn't look up at the sky, could care less about what goes on around him, and is far too busy looking at his smartphone or taking selfies. This is a sad fact of human beings that actually works in our favor.*

"*We're not at the zombie apocalypse yet, but we're getting close. There are a lot of shallow brain-dead people walking around, too self-obsessed to care about some weird looking clouds. And, we'd rather take the chance on having to explain chemtrails than having to explain Gargantuan.*"

Wyatt took a long sip of his *Tim Horton's* dark roast coffee, and gazed once more at the rapidly rising sun. Nope, nothing there...although he knew now that it *was* there. He marveled at how fast the chemtrails had expanded outward in just the last few minutes. They were actually starting to look like genuine clouds now. He shook his head in astonishment.

Sheer genius.

Suddenly, there was a gentle hand on his shoulder.

"Penny for your thoughts?"

He turned around and smiled. Allison was standing behind him with her own cup of coffee, adorned in a dark blue dressing gown that fell all the way to her ankles. It brought out the blue in her eyes, which this morning had the hue of an azure sea. The gown was slightly open in the front and Wyatt fought the urge to steal a glance.

He chuckled. "I think you can guess what thoughts your penny would buy you this morning. Sleep well?"

"Yes, I sure did. That guest room of yours is lovely, and the bed is the most comfortable I've ever slept in. I didn't even hear you snoring—the walls are nicely soundproofed."

"Not that soundproofed. I heard you as clear as if you were in the same room."

"You did not! You're lying! I don't snore!"

"Oh, yes you do, dear lady. Hate to break it to you."

Allison pretended to sulk. "There are some things you shouldn't be honest about with a lady. Didn't your mom ever teach you that?"

Wyatt shook his head. "No, in fact, she warned me about ladies who snore. She said they're too darn smart for their own good."

"Ah, a back-handed compliment. I'll accept it."

Wyatt grimaced. "No joke, you are very smart. It's kind of intimidating at times, but also very stimulating. I love it."

"Thanks, but don't be intimidated, Wyatt. Please—just tap me on the head if I start blowing my horn too much. I get carried away with the things I know about. Everybody has a different kind of intelligence, I think. Mine was borne from many years in school. It takes a long time to become an astrophysicist, and I think all that time in school can make some of us kind of 'bookish,' almost professorial."

Wyatt squeezed her hand. "No need to explain your smarts to me. I love it, and I don't think you got it from school—you were just made that way. It makes you a very intriguing woman."

She smiled warmly at him. "Thanks. I do feel comfortable around you, so I appreciate your saying that. It's nice that I can just be myself, and that you're secure enough to handle it."

Wyatt took his cup off the railing and walked over to the umbrella table. "C'mon, let's sit here and look out at the lake while we sip our coffee."

Allison joined him and sat on one of the chairs facing the lake—careful not to let the dressing gown open up and show off too much of her legs.

Wyatt sighed. "That was quite the bombshell you laid on us last night. I'll have to ring my parents today to see how well they're adjusting to this new world we suddenly find ourselves living in."

"We could just drive over there, Wyatt. They might need me to fill in the blanks for them on a few things."

Wyatt nodded. "That might be a good idea, but you were pretty detailed. Might be too much information for them already."

"Maybe for you, too. You were quiet at dinner last night. I made my roast lamb specialty and you either loved it so much you couldn't talk...or, you were in shock."

"I loved the meal—and I'm sorry I wasn't great company. I was just trying to absorb everything you'd told us. It was a shock. You've known about this for a long time, but for us to suddenly find out that our world may be coming to an end..."

Allison reached over and rubbed his arm. "I did enjoy working with those shiny appliances, though. You were right—they are like brand new. You should learn to cook."

"I know how to cook—I just can't be bothered most of the time. Tell you what—I'll make dinner for you tonight. Can you stay in town a bit longer?"

"I'd love to. Maybe for a couple more days, then I have to fly back to Penticton."

"What's there?"

"Well, from there, I'll be driving down to Osoyoos. I own a vineyard there, and there's someone waiting for me—it's all related to this subject. I'll tell you about that over dinner tonight."

"So, you told us last night that you're able to read minds. A power that passed down to you from your dad. Sounds like he had the exact same experience that my dad did—zapped by a beam from one of those alien crafts."

Allison crossed her legs and took a sip of her coffee. "Yes, his DNA was changed like your dad's was, and when I was born I had a transcended version of that new DNA. I think that's the only power I have, but who knows? But…you must have inherited something, too, Wyatt. You haven't volunteered what that is. Tell me…I know there's something."

He let out a long sigh. "I've discovered that I'm a 'remote viewer.' That's how I managed to track down my mom when she was kidnapped. I was able to project myself and see the whole thing. It was weird."

Wyatt could tell that she didn't even seem surprised.

"I know all about 'remote viewing.' It's a real phenomenon. Used by most of the world's intelligence agencies. Sometimes, they hit on things, and sometimes they don't. It's an erratic talent, but, when it's in full force, it's very powerful and very accurate."

"Aside from saving my mom a few weeks ago, I can't see that I'd want to use it that often. It's very eerie—actually, quite disturbing."

"In your job, you could use it to solve crimes."

Wyatt laughed. "Back at the RCMP, I could have used it a lot, but here in Nelson the most serious crime we usually have is spitting on the street."

"Well, I'm thinking of a purpose for it."

"What's that?"

"I don't want to talk about it right now. I will, though—have to give it some thought. One thing I've learned about remote viewing, is that it's most effective when the performer doesn't have a lot of time to think about what he's going to focus on. Works best when it's fairly sudden and spontaneous."

"I think you're right—that's how it happened when I used it on my mom. It wasn't planned at all, because I didn't even know I had the skill. It just happened when I was standing out in the alley talking to witnesses."

"Yes, traumatic events can sometimes trigger it." Allison grinned. "We may have to find a way to traumatize you again."

Wyatt frowned. "I don't know if I like the sound of that. So, tell me about your mind-reading skill. You said you only get it for a few seconds at a time, and you have to do something to trigger it?"

Allison inserted her index fingers into her ears and immediately popped them back out again. "That's all I have to do. Do you want me to tell you what you're thinking?"

"Yes."

"You're thinking that there's no way I'll be able to read your mind because you're focusing it on emptiness."

Wyatt laughed. "Geez, that's exactly right."

"Now, you're thinking that you'd love to kiss my lips. I can actually see an image of you puckering up."

Wyatt put his hands over his eyes. "Stop it! I'm embarrassed now!"

Suddenly, he felt gentle fingers prying his hands away from his eyes. He opened them and there she was, leaning over him, dressing gown hanging slightly open.

Her voice was soft. "Don't be embarrassed. You can't read minds, but if you could you'd know that I was thinking the same thing. So, pucker up, Chief."

She kissed him, slowly and gently, and he responded willingly. Her lips were just as he'd imagined them to be—luscious and seductive. It was only a short-lived moment, but it was a romantic one and, in Wyatt's mind, it held the promise of more moments to come.

Their faces pulled back at the same time and they smiled at each other.

Wyatt didn't know what to say, and he was relieved that Allison decided to break the silence. "Well, I'm glad our first kiss is over with. What's for breakfast?"

Wyatt laughed so hard he started choking. "That was…the best icebreaker…I've ever heard."

"How's this for a sequel? We know now that each of has at least one DNA gift passed down by our fathers." She smiled in that cute mischievous way that showed off her dimples. "I wonder if we have any more gifts, huh?"

"I'm willing to find out, if you are."

She grinned again. "I sure am."

Wyatt nervously jumped to his feet. "Okay, time for another icebreaker—or a cold shower! I think I should start breakfast."

"You do that, Mr. Policeman."

Wyatt grabbed their empty cups and started heading back inside. But, then he turned around. His cheeks felt flushed, but at this moment he didn't care if she noticed, especially since hers had also turned a nice crimson color.

He had something he wanted to ask her and it couldn't wait.

"Allison, is all that you told us engrained in stone? Is it inevitable?"

She shook her head.

"No, as I mentioned to you all yesterday, what I shared are predictions. Scientific stuff—best guesses. You now know, though, that the weird weather and changes that have been taking place are due to Gargantuan. That's fact.

"Will it get worse? Yes. Might it get better? Yes—after Gargantuan makes its closest pass and begins moving back out again.

"How much worse will it get? We don't know for sure, but we've planned for the worst case scenario. It will come within fourteen million miles and, when you consider that the Sun is about ninety-two million miles from us, that gives you an idea of how close it will be.

"Right now, Gargantuan seems to be about 120 million miles away, and the puzzling thing about it is that its progression towards us seems to stall from time to time. Which doesn't make much sense, considering that it's in a definite orbit. It should continue towards us at a reasonably consistent pace."

"Why would that be?"

"We think that there's an artificial means, on, or inside the planet, of controlling its rate of orbit speed."

"From the aliens that live there?"

Allison nodded. "Yes, they seem to have some means of controlling the planet's position in orbit. Sometimes, it moves at a consistent rate, and then sometimes it seems to stop dead in its tracks—in astronomical terms, of course."

"How is that possible?"

"Well, we have to plan for the fact that they're an advanced intelligence. They might have figured something out that suits their purposes, whatever those purposes may be. We think we know what it might be, though."

"What?"

"Something we're also doing ourselves. Something that may be a solution if we decide that the worst case scenario is going to happen. It might buy us a few extra years, or might even give us a permanent solution."

Wyatt came back to the table and sat down. "I'm intrigued. Continue."

Allison clasped her hands together and began cracking her knuckles. "It's a project I was assigned to…back in its earlier stages, when I worked…at the Jet Propulsion Laboratory. NASA and the JPL were both involved…in a big way. I'm…still involved as a member of Majestic 12;

the communications liaison director."

"You seem hesitant talking about this. Your voice is shaking a bit. What is it, Allison? Spit it out."

"You've heard of the project. In fact, Stephen Hawking got a lot of publicity a couple of years ago when he spoke out against it. He's been silent since then, because we brought him in on it and he now knows the true purpose.

"It's huge, Wyatt, and it's scary as hell—but it may be the only chance we have."

Wyatt felt his heart racing. "I'm waiting."

"It's located deep underneath the Franco-Swiss border, an engineering marvel to say the least. We don't even know exactly what it may unleash upon us, it's that scary. But, it also may be a planet-saver.

"You've read about it, I'm sure—the Large Hadron Collider, known to the world as CERN."

CHAPTER 43

Wyatt walked over to the kitchen sink, turned on the tap, and splashed cold water on his face. Lots of cold water. He wanted to wake up from what was starting to feel like a bad dream.

Could this summer get any stranger?

He yanked a dish towel off the rack on the oven and dried himself. Allison was sitting at the dining room table, patiently awaiting his return.

Just a mere hour ago, they'd been enjoying the spectacular view of the lake out on his deck.

Then, she'd dropped the bombshell.

He'd tried his best to absorb what she was telling him, but the facts just got jumbled around in his brain. The specifics were mind-numbingly technical and the implications were beyond belief.

It seemed like a bad dream—one of those fantasies that seemed to make sense when you were asleep, but quickly veered to the bizarre once you were awake. When rational logic and common sense finally took over from the subconscious.

Wyatt shook his head in an effort to clear the cobwebs as he walked back to the table to join her. He pulled his chair out to the jarring sound of the feet scraping along the hardwood floor, and plopped his weary body down.

His weariness came from not getting a break from this—the entire summer had been consumed by one revelation after another. Ever since his very own father had been betrayed by an x-ray machine.

And, now, this.

He'd almost gotten used to the idea of an incoming heavenly body called Gargantuan, but then she'd hit him with one more terrifying twist.

From the luscious mouth of a beautiful mysterious lady, whom he knew now without the shadow of a doubt he had strong feelings for.

That fact complicated things even further. He found it difficult to be angry with her for deceiving him and his father. These revelations she'd laid on him put the deceptions themselves way down on the totem pole. They seemed petty compared to what she'd told him. Being lied to was hardly a big deal when stacked up against the shocking knowledge she'd shared with him.

He stared into her hypnotic blue eyes and just locked on for a second or two. Then, in a whisper, he said, "You mentioned that a plane went down. Which one was it? Did I read about it?"

Allison nodded. "You must have. It was that Germanwings airliner; 150 people died. A story was concocted about the co-pilot committing suicide—locked the captain out of the cockpit and put the plane into a dive."

"Yes, I remember that. Horrifying. But, didn't they give a lot of details after the crash about the co-pilot researching methods of suicide online?"

"Sure. Amazing, isn't it? How these things just seem to materialize after an event? It's called 'creating a backstory.' That's all it was."

"So, you're saying that CERN was responsible for this?"

Allison nodded. "I'm not just *saying* it was—I *know* it was. There was an amazing coincidence that day, and virtually no one connected the dots. CERN had been shut down for a two-year maintenance program, getting prepared for gearing back up again for its next big thrust—power to be amped up at twice what was used when the Higgs-Boson 'God Particle' was discovered in 2012. The Large Hadron Collider was going on steroids, and March 24th was the big day.

"At around the exact same time as the LHC hit full power, the Germanwings aircraft went down—descended from 38,000 feet in eight minutes and slammed into a mountain. The point of impact was 190 miles from CERN. The plane was on its way from Barcelona to Dusseldorf, and it began its fatal descent almost directly over the French/Swiss border, where CERN is located. Eight minutes later, it hit the mountains."

Wyatt leaned forward across the table. "What brought it down?"

"Magnetics."

"But, planes are made of mainly aluminum. Aluminum isn't magnetic."

Allison rubbed her tiny fists against her eyes. Wyatt could see that they were getting bloodshot.

"Not at normal magnetic levels, you're right. But, one thing about 'matter'—everything is magnetic when forces reach extreme levels. So, it's conceivable that the aluminum became magnetic. And, the jet engines were made of titanium, which is known as a paramagnetic metal. It has no magnetic field of its own under normal conditions, but it develops one if it's exposed to an externally applied magnetic field.

"In the case of the LHC, it has 9,300 magnets and the environment in the tunnels is super-cooled to minus 456 degrees Fahrenheit to enhance the power of the magnetic field. The result is a field that is 100,000 times more powerful than the actual magnetic field of Earth itself. This massive magnet literally sucked that helpless plane right out of the sky to its doom."

Wyatt shook his head back and forth. He could feel a headache coming on, and he wasn't surprised.

"So, if I understand it right, this monstrosity caused the deaths of 150 people and they created a story making the co-pilot out to be some kind of psycho. And, they never admitted the danger of this thing? No warnings to other planes going over that flight path?"

Allison grimaced. "That's the gist of it. Not only that, as soon as they realized what had happened, they shut the LHC down cold. They were shocked at what it had done. Then, the gremlins went to work online, erasing any reference to the LHC having been started up that day. If you search online now, you'll see that the re-start was in April, not March. If anyone has any old newspapers from that fateful day of March 24th, they will see that it was indeed fired up—but who reads newspapers anymore? And, if they do, who keeps them?"

Wyatt leaned back in his chair and crossed his legs. "I've read about this LHC over the years, but never paid too much attention to it. Quantum physics was never my strong suit. But, I always understood it to be merely an experiment to discover the God Particle, the origins of the Big Bang, the wonders of the creation of the universe and all that crap. I always wondered why they hell they were even bothering—like, who the hell cares? Why do we need to know this? And, you're now saying that all of that was just a smokescreen?"

Allison nodded. "Yes, sort of. They did have to discover the Higgs-Boson particle, better known as that God Particle, before they advanced to this final stage. So, that was the first step in the process. They've now reached the final step, the real purpose."

"How long have they been planning this thing?"

"After the incoming path of Gargantuan was confirmed without a shadow of a doubt, they started construction. It took ten years, and was completed in 2008. They were slow off the mark, despite the fact that we've known about Gargantuan for many decades now. They just refused to believe it was true.

"Then, when there was no more room for denial, the best physicists in the world came up with a plan. A workable plan—to a point. Over 20,000 scientists have been involved with the CERN project—the best minds in the world. But, the world's leaders were still in denial. It took far too long for them to react. When they finally did, twenty-one countries funded the project at a total cost of seven billion dollars, and an annual budget of 300 million.

"And, you wonder why your taxes keep going up, and why you seem to be taxed constantly for carbon emissions and climate change? Well, now you have your answer. That's where the money's been going, as well as towards private bunkers and massive government underground cities."

Wyatt stood up and walked over to a window overlooking the lake. "Where exactly is this LHC thing?"

"Geneva, Switzerland. About 300 feet underground."

He put his hands up against the window and leaned forward until his forehead was resting against the glass. "When you were talking about this before—you were skipping around quite a bit—you mentioned that the LHC might be the solution to Gargantuan."

Allison cleared her throat. "It's possibly a solution, but no one knows for sure. And, it might save us, for a period of time. It would perhaps buy us time to get better prepared."

Wyatt turned around to face her. "What do you mean?"

He noticed Allison swallowing hard. He'd hardly ever seen her nervous before, but at this moment she was.

"As I said before, it took too long for those in power to appreciate the gravity of the situation. Too long to face the fact that Gargantuan could possibly be an extinction level event. Not necessarily in the havoc that its magnetic pull would have on our planet, but in the other implications. It's been slowly but surely pulling the Earth apart for decades, and that's getting worse as it gets closer. But, if we could somehow survive that, once it makes its circle around the Sun, we won't see the beast again for another 3,600 years.

"So, if Gargantuan's magnetic effects weren't concerning enough for us, the possible predatory nature of its inhabitants is the big unknown. With their advanced intelligence, who knows what weapons they might possess? We can only imagine. Look at what happened to my dad and yours. That was decades ago. The world's armed forces couldn't deal with those alien scout forces back then. We couldn't fight them—they turned our own weapons back against us. When their crafts appeared in the sky, we couldn't catch them. They're far too fast. In fact, we've been running away from them. We wouldn't be a match if they wanted to take over our planet. We're guessing that human civilization would be dead within perhaps a day or two, with our beloved planet left vacant and safe for them to take over.

"We have a few of their craft and several alien bodies—not because we were successful in bringing them down, of course. We've never been successful at that. We have them only because they crashed. And, we've made some good progress reverse-engineering their technology, but we're decades away from mounting a proper defense. We need a few more decades of taking this threat seriously."

Wyatt sat down again and put his feet up on the table. "So, what are you planning to do? Fire the sucker up again and chase them away with its massive magnetics?"

Allison rested her elbows on the table and leaned forward. "No, that wouldn't work."

She paused to catch her breath. "We're going to send the Earth back in time. To buy us a few more decades until we have to deal with this again, at which time, we'll be better prepared."

Wyatt found himself choking on his own saliva. "What? Are you nuts? Tell me this is all just a dream, please?"

"I wish it were a dream, Wyatt. And, maybe we are nuts. But, we think it's possible—we won't know until we try. The alternative is the likely end of civilization."

Wyatt's headache was getting worse. He wrung his hands together and cracked his knuckles.

"The way I understand it, this Large Hadron Collider rams particles together at high speeds—protons and neutrons—and tries to create a reaction."

"Yes, in simple terms, that's correct. The objective was to have the protons reach almost to the point of the speed of light—which is essential for any concept of time travel. But, on its last run, it managed to go beyond the speed of light, which was an amazing accomplishment. And, through that process, it actually created a wormhole—which is another essential element of time travel. That wormhole has been saved and quarantined—it's a living, breathing, pulsating tunnel to the past now, waiting to be thrown into action."

Wyatt growled. "This is crazy! How the fuck do you quarantine a wormhole? I lock prisoners up in a cell when I want to quarantine them. What do you guys do? Lock it up and feed it three times a day?"

Allison smiled. "I understand that you're getting frustrated here. It's a lot to handle. All we do is isolate it in a section of the LHC ring and continue to bombard it with protons at a lower speed—this settles it down and saves it for when we want to use it. When we do, we'll bombard it at higher speeds again and let it grow to the point we need it to. They've done exhaustive calculations as to how big it will have to be to get us back to a certain point in time."

"Why don't you just send us *forward* in time, away from Gargantuan?"

"It doesn't work that way. First of all, our experiments have shown that we can only go back in time, not forward. And, even if we could go forward, that would do us no good at all. We're only altering space/time—not the position of Earth in the universe. We would only be moving forward to a point when the destruction would have already happened. We would, in effect, be exterminating ourselves. We can't escape Gargantuan—we can only delay our meeting with it.

"So, we can go back to a point when we can make the technological advances to protect and defend ourselves for when we reach this point in time again. We'll be better prepared to handle the blow. We have the advantage of going back in time from the future—our knowledge and reverse-engineering will enable Earth to get a head start for when Gargantuan makes its run towards us in the future 2015, rather than the present 2015. We won't be so naïve or complacent the next time around."

Wyatt rubbed his chin. The pain had shifted from his head to his jaw, and it was throbbing non-stop. "How will we all survive this time travel? If we all go back, that will at least double the population of Earth in whatever time we go back to."

Allison stared at him for a few seconds before answering. "We won't all survive. The way the wormhole works, only structures and people underground will move with Earth to the past. Everything above ground, and everyone above ground, will simply vanish. They will, of course, exist in the past in their younger states. But, those who are lucky enough to be underground at the time the transition takes place will in effect be in an alternate universe. The older versions of them, and their younger versions if they had been born at that time, will exist together on Earth in the new dimension."

"Christ Almighty! Each question I ask digs this story into an even deeper hole! Okay, one more question and then I think I may have to throw up—what period have these CERN geniuses calculated to take Earth back to?"

Allison reached across the table and rubbed Wyatt's shoulder.

"Before I answer that, let me just say that you and your parents will be underground with me when it happens. Okay? And to answer your last question—we had to decide on a period when civilization had a leader who was clever enough, and somewhat of a hero at the same time.

"Someone who wanted to change the world for the better, and was able to think outside the box. A person who might listen to us and not discard what we had to say. A leader who had an interest in knowing what was going on, in fact demanded to know what was going on—even though he was thwarted every step of the way.

"We decided we needed that one leader who showed that he was enough of a visionary to put the wheels in motion to land a man on the Moon."

Allison took a deep breath, and then exhaled slowly. "We're going back to 1963. To the era of John Fitzgerald Kennedy. To the time before he was assassinated."

CHAPTER 44

Aside from being awestruck by the mere expanse of CERN, visitors to this massive complex near Geneva, Switzerland are greeted by a statue.

Not just any old statue. No, this one has a message, and the message can be taken in different ways, depending on who does the interpreting.

Most people might not even give the statue a second glance. Some might point, or stop for a second and gaze at it, but most wouldn't think to ask what it means, what it represents, or even read the plaque adjacent to the work of art.

It depicts a dancing figure who goes by the name of Lord Shiva, a mythical Hindu deity, donated as a gift from India in 2004. The essence of Shiva is that he is the god of the creation of the universe, dancing it into existence and sustaining it with his rhythm.

But, he is also the god of destruction. Indeed, the plaque, if anyone took the time to read it, talks of how the deity is dancing the universe into extinction—specifically, the vibration of the drum held in his right hand stands for creation, while the fire on his right arm symbolizes destruction.

Shiva does his cosmic welcome dance mounted on a platform between buildings thirty-nine and forty. He no doubt receives plenty of compliments throughout each and every day, as eager science buffs make their way to the Visitor's Center.

There are well over 500 buildings at CERN, but there is only one area where visitors are permitted. The 'Globe of Science and Innovation' is a veritable playground for physics geeks. And it is indeed an amazing journey, one that takes alert guests all the way back to the Big Bang.

CERN is an amazing scientific accomplishment. The acronym stands for 'European Organization for Nuclear Research.' It was actually founded in 1954 for various collaborative quantum physics experiments on behalf of its member countries. Tens of thousands of scientists are involved in CERN, and the complex itself has 2,500 permanent employees. The organization has assured the world that it does no military research whatsoever, and so far it hasn't behaved in any way that would cause doubt of that assurance.

CERN is much more than just the Large Hadron Collider, even though it is most famous for that invention. The LHC put CERN on the map, but it's unfair that it doesn't get recognition for the other astounding innovations that came out of the experiments performed there in the last half century. Most people wouldn't know that superconductors, electrical chips, advanced computers, grids, and networks all came from research at CERN. Not to mention the most world-changing invention of them all—the internet.

Yes, indeed, the internet was invented by CERN.

In 1998, construction started on the Large Hadron Collider. Funded by more than twenty countries, it was completed and put into operation in 2008, heralded as the largest and most powerful particle accelerator in the world. An interactive science lab, allowing physicists to discover what the vast universe is made of and how it works.

And…how it was formed.

The instruments used in the LHC are particle accelerators and detectors. The accelerators boost beams of particles at high energies hovering around the speed of light, causing the particles to collide either with each other or with stationary targets. The detectors then take over and record the results of these collisions.

While the LHC is the world's largest accelerator, only about 1% of accelerators around the world are used for research facilities at places like CERN. Most people would be surprised to learn that the other 99% of accelerators are used for more common applications, such as radiotherapy, cargo and luggage scanners, steel hardening, asphalt strengthening, food sterilization, and the creation of computer chips. Even for two of the most benign applications imaginable—the sealing of potato chip bags and hardening of paint on pop cans.

Visitors to CERN aren't able to visit the actual LHC—however, they can witness live collisions of particles on screens in the Globe center. The Large Hadron Collider is, by all accounts, 300 feet below the surface of the ground, but some other estimates put it at least 600 feet down. It's actually circular in shape and the circumference is a full seventeen miles. The protons circulate the massive ring 11,000 times every single second. The operating temperature of the structure is minus 456 degrees Fahrenheit and the air inside the ring's beam line is actually thinner than the air in outer space.

For guests who start developing headaches from all of the mind-boggling scientific data, there's a gift shop, three restaurants, cash machines, and even a travel agency on site.

There's also a medical clinic…just in case.

The first attempt to build the largest collider in the world was actually undertaken in the United States. Called the 'Superconducting Super Collider,' construction began in 1991 in the state of Texas. By 1993, after two billion had already been spent, the project was abandoned when it became clear to Congress that the ultimate costs would exceed twelve billion dollars. When it was cancelled, fourteen miles of tunnels and seventeen shafts had already been dug and all the surface structures had been completed. It sits derelict today, bearing the label of being the most expensive white elephant in the world.

CERN's scientists believe that the universe began with every speck of its energy rammed into a very small point. This dense point exploded with incredible force, thus creating matter and expelling it outwards to create the billions of galaxies of the vast universe. This is the event that scientists refer to as the Big Bang. Since there was no air—or no anything, really—the Big Bang didn't have to expand through resistance. It was just nothingness at the beginning of time. So, in effect, the massive explosion created space and stretched it outwards with no resistance whatsoever. The universe expanded at will.

Astronomers are actually able to verify their theories about the origins of the universe and matter, by looking at distant clouds of gas through high-powered telescopes. A surreal fact, which most people have a tough time comprehending, is that these telescope viewings are actually looking way back in time. Because light from these distant clouds takes billions of years to reach telescopes, astronomers are in reality viewing the way those objects looked billions of years ago, and not at all how they look today. It's not even known if they still exist today.

Without a doubt, CERN's Large Hadron Collider is one of the most remarkable engineering achievements ever. And, in its short history, CERN has already contributed immensely to the modernization of society. Things society takes for granted, almost to the point of never giving them a second thought, originated at CERN. Innovations and inventions that have changed life for the better...and also, if truth be told, worsened it in equal doses.

CERN is a testament to not only the power of the human brain, but also to man's quest for knowledge, his restless spirit, and his pursuit of betterment.

Some people may ponder the real message of Shiva. Dancing in stoic silence in front of the world's largest particle collider, is Shiva telling the world something? Shiva—the deity of creation and destruction. Is he encouraging man to play God? Or, instead, warning what is to come?

Several scientists, including Stephen Hawking, have expressed alarm at how far the pendulum has swung with the LHC, and have questioned, as well, how far it should swing.

The Higgs-Boson particle was discovered by CERN in 2012, but that wasn't the end. It wasn't enough that the God Particle—the origin of the Big Bang—was re-created. The LHC was compelled to push the pendulum further. It was merely the beginning.

Before even the remarkable discovery of the God Particle, a famous scientist was quoted as saying: "The men who would play God in search of the 'God Particle' are truly going to find more than they bargained for as they open up the gates of hell."

CHAPTER 45

Wyatt cranked the starter of the two-year-old Sea Ray and the powerful dual inboard engines roared to life. Their combined output was 250 horsepower, enough to allow the sleek police boat to outrun any other craft on the lake.

The hull was white with red stripes, and along the sides were the words, 'Nelson Police,' painted in large black lettering. It had a removable canopy, a proper police siren, and the usual array of warning lights, similar to what a typical police cruiser on land would have.

The marina's moor master untied the ropes. Wyatt slipped the craft into gear and guided it slowly out onto Kootenay Lake.

Today, the top was down as it was a warm and sunny afternoon. The boat had Captains' seats up front, and a wrap-around leather lounger for four in the rear. Seating for two more was up in the bow, just past the windshield of the cockpit.

Allison was stretched out in the rear, her shapely legs curled up in the curve of the lounger. She was wearing a bright yellow halter top, green shorts, a white sun hat, and gold-framed Oakley sunglasses.

Wyatt could barely make out her reflection in the windshield, but it wasn't the perfect image he wanted so he turned his head around and stole a quick 'live' glance.

She was indeed the picture of perfection.

She always dressed so casually, which impressed him. It was a mistake to stereotype—being a police officer he knew how erroneous that always was—but he'd never pictured a billionaire being so unassuming.

She looked like a million bucks, but not because the clothes were expensive. They weren't. She just looked good in anything, and he was pretty sure she knew it, too.

Allison never wore jewellery, which also surprised him. It was almost as if she deliberately went out of her way to *not* look rich. But, Wyatt also knew that she wasn't the typical 'born with a silver spoon' girl. She'd shunned the family business and educated herself instead in astrophysics. She only came into the business by default when her parents and husband had died in that car accident—the one that turned out not to be an accident.

Over the last couple of days, Wyatt had absorbed more information than he'd probably digested in the last decade.

This beautiful woman was a member of a mysterious group called Majestic 12, a group that she admitted had ordered the deaths of dozens of prominent scientists, astronomers, journalists, and politicians in the last half-century. He'd tried to pin her down on the actual number, but she refused to speculate. Which made Wyatt think that the number was off the charts—saying it was "dozens" was probably an understatement.

And, here he was, a policeman, hearing someone confess to ordering the deaths of countless innocent people. He thought that was weird—not because it was coming out of Allison's mouth, but weird because he didn't feel any duty to do anything about it. He wasn't about to arrest her, and had no inclination at all to blow the whistle. It was as if the deaths themselves were minor in the scheme of things.

And, after all that he'd heard, they were indeed minor and he wasn't experiencing any pangs of conscience for not doing his duty and slapping the cuffs on her.

The people had been murdered to keep the lid on ominous events—truths that people would have a tough time swallowing.

Wyatt knew that the average person enjoyed fantasizing about UFOs and aliens, especially since no one really and truly believed they were real to begin with. But, if they found out they were real and that a massive planet called Gargantuan was on its way, possibly inhabited by hostile aliens, mayhem would result. No doubt. Too much to handle for the average person.

He also understood Allison's cynicism. She was too close to it, and now knew that her own parents and husband had been murdered by Majestic 12. All because her father wanted to blow the whistle. Now, she herself was torn between thinking that her father was right and that she should blow it wide open—or, instead, following through on the plan to try to send Earth back in time.

She'd told him this morning that if the CERN solution didn't work, she might just blow the whistle. Give people a chance to prepare, a last chance to live and love. But, Wyatt knew that was the romantic idealist in her talking, and he wasn't convinced at all that she thought that was the best thing to do. If push came to shove, he believed she'd keep her mouth shut for the greater good.

The policeman inside of him, the man who'd seen lawless chaos at times during his years with the RCMP, knew that was probably the right thing to do.

He spun the wheel towards the south, and continued cruising along at a snail's pace.

She called out to him from the back seat. "Where are we heading to, Captain Hook?"

He turned to face her. She was giggling, the sunlight glaring back at him off her sunglasses.

"We're gonna head to a little cove down the lake a bit. A perfect place to enjoy that nice picnic lunch and bottle of wine you packed for us."

"Is booze allowed on private boats?"

"Sure, as long as the driver doesn't drink."

"So, that means you're not going to have any?"

Wyatt laughed. "Of course I'm going to have some. That law only applies to civilians—I'm the police chief, remember?"

"Oh, double standard, huh?"

"Yep. But, only because you're with me, and only because pretty soon the laws won't matter anyway."

Allison grimaced. "It sounds like we need to talk some more."

Wyatt turned his eyes back to the sparkling view through his windshield.

She called out, "Hey, can you turn on the police siren?"

Wyatt flipped the switch and the shrieking sound caused him to jerk. He couldn't recall ever having used the siren before, and he was shocked at how loud it was.

Allison was laughing her head off in the back seat, yelling, "Woo! Woo!"

He smiled at her girlish silliness—he loved that about her. Vivacious, full of life, finding reasons to laugh despite how serious everything was right now.

"Go full speed! C'mon, Chief—be wild and crazy!"

Wyatt yelled back. "Okay, hold on tight, you little nut!"

He rammed the throttle forward and the bow rose high in the air as the craft struggled for equilibrium. Then, after a few seconds, it slammed back down again. Now, that the boat was level on the water it picked up speed like a rocket, and they were streaming across the almost empty lake. It was early fall, so there weren't many other boats out on the water. And, since Kootenay Lake was so huge, it wasn't difficult to find empty space to put a boat through its paces.

Suddenly, he heard a scream.

He spun around in his seat and saw Allison laughing, her long brown hair blowing in the wind.

"My hat!" She pointed behind them.

Wyatt pulled back on the throttle and spun the boat into a tight circle. Allison leaned over the side as they headed back in the direction they had come from.

"There it is!"

Wyatt pulled slowly alongside the spot she was pointing at, and shut off the engine.

Then, she cried out, "Damn! It just sunk!"

Allison stood up on top of the lounger and yanked her halter top up over her head. Then, she wriggled out of her shorts and tossed her sunglasses onto the seat.

She had a bikini on underneath, bright red with white polka dots.

Wyatt caught his breath.

She dove over the side and disappeared beneath the clear blue water.

Wyatt dashed over and yanked the extendable ladder out from a hatch in the hull, and slipped it over the side.

He peered down, but couldn't see any sign of her. Panicking, he yanked off his t-shirt and shorts. Down to just his bathing suit now, he stood on the edge of the boat ready to dive in as well. Then, he heard her voice from the other side of the boat, and felt her soaking wet hat smack him in the back.

"I'm over here! And, it's cold!"

"The ladder's over on this side. Get over here."

She disappeared under the boat and a few seconds later reappeared with her hands on the lower rung. "Be a gentleman and give me a hand, Chief."

Wyatt helped her back into the boat and slid the ladder back into its slot. She stood there shivering, long hair plastered across her face. Wyatt opened a locker, pulled out two large towels and wrapped them around her. She cozied up to him and he hugged her.

With her teeth chattering, she said, "I think…now would be a good time…for a glass of wine…don't you think, Chief?"

"Good idea."

He gently lowered her down to the lounger and tucked the towels around her. Luckily, even though the lake water was cold, it was a sunny hot day and she'd dry off fast. He reached down to the picnic basket, opened it, and pulled out a bottle of Bordeaux and two wine glasses.

"Do you want to eat first?"

She shook her head.

"Okay, wine it is."

Wyatt poured and handed her a glass. She moved in closer to him and laid her head on his chest. He pulled the towels around her exposed legs and wrapped an arm around her shoulders.

They sipped their wine in silence for a few minutes as the boat drifted along lazily with the current.

"Do we need the anchor?"

"No, this lake is deep—we'll be fine. It's nicer this way, don't you think? Just drifting along?"

She nodded.

After a few minutes of silence, Wyatt broke the spell. "This doesn't seem real. Us sitting here like this—everything seems so peaceful, so right. It's hard to believe that a cataclysm is on its way."

"It is nice. At times like this, the world is a beautiful place."

Wyatt pointed to the south, in the direction of the Sun. "It's somewhere up there right now, isn't it? Coming towards us, hidden from view."

"Yes. It's coming in from slightly behind the Sun. That's why at this time of day you can't see it. The Sun is far too bright. And, there are no chemtrails up there right now, so the atmospheric conditions must be okay today."

"Do you think it'll work? Going back to 1963?"

Allison took a long sip of her wine, then held out her glass. "More, please?"

Wyatt poured and filled his own glass, too.

She sighed. "I have to hope that it will—the science seems right. But, we won't know until we try."

"Why 1963? That's the year Kennedy was assassinated. Cutting it kinda close, don't you think?"

"It was a tough choice. But, he was elected in 1960, so that wouldn't have been a good time. He was too new in the job. Then, in 1961, there was the ill-fated Bay of Pigs invasion of Cuba. That was an embarrassing disaster for him, and he was distracted recovering from that for the rest of the year.

"In 1962, he had the Cuban Missile Crisis to contend with. America and Russia came close to nuclear annihilation, and he came out on top. So, that year would have been a bad one, too, because post-crisis diplomacy with Russia and America's allies took up most of his time.

"We decided that 1963 was the only time we could do it—and, of course, he was killed on November 22nd of that year, so we need to get Earth back to a date well before then.

"It will be a good time in another respect as well. Kennedy was concerned about UFO and alien activity and he demanded that the C.I.A. brief him in detail. They refused, and Kennedy gave them a deadline. It was to be February of 1964, but, as we know, he didn't live that long.

"So, we know that he was suspicious of the C.I.A. and in fact wanted to dismantle it. He was vitally interested in the UFO topic in 1963. Our going back to that time will be good, because we know from history that it will be foremost on his mind. He'll give us an audience."

Wyatt gazed up at the sky. "Here's an uncomfortable question for you. In the quest to keep the lid on the UFO and alien crises, did Majestic 12 have JFK killed?"

Allison was silent for a few seconds. "I don't know. And, that's the honest truth. It's possible. I've heard some rumors, but lips have been sealed on that one, for obvious reasons. But, if we did, wouldn't it be ironic if we succeeded in going back in time to save his life? The life we stole?"

Wyatt whistled. "That would be surreal."

He pulled her in tighter to him. She felt so good. Her body was warm underneath the towels, yet her little button nose felt cold against the side of his neck.

His mind was filled with a million questions, most of which he guessed she couldn't really answer. He asked another one, anyway.

"How will you even get through the front door of the White House? Since you folks will be from the future, he won't have a clue as to who you are. He won't give you the time of day, and neither will the Secret Service."

She smiled. "We'll find a way. Trust me."

Wyatt drained his wine. "If this works, it will be so strange for all of us to be back in that era. You and I won't even have been born yet, and my mom and dad will be able to see themselves as young adults."

Allison shook her head. "We need to warn them to stay away from themselves. There can't be any contact between the present and past of the same people. We can't predict the outcome."

Wyatt nodded. "Okay. Too weird to even imagine, anyway."

He paused for a second before asking his next question, which he couldn't have known at that moment was going to be his last for a while. "You mentioned you had an underground facility that we'll be going to. Where is it?"

Allison sat up straight and shrugged the towel off her shoulders. Then, she wrapped her bare arms around Wyatt's neck and moved her face within inches of his.

She whispered, "Enough of this depressing talk. It's high time you and I had a 'moment.'"

Her beautiful blue eyes were intoxicating, strangely enhanced by the wet strands of hair that snaked across her face.

She kissed him. A different kiss than the one she'd laid on him when they sitting on his deck. This one said so much more.

He kissed her back and, within seconds, their tongues were swirling, exploring. She sighed as he unfastened her bikini top. Allison slid on top of his lap; he slipped his hands under her bikini bottoms and in one swift move dropped them to the floor of the boat.

For just a split second he thought about how they were out on the lake, in an open boat, with no protection whatsoever from prying eyes. Drifting along in an easily recognizable police craft. However, the one bit of solace he got was knowing that most boats wouldn't allow themselves to come within spitting distance of a police boat—most boats had liquor onboard, and most of the drivers drank. Just like Wyatt.

He hadn't even noticed that she'd already slid his bathing suit down to his knees. He reached down and pulled it off.

She raised herself up, inviting his lips to caress her breasts. He started with his tongue and pursed his lips over one nipple—then the other—back and forth until gently grasping a nipple in his teeth and squeezing. A long, drawn-out moan expelled from her mouth. She flung her head backwards while at the same time grasping his penis in her hand and pulling it up against her vagina. She slid it in and out, back and forth, until finally allowing it to find its own way.

As they swayed and rocked in rhythm together on the back lounge of the Sea Ray, the Sun beating down on their skin, Wyatt's brain was still working. He tried to remember the last time he'd had sex—but he couldn't. He knew it wasn't that long ago—maybe just a few months—but, whenever it was, it was totally forgettable right now. He couldn't even remember who he'd been with. He looked up at her face at the exact same time as she looked down at his. She smiled in a lazy sort of way and pursed her lips. He accepted the invitation.

As their tongues swirled against each other in passionate excitement, Wyatt's brain punched out another thought.

How could this be happening?

He knew he was in love with the stunning Allison Fisher.

What had he done that deserved being dealt a cruel hand like this?

Hopelessly in love…and Gargantuan was coming.

CHAPTER 46

She was standing at the kitchen counter, peering into the backyard at what seemed to be nothing in particular.

Wyatt and Allison strode quietly up behind her. He gently touched her shoulder.

"Mom?"

She took a second to respond, then turned her head slowly. In a weary voice, she responded. "Oh, hello, Wy. And, Allison—so nice that you're still visiting with us."

Allison stood beside her and gazed out into the garden. "You look worried. What's out there, Helen? A bear, or wolf?"

"Oh, no. I can only wish for something simple like that."

Helen turned and looked at her son.

"It's happening with your father again. The surgery worked—his strength and vitality are back—but so are his little spells. He's out in there in the studio right now."

Wyatt gave his mother a hug. "Mom, the alternative would have been worse, don't you think? He was aging right in front of your eyes."

"Yes, Wy, you're right. But…I still worry. He gets that look in his eyes, starts to glow and that transparency thing comes back again. When that happens, it's like he's possessed. He just goes right out to the studio, sometimes without even bothering to dress."

Wyatt rubbed her back, reassuringly. "We'll go check on him, okay? Do you want to come with us?"

Helen shook her head. "Thank you. Yes, please go. But, I'll stay here. It upsets me too much to see him like that."

Wyatt nodded.

"Mom, I should warn you that sometime in the future, you, Dad, and I are going to go with Allison to a special place she has. You know all about what might happen now, even though we don't know exactly when that will be. But, Allison has a safe place for all of us to go to. I don't want you to worry—she'll take care of us. Might be a smart thing, though, to pack a bag for you and Dad. In case we don't have much time."

Helen's eyes opened as wide as saucers, and she looked at Allison. "This sounds serious. Is it going to be sooner than you thought?"

Allison shook her head. "No, Helen. We're fine for quite a while, I can assure you. There's no imminent danger. But, Wyatt's advice is smart—best to be prepared."

Helen took off her apron, and walked to the foot of the stairs. "I'll do that right now, then, while you check on Willy."

Suddenly, she grabbed onto the banister and gasped. "Did you feel that?"

Wyatt opened his mouth to answer, but then noticed out of the corner of his eye the chandelier swaying in the dining room. Then, the silence was shattered by the shrieking sound of car alarms out on the street.

He jumped up, ran over to his mother, and held her tight.

He could swear that the floor was shifting under his feet—very gently, but noticeable. Like an undulation, pulsing up and down.

"It's an earthquake, Mom. Just hold onto me—it won't last long."

Helen struggled to talk. "We never get earthquakes here, Wy."

Wyatt winked at Allison. "Oh, sure we do, Mom. Your memory isn't as good as it used to be."

Suddenly, it was over, except for the car alarms and the gentle swaying of the chandelier.

Helen squeezed his arm. "Wy, I don't think I want to go upstairs right now. I'll wait in the garden while you and Allison visit with your dad."

"Okay, Mom. That's probably a good idea."

Wyatt led the way out the back door and into the garden. Helen sat down on a Muskoka chair just outside the back door. "I'll wait here for you."

As they approached the studio door, Wyatt caught a glimpse of his dad through the window, pacing back and forth inside.

Allison whispered. "You were lying, weren't you? You've never had an earthquake here before, have you?"

Wyatt shook his head. "No, but she doesn't have to be reminded of that."

He raised his hand into the air with a flourish. "Look around you, though. We're surrounded by mountains, most of them dormant volcanos. It was only a matter of time. The epicenter was probably a long way from here—maybe Vancouver, which is a severe earthquake zone."

Allison remained silent.

Willy didn't seem to notice them when they entered the studio. He just kept pacing, one hand on top of his head, the other one swinging at his side. As Helen had told them, Willy was glowing and his skin was slightly transparent. If he'd noticed the earthquake, he certainly didn't show it.

Wyatt glanced over at Allison, who didn't seem the least bit shocked. He reminded himself that she was familiar with Willy's condition, with what she'd known about her own father. Plus, Wyatt was pretty sure that there wasn't very much that could shock the very-much-in-control Allison Fisher. At least, not that she would betray.

"Dad? Are you all right?"

Willy whirled around, hair disheveled, eyes wild. At that moment, he looked like a mad scientist.

Except for the attire. He was dressed only in boxer shorts, and seemed so distressed and distracted that he showed absolutely no shame at Allison seeing him that way. Normally, Willy was a proper gentleman, with old-fashioned modesty.

"Oh, hi, Wyatt, Allison. I don't know what I'm doing in here. I'm just...all mixed up today."

Wyatt walked over to the center of the room and stared across the expanse of floor. The large granite sphere had been moved. And, the carved tunnel entrances in the sphere had been opened up, made larger.

But, more puzzling than that were two other balls that were now on the floor, arranged in a way that made kind of a triangle between all three. Both had obviously been carved by Willy, just like the big granite one. The one at the top of the triangle was the largest and its stone type was different from the other two as well. It was a lighter, almost golden material—Wyatt guessed marble.

The original sphere was positioned about ten degrees down to the left of the big golden one. The third sphere was positioned well down from the other two, and it was also the smallest of the three.

It had been a long time since Wyatt had studied geometry, but he recognized the triangle formed by the three balls to be in the category of 'obtuse.' He didn't know what to think about this latest puzzle, so he looked over at Allison with a question in his eyes.

She showed no emotion as she looked down at the floor. She pointed at the small sphere. "That's Earth. And, that golden one is the Sun. Of course, we now know that the original one on the left there is Gargantuan."

Allison turned to Willy. "Any sensations when you were doing these other two? Or, when you were arranging them like this?"

The glow had left him, and his skin was no longer transparent.

Willy suddenly became modest as well—he pulled a work apron off the bench and tied it around his waist. He shook his head.

"Just the usual—a trance, hands knowing what to do. But, the force in my head was strong, overwhelming."

Allison nodded and looked down again.

Wyatt whispered. "What does this mean?"

"You'll remember I told you that your dad was a 'receptor,' just like my father and the dozens of others who'd been hit by beams. We don't think it was intentional by the aliens to have them be this way—it was merely another side effect. Willy is connected magnetically to Gargantuan and it creates a psychic energy inside of him. All of the 'receptors' around the world are kind of the 'canaries in the coal mine' for us. They tell us how close it's getting and how strong the magnetics are becoming. It will get worse for him."

Wyatt gestured with his hand at the sphere display. "What the hell does this tell you?"

Allison sighed, and pulled her phone out of the holster on her hip.

"Gargantuan is a hell of a lot closer than it was a month ago—disproportionately closer, considering the time factor. The triangle shows that it has now moved past the Sun on its run towards Earth. You can see that Gargantuan is about ten or fifteen degrees below and to the left of the Sun. That indicates it's only about eighty million miles from us now—so forty million closer than just last month. And, Willy has opened up the tunnel entrances much wider—indicating that preparations are being made for aircraft, symbolizing test exits and entrances. Your dad senses this activity without realizing it."

Wyatt found that his mouth had suddenly gone dry. "How could it have moved that fast towards us in just a month?"

"I told you that Gargantuan seemed to have the ability to slow down its rate of advance in its own orbit. So, on the converse, it must also have the ability to speed it up. We think they might have their own version of CERN under the surface of the planet. The ability to magnetically pull itself along at whatever rate of speed they wish. Much more advanced than our version of the LHC, which should be no surprise. Everything they have is probably more advanced—we already know their weapons are well beyond what we have."

Allison punched a speed dial number on her phone.

"Who are you phoning?"

"Shh…the Vatican."

Wyatt opened his mouth in shock, but the stern look in Allison's eyes shut him up. He resigned himself to just listening intently to the one-sided conversation.

"Cardinal Valenti, please?"

A few seconds of silence, then, "Cardinal, it's Allison Fisher."

"Yes, just fine, thank you."

She nodded and murmured for a few minutes, without saying anything intelligible.

Then, "The entire Pacific Rim?"

"What's your latest reading?"

"I agree. I'm guessing eighty million miles. One of our 'receptors' has given me some clues."

"And, you're still not seeing it clearly?"

"Cloaking?"

"Okay, have you talked with Chad?"

"And, how about CERN?"

"Well, they're going to have to be ready. We need to pick a date. They'll only get one shot at this, and it's starting to look like the sooner the better. Call them back, and then let me know. You have my number. Goodbye for now, Cardinal."

Allison clicked off. Wyatt stared at her.

"Vatican? Cardinal? Were those just code words?"

She grimaced. "No, they weren't code words. That was Cardinal Valenti of the *real* Vatican. But, I wasn't talking to the Vatican in Italy—I was talking to their branch in Arizona."

Wyatt knew his face reflected his incredulity. "The Vatican has a branch in Arizona?"

She nodded slowly. "I'm sorry to hit you with one shock after another. But, I'm not hiding anything from you now. It's too late for that. Yes, they have the largest 'near infra-red' telescope in the world in Arizona, more powerful than any country has. It's located at the Mount Graham International Observatory. They have another one in Castel Gandolfo, Italy, but it pales in comparison to the power of the one in Arizona."

"Why would the Vatican have telescopes?"

"The Catholic religion has no choice but to publicly deny the existence of aliens, but they've always known that they exist. The religion would have been weakened considerably if the Vatican admitted they believed in things like the Big Bang and extraterrestrials. But, they do. They know there's no such thing as 'God.' If truth be told, none of the leaders of the civilized religions believe in 'God.' Like most other institutions in our lives, religions exist to keep people in order, keep them fearful of what the afterlife will bring. And, give them hope."

Wyatt shook his head in disbelief. "So, what does the Vatican have to do with all of this, aside from their monster telescope?"

"They're partners in the CERN complex and have invested heavily in the technology. Their own observatories in Italy and Arizona are run by Jesuits, and Cardinal Valenti is the managing director. The Jesuits are the most highly trained astronomers in the world; one of the world's best kept secrets. The Vatican is our main conduit to the scientists at CERN. They all speak the same technical language. And, you may find it ironic to know that their powerful telescope in Arizona is nicknamed 'Lucifer.'"

Wyatt started pacing the room. He noticed that his dad was now leaning up against the workbench, eyes fixated on Allison, clearly absorbing every word she was saying. Willy jumped into the conversation.

"When you were on the phone, you mentioned the Pacific Rim. What was that about?"

Allison turned to face Willy. "Did you feel the small earthquake we had, Willy?"

He shook his head.

"Well, we had one. And, the cardinal was telling me that they've been rolling all along the Pacific Rim today. The entire 'ring of fire,' from Alaska right down to Patagonia, over to New Zealand, and up through the Asia rim. None of them destructive, all in the four and five range on the Richter scale, but large enough to cause some panic. What was unusual was that it was kind of a rolling effect, like when you shove your legs under a blanket."

"Gargantuan?"

"We're guessing that. The cardinal agrees that the planet has accelerated in its run towards Earth. But, surprisingly, even though it's closer, it's become impossible to see even with their 'Lucifer' telescope. We're thinking that Gargantuan has some kind of cloaking technology that's been activated now that they're coming closer to us, making it invisible. The cardinal said that he's talked to CERN and they've expressed the fear that they're not ready. He'll get back to me after he talks with them again. The bottom line is, we may not have the luxury of *not* being ready—no option of doing more testing. CERN may have to just pick a date, activate the wormhole, and we'll all cross our fingers, toes, and anything else we can think of."

Willy walked to the door. "I don't know what you're talking about, Allison. This CERN stuff and picking a date or whatever. I think I'm out of the loop here."

Wyatt followed him. "I haven't told you everything yet, Dad. CERN is a possible solution, and it's about as science fiction as things can get. We'll all sit down and talk about it. Allison filled me in on it all, and we were going to tell you and mom the whole story today."

Suddenly, Allison's phone rang.

"Hello?"

"Gerndle, calm down. Speak slower."

Her eyes widened.

"Did they ask about anything else?"

"Where is the senator right now?"

"Okay, tell him to stay down there—not to come out again. I'll be there soon."

Allison's finger was poised above the 'end" button, but she paused to ask one more question.

"Gerndle, do you know if he used his cell phone when he was outside?"

"Of course, I understand, Gerndle. There's no way you could have watched him every minute. Not your fault. But, he's pretty strongminded. I warned him not to use his mobile, but he probably thought it was safe. I should have known better—should have taken it away from him. Okay, be there soon."

CHAPTER 47

They all adjourned back to the kitchen for some cold refreshing lemonade. Throats were dry from the shock of the earthquake, and Wyatt noticed that concern had masked Allison's face since those two strange phone calls.

She could probably use something stronger than lemonade. While she was clearly a battle-hardened boardroom warrior, he was getting accustomed to the reality that in front of him she had difficulty hiding what she was feeling. He took that as a compliment.

"What's going on, Allison? Tell us."

She ran her fingers through her long dark hair, and then shook her head in dismay.

"I'm just a bit worried. A good friend of mine has made a mistake, and it may have opened a can of worms."

"That friend you mentioned to me, the one you said was down in Osoyoos?"

She nodded. "He's a U.S. Senator—John Hartford."

"I've heard of him. From Vermont, isn't he? A possible presidential candidate?"

"Yes. We got out of a difficult situation back at his home in Vermont, and I brought him here to Canada. Stashed him at a spot I own in Osoyoos, to keep him safe. But...looks like he's used his cell phone, and now he's been traced. Someone dropped by and enquired about him. It may be nothing, but my instincts tell me I'd better get back there fast."

Willy walked over to her. "What happened down in Vermont?"

Allison sighed. "Some information fell into his hands about the... subject...you're all aware of. He was going to blow the whistle as part of his election campaign. Majestic 12 put a hit out on him, and I got him out of it just in time. Now, it looks like they've tracked down where I've hidden him."

Wyatt rubbed his chin. "Why did you save him from the hit? You didn't save others—why him?"

Allison lowered her eyes. "It all started becoming personal after I discovered that they'd killed my family. I told you that—that's not news. You know I've been conflicted. As for Senator Hartford, he's one of the good guys, just like my dad was. He fights injustice, looks out for the little guy…and he's done that his entire career.

"He's a rare leader who wants to bring about serious change to make this country better. God knows it needs it. I took it upon myself to save him—whatever happens to us all, we need leaders we can trust. And, he's one of those rare leaders."

Wyatt forced himself to ask the question that was at the forefront of his mind, knowing full well that it was a selfish one—and in the grand scheme of things right now, totally irrelevant.

"Was there…something…between the two of you?"

She wrapped her arms around his neck and kissed the tip of his ear. "No, Wyatt. There was nothing between us at all. I haven't been with anyone since my husband died. Until you…"

He felt foolish now for asking, but he was glad he did. It was out of the way now. He kissed her on the cheek. "Okay, I had to ask. Sorry."

"Nothing to be sorry about."

Suddenly, there was a low rumbling sound—faint at first, but it increased in intensity quickly. The car alarms started up once again, and the chandelier resumed its sway.

Wyatt held onto Allison tightly, and Willy did the same with Helen.

Over the incessant rumbling, Willy yelled, "Okay, this time I feel it! What's going on?"

There was a noticeable pulse underneath Wyatt's feet, like a heartbeat on steroids. That was the only warning he got. Suddenly, the hardwood floor cracked and heaved upwards. He and Allison jumped back, and he swung his gaze towards the big picture window in response to a ghostly creaking sound. Then, watched in horror as the roof over the front porch groaned and crashed to the ground.

Helen screamed. "My God! We're going to die in here!"

Wyatt pushed Allison towards the front door and motioned at Willy and Helen. "Outside! Now!"

Out on the porch, they crawled carefully over the debris from the collapsed roof and made it safely to the front lawn.

Helen was pointing and sobbing. "Look at our porch, Willy. Where we've spent so many lovely afternoons."

Willy hugged her tight. "I'll fix it, sweetheart. Don't worry. It's just a house. The main thing is we're safe."

Allison glanced over at the two of them. "No, Willy, I don't think you'll be fixing this house. It's started, and it will get worse. You'll have to leave."

"What do you mean?"

"The beginning of the end has started. We need to hurry up our contingency plans. You all need to come with me."

Willy and Helen just stared at her, mouths open in shock.

"Up until now, it's just been talk—you've heard me telling you what's been going on, what's coming. But, the timetable has been moved up on us—not by our choosing. And, it sounds like we're not even ready."

Dozens of people were out on the street now. Wyatt glanced down the long row of houses and saw that a few others had been damaged as well. Not too seriously, but enough to scare the shit out of people. Especially since even just mere tremors were a rarity in Nelson.

The shaking had ended and neighbors were once again busy disabling their car alarms—for the second time in the past hour.

Wyatt adjusted his gun holster, which had slipped forward on his belt while they were climbing off the porch. "What do you mean? Isn't this CERN thing almost ready to go?"

Allison shook her head. "Not according to Cardinal Valenti. He said they're panicking, and don't feel they have the science totally figured out yet. Let's face it—taking the Earth back in time to 1963 is hard enough to wrap our heads around as a concept, let alone imagining how scientists could possibly figure out how to do it. I'm a physicist and I don't even really understand it. These people are geniuses, but…there are limits."

"Maybe this is just a blip? An earthquake swarm?"

"I don't think so, Wyatt. This swarm, as you call it, is happening all along the Pacific Rim. That's never happened before, all those countries at once. And, when we were in the studio with Willy, you and I saw what he'd assembled. He'd added two more spheres to his display—the Sun and the Earth—and his coordinates tell us that Gargantuan has moved 40 million miles closer in the past month. The magnetic pressure of that closer proximity is tearing us apart.

"Cardinal Valenti agrees—he also calculated that it's only 80 million miles away from us now, without me even telling him what Willy had done. Willy's a receptor—that's why we've kept an eye on him and the others over the years. We knew that the magnetic attraction would cause these people to autonomously react. We can't ignore the warnings he's unwittingly giving us. That would be stupid of us."

Wyatt folded his arms across his chest. "Is the cardinal sure he can't see the damn thing through that Lucifer telescope? Can't he keep trying? Maybe at a different time of day?"

Allison shook her head. "No. He thinks they've turned on some kind of cloaking device. It's invisible, but it shouldn't be now that it's moved to the frontal zone of the Sun. And, the fact that it's so much closer now, means we should be able to see it clearly. But, we can't—so they have some technology that we didn't predict.

"As I told you, at times we have been able to see it—and that was when it was much farther away. That was the reason for all the chemtrailing in the sky. But, now, it's become a goddamned ghost. We won't need the chemtrails anymore now that Gargantuan's cloaked itself. And…I guess it won't matter anyway. Even Majestic 12 doesn't matter anymore. Its purpose is redundant now. Keeping secrets no longer matters. In fact, the Cardinal told me that most of the Majestic 12 members have retreated underground…literally."

Wyatt sighed with exasperation. "I'm just a lowly police officer, so I'm clueless on this shit, but if this giant planet is able to alter its orbital speed—come to a virtual standstill, or speed up as it's now done—isn't it possible that when we go back in time, it could do the same? Or worse?"

Allison took a deep breath.

"Yes, anything's possible. They're probably far more advanced than we are. Going back in time is not going to guarantee defeat against Gargantuan and its inhabitants. All we're trying to do is buy time. Get a head start back in 1963 on the technology side with reverse engineering of the alien technology we've found, and start building CERN thirty years sooner.

"Those things may give us an edge, so that when we do finally reach 2015 again, we'll be far more advanced than we are now, and better prepared to defend ourselves.

"But, you're right—it's all a crapshoot. We have no idea how advanced they are. Our 'do-over' may not save us when we move through the decades into the twenty-first century again. All I can say is that the best and brightest minds on the planet believe that going back to the twentieth century is our best chance to survive the twenty-first."

Willy was staring at a frantic neighbor down the street, who was busy dragging branches of a tree off his car hood. Then, he turned his gaze back to Allison. "You said we have to go with you. Where?"

"As I said, I have a place in Osoyoos. That's where Senator Hartford is right now. Underground dwellings, very comfortable, very safe. If the worst happens and CERN can't stop the destruction Gargantuan and its inhabitants foist upon us, underground is the best place to be."

She gestured with her hand, waving it in a wide circle. "All of this havoc today is just evidence of the magnetic pressure this rogue planet is exerting upon us. It's been building for decades. It will get worse. In fact, it will probably be a living nightmare, sad to say."

Willy nodded his understanding. "Okay, but what if CERN does work? What if they are able to send Earth back in time?"

"Again, underground is the safest place to be. The theory is—and it is just a theory, I have to warn you—the wormhole, which is currently in quarantine, will be unleashed and pounded mercilessly with protons faster than the speed of light. It will be an Earth-crust directed force, calculated with precision to take the planet back in time.

"The science of it, with the force directed laterally, is that only the sphere itself and everything within it—in other words, underground—will transcend time. Everyone and everything *above* ground will vanish with the time transfer—painlessly, and instantly. They'll be replaced by the actual people and structures above ground that exist back in 1963."

Helen gasped at hearing that, and thrust her hands up to her mouth.

Willy whispered, "Jesus Christ...this is too weird."

Allison wrapped her arms around Helen and hugged her gently.

Then, she spread her glance around to all three of them. "Quantum physics is fascinating, although scary as hell. But, fate has brought us together at this point in time, for whatever reason. Willy's encounter with the x-ray machine happened for a reason, I think. We were all meant to meet in the here and now, and Willy was meant to give us warnings about the imminence of Gargantuan."

She smiled warmly at Wyatt. "And I was meant to fall in love with you."

Wyatt mouthed the words, "*I love you, too.*"

"So, either way, you're safest underground with me, folks. What's it going to be? My chariot is waiting for us at the airport."

Willy walked over to his son. "Wyatt, it's your decision. We're with you, here or there, whatever you decide." He turned his head in his wife's direction. "Right, Helen?"

She nodded nervously.

Wyatt looked down at the ground, and shuffled his feet. The conflict in his mind and in his heart caused him to hesitate. "All these people. Our friends. This city. I'm the police chief. I have responsibilities. It feels as if I'd be running away."

He looked up at Allison, and saw that her eyes were beginning to mist over.

She whispered, "You can't help them, Wyatt. And, we can't save everyone. If it helps with your decision, think of it this way—you have a responsibility, first and foremost, to live. And, to love…"

They were all silent for a few moments until Allison finally broke the stillness again. She wiped the corners of her eyes, turned on her heel, and walked across the lawn without a single backward glance. Wyatt heard her cry softly, "May God be with you all."

This time, there was no warning rumble. It could only be described as a crash, followed by a loud roar reminiscent of the collapse of the Twin Towers.

Five parked cars disappeared in a heartbeat.

The road split right down the middle, expanding into a sinkhole about 50 feet wide. The dark chasm snarled like a T-Rex from Jurassic Park, and spewed steam and black particulates upward like a fountain. An ash cloud wasted no time in spreading its ghostly fingers out in every direction.

Wyatt couldn't get the words out fast enough.

"Alison, wait! We're coming!"

CHAPTER 48

Except for the smooth hum of the jet engines, it was as quiet as a mausoleum. But, it sure didn't look like one.

Wyatt allowed his eyes to wander around the cabin, admiring the walnut paneling and grass cloth window shades. He ran his fingers along the supple beige leather of his seat, and pushed the recline button. Unlike commercial jets, this plane's seats actually reclined—flat.

Of course, there was more room in this jet than a commercial airline, being that it was outfitted for only twelve passengers. Wyatt thought that was ironic, considering the owner was a billionaire member of a group called Majestic 12.

This was certainly the way to travel if you could afford it.

Soon, though, luxuries like this would mean nothing. In fact, in Allison's case, she'd have to leave it behind when she transcended back to 1963, including her massive wealth. Assuming, of course, that the plan worked.

He tried not to think of the chaos he'd left behind in Nelson. His conscience was tugging at him; the feeling that he'd abandoned both his community and his responsibilities was a tough thing to reconcile.

But, then, so was the rest of this hocus-pocus.

It was still a blind spot in his brain. He couldn't, no matter how hard he tried, wrap his mind around the concept. She'd explained it as best she could, but Wyatt just didn't get it.

He turned his head and glanced towards the back of the cabin.

Allison was sitting at a conference table with Willy and Helen—they were playing some kind of card game and talking together in hushed tones. They must have thought he was asleep.

He stood up, stretched, and walked back to where they were sitting.

Slid into a seat, then covered the card deck with his hand stopping the game's progress.

Allison smiled at him. "You're awake. Do you want to play?"

"No, I want a science lesson. I know it doesn't really matter whether or not I understand this stuff, but my head is spinning."

Willy nodded. "Me, too. I wasn't the best science student in school, but this wormhole business is beyond anything I could have even imagined."

Allison clasped her fingers together and looked from one to the other.

"Okay, I probably haven't explained it properly.

"And, you have a right to try to understand it, because you're all going back with me to 1963. If it works, that is, and I pray that it does. Not just for us, but for all of mankind."

Willy scratched his forehead. "But, if it does work, what happens to everyone here? You said they'd all just disappear. I don't get that."

"Well, picture it this way. The wormhole is kind of a time machine, but not really. It's more of a mechanism for an alternate universe. Since it's located deep underground, its energy force will be confined to anything beneath the surface.

"Everything above will cease to exist, instantly, with the transference. It will be as if none of it was ever there in the first place."

Wyatt tapped his finger on the table. "That's the part I'm struggling with the most."

"I understand, Wyatt. As I said before, a lot of this I just don't get either. It's bizarre, to say the least. But, we're tampering with time and space. We've learned a lot about matter, density, the Big Bang, Black Holes, and...wormholes.

"The public hasn't heard too much about wormholes because they're just too impossible to fathom...and they're scary as hell. In a lot of ways, we're playing God when we fool around with these things that we don't quite understand yet.

"But, we have an extinction level event on our doorstep, and the time for experimentation is over. We don't have the luxury of time any longer. So, we have to trust the instincts and brains of our brightest people.

"Let me tell you, some of these scientists at CERN are scary—their brains are off the charts. You'd be spooked if you chatted with them. A lot of them are actually autistic savants—scary smart. Makes me think sometimes they themselves have alien DNA!"

Willy picked up the deck of cards and started shuffling it. "Allison, if we all manage to go back, Earth, the way I see it, will be two different worlds. An underground world, and an above-ground world. Is that basically right?"

She nodded. "That's it in a nutshell, Willy. As I said, kind of an alternative universe, rather than time travel, but in essence they're the same thing—and time travel is probably the easiest way to understand it. But… as of the moment of transference to 1963, Earth at that time changes to include those of us from 2015 who are underground, and excludes all those from 2015 who were above ground. Alternate universes—2015 underground, and 1963 above ground."

"What are people going to think once we start crawling out of the ground?"

"It will be as if we'd always been there. The structures we've built underground will be intact, and we will come out just as if we were merely hiding in a bomb shelter, which of course was quite common anyway back in the sixties.

"Anything we change while we're there will change the future 2015, just as if this current 2015 never happened. Going back is like creating a clean slate for that time, and fixing things back then will clean the slate for the future."

Wyatt rubbed his tired eyes. "I guess this is all like believing in God. No one can really understand it, but they believe it anyway. I mean, we scoff at things like what you're talking about that just sound crazy and unbelievable, yet we'll go to church and pray to a God we've never met, who's supposed to be comprised of three spirits—one of whom was born to a virgin. And, that he died and rose from the dead. And, that his father in heaven created the universe in a week's time. And that he lives, but doesn't really live—in fact, he's timeless. And, if we're good, we get to go to a place called heaven, and live for eternity. If we're bad, we go to a fiery hell. Now that I've just recited all that bunk, what you're telling us is starting to sound pretty realistic!"

Allison chuckled. "That may be the best way to look at this. Just believe, as we've been taught to do without question from day one about religion. There are some mysteries we'll never truly understand, I guess, including where the hell we came from, and who created us. For now, until we know better, some of us will believe in the only thing we know, and that's God."

Helen shook her head, and jumped into the conversation. "But, wait—we're going to look different than the rest of them back in the sixties, and we're going to have tools that they didn't have—like computers and iPhones."

"Good point, Helen. But, the looks part won't matter. No one really pays much attention to people who look different and, as you well know, the people in the sixties all strived to look different and…individual.

"As for the tools, naturally our phones won't work because there won't be any cell towers, so no need to carry those around with us. But, we have laptops that will just need to be plugged into a power source."

"There was no internet back then."

"No, Wyatt, but we won't need the internet. We'll have all of the information from the future downloaded onto our hard drives, so we just have to plug in and show them.

"That's where our meeting with Kennedy will be important. We'll be able to show him all he needs to know to convince him to start building CERN. We'll be able to demonstrate the reverse engineering we've done of alien technology, and show him the kind of defenses that Earth is going to need when it finally reaches 2015 and the threat of Gargantuan is again on our doorstep. The Earth will be better prepared than we are now, if we get a head start. Kennedy will give us that head start, if we're able to convince him.

"All of the CERN scientists I talked about will be safely underground when the wormhole sucks us back, as will many other scientists around the world. We'll be adding to 1963 an element of advanced intelligence that will be simply overwhelming, and extremely beneficial to mankind. Maybe by 2015, we'll even be far more advanced than Gargantuan's inhabitants. Which means we'll win…and survive."

Wyatt rested his elbows on the table, and stared into Allison's hypnotic blue eyes. "Meeting you has turned our world completely inside out—no pun intended. I feel like this is just a dream. A dual dream—happy having you in my life, but a nightmare with what you've told us."

Allison squeezed his shoulder. "We play the hand we're dealt, and this is it. Ninety-nine percent of the population knows nothing about any of this, so I guess in that respect we're the lucky ones."

"Are we, though? We're going back, but we have to live with the knowledge that all of these people are going to die."

Allison shook her head furiously. "No! That's the one point you're missing! There's no concept of 'death' with what we're doing. If this works and we go back to 1963 and manage to convince Kennedy to begin preparing the Earth for the future, then all of these people will still exist—they'll just get a do-over. They'll still be born, grow up, and reach 2015 in a safer state than they're in right now."

Willy poured himself a glass of juice from the jug on the table. "That wouldn't be entirely correct, would it? I mean, if we can change that one aspect you're talking about, we will all probably change a lot of other things, too. We'll be populating their world now—probably in the tens of thousands considering how many bunkers like yours exist around the globe. Some people we know now may not exist in the future 2015 if we put our interfering stamp on things."

Allison nodded slowly. "Yes, Willy, that's right. I stand corrected. We have to look at mankind as a whole instead of the individuals we know and love. So, collective mankind will still be alive in 2015 and will have a better chance of survival if we do this right. But, some of the people we know now won't be here then. There's no doubt that we'll change a lot of things, so the world could indeed look considerably different in the new 2015 than the old one we're used to now. That, alone, will be fascinating—our memories of what once was, against what we watch it become."

"What about me? If I go visit myself as a younger Willy, and perhaps cause the younger me to have an accident and die, would both of us disappear?"

"First of all, Willy, I must warn you not to do that. We don't know what having contact with your younger self would do. It's a scary unknown. But, as far as your younger self dying, no, I don't think that would have an effect on the older you.

"You're thinking of that movie, *Back to the Future*, where Marty starts to fade away. That movie was based on the fantasy concept of time travel, which isn't really what we're doing. As I mentioned, our approach is really an 'alternate universe' for those beneath the ground that we're sending back. So, you'll exist back then no matter what might happen to your younger self. Understand?"

Willy laughed. "No, not really, but I guess I'll just have to suck it up. This is the strangest stuff I've ever heard—even stranger than my side effects from an alien beam weapon."

Allison chuckled, and then looked up as the co-pilot approached their table. "Ready to land, Dave?"

"Yep. If you could all get back to your seats and buckle in, we'll have you on the ground in about fifteen minutes."

"Great. Okay, folks, after we arrive in Penticton, we'll be driving down to Osoyoos. If you think all of this is strange, wait until you see your new quarters!"

Wyatt got up and started heading for his seat. "Do you think your friend is safe? Any updates?"

Allison nodded. "Yes, I think everything's fine. Gerndle texted me to say that the guy who was asking about the senator never came back. So, she must have convinced him that he wasn't hiding out at the winery. She's a good actor, and she's German. Those Germans can be pretty poker-faced; hard to recognize their emotions sometimes."

CHAPTER 49

"This one doesn't feel right to me."

Cliff steered the black Lincoln onto the secondary road and drove through the tunnel of lush grapevines and fruit trees.

He turned to his partner. "Bert, once they start feeling right, you'll know you've completely lost it."

"But, you were here this morning. She said he wasn't there. What are we going to do, torture her?"

Cliff blinked his eyes several times—the dust from the road was finding its way through the car's filters. "We'll just scare her a little. She'll give it up."

"But, what if he's not here? How do we know for sure?"

Cliff shook his head. "No, he's here. The technology is solid. The cell signal came from this winery."

"What did they say to you?"

"They told me to go back and try again. That this is an important one."

Bert looked at the image on his cell phone. "The guy's a famous senator. High profile. I don't like this type of job."

"That's why the payday's so lucrative, Bert. Don't complain."

"Why do they want him dead?"

Cliff shook his head. "It doesn't matter. We're never told why anyway, you know that."

"Yeah, but I figured in this case you might have been given a hint."

"No, not at all. You never get the assignments—they all come through me. So, as I've told you before, I never even know who's assigning the jobs to us. These things are done through double and triple blinds; even the voices on the phone are electronically altered, and the phones they use are untraceable. Probably satellite."

Bert looked out at the dense foliage they were driving through. "Feels like a trap to me. Christ, people could be hiding amongst all this crap and we wouldn't even see them."

"The manager's just a harmless little lady, Bert. And, this is just a fucking winery. It's not a trap. Why would anyone want to trap us? We're not important, not relevant. We're just machines."

Cliff could feel Bert's eyes boring into him.

"I can handle popping people, Cliff, but torture's not my thing. If that's what you're planning, count me out. Tell me before we go any further along this fucking jungle road."

"We're not going to torture anyone. I promise. We'll be in and out. It's a goddamned winery. Aside from the trees, where could he hide? Maybe a wine barrel?" Cliff laughed at the image he'd created in his mind. "Yeah, a wine barrel—I like that. We could just roll him out of here."

Bert wasn't amused. "I'm surprised they didn't just cancel the hit once you told them he wasn't here."

Cliff smiled wryly. "You seem to have forgotten. Orders are always irrevocable. We don't even know who's giving them to us, so how could they be cancelled? How would we know if the proper authority in charge was giving the order to cancel? No, Bert, the only way an order can be cancelled is to execute us. That's the only way it can be stopped. That keeps the certainty part of our business intact. We do it, get paid, and the customer's happy. Hell, we've already been paid half for this one. Do you really want to return your quarter million? I sure as fuck don't."

Bert shook his head. "No. But, for some reason this one just doesn't feel right."

The road widened and the dense foliage came to an end, replaced now by a circular driveway that led them to the front of a futuristic glass and stone building. Cliff parked the car.

They got out and walked up the front steps, into the front foyer. There was a reception counter and a long hallway that led to the rear of the building. Cliff could hear the faint sound of a bell ringing.

A middle-aged blonde woman rushed out of an office down the hall and came up to greet them at the counter.

Once she recognized him, she couldn't hide her shock at seeing him again. In a halting, heavily accented voice, she said, "Oh, you again. I told you already that he's not here."

Bert stepped forward. "Hello, ma'am. We're sorry to bother you. But, it's an urgent family matter. We have to reach this man named John

Hartford." He held out his phone to her. "Here's his photo. He may be going under a different name. Are you sure you haven't seen him? It's very important."

The woman glanced at the phone and just shook her head. "No, I haven't seen him."

Cliff was starting to lose his patience. He glanced at his watch. His many years of experience had taught him that these things had to be done quickly. And, preliminary matters tried his patience. The real job lay ahead, and this woman was just a nuisance in the way.

He glanced around, and allowed his finely tuned ears to search for sounds of life. "Do you do tours here, ma'am?"

"No. This is a private winery."

"So, are you the only one here? No staff?"

She hesitated. "No need for staff except at harvesting time. The winery runs itself, and as you know, wine just ages nicely when left alone."

Cliff reached under his jacket and pulled out his Glock. He pointed it at her head. "I'm done being nice. We know that man, Hartford, is here. So, do yourself a favor and show us where you're hiding him."

The lady staggered backwards at the sight of the menacing pistol. She put her hand up to her mouth and gasped.

Suddenly, the sound of footsteps. Cliff glanced to the right and saw a man walking quickly towards them. He was short, balding, and a bit on the chubby side. Wearing a rubber apron, rubber gloves, and holding a clipboard in his hand. He was studying the clipboard as he walked and hadn't noticed them yet.

The woman had heard his footsteps, too. She whirled around and yelled, "Derik! Run!"

He jerked his head up, and his eyes and mouth opened wide as he took in the shocking scene in front of him. He dropped the clipboard, spun in a 180, and started running back down the hallway.

Cliff reacted on instinct. Images from Iraq flashed through his brain. The enemy throwing grenades at him and his comrades, then turning like a coward and running away. The soldier inside of him couldn't consent to retreat. Retreat and escape weren't permitted.

He raised his pistol and fired once. The blast reverberated within the walls of the small lobby, and echoed down the hallway.

The enemy went down. The woman screamed.

* * * * *

Allison led the way into the winery.

She called out. "Gerndle? Derik?"

Silence, except for the faint sound of the warning bell announcing their entrance, ringing down in the office area.

She turned to the others. "They must be down in the oak room. We'll wander down there after. Follow me."

Down the long hallway they went. Allison in front, with Wyatt, Willy and Helen pulling up the rear.

"My dad built this winery, and we have four residences underground—nicknamed the 'Treehouse.' Clever, huh?"

Wyatt moved up beside her as they walked. "So, down there is where the senator is?"

"Yep. And that's where we'll all be. I'll take you there first, then I'll introduce you to Gerndle and Derik after that. They run this winery by themselves, so when it's wine-tasting time they're both usually in the oak room together. This place keeps them pretty busy."

She led the way out the back door and along a small path until they reached the small stone crypt-looking building that housed the hatch entrance to the 'Treehouse.' Allison took a remote unit out of her purse and pressed a button. The door lock clicked and she gave it a shove. The heavy door creaked open and they stepped inside.

It was pitch black in the windowless room. She flicked the light switch on the wall.

The scene inside made her stomach turn.

A man was standing over the hatch in the floor, with a gun pointed towards Allison's head. "Welcome. Heard you coming, so we decided to turn off the lights and give you a surprise party."

Behind her, Helen's heavy breathing gave a dose of reality to the scene in front of her. There was another man off in the corner, also with a pistol in his hand. Derik was lying on the floor, wearing an orange apron and gloves. Blood was pooling on the floor underneath him.

Gerndle was stretched out on the floor, head leaning up against the stone wall, holding her hand over her chest. She seemed to be in shock, breathing shallow, eyes glazed over.

Allison found her voice. "They need help. Please, let us tend to them and then you can tell us what you want."

The tall man standing over the hatch shook his head. "Only one needs help, and you can deal with that afterwards. The man's dead. An unfortunate circumstance, but it couldn't be helped." He nodded in his partner's direction. "Frisk them."

The shorter man, who hadn't yet said a word, stuffed his gun into a holster under his jacket, and began frisking each of them one by one. When he reached under Wyatt's jacket, he pulled the 357 Magnum out of its hip holster and exclaimed, "Well, what do we have here? Police issue! Who are you, buddy?"

Wyatt spoke through clenched teeth. "Good guess. I'm a police officer."

The tall one chuckled. "At least we have someone here who understands that we're serious dudes. Tell your friends to behave themselves, copper, and they'll be okay."

Allison took a step towards Gerndle.

"Hey! Stay where you are!"

"She needs help. What have you done to her?"

"Nothing at all. Seems she had a heart attack. She'll be fine."

"No, I don't think she will. Let us at least get her some water and an aspirin."

The tall man shook his head. "We want Senator Hartford. He's down there, according to the lady. She agreed to phone him on the direct line to try to convince him to come out, but he didn't fall for the bait. Apparently, she can't open the hatch from up here because the sly man engaged the safety lock. He won't release it."

Allison nodded. That was a safety device installed to protect the inhabitants down below, in case of attempts at intrusion from above. The senator, while having been careless with his cell phone, was now at least on his guard. She was glad. But, it presented an extra challenge for them now. Her mind was whirling.

"Well, the senator was being smart. What do you intend to do with him?"

"Lady, I know who you are. Allison Fisher. We were given information about you. I know you own this place, and I know you're a good friend of the senator's. He probably barely knows these two sauerkrauts lying here, but I'm sure he knows and trusts you."

"You didn't answer my question. What are you going to do with him?"

"I'm not going to bullshit you. We're going to kill him, because that's what we're being paid to do. We're not being paid to kill you or the others—one's dead, but that wasn't intended. If you let us have Hartford, we'll let the rest of you live. We're running out of time here."

Allison bit her lip. "First, you need to let me make a phone call. To Atlanta. I promise you that it will not put you in any danger. It has to do with this…job…you've been assigned. After I make the call, you'll have my cooperation."

The man pondered her request for a second or two. "I guess there's no harm." He walked over and stood beside her. "I'll watch your phone to make sure you're indeed calling Atlanta and not someone local."

Allison pulled her phone out of her jacket pocket, and punched in the number.

"Powers, here."

"Chad, it's Allison. Call off the dogs."

"What are you talking about?"

"I'm standing here with your two killers. Talk to them and end this. You know there's no point anymore. You've talked with Cardinal Valenti and I'm sure CERN as well. It doesn't matter now if Hartford blows the whistle. The deadline has moved up."

"I've already ordered the hit stopped. I did that yesterday. They should have received that message through our blind."

Sarcasm dripped from Allison's voice as she quipped, "I don't think they got the memo." She held her hand over the phone and turned to the tall man. "My contact says the hit was cancelled."

The man chuckled. "No one told us anything, and even if they did, the order can't be reversed. There's a 'failsafe' in our profession, lady. Orders stand."

Allison put the phone back to her ear. "He says the order can't be cancelled, Chad. You've really set the wheels in motion here, haven't you? You prick!"

He growled back at her. "Fuck off, Allison. I have more important things to worry about than your senator buddy. Deal with it. Let them have him. You should have just let him die back in Vermont instead of sticking your pretty little nose in. Serious stuff going on now—all hell's breaking loose. All of the Majestic 12 board have disappeared, and I'm about to do the same. So, if you think I give a shit about a stupid politician, think again."

The phone disconnected.

Allison turned to the tall killer.

"I'll pay you double, triple, or whatever—to *not* do this."

"Sorry, lady. We have ethics in our profession, too. Our reputations would be toast if we did things like that. We'd probably be dead ourselves in short order. So, get on that phone hanging on the wall over there and phone the good senator. Then, we can all go home."

Allison didn't believe his promise that they'd be allowed to live. Once the senator was killed, she was sure they'd all suffer the same fate. But, she was running out of options.

The tall man walked over to the trembling Gerndle and put the gun to her head.

"I'll count to three. If you haven't picked up that phone by then, she's dead. Then, one by one, each of your friends, too—until it's just you and us."

Allison put her hands up. "Stop. These people mean a lot to me, much more than the senator does. I'm not going to watch them all die over him. You can have him. And, he'll listen to me. He'll open up."

The killer moved his gun away from Gerndle's head.

"Smart lady. Okay, make the call."

Allison walked over to the wall and, before pulling the phone off its cradle, she turned towards the killer. "Did Gerndle tell you that the safety lock is on a timer?"

He shook his head.

"You'll have to be a wee bit patient. Once he releases it, it will unlock automatically after ten minutes. Understand?"

"Okay, makes sense. A true safety lock—good thinking on your part. Make the fucking phone call."

Allison pointed her remote at the hatch and pressed a button.

"Okay, the topside lock is released now. Once we hear the click of the safety lock, we can lift up the hatch in exactly ten minutes' time."

"Phone him!"

Allison picked up the phone and punched the button.

"Hello?"

Allison kept her voice steady and cheerful.

"John, it's me, Allison."

"Oh, good. You're back. I'm sorry—I really screwed up on that cell phone thing. Should have listened to you."

"It's okay, John. Someone enquired about you, but they haven't been back. It's safe now."

"Gerndle advised me to stay down here and put on the safety lock, told me not to release it. But, then she phoned me a few minutes ago and told me to unlock it. Something in her voice didn't sound right. So, I decided to wait until you were back. Are you sure it's safe?"

"Yes, it's okay now. I have three friends with me who are going to be joining you down there. And…good news on the Homefront. Everything's calmed down and you're no longer a target. I've talked to your campaign headquarters. Sounds like it's time for you to announce."

"Really?"

"Things are moving along fast, John. It's best you announce sooner rather than later. The nation needs leadership right now because things are spinning out of control. Okay?"

"Hmm…well, we'll have to chat more about this. I'm not sure."

"Disengage the safety lock now, John. We can fly back to Vermont in my jet. And, you'll be pleased to know that your daughter got in touch with me. She just flew in from Spain. Wants to help with the campaign."

"Gotcha."

Allison hung up the phone, and nodded at the killer. The click of the safety lock reverberated around the walls of the crypt room.

He smiled, and glanced at his watch.

"You did good. Counting down…."

*****

John punched the safety lock button as soon as he hung up the phone. He knew they'd hear the sound of the lock topside. And, he knew also that he had no longer than ten minutes.

He dashed to the back of the apartment and into the storage room. He opened up the gun locker and chose an Uzi machine pistol, shoved in a magazine and put an extra one in his pocket. He'd used one of these before, in a war games exercise. Of course, at that time he'd been firing blanks. This time he wouldn't be.

The senator shoved open the blast door, revealing a passageway which connected with the main tunnel towards the emergency escape hatch. He recalled Allison telling him that the tunnel was about 100 feet long and could only be opened from the inside. It would take him out into an overgrown area of the vineyard, only a short jog back to the crypt building.

As he raced through the tunnel, the menacing Uzi stuck inside his front waistband, his life flashed across his mind. All the wonderful things he'd done, and all the wonderful people he'd known.

He thought about his regrets, too.

One in particular—that he'd never had children. Allison's comment about his daughter flying back from Spain was clever indeed, but it also made him sad for a brief moment.

A moment when he wished it were actually true.

CHAPTER 50

Allison stole a glance at her Rolex. About seven minutes to go. When that precious time expired, these two killers would be expecting Senator Hartford to open up the hatch and climb out. At which time, they'd shoot him dead, along with the rest of them.

Of course, he wouldn't be opening the hatch at all. Allison knew he'd picked up on her warning. But, what he would do instead, she had no idea. If he did poke his head out of the hatch, he'd probably be armed—so a gun barrel would come out first, instead of his senatorial head. Then, there'd be a gunfight, which in this small confined space would guarantee multiple casualties. John was smarter than that.

She'd already shown John where the gun locker was, so that was probably where he headed first after hanging up the phone. Allison had also shown him the blast door that led to the emergency escape tunnel. She prayed he remembered that. He could take that route and, once outside, use his cell phone to call for help. But, it would take time for the police to get there, considering how far outside the town of Osoyoos the winery was.

They certainly wouldn't be able to get there in seven minutes.

She glanced over at Gerndle, who was slumped against the wall next to Derik's prone figure. Derik's blood had spread across the floor, and Gerndle's beige trousers had soaked it up like a sponge. Her eyes were closed, right hand still clasping at her chest. Time was running out for her. If she didn't get help soon, she would die right alongside her husband.

Allison turned her head toward Wyatt. He was staring at her, no doubt wondering about what she'd said to the senator over the phone. He knew her well enough by now to know that she wouldn't have just summoned him to his death. He'd probably guessed that she'd given him a clue of some sort.

He flashed her a wry smile and she returned it with a quick wink.

Willy eased Helen down to the floor. Her face was as white as a ghost, and Allison knew that she'd been through hell a few weeks ago with the kidnapping. She had just recently started returning to normal, according to Willy. But, the earthquake had literally shaken her world again…and now this.

Willy sat down beside his wife and wrapped his arm tightly around her shoulders. She closed her eyes and breathed a heavy sigh.

"Five minutes to go, Ms. Fisher. That safety lock should release completely and the good senator will come crawling out of there."

Allison turned her gaze toward the tall killer. "Yes, not much time left now. However, he may not be able to open that hatch. It's heavy, and he's not a young man. He may expect us to lift it open for him."

The killer smiled. "We'll just have to see, won't we?"

He beckoned with his index finger. "Be a good girl and stand over here, right smack in front of the hatch. I want your comforting face to be the first thing he sees when he opens up."

Allison walked over and stood near the edge.

The killer then pointed at Wyatt. "You, copper, come over here and stand on the other side of the hatch. If he doesn't open up, you can do the honors."

Before Wyatt could move, Willy unwrapped his arms from around Helen, stood up, and walked over to the hatch. "Let me do it, buddy. My son dislocated his shoulder a while back and might not be able to lift it. That hatch looks heavy."

The killer laughed. "Father and son, huh? Well, aren't you the caring daddy—sure, you can lift it if you want. For an old fart you're quite the stand-up guy, aren't you?"

Allison noticed the cold hard look that had suddenly appeared in Willy's eyes.

And, she noticed something else as well. His jawbones seemed to protrude a bit more than they had just a few short minutes ago. In the dim light of the crypt building, he seemed to be glowing. The killers probably thought it was just a trick of the light in the room, but Allison knew what it was. It was happening right in front of their eyes, just the way she'd seen it happen with her own father once upon a time.

*****

John ran as fast as his aging legs could tolerate.

He was still in pretty good shape, but hadn't done any running in quite some time. He could feel it in his knees, but pushed himself to keep going.

He came to the end of the tunnel, climbed up the short ladder, and twisted the wheel on the hatch. He heard a hissing sound as the hydraulics lifted the hatch skyward.

He dragged himself out onto the long grass and took a second to get his bearings.

He was in the middle of a wild, unkempt vineyard, with no discernable path to anywhere. It was too thick to see more than 20 feet in front. But, he remembered Allison telling him that the crypt building was south of where the escape hatch opened up.

He looked up and saw the Sun.

Luckily, this area of the world was sunny most of the time, otherwise John wouldn't have had a clue as to which direction to run. His watch told him it was 3:00 in the afternoon, so he knew he had to aim roughly in the direction of the Sun.

He took several deep breaths and then began his dash through the thick underbrush, grapevines slapping his face as he fought his way along. A couple of times, he tripped and fell hard, made all the more painful by the Uzi pistol stuck in his waistband. He thanked his good judgement in leaving the safety on.

It only took a couple of minutes to break out into the open.

And, there it was.

The stone crypt building, where, any minute now, he was expected to open the hatch and emerge. The building where Allison and her friends were being held hostage at this very moment.

Allison Fisher—the woman who had risked her life back in Vermont to save his.

Now, John would have the chance to perhaps return the favor.

He glanced at his watch. Eight minutes had gone by since he'd started his mad dash down the tunnel.

Two minutes to go.

John thought of phoning the police, but realized that was foolish. They would take far too long to get here, assuming they could even find this remote place.

He realized the only choice he had was to burst through the door and hope that he shot the right targets. But, Uzi machine pistols, while deadly, were notoriously inaccurate. They were slaughter weapons, firing several rounds a second. He knew it could be switched to 'single shot,' but he didn't know how to do that.

He walked cautiously up to the building and rounded the corner towards the one and only door, his heart pounding out of his chest.

Suddenly, he noticed something.

Something which caused him to remember a conversation he'd had with Gerndle on one of the times he'd come out for some fresh air and sunshine.

About twenty yards from the crypt was another little building. A building that contained nothing but electrical panels, maintenance equipment…and the control panel and piping system for the winery's fire suppression system.

Gerndle knew the winery inside and out, as well as all of the machinery that kept it working…and kept it safe. She had proudly taken John on a tour, even down to the oak room where rows and rows of oaken casks fostered the fermentation of Diamond Winery's award winning vintages.

During the tour she gave him, John had noticed that there were sprinkler heads in the ceilings of every building, including the crypt structure. Gerndle explained that the entire winery was protected by what was known as a Deluge sprinkler system, which was vastly different from the Wet Pipe systems that were more common.

In Wet Pipe systems, there was always water in the pipes, ready to burst free as soon as the fusible links in the sprinkler heads were melted by fire at a pre-set temperature. But, the disadvantages to systems like that were possible water damage if there was leakage, or freezing of the pipes if the heating systems failed—which would cause one hell of a mess.

In a Deluge system, there was no water in the pipes. It waited patiently until someone activated it manually. Or, it could be connected to the fire alarm—once the alarm went off, the system would activate automatically and the deluge would commence.

At Diamond Vintage Winery, the Deluge system could be activated either way. And, making it even more interesting, Gerndle explained to him that it was engineered to be even more effective in fire suppression than just a mere water system. It had two piping networks that joined together at the entrance point to each building.

One network contained water and the other one contained a foam solution. When the two mixed together, a ferocious liquidy foam substance blasted through the ceiling-mounted sprinkler heads, thoroughly smothering whatever fire might exist below.

John dashed over to the little services building, opened the door and ducked inside. He glanced at his watch. Thirty seconds left.

His eyes scanned the controls. He could activate the fire alarm and the suppression system would automatically explode into action. Or, he could just manually trigger the system without the alarm.

He chose to go without the alarm. It would be too loud, and if Allison or the others were shouting instructions, they might not hear each other.

John's fingers slid across the control panel until they came to a button which was labelled 'Hatch Building.' He punched it, which would ensure that only that little crypt building would be deluged. John figured doing only that building would ensure maximum pressure in the system.

Another set of controls allowed for a choice as to timespan of suppression. John chose fifteen minutes.

His fingers slid down the screen until they came to the final button.

Senator John Hartford pulled the Uzi out of his waistband and clicked off the safety.

He took a deep breath…and then another.

Through clenched teeth, he muttered to himself, "Do it, John."

Without another moment's hesitation, he pressed the button labelled 'Activate.'

CHAPTER 51

The tall killer was staring at his watch and counting down. "Ten, nine…"

It occurred to Wyatt that he actually seemed happy, excited. His voice also bore a tinge of sarcasm and taunting. Verging on victorious.

Wyatt didn't know what to expect when the countdown ended. Would the hatch actually open? Was Allison telling the truth when she explained about the time delay on the lock? Would the senator open it? Or would Willy have to do the honors?

If he did emerge from down below, the senator would be an instant dead man.

Wyatt was certain that the rest of them would be close behind him on the trip to the hereafter. Instead of the plan to wormhole their way back to 1963, they would now just cease to exist.

His life over the last few months had gone through incredible twists and turns. The world and all that he thought he knew about it had been turned on its end.

The horror of what was about to happen to the planet, and the pie-in-the-sky plan to use CERN to circumvent fate, was enough to make his head spin.

But, now, these killers.

In an odd way, he felt annoyed, like they were just pesky little insects that needed to be squashed. The type of insects that were elusive and painful, the ones that ruined a good day of golf or a picnic in the park. No matter how hard you swatted at them, you just kept missing, and they just kept buzzing, biting.

These hired guns obviously had no idea what was going on. They had no idea that the world was in peril. They were just obeying orders, orders that the tall one already told Allison couldn't be rescinded. So, they would kill, collect their money…and, unbeknownst to them, there would be very little time left to spend it.

They were now standing in the way of refuge. Standing in the way of a plan, despite how ridiculously remote that plan sounded. But, it was at least something that had given each of them hope, something to hang on to.

And, now, right when they were on the verge of some semblance of safety and a possible solution, they might not live to see it through.

"Okay, old man. I don't hear that hatch opening, so you're on. Give it a heave."

Willy reached down to the handle on the hatch and pulled upward.

The heavy hatch creaked as it retreated from its mooring. Wyatt caught his breath as he noticed the dramatic change in his father's appearance. His strong hand gripping the handle of the hatch accentuated the bone structure. In his bent-over position, the rays from the single light in the room seemed to catch his face just right.

Willy was now, once again, a living skeleton.

With his back to the killers, they hadn't yet noticed the horrifying apparition.

The hatch was now completely open, revealing its dark haunting abyss.

Senator Hartford was nowhere in sight.

"I can't see a fucking thing. Lady, aren't there lights you can turn on?"

Allison extended the remote and pressed a button. Suddenly, the shaft illuminated, all the way down as far as the eye could see.

"Fuck! Where is he? Is there another exit out of that tomb?"

Allison shook her head and lied. "No. For security reasons, this is the only way in or out."

"I don't know if I believe you—but, okay. Plan B."

The killer suddenly rammed the barrel of his Glock into the back of Willy's head. Wyatt could hear the impact from where he was standing on the opposite side of the room.

"Climb down there, old man, and bring him up. Tell him there's an emergency with Ms. Fisher—and, if he doesn't buy that, just tell him we're going to kill her and everyone else. If he's a good senator, I'm sure his conscience won't be able to handle that."

Willy slowly turned and faced the killer.

Wyatt had seen countless horror movies over the years, but very few compared to the scene in front of him right now. His dad—a haunting glow adorning the three exposed areas: his face, and both hands.

Totally transparent, his skeletal face accented by effervescent blue eyes. The macabre sight of an aperture that was supposed to be a mouth, opening and closing in a menacing whisper.

"You're a dead man."

The killer lurched backwards. The look on his face was indescribable. In the split second that he saw it, it reminded Wyatt of the frozen expressions of the unfortunate victims in the movie, *The Ring*, after they'd laid their eyes on the demon girl climbing out of the well.

A blood-curdling scream escaped the lips of the tall man as he backpedalled away from Willy, followed by a "Jesus Fucking Christ!" from the shorter partner standing against the wall.

Instinctively, the killer fired his pistol in Willy's direction, but it was poorly aimed. It caught him in the shoulder and spun him around.

But, it was only a momentary distraction.

Willy kept coming.

* * * * *

John listened carefully for what he'd expected would be a sudden rush of liquid through the pipes.

All he heard was a slight humming sound. Not the deluge he'd expected.

He cursed, and ran out of the building towards the front door of the crypt. Maybe there was a delay on the deluge the same way there was a delay programmed for the safety lock in the hatch.

John reached the front door, Uzi held in front of him at waist level. He knew that beyond this door was a tragedy waiting to happen.

Allison and her friends were in danger because of him.

And, by now, they must have realized he wasn't in the shaft and wouldn't be coming up.

How the killers would react to that, he could only guess.

They might go down to search for him, but he suspected they'd be reluctant to do that, fearing an ambush.

John reached his free hand out towards the door handle.

Then, he stopped himself.

He still faced the same problem he was worried about before. Going in, gun blazing, could only result in innocent people being killed. Adding to that worry was the fact that he didn't even know who Allison's friends were. In the split second it took to pull the trigger, would he be able to tell the good guys from the bad?

His idea of using the fire suppression system as a diversion didn't seem to be working. Was there something else he was supposed to do to activate the system? Something he'd overlooked?

John swore again, whirled around, and dashed back inside the services building.

He wiped the sweat from his eyes and once again studied the control panel. Double-checked everything he'd done.

He was puzzled. It appeared as if he'd followed the proper procedures.

Then, he noticed it.

A small switch on the side of the panel console.

With the label: *System delay override.*

*****

Willy grabbed the killer's gun hand and flung it upwards. The man swung his free hand at his skeletal face and made contact, but Willy just shrugged it off. He twisted the man's arm backwards until the shoulder popped out of its socket. The killer screamed in pain and shoved his knee up into Willy's groin. Another shrug, as Willy slammed the man up against the wall.

The tussle had only taken a couple of seconds, but to Wyatt it had seemed a lifetime. He was in awe watching his father in action, while at the same time being aware of Allison dashing over to Gerndle and covering her with her own body.

The second gunman was now trying to position himself to get a shot at Willy without hitting his partner.

Wyatt was just about to rush the man when there was another kind of rush.

Actually, more like a 'whoosh.'

It reverberated loudly through the ceiling of the crypt for a second or two until the source of the sound made its appearance. He looked up just as a white foamy substance poured out of the sprinkler heads in the ceiling.

Suddenly, the room and everyone in it took on a different appearance. Like a blinding snowstorm, but worse than that. A thick slippery foam that stuck to everything it sprayed.

The short killer was trying his best to ignore the foam storm, and began angling around the room, still trying to take aim at Willy to save his partner.

Wyatt made his move. He dove forward onto his chest and slid across the room along the foam that had now completely covered the floor. Its slipperiness carried him forward with ease, just as if he were sliding into home plate.

At the last second, the man saw him. But, it was too late. Wyatt's forward momentum carried him hard into the killer's legs, taking him down. He then scrambled on top of him and slammed his foam-covered fist into his face. The sickening sound of cracking bones told Wyatt that his fist had done serious harm to his nose. He started snorting as the blood gushed across his face.

He still had the Glock in his hand, and Wyatt scrambled farther up the man's chest and pinned his upper arm to the floor.

Just as he clasped his free hand on the man's gun, he glanced up to check where Willy was.

What he saw was a blur of motion, encased in white foam. Willy lifted the tall killer high in the air and then slammed him down to the concrete foam-covered floor in a move that most professional wrestlers would have had a tough time mimicking.

Part of Wyatt's brain told him to look away now, but for some reason he couldn't.

It was brutal and animalistic, but perhaps because it was his father doing it, it became less so.

His brain also told him that these men had to die.

For a second or two, he remembered how scenes like this were portrayed in movies. Most of the time, when the killer was down and out, the good guy walked away without checking to make sure he was really and truly dead. Followed by the tiresome and traditional miracle—the bad guy would somehow come to life and reach for the gun lying on the floor.

Wyatt was fully aware that in real life it wasn't like that.

During his years in the RCMP, he'd brought many lives to an end, lives that deserved an ending because of the fickleness and unpredictability of a courtroom.

And, now, his dad was doing the same thing.

For Wyatt, it was like a bad dream—but also a good dream. Just like when Willy had ended the lives of the kidnappers who had terrorized his wife, he was doing it once again. Exacting his own sense of justice that his amazing strength and induced brutality was allowing him. Without conscience. The offshoots of DNA that had been permanently altered.

Willy picked up the still-breathing killer like a ragdoll and threw him on top of the shaft opening. Then, he dragged him slightly backwards until his head was positioned just right. Almost like the care he put into the works of art perfected in his studio.

Then, without hesitation, Willy Carson grabbed the edge of the heavy metal hatch cover and slammed it down on top of the dazed killer's head.

Wyatt gulped and turned his attention back to the man underneath him. The killer's hand was still wrapped tightly around the butt of the gun, but Wyatt managed to slide his index finger in between the trigger and the guard as a precaution. For now, the gun couldn't be fired.

He was just getting ready to break the man's wrist to get the gun out of his hand when suddenly the door to the crypt was kicked open. Wyatt twisted his head around and noticed a tall distinguished looking man standing in the doorway, holding an Uzi pistol. He looked somewhat like the actor, Donald Sutherland.

Allison called out. "John!"

The one remaining killer took advantage of the moment's distraction and wiggled his hand free from Wyatt's grasp. He lifted his gun hand and aimed it towards the doorway.

A volley of bullets came, tearing into the gunman's hand and forearm. He let out a guttural scream as flesh and bone were torn to shreds.

The Glock fell harmlessly to the floor. Wyatt scrambled to his feet and retrieved it out of the thick foam. He pointed it down at the would-be assassin's head.

The man from the doorway sloshed his way through the foam and joined him. Wyatt held out his hand and they shook.

"Senator Hartford, I presume?"

"Yes, that's me alright. Thank God I didn't hit you. And, thank God you're one of the good guys! I fired on pure instinct and it looks like I'm a better shot than I thought."

"You are. Thanks, Senator. For the shots…and for the foam, too. I'm assuming that was your mischief as well?"

John grinned. "Yeah. Worked pretty good, huh?"

"Gave me a bit of an advantage for a few precious seconds."

John nodded down at the floor. "What about him?"

The killer had pressed his mangled arm between his legs, wincing in pain.

He forced out the words he wanted them to hear. "This…job is… done. Don't worry, it's…cancelled. Let me go…and…you won't have to worry."

Wyatt frowned down at him. "Didn't I hear your partner say that a hit can never be cancelled?"

"That…was him…talking. Not…me."

Wyatt shook his head. "Sorry, buddy. There's only one way your hit on the senator can be cancelled. And, this is it."

Wyatt leaned down and placed the barrel of the killer's own gun against his temple.

Then, he calmly fired one bullet into his brain.

CHAPTER 52

The sling was on a pulley system.

Actually, the sling itself looked like a hammock, although this hammock wasn't designed for leisurely naps.

It folded down neatly from inside the top of the shaft and then jerked and shook its way to the lowest level, guided by human hands on red colored levers.

The lowest level was number four.

The first level contained the four apartment units, the second level was dedicated to composting, and the third level was the massive vegetable garden.

But, sixty feet below the apartment units was level four, and there was a reason why it was the deepest point in the underground complex.

It was the last one anyone alive would want to visit.

Unless they absolutely had to.

And, today, Wyatt and John had to.

They volunteered to sling the four dead bodies down to level four, which was the mausoleum floor. John worked the pulley system from the top and Wyatt handled the transfer down below.

The bodies of the two mangled killers were taken down first and Wyatt placed them in two of the dozen or so concrete coffins.

Next came Derik's body.

And, finally, Gerndle's.

Wyatt had never seen Allison cry before. The history that she'd had with Gerndle and Derik was a beautiful one, and of course her father had been very close with them before Allison had entered the picture.

They had been loyal employees for decades, but more than that, they'd been like family.

While the desperate struggles were going on in the crypt, Allison had covered Gerndle with her own body to not only protect her from more harm, but also to shield her eyes from what was going on. Since she'd already suffered what appeared to be a heart attack after seeing her husband shot dead, the sight of more violent images was the last thing Allison wanted her to witness.

But, it didn't matter. When the danger was over and Allison had pulled herself off her, Gerndle had already passed away.

Wyatt was saddened to see her so upset, but, strangely—or, maybe not so strangely—it also made him feel closer to her.

They sat together on the foam-covered floor for at least half an hour, and he held her tight as she sobbed uncontrollably. Once in a while, she'd utter a memory of Gerndle and Derik—things they'd done together as families, the wine-tasting festivals that they'd hosted in Osoyoos, and the celebratory nature of harvest times.

She had wonderful memories of them, and, while it was good for her to speak of them, every memory made her cry just a little bit harder.

Wyatt knew by now that he was in love with Allison, but the woman he thought he'd fallen for was only the tip of the iceberg. Beneath that efficient, take-charge exterior was a woman with deep emotions, and this was the first time he'd seen that side of her.

Her ability to cry and lament her loss, her willingness to show weakness in front of him.

He cried right along with her, even though he hadn't even known the couple. But, he wasn't crying for them—he was crying for Allison. For her loss, and for her humanity.

And, he cried because he just loved her so darn much, and on this day he'd come so close to losing her. The inner release of that fear of loss brought a cavalcade of tears in concert with hers. It was the most intimate moment he'd ever shared with a woman, and it had taken place in the most unexpected of places, at the most unexpected of times.

When Wyatt and John had finished their gruesome task, they made their way back up to the apartment on level one.

Allison, Willy, and Helen were sitting at the kitchen table; Willy naked from the waist up.

Allison and Helen were examining his shoulder wound. The tall killer had delivered a shot directly into Willy's upper shoulder, and while it had spun him around at the time, it hadn't seemed to impair his ability to fight back. And, fight back he had. In spades.

"How's the patient?"

Willy smiled. "I'm okay, son. No big deal."

"Dad, a bullet is always a big deal."

"No, I just got grazed."

Allison laughed. "It wasn't a graze, Willy. It went clear through you and out the other side."

She turned to Wyatt and beckoned him closer with her index finger.

"Come here. Take a look at this."

Wyatt took a seat beside his dad at the table, and examined the shoulder wound that Allison was pointing to.

It had completely healed over. No blood, no holes, just scar areas on the front of his shoulder and on the back where the bullet had come out. They already looked like old scars, not red or raw like you'd expect with recent wounds.

Like he'd had them for years.

Wyatt looked up at Allison. "DNA?"

She nodded. "Yep. Just another little surprise. He's healed up good as new. No loss of movement either. When he moves his shoulder, he doesn't feel any pain at all."

John Hartford slid his finger over one of the scars. "Actually, quite smooth, too. So, Willy went through the same thing that your father did, Allison?"

"Yes, but at a different place, different time. My dad was on the HMS Diana when it happened, and Willy got beamed during the Korean War."

"And, your dad used to get transparent like I saw in Willy up there in the crypt? And, with the same kind of strength?"

She grimaced. "Yes. Identical. Although, I never saw him heal over from injuries like this. Getting shot isn't a normal injury, of course. Usually there's muscle damage, infection. In Willy's case, there's nothing except the scars. He's completely healed—and in a matter of just a couple of hours. It's absolutely amazing."

Willy laughed. "Okay, it's not that amazing." He pulled his shirt back on. "I'm tired of being a lab rat here. Let's eat something. I'm hungry from all that exercise up there."

Allison stood up. "Well, since the good senator has been holed up here for a few days, maybe he can whip something up for us. He knows where everything is by now."

John rubbed his hands together. "Oh, boy. I love cooking. If you'll all trust me, I have some wonderful steaks already thawed. And, we have some fresh veggies that I picked from the garden level. Sound good?"

Somber nods from around the table.

Wyatt opened the fridge and took out a can of beer. The cold can felt good against the palms of his hands, which were starting to feel like they were on fire.

"I'll help you, John. But, first, I think we need to talk about next steps before we all eat and doze off. We've had a disturbing day, to say the least, and I know we're all avoiding talking about that. Which is probably a good thing. But...we have some serious times ahead of us."

He nodded in Allison's direction. "Sorry, dear, but I'm looking at you. We need you right now."

She inserted her index fingers into her ears, and immediately popped them back out again. Wyatt could feel her eyes boring into him—not in an angry way; more just penetrating, deep, challenging. He felt strange.

He put down the beer and started rubbing his hands together—a fiery tingly feeling was cascading up and down his fingers. He went over to the sink and ran them under cold water.

Allison gestured to John and Wyatt. "Sit down at the table, guys. And, John, turn the dimmer down on the light. I want to try a little exercise here with our remote viewer."

Wyatt scratched his head. "You told me before that you had some plan for me to use that skill. But, I don't think it will work. It only happened once, that time when Mom was kidnapped."

"Shush…it will work. Just concentrate on what I'm about to say. I've worked with many remote viewers over the years. They never think it can be turned on, but it can be. Most are afraid to admit they even have the power, but it's the most sensational of all the psychic skills. And, you received yours from the altered DNA of your father, just like I received my mind-reading skill from the altered DNA of my own dad."

"The one time it worked for you was under stressful circumstances. You've just endured an entire day of stress, so the environment is perfect for you."

Wyatt shook his head. "I'm not feeling or seeing a damn thing."

"Oh, yes you are. I'm reading your mind right now. For the last few minutes, you've been feeling tingly, your fingers are on fire. I saw you squeeze the life out of that cold can of beer, and, for no apparent reason, you ran your hands under the tap.

"'I know what's going on. It's happened the same way with other remote viewers, and it happened before with you—that fiery tingly feeling was with you out in the alley behind your dad's house when Helen was kidnapped."

Her brilliant blue eyes were still boring into him, and all of a sudden they felt strangely hypnotic.

"I want you to make a connection, Wyatt. Hold Willy's hand—tightly. As soon as you do, I want you to concentrate on the anxiety you might feel for your father if he were outside, sometime in the not too distant future.

"I want you to picture him standing on the top of a mountain, looking off to the west. Sometime in the future. If you can pin it down, that would be great. But, doesn't matter. I want you to focus on a stressful time through your father's eyes, outside, surveying the world around him. Perhaps it will be just as simple as a mere thunderstorm. If that's the case, we can all feel more at ease. Allow your brain to peak at the most stressful moment your father may experience, and repeat out loud to us what you see while you're seeing it."

Wyatt nodded. He understood what she was trying to do. And, she was right. The fiery tingly feeling was in his hands the same way it had been during the kidnapping ordeal, when he'd been able to soar above the route of the bad guys all the way to their farmhouse.

Worth a try.

Willy held out his hand and Wyatt grasped it, making a joint fist together.

Then, he closed his eyes.

At first, the only thing he noticed was that the tingling had stopped.

But, suddenly, an electric jolt ran up his arm and into his neck. He trembled, gasped at the flash of pain. It only lasted a second or two, but it was how he envisioned what it would feel like if he stuck his finger in a light socket.

As suddenly as it came, it went.

He was soaring now. Along the treeline towards the base of a mountain. It was the tallest mountain in his vision and he steered his body towards it. He knew that was where his father would be.

He could almost feel the tops of the trees scraping his stomach as he steered his body along the rolling foothills. Then, up the mountain slope until he reached the snow-capped peak.

Hovering in the air now, he looked from side to side.

Then, he saw him.

Standing on top of a craggy rock, on the highest point of the mountain, with his arms spread out as if reaching for the sky. His back was to him, and he was gazing off towards the west.

Towards the Pacific Ocean.

Wyatt swooped forward and, just like a magnet, he was sucked in.

Sucked into his father's body.

Looking to the west.

His dad's eyes were now his own, and he could feel the sensation in Willy's brain, and the electricity in his arms as they reached for the sky.

There was a connection…with something. Almost magnetic.

He gazed right into the setting Sun, even though he knew that was a dangerous thing to do.

But, it seemed okay, it seemed safe.

He could see the fiery ball clearly. There were no chemtrails in the sky, which was unusual. The Sun was the clearest it had ever been, even to the point of the gaseous filaments leaping outwards from the surface.

Suddenly, he felt a jolt through his body as his eyes wandered to the left. There was another ball in the sky, poking out through the filaments. Not a Sun…something else. Huge, ominous, dark and brooding. Despite seeming so close to the Sun, it wasn't reflecting any light. It was illuminated on the outer edges, but not all aglow like the Moon normally looked.

His eyes moved to a lateral view now—directly westward. Towards the Pacific.

His knees felt weak as the scene in his vision assaulted his senses. At first glance, the ocean seemed very far away, too far to see any detail. But, just as if looking through a telescope or binoculars, the scene quickly magnified.

It was now right in front of him.

A wall of water that was still far out from shore, perhaps a few hundred miles. But, the magnification allowed him to observe the swirling cauldron, the power of its force.

The wall was getting taller by the second. Normally, scale would be a hard thing to determine, but, in this weird vision absorbing his brain, the scale was strangely obvious.

His brain was telling him how high the wall of water was.

It gave him scale, something that was already in his brain from what Allison had told him about where she lived in Chicago. And, from the photos he'd browsed on his computer out of curiosity.

After all, he was in love with her. Why wouldn't he want to see where she lived?

Even though she didn't live near the ocean, this disturbing vision of calamity put her building right there. Right in front of the massive wave as if it were floating on water.

To give him scale.

From atop the highest mountain in the Rockies, Wyatt, through the eyes of his father, watched in horror as the giant swirling wave completely overwhelmed the ninety-two storey Trump Tower.

CHAPTER 53

She'd been topside for three hours.

Wyatt had made several trips up the ladder just to make sure she was okay. Paranoid that perhaps other assassins had arrived to take the place of the two they'd killed.

Each time he'd made his climb, Allison was on her cell phone, pacing back and forth in the main lobby of the winery. She impatiently waved him off each time he tried to interrupt.

She looked worried, agitated. Put her finger up to her lips to shut him up.

He knew something was wrong.

She had climbed to the outside world right after Wyatt had finished his 'remote viewing' episode. Said she had to call her CERN contact, who Wyatt now knew was Cardinal Valenti, the managing director at the Vatican's Arizona observatory.

Allison insisted that Wyatt and the others stay down in the bunker, and said that she wouldn't be long.

That was three hours ago.

Wyatt's vision of the calamity that was to come had left everyone silent—except for their heavy breathing. When he emerged from his vision, he could see that every face in the room had taken on a shade resembling a pale August moon.

Allison hadn't even let him finish his remote viewing session. After he'd described his vision of the giant tidal wave, she shook him out of his trance.

"*That's enough,*" she said. "*We don't need to hear any more.*"

Then, she picked up her phone and was gone.

After the shock of Wyatt's eerie travelogue had sunk in, Willy and Helen tried distracting themselves by wandering around the spacious apartment.

Senator Hartford's way of coping was pouring himself a glass of whisky, raising his eyebrows at Wyatt in a silent invitation. He nodded eagerly.

They sat in the living room and raised their glasses.

"What should we toast to, Chief?"

Wyatt allowed a weak chuckle. "I guess there ain't much left, Senator."

"No, that's not right. We all now know about this CERN plan. While it sounds ridiculously impossible, it's at least a faint hope."

"Okay, let's toast to 'faint hope.'"

The tumblers clinked and the bronze liquid swirled and danced soothingly. They both drained their glasses and sat, side by side, staring at the wall.

John poured refills just as Willy and Helen came into the room.

"You two want some?"

Willy nodded. "Absolutely—for me anyway."

Helen let out a sigh. "Me, too. Make it a tall one."

Willy laughed and retrieved two glasses out of the bar cabinet. John poured again and they all toasted.

"To miracles."

Willy picked up his sweater off the ottoman and pulled it over his head. "It's comfy down here, but kind of chilly."

John pointed. "There's a thermostat on that wall. We can crank it up if you want."

Willy shook his head. "No, probably best we conserve energy down here. Who knows how long we'll need it for?"

Helen shuddered at that comment. Willy wrapped an arm around her shoulder. "It might not be too long, dear. Don't worry—we're together, and for now we're safe."

Willy turned to Wyatt. "In that vision you had, did you have any sense as to how soon?"

Wyatt shook his head. "No definite time, Dad. Just a feeling that it was close, very close."

John stretched his legs out and rested his feet on the coffee table. "What do you think of this CERN plan, Wyatt?"

"It's crazy, John. Hard to fathom. But, when I think of how far society and science have come, maybe it's not so crazy. Science seems to have cracked the ceiling over and over again with unbelievable innovations. We take them for granted—a lot of them we use every single day. But, we seldom try to understand how they work. When we do think about them, our brains just get scrambled."

He pointed at Willy. "And you saw my dad up there in the crypt—how he looked, what he did, how fast he healed from that gunshot. That's right out of a science fiction movie—but, it's real, that's how he is. We know what caused it many decades ago. It happened to Allison's dad, too, along with dozens of others. If those aliens are that far advanced, perhaps we're more advanced than we know, too."

John nodded thoughtfully. Then, he whispered, "Very soon, this big ball we live on may transcend time and space. Back to 1963. Mindboggling."

"No, it won't."

They all turned their heads at the sudden intrusion of a new voice.

Allison stood at the entrance to the living room, arms hanging loosely at her side, one hand holding her cell phone.

Wyatt rose from the couch. "What? What are you saying?"

Allison let out a long sigh.

"I'm sorry. The plan won't work. CERN has completed their tests on the wormhole they have in quarantine. Don't ask me to explain the science or the logic, because even I don't understand it. But, in a nutshell, if the wormhole is set loose within the Earth's crust and mantle, the planet will collapse within itself. It won't transcend time; it will simply contract into a tiny ball of dense matter."

John poured himself another scotch. "Do you want one of these, Allison?"

She walked over to the bar and grabbed a tall glass. "Yes, absolutely."

He poured and she took a long sip; then gasped as the warm burning liquid did its soothing deed.

Wyatt wrapped an arm around her shoulder. "Was it the cardinal who gave you this news?"

"Yes, then I talked to a couple of the scientists at CERN as well. They're frantic. They thought they had this figured out, but new tests and calculations told them it would be planetary suicide."

"Why didn't they do these tests earlier?"

"Wyatt, they thought they had more time. When these earthquakes began rolling around the Pacific Rim, panic set in. Everyone realized they had little time left. And, then, Gargantuan became strangely invisible. Even the Vatican's Lucifer telescope couldn't see it. The fact that it began cloaking itself told us that it was closer than we thought, and more imminent than we thought.

"You and I deduced that ourselves when we saw Willy's arrangement of the sculptures in his studio. He had the Earth, Sun, and Gargantuan arranged in a way that told us that Gargantuan had suddenly accelerated its pace along its own orbit. In essence, racing towards us. Then, your vision told us the calamity was coming. You couldn't tell us when, but you were left with the feeling that there wasn't much time left."

Wyatt looked over at Willy. "Yeah, Dad was doing those things without realizing why. I guess he was getting magnetic signals that became stronger the closer the thing got to us."

"Exactly. Anyway, after the quakes started rolling around the Pacific and Lucifer lost sight of Gargantuan, Cardinal Valenti ordered that the pace at CERN be sped up. They pulled out all the stops, realizing we didn't have the luxury of time any longer. And, they concluded that it just wouldn't work. The science isn't solid.

"The transcendence idea itself was solid and calculated down to the exact year and month, but the stability of the wormhole was the red herring. It turns out that it can't be controlled through the Earth's mass. In fact, once it's no longer contained, the resistance of the planet's mass will cause the wormhole to expand—at an astonishing rate.

"If it just kept its size constant, it would have been okay. But, it won't—it will expand and just keep on expanding until the Earth collapses. It's the resistance of the Earth's mass that the physicists hadn't properly considered in their calculations. They made a huge mistake."

Senator Hartford leaned forward on the edge of the couch and drained his glass.

"So, that's it, then. We just wait down here and see what happens."

There was an eerie silence for a minute or two, as John's ominous statement sunk in.

Allison walked to the center of the room and faced them.

"No, there is a Plan B. It's a long shot, but, at least it's a plan."

Wyatt looked into her beautiful blue eyes for a sign, searched for some of that famous confidence, the take-charge attitude he'd come to know and love.

It wasn't there.

Her mesmerizing eyes were no longer mesmerizing.

They were just worried, bloodshot, and blinking rapidly. Whatever this Plan B was, it clearly wasn't something that was giving her any joy.

"Tell us, Allison. Just spit it out."

She folded her arms across her chest and took a deep breath.

"What I'm going to tell you is the only hope we have left to still do what we'd planned to do. Again, we want to go back to 1963, before Kennedy's assassination, to convince him about the perils facing Earth in the future.

"Convince him to begin preparations to build CERN decades sooner, and share with him the alien reverse engineering that is available to us today that wasn't available back then. By using the hard drives on our laptops, we can provide enormous amounts of advanced scientific information that can enable that to happen.

"We can also show him and his advisers videos of what life will look like in the future, the technological advancements that have been made. We'll even be able to show him historical videos of himself, to help make the case that we are indeed from the future.

"We'll show him the Zapruder film. He'll be able to watch himself being assassinated. And, the news reports—he'll see Walter Cronkite crying on air as he announced his death. All of this will force him to take us seriously."

Senator Hartford, voice slightly slurred from the scotch, interrupted her.

"All that's fine and dandy, Allison. But, you just finished telling us we can't go back. So, what's the point?"

She took another deep breath, an extra-long one this time. When she replied, Wyatt detected a slight choke in her voice.

"That's what Plan B is. A handful of us might be able to go back. A different concept than what was planned before. Instead of a transcendence of time and space for the planet itself, it will be actual time travel, just as we all think we understand the concept to be."

Wyatt clasped his hands behind his head. "What the hell are you talking about?"

"Hear me out. The wormhole can't traverse laterally through the Earth's crust and mantle due to the resistance of the planet's mass. But, it can be routed upwards, through the surface, and a short distance into the atmosphere. A few thousand feet. No resistance.

"It's been under quarantine, as you know. CERN has calculated the exact sequence and strength of proton bombardment, faster than the speed of light, that will be needed to propel the wormhole into sending an object back in time to the exact era we want—down to the month and year. It will be September, 1963—two months before the assassination."

Wyatt glanced around the room. Everyone's expression looked exactly like his felt. Shocked. Puzzled.

Allison continued. "I know this is hard to grasp, but we're going to have to just trust the science. It's possible. They've done it before, on a smaller scale—object transfer. And, it worked.

"This time it will be a bit larger. An airplane. And, it will have to be at a specific height, at precise coordinates, directly over the CERN complex in Geneva at an exact moment in time. The wormhole will be released upwards through the surface of the Earth and timed to intersect with the plane. Both the plane and the wormhole have to be coordinated exactly. If they're out of sync in any way, the opportunity will be missed. A one-time shot, because there's only one wormhole in quarantine. It's the only one we have.

"There's a huge risk. Just like that Germanwings jet that I told you about, Wyatt. That jet was sucked in to the side of a mountain by the enormous magnetic pull of the Large Hadron Collider at CERN, which was reactivated on that very day and time that the jet went down.

"It was reported in the media as a suicide by the co-pilot, but that wasn't the truth. There's a chance that the LHC, which will be needed to propel the wormhole upward, could cause another magnetic disaster. This plane could crash into a mountain, instead of traveling back to 1963."

Senator Hartford stood. "This is just one plane you're talking about. How does this affect us? We're down here."

Allison cleared her throat.

"The plane can't be big. It has to be a certain size, like my Gulfstream. I've volunteered my plane.

"The President and the Pope put out a call for volunteers amongst the few who know about all of this. No world leader wants to chance it and, naturally, with the risks involved, very few have the stomach for it. It's kind of like volunteering for a one-way trip to Mars. Some wackos lined up for that Mars opportunity, but those aren't the types we need, nor are they in the know on this. Very few are. You folks are in the know only because you know me.

"Every world leader who knows about this is choosing to stay behind, to maintain order and coordinate a military response, if one is viable, against the inhabitants of Gargantuan. And, a defense may not be viable at all, if the kind of cataclysm that Wyatt saw in his remote viewing episode comes to pass. The aliens from Gargantuan will then simply come in to mop up after the carnage.

"Of course, if we're successful in going back and changing the future for the better, none of this is going to happen in the present."

Wyatt muttered. "For God's sake. I'm getting a headache trying to process this."

Allison grimaced and nodded.

"I understand, Wyatt. Let me finish, then we can discuss. I've volunteered my plane and myself as one of the guinea pigs. Cardinal Valenti will be accompanying me, as well as several brilliant scientists from CERN. Together, we'll have a strong contingent of scientific knowledge and data. We need a politician as well—someone who knows his way around Washington, someone who will know the right things to say to get us through the doors of the White House."

She pointed at John. "Senator, I'm enlisting you. I've always thought of you as someone who could save America, so now's a good opportunity for you to step up and do just that. There would be no greater accomplishment than this. Being president wouldn't come close to the impact you'd make if we were successful with this…mission. You can decline, if you wish—I would understand, believe me. But, I hope you won't."

Allison's eyes passed slowly from Wyatt, to Willy, and then to Helen.

"I want you to go with us, too. There's just enough room on my plane for all of us. The alternative will be to stay here and take your chances. I hope you won't. But, you know the risks of taking this flight—I've been totally honest about that.

"We could get sucked into a mountainside, or this wormhole could go rogue and take us virtually anywhere. We're hoping the science is right and that we'll be back in 1963, but, let's face it, this concept is bizarre and for the most part untested.

"We could literally end up anywhere, at any historical point in time. I admit, it's scary to think of.

"We could even just vanish into a puff of cosmic vapour."

CHAPTER 54

The bedroom was dark.

Even with the light on, it was dark.

The absence of windows had a powerful psychological effect. The drapes hanging on the wall pretending to cover a view that didn't exist only fooled the mind for a few minutes.

The darkness was a psychic one—claustrophobic, smothering.

There was a way to escape to the great outdoors, but one had to climb a metal ladder embedded in granite rock in order to do it.

There was no easy stroll out to the backyard or the front porch. You couldn't just lean over the fence and wave at neighbors—or crack a smile while watching happy children bicycling along the sidewalk.

Decisions used to be easy.

What to eat for dinner, what time to get up in the morning, which newspapers to read. Choosing a video to watch in the evening. When the next party would be, and the theme. Who to invite.

Inane little events like Helen's next date at the beauty salon, which usually coincided with Willy's appointment at the barber. They'd always planned simple things that way, so they'd have as much time as possible to spend together.

Willy's hair was always finished before Helen's, of course, and he'd wander down to the salon and wait for her in the lounge. There were always magazines to read, albeit just fluffy, girly stuff, not the sports or car magazines that populated the rack at his barber's.

But, he never minded. Because he was waiting for her.

The stylists always made a fuss over him. He had to admit he enjoyed that, while at the same time noticing Helen beaming with pride at her charming husband being the center of attention.

The routines they took for granted.

Until now.

Going to church on Sundays, meeting the guys afterwards for coffee at the local café, trudging out to his studio to sculpt another masterpiece, traveling to Lake Louise in February of every year to compete in the annual Ice Magic festival.

Many times he'd reflected that perhaps his life wasn't so meaningful anymore, had lost its purpose. He'd never confessed those feelings to Helen, because she would have taken it personally. And, it never had anything to do with Helen at all, but she wouldn't have understood. Willy rationalized that it was probably something everyone his age thought about. Looking back, taking stock, wondering what else…or more…they could have done.

Was anyone ever satisfied? Was there really such a thing as contentment? Or, was that an illusion, too, just like all the other things he was now sadly aware of?

The weather extremes were an illusion, because they weren't just naturally occurring things like he'd always believed they were. The traumas the Earth had been experiencing were being caused by the powerful magnetics of an intruder—an intruder that probably wanted to confiscate the planet and everything on it.

And, Gargantuan itself had been hidden for years by another illusion.

Chemtrails.

Those fake clouds that suddenly appeared out of nowhere, birthed from streams of chemicals from the nozzles of specially-equipped planes, and then insidiously spread into "clouds." An illusion that no government official ever had to explain, because hardly anyone ever bothered to ask. And, if anyone had asked, they would have been lied to anyway.

Illusory clouds whose primary purpose was to hide the approaching monster from outer space.

Earthquakes rolling around the world, and volcanoes blowing their tops, weren't being caused by normal Earth gyrations. They were being caused by the approach of Gargantuan. But, normal crisis preparedness still continued in the affected cities and towns, just as if the events were not out of the ordinary at all.

Illusions.

The CDC clinic down in Atlanta had been an illusion. It existed for one purpose only—to suppress the altered DNA of victims like Willy, and to cause them to rapidly age. To hide the effects of what had happened to them during their military service for their country.

Majestic 12. Another illusion, designed to protect the naive public from knowing the truth. Created in 1947 by a president who considered himself a great man because he'd made the decision to annihilate 200,000 innocent Japanese citizens.

The very first, and still only, leader in the world to have ever used nuclear bombs.

His presidency was an illusion—it wasn't a great legacy as the American people were led to believe. Just like Pearl Harbor was allowed to happen by his predecessor to anger Americans enough to draw the country into a war that Roosevelt wanted, Hiroshima and Nagasaki were unnecessary slaughters by Truman.

To this day, very few Americans knew that the Japanese had offered surrender days before the bombs were dropped. But, with the Russians poised to invade Japan, America didn't want them to have a foot in the door. The war had to appear to the world to have been ended by the U.S.A., not by their reluctant ally. The surrender was ignored. The attack was an illusion.

Because, "to the victors go the spoils" and, decades later, the Americans still had their massive military stamp on the Far East solely because of the horrific weapons known as "Fat Man" and "Little Boy." And the victors always got to write the history books.

All illusions.

Majestic 12 had ordered the deaths of dozens, if not hundreds, of influential people over the last sixty years to keep secrets hidden. Most of the deaths were disguised as accidents, of course, or death by natural causes.

All illusions.

CERN was an illusion.

A massive multi-billion-dollar undertaking that had been presented to the world as just a giant physics experiment. When, in actual fact, it was designed for something entirely different. A noble pursuit, no doubt, but one that also attempted to play God.

And, after all this time and money, its intended purpose—to cause the planet to transcend time and space—wouldn't even work. All it *might* be capable of doing, was to send a small planeload of brave, desperate people back in time. They were Earth's last hope.

Even the Vatican was an illusion.

The Catholic religion's royalty, rich beyond belief, and hypocritical in the extreme, had always believed in evolution and the God Particle. Publicly, they denied evolution, of course, because accepting it would have torn the curtain away from the great and powerful Oz.

The Vatican had been one of CERN's major benefactors, which most Catholics would have been surprised to hear. Adam and Eve were just a joke, yet they were a joke that was perpetuated over centuries just to keep the coffers full. And to keep control over a population that would prefer to believe that a divine spirit created the universe in seven days, rather than face the fact that their precious surgically-enhanced bodies actually got their origins from exploding matter.

A lie, told often enough, becomes the truth.

How many people who practised the Catholic faith knew that the Vatican owned and operated the most powerful telescope in the world, located in Arizona of all places? A telescope that was ironically named 'Lucifer.'

For a religion that had convinced entire societies and the history books that it believed in divinity and absolute spiritualism, the Jesuits were, ironically, the most highly trained astronomers on the planet. A religion that pretended to believe in the Father, the Son, and the Holy Spirit, was actually obsessed with science and the formation of the universe.

Illusions.

The proposed hotel in Nelson had been an illusion, just to get close to Willy. To make sure that he didn't get out of control. To keep a lid on him after his accidental x-ray procedure. Radiation that had caused him to flare up into this otherworldly being that he now knew he really was deep down inside the labyrinth of his DNA.

The Diamond Vintage Winery was an illusion. Who could know from the innocent exterior that it was merely camouflaging an underground doomsday shelter? How many other facilities like this existed? How many people around the world would be climbing down metal ladders installed in granite rock over the next few days and weeks, to escape a cataclysm?

And, the poor oblivious souls walking around above ground would be left wondering where their government officials went, why the chieftains of conglomerates were nowhere to be found, and where all the wealthy celebrities had suddenly disappeared to.

All of a sudden, over a very short time frame, they'd all be gone. Hiding. And, people would be left scratching their heads wondering why. Until the day, hour, minute, and second that it happened. At that moment of truth—that shocking moment of awareness—there would be a mass awakening.

But, by the sounds of it, that moment wouldn't last very long.

There might be just enough time to grab family photographs and scoop up kids and pets.

There might be enough time to run for a stretch, but no one would know which direction to run in.

There might be enough time to scream.

But, no time to analyse.

And, certainly no time to understand that virtually everything they thought they knew had just been one giant illusion.

Helen was sitting on the edge of the bed, resting her chin on her tiny fists.

Willy walked over and sat down beside her. He draped his arm around her shoulders, lowered his head and looked deeply into her eyes.

Into her soul.

They communicated without saying a word.

Her eyes asked the questions and his eyes gave the answers. He knew what she wanted to do, and she knew that he felt the same way.

He nodded his head and smiled knowingly.

She smiled back at him, a smile that was one-part resignation, the other part contentment.

Helen whispered a question. "Maybe we could even rebuild our front porch?"

He whispered back, "Yes, dear, we will. And, we can help the neighbors rebuild theirs, too. After we've finished all that work we can host one of our famous parties—assuming of course that the earthquakes leave us alone for a while."

"Can we invite all the old draft-dodgers?"

"Wouldn't be much of a party without them."

"Smoke a few joints, maybe?"

"Why not?"

They both giggled like school kids.

Willy stood up, reached down, and gently held her soft hands. He eased her up off the bed and, arm in arm, they headed through the doorway together.

Back to the living room where Allison, Wyatt, and John were chatting in low tones.

Willy cleared his throat to get their attention.

"Allison, we're not going with you. When you folks fly out of here, we want you to drop us off in Castlegar and we'll drive from there. Back to Nelson. Back to our home and our friends."

Willy looked at his son. Wyatt was about to say something, but the look in Willy's eyes no doubt told him it was fruitless.

"No, Wyatt. Don't bother trying to talk us out of it. Our minds are made up. Nelson is where we belong and, if things are going to come to an end, that's where we want to be. We've already lived the sixties, a turbulent time that we don't want to live through again. And, we're just too old now to do it. We've had a good life.

"And don't offer to stay behind with us. You need to go with Allison and John. Help them make this work. You three, and the others going with you, are Earth's last hope. Make it count. Be the heroes. The world needs a few heroes right about now."

Wyatt got up from the couch and walked over to his parents.

With tears in his eyes, he said, "I understand. I won't try to talk you out of it. And, I'll be seeing you back there in the sixties. You won't know me, but I'll definitely know you."

CHAPTER 55

The executive hangar lounge at London's Gatwick airport was quiet, which Wyatt thought was unusual for a Friday afternoon. The eerie emptiness added one extra element to the anxiety Wyatt was feeling. Almost as if the hangar had been reserved just for them—the calm before the storm. But, Allison explained to him that most of the private jet traffic took place in the early mornings and evenings.

The Vatican representatives, Cardinal Valenti and his aide, Monsignor Conti, were already at the terminal when they arrived.

Both of them were dressed in normal priestly garments, nothing garish or flowing. Wyatt had been expecting Valenti to be adorned in the traditional cardinal garments, complete with gown and cap. He was very tall, around six and a half feet, handsome, and with a dark complexion that reminded Wyatt of the Vatican characters featured in one of the *Godfather* movies.

Conti was the exact opposite—bookish, short and skinny, with thick-lens glasses. He looked like the stereotypical aide.

Wyatt was aware that Valenti, a Jesuit, was high up in the Vatican hierarchy and a noted astronomer—and, of course, the managing director of the Arizona observatory. Wyatt was curious, though, as to what the man's exact role would be on this mission, since high-level scientists from CERN would already be along for the ride, as well as Allison, who was an astrophysicist herself.

He pulled her off to the side so that Valenti and Conti couldn't hear him.

"Why are the cardinal and the monsignor going with us? Unusual choices, considering this is mainly a scientific and political venture. Of course, I don't really belong here either, but I was just curious."

Allison brushed the back of her hand against his cheek, then squeezed his shoulder affectionately.

"Don't say you don't belong here. You're with me, so that gives you the right. And, I get to say who comes."

She smiled mischievously. "After all, it is my plane."

"Yeah, but…"

Allison shook her head. "No 'buts' about it. I want you with me. We're going to succeed in this mission and, because we will, I want someone like you to hang out with back in the sixties."

She giggled. "Only because I think you'd make one fine looking hippie!"

Wyatt laughed at the image. "Okay, at least now I know your motivation. And, you'll be a flower child, I assume?"

"Sure. And…here's something to get excited about. Haven't you ever wished you could have been at Woodstock?"

"That would be quite something, wouldn't it? But, at our ages we'll look a little out of place."

"We'll pretend to be organizers—grow your hair out a bit, put some beads in mine, then we'll go make love in a muddy field, gyrating to Carlos Santana. It'll be…groovy!"

Wyatt wrapped his arms around her waist and gave her a quick kiss on the lips. "You've got a deal. We'll do it. So, answer my question about our Vatican friends."

"Cardinal Valenti is our way in the front door."

"How's that?"

"You're forgetting that John F. Kennedy was the very first Irish Roman Catholic ever elected president. Even though he broke at least one of the Ten Commandments over and over again, he was a staunch Catholic in his public persona. Being Catholic meant a lot to the Kennedy family. They held any representative of the Vatican in high reverence."

"Yeah, but back then there would be no record of Valenti being a cardinal. And, just being a cardinal isn't going to open the White House doors."

Allison nodded. "You're right. But, we're not going to the White House right away. Our way in the front door will be through Hyannis Port, Massachusetts. The Kennedy family compound. Where JFK's parents, Joe and Rose, lived."

"Why?"

"Because, first of all, it will be easier for us to get a reception there.

Joseph, the family patriarch, would open any door to someone like the cardinal, a representative of the Pope. And, since he was the ultimate puppet-master in the Kennedy family, having singlehandedly manipulated the election that brought JFK to power, he's our 'in' to the president.

"His son will listen to whatever he has to say; he always did. If Joe says that John has to meet with us, he'll meet with us. And, we may not even have to visit the White House. I'm guessing that Joe will command John to travel out to see us at Hyannis Port. Which is probably better for our first meeting, anyway. Away from all the Oval Office controllers and hangers-on.

"As well, we will have a bona fide senator with us as well. Hartford speaks their language, and he has an insider knowledge of the corridors of power, which haven't really changed all that much in the last half century."

Wyatt cocked his head to the side. "C'mon, Allison, we still have the problem with neither the senator nor the cardinal being on anyone's records or radar back then. They'd be deemed imposters."

"True. But, we have an ace in the hole. Two aces, actually.

"John's briefcase contains some highly classified material that the senior Kennedy is well aware of. It pertains to Majestic 12, which Joe Kennedy was an early member of. It was given to Hartford by one of our members, who was killed a few weeks ago because of it. I told you about him—an oil tycoon named Farmington. That information from the fifties and sixties, as well as subsequent decades, is what led to the hit being put out on Hartford."

Wyatt folded his arms across his chest. "Okay, so that will get the father's attention, and give Senator Hartford credibility."

"Exactly. Again, our aim is to show enough information from documents, or from the hard drives on our computers, to convince them we mean no harm. And, that we are indeed from the future. Once they're convinced of that, they'll listen to us about what needs to be done to prevent a calamity fifty-two years into the future."

"You said you had two aces in the hole. What's the other one?"

"Joseph Kennedy had a stroke in 1961, paralysed him on the right side of his body. He regained some movement and the ability to walk...sort of...and, luckily, his mind was still alert.

"After this stroke, he became circumspect about his life. And, about his religion. To the world, Joe was thought to be a devout Catholic...but he wasn't. It was all a scam. He used it to mix within all the proper circles. It was good for his image.

"But, after the stroke, he started having regrets, knowing that his life was coming to an end. He entertained prominent Catholics regularly after the stroke, almost as if he was looking for forgiveness for a life that was rich and full…but, sordid in the extreme.

"So, religion was his Achilles Heel. His vulnerable spot. He'll listen to anything pertaining to the Catholic religion. And, we have something shocking to show him."

Wyatt was getting more intrigued with every word Allison was uttering. He could feel the warmth of the blood rushing to his cheeks.

"You have my attention. What is it?"

Allison lowered her voice a notch.

"You've heard about the Three Secrets of Fatima, I'm sure. In 1917, three shepherd girls, Lucia, Jacinto, and Francisco, were visited six times over a period of several months, purportedly by the Virgin Mary. Three secrets were revealed to the girls, and the first two were announced to the public.

"And, let's face it, who knows if this event even really happened? It could be just another Vatican con job. But, the important thing is that Catholics believe that it happened, so we're counting on that.

"The first secret gave a graphic and horrific description of hell.

"The second secret predicted that World War One would end, followed a couple of decades later by World War Two.

"But, the third secret wasn't revealed until the year 2000, long after Joseph Kennedy died. So, Kennedy never knew what that secret was."

"Wasn't it something to do with an assassination attempt on the Pope?"

Allison nodded. "Yes, when it was announced by the Vatican, it told about that attempt back in 1981 against the life of Pope John Paul the Second. But, let's face it, it's pretty easy to predict something twenty years after it already happened. So, there was immense scepticism about that third secret and the Vatican has been under heavy criticism ever since that year 2000 announcement. No one believed what they announced—it was felt that the real secret was too frightening to release to the public."

"Okay, so what?"

Allison took a deep breath, then exhaled slowly.

"It was indeed a farce. That wasn't the third secret. Our Pope has given Cardinal Valenti all three written secrets, complete with the official Vatican seal, in their original envelopes back when they were written out.

"It's true that the real third secret was never intended to be announced, because it was just too horrific.

"It pertains to Gargantuan.

"Valenti will share all three of the 'Our Lady of Fatima' secrets with Joseph Kennedy."

Wyatt whistled and exclaimed, "Wow!" Then he scratched his chin. "But, Joe Kennedy might think this is all being made up, forged."

"He might—except the old documents are pretty authentic-looking. The cardinal does, however, have other stuff in his briefcase; things that Joe will recognize, him being a student of the Catholic religion. I don't know what they are, but the cardinal says they're convincing. Artifacts from the Vatican, the Sistine Chapel, and St. Peter's Basilica. Famous items that any Catholic would recognize. All of these things will get his attention and, most importantly, will get us an audience with the president."

Wyatt glanced over at the cardinal and his aide. Senator Hartford was chatting with them, and four other men had just arrived, each carrying computer cases.

He pointed. "I think your CERN scientists are here, Allison."

She glanced over in their direction. "Yep. Looks like we're good to go. I'll let the pilots know, and we can be on our way."

"Okay. I'll join you guys shortly. I just want to think by myself for a minute or two."

Allison rubbed his shoulder. "I know, it's a lot to handle, isn't it? Don't worry—we're going to pull this off. I have a good feeling."

She turned and walked away in that confident stride Wyatt had become lovingly accustomed to.

He strolled over to the large floor to ceiling windows and gazed out over the tarmac. He rested his eyes on Allison's gleaming Gulfstream, being fueled for the very last leg of their trip. Several mechanics were also busy doing last minute checks and he could see the heads of the two pilots through the cockpit windows.

He gulped.

This was it.

That beautiful jet had made quite the long journey already. After leaving Penticton, they'd flown right to Castlegar and dropped off Wyatt's parents.

It had been a sad goodbye.

Wyatt's eyes welled up as he thought about the last hugs and kisses he enjoyed with Willy and Helen before watching them walk off towards the car lot. He would never see them again that way. If he and the others were successful in going back to 1963, his parents would be young adults. Wyatt would be older than his very own mom and dad. And, they wouldn't even know who he was. Wouldn't know their own son.

He sighed, and wiped a tear from his eye. Life had sure taken a bizarre turn.

After Castlegar, they flew to Halifax on the east coast, refueled again, and jetted from there to Reykjavik in Iceland. Another refueling, then the second last leg of their trip—London.

And, now, as he looked out the window at Gatwick International, his stomach warned him that the last leg of their trip was imminent.

London had been their meeting point with the cardinal, the monsignor, and the four scientists. They were all here now. Nothing left to do. Nothing except Allison's instructions to her pilots as to what the last leg would be.

Geneva, Switzerland. A ninety-minute flight from London.

And, they wouldn't be landing. At least, not in this year.

Instead, they would circle around until the exact moment. The pre-arranged moment.

A dinner-hour date with some invisible fucking thing called a wormhole.

At precisely 9,000 feet above sea level.

At exactly 46.23417 degrees latitude North, and 6.05278 degrees longitude East.

No later, and no earlier, than 6:00 p.m. Central European Time.

Wyatt felt his stomach churning.

Easy-peasy. What could possibly go wrong?

CHAPTER 56

Wyatt felt, rather than heard, the twin Rolls Royce engines fire up; a power plant that was capable of propelling the Gulfstream G650 at close to supersonic speeds.

Allison's jet was, without a doubt, the quietest airplane he'd ever traveled on.

The cardinal and his aide were sitting side by side, opposite him on the starboard side of the craft. They were talking in Italian, either out of convenience, or, more likely, because they were speaking of things they didn't want anyone else to hear.

The CERN physicists were scattered about the plane, each with their laptops open, fingers moving quickly…and frantically…across keyboards. No doubt some last minute calculations, and probably communications with the Large Hadron Collider folks at CERN.

Allison, Wyatt, and John were sitting together at the conference table. They'd have to move over to their regular seats in a few minutes once takeoff commenced, but for now they were enjoying just chatting together.

Wyatt guessed that the other two were just as nervous as he was, although Allison was bravely soldiering on, trying hard not to show it. The senator was cracking his knuckles a lot, something he'd never seen him do before in the short time he'd known him.

Wyatt liked John, and he could see why Allison did, too. He was a straight-shooter and one of those rare politicians who actually believed he could change Washington.

Up until this Gargantuan thing became suddenly critical and imminent, John had indeed intended to run for president. He thought he could make a difference. He'd talked about it with Wyatt, some of the things he would have done with the tax code and financial institutions, both of which he believed were out of control.

Wyatt also liked his ideas on foreign policy; that the U.S. had allowed itself to be dragged into far too many conflicts with no consideration of the cost in lives and dollars. With the country now approaching a national debt of a staggering twenty trillion, it was in serious trouble, with most people not being even slightly aware of how serious it really was.

As well, John felt there were far too many secrets and, in order to change the direction of the country, he felt that some of those secrets had to be revealed. As long as things remained secret, power was unbridled because no one was ever held accountable. When there was always the comfort of knowing that virtually anything could be covered up, then anything at all could be done.

Anyone could get away with anything.

He believed that the C.I.A. should be disbanded, and the activities of the NSA curtailed. Wyatt thought those two ideas alone would probably have gotten the senator killed. But, instead, the thing that had put his life in danger was his knowledge of Majestic 12. The leaked papers from Farmington.

Footsteps approaching, owned by the captain, Cole Howard.

"Hey, guys. Wanted to let you know we'll be ready to take off in a few minutes. I've filed that flight plan you gave me, Allison. They gave me a bit of a hard time about the descent to 9,000, but I finally got it cleared."

Allison smiled. "Well, they always gripe, don't they? Especially the air traffic controllers in France."

"Yeah, a bit of a power trip, I think. But, once I mentioned that it was a CERN experimental flight, they got in touch with the folks at the facility and I'm guessing they got their marching orders. CERN seems to carry a lot of weight in both Switzerland and France."

Allison nodded her head in agreement. "With CERN straddling the border with both countries, and the massive investments they've each made, maybe that project has actually forced them to get along. Hey, perhaps that's the secret to peace? Build a massive scientific community under every shared border in the world? It would force everyone to talk nice to each other. Perhaps even North and South Korea would get along?"

Cole laughed. "Oh, I love your optimism, Allison. Maybe someday, huh?"

Cole seemed to be about fifty or so—grizzled features, but easy on the eyes; probably a former fighter pilot, like a lot of the commercial flyers were. He had that look about him—kind of a combination of Harrison Ford and Daniel Craig.

The co-pilot came out of the cockpit and sauntered down to join them. Dave Hall was quite a bit younger than Cole; thirtyish, blond hair, blue eyes. Looked the part of a California surfer.

He tapped Cole on the back and waved his wristwatch in front of his eyes.

"It's 4:00, Captain. Time for us to scoot."

"Yep, we're good to go. Okay, folks, strap in."

Wyatt stood. "Smooth flight today, Cole?"

He nodded. "Should be, Wyatt. But, you never know when flying around the Alps. And, Geneva has the Jura mountain range as well. Occasionally, the weather systems from the two chains fight against each other. We'll see. Forecast looks pretty good, though."

Allison and John moved over to the single seats. Wyatt chose one across the aisle from her.

She looked up at Cole. "So, you guys understand what it is we're doing? And, why it's important we be at those coordinates I gave you…at exactly 6:00?"

Cole nodded. "No problem. It's 4:00 now. We'll be on site at around 5:40 and we'll circle at 9,000 feet. We'll time it so that we're right over those GPS numbers at 6:00. You said there's some experiment you have to observe right at that moment. So, don't worry, we'll get you there. It must be one hell of an important experiment for us to be flying this unusual route."

Allison fastened her seatbelt. "Yes, CERN is releasing some low-level magnetic waves, which will interact with chemtrail clouds at the 9,000-foot level. No danger to an aircraft like ours, but we need to see the effects those special waves have on the metal particulates in the clouds. I repeat—it's crucial, Cole, that we be at exactly 9,000 feet, at those coordinates, at exactly 6:00. Failure is not an option."

Cole shook his head. "I'll never understand you scientist types—and you happen to also be a hotel magnate. But, I guess, as they say, you can take the girl out of the physicist, but you can never take the physicist out of the girl. This experiment sounds drab as hell, but, as usual, we'll do our duty for you."

Allison smiled. "I know you will."

"Hey, if you get bored, come on up to the cockpit. You can take over the controls for as long as you want."

She laughed. "I think I'm a bit rusty. Been lazy for the last two years, letting you guys do all the flying. Haven't even had my mandatory medical checkup."

Cole turned to walk up the aisle. "Well, we'll leave the door unlocked if you change your mind."

After Cole disappeared, Wyatt leaned across the aisle.

"So, you're a pilot, too?"

Allison smiled modestly.

"Yes, I learned a long time ago. Instrument-rated, too, so I'm qualified on this jet. But, I wasn't kidding—I am rusty, and I've been a pampered little princess over the last few years. These guys are so good, I just relax now and let them do all the flying. It's kinda nice. Like when a person takes the train to work once in a while instead of the car. A nice treat not to have to worry about driving, and just be able to lean back and read the newspaper."

Wyatt looked into her smiling eyes, and at that moment he didn't know what he felt. Probably a combination of love and hero worship. The most amazing woman he'd ever met. He would trust her with his life…and, ironically, he was doing exactly that today.

He knew in his heart she would trust him with hers, too.

He whispered. "I love you. Do you know that?"

She reached across the aisle and rubbed his arm. And whispered back, "I love you, too."

Wyatt put his hand across hers and lowered his voice to an even softer whisper.

"It sounds like these pilots have absolutely no clue about what we're really doing. You made up a cover story. Why?"

"Judgement call. First of all, too much to tell. The story is too long and the science is too surreal. You and John have had lots of time to get used to all this, and you've seen some of it up close and personal already. With the attempted murders, the bunker, Willy's bizarre transformations, your 'remote viewing' episode. It's been a lot to absorb, but for you guys it's been a long stretch already. And, I've had time to explain it all to you, including this wormhole concept.

"But, these are my pilots. That's all they are. Nothing more sophisticated than that. They're clever and capable, but this is all way beyond them. They would never sign on to a mission like this. I know them—they're the types who crack open a can of beer every night and watch a baseball game. Meet up with the boys in the pub on nights when they're not flying. They're not deep, they're natural sceptics, not the least bit curious about anything beyond their tight little worlds. I decided I couldn't take the chance on telling them. If they refused, we'd be in trouble trying to line up someone else at the last minute.

"We also had absolutely no time to indoctrinate government pilots into doing this run. Only a few people know about Majestic 12 or this Gargantuan threat, and hardly anyone stepped forward to volunteer even to be just a passenger on this mission, let alone a pilot. Except for our own little band of pioneers, that is.

"All of the members of Majestic 12 have gone into hiding now, including that bastard, Chad Powers. Bunch of cowards. None of them volunteered any expertise for this mission. I think once we're back there, Wyatt, I'm going to track that Powers prick down and kill him myself. A wooden stake in the heart, maybe? The world will be a safer place in the future if I transform into a child killer for just that one menace. He can't be allowed to grow up into the munitions manufacturing Satan that he is."

Wyatt squeezed her hand. "Calm down, hon."

She giggled. "What makes you think I'm not calm?"

Wyatt laughed, and changed the subject. "It sounds like you could have just flown this plane yourself."

"No, Wyatt. That would be taking a chance. I haven't flown in two years."

"Don't you need to maintain a certain number of hours to renew your license?"

She shook her head. "In the U.S., there is no renewal of pilot licenses. They're issued for life. But, for my rating, I need a complete medical every five years and a flight review if I haven't flown for six months. I'm way overdue for both. Sure, I could fly this thing, but to make sure this mission goes off without a hitch, I had to have the best pilots for us."

Allison gestured her head in the direction of the cockpit. "And, those two guys are the best there is, believe me. Both former fighter jocks, skilled as hell."

"Do you feel a bit guilty deceiving them?"

Allison grimaced. "I did at first—but not for long. This is just too important to worry about guilt. And, if it works, they'll be going back to the sixties with us, of course."

She giggled. "I guess once they notice that Elvis and the Beatles are at the top of the charts, I'll have no choice but to explain everything to them!"

Wyatt frowned. "When this happens, and we're back in 1963—where the hell are we going to be?"

"You mean location?"

"Yeah."

"Right here, over Europe. In fact, right over where this is going to happen. Geneva. CERN."

"But, there won't be a CERN."

"No, it will just be open land between two mountain ranges. There will be a Geneva, of course, and that's where we'll land. Although, the airport controllers will be a wee bit shocked to see a jet like this suddenly appear on their screens coming in for a landing."

Wyatt shook his head again. Then, he leaned back in his seat as the plane began its taxi towards the runway. His stomach was gurgling away as he wiped his sweaty hands against his pant legs.

In a few seconds, they'd be in the air.

Heading for Geneva.

And, after that, where the hell they'd end up was anyone's guess.

CHAPTER 57

Allison was in dreamland. The smooth motion of the plane had soothed her to sleep, the same kind of soothing she remembered from back when she was a toddler. Cradled in her mother's arms on road trips, her dad at the wheel humming a tune to himself, the swaying motion of the car rendering comfort almost identical to a rocking basinet.

Motion always had that effect on her. And, funny, in all of those motion-triggered dreams, including this one, she knew it was only a dream. A part of her was still aware of the conscious world, while another part was firmly entrenched in whatever images she was dreaming about.

Her head was resting against the seat's window ledge. She'd left the blinds open, enjoying the warmth of the setting Sun against her cheek. For the most part, the flight had been smooth, except for the occasional little jolt.

Images were racing through her brain. Her and her brother with their parents enjoying Christmas morning in the old Chicago family home; summer at the lake splashing and frolicking in the sparkling water; playing Monopoly out on the sauna deck on warm evenings; diving off the dock into the dark forbidding water late into the night.

And, skinny-dipping when she was all alone.

Then, her dream skipped to 1963, at least how she thought it to be from books, movies, and documentaries. A different era, and an era at least as troubled as the one she was in now. Even that decade had faced the danger of extinction.

The Cuban Missile Crisis, when nuclear annihilation had been so close it had been palpable for the people who had lived through it.

Allison visualized in her mind what that world would look like.

The old cars, made with a hell of a lot more character and pizzazz than the ones in her era. The method of dress—at one extreme still old-fashioned, styles from the 50s hanging on for dear life. Contrasting with the 'Beatle' haircuts on the boys, the long stringy hair on the girls, and the flowing gowns of the flower children.

Beads, braids, beards, free love, nakedness embraced, torn bell-bottom jeans and shared marijuana joints.

In some ways, similar to 2015, but, in reality, a lot more innocent, pure, and simple.

The 60s didn't seem to have the phoniness that 2015 presented. And, strangely enough, women had come a long way by the 60s, but it seemed to Allison that in a lot of ways women had taken a step back by the time the 2000s rolled around. More demeaned, more objectified, and more willing to be seen as sex objects. Whereas, women in the 60s seemed more defiant, more confident.

She pictured her and Wyatt strolling along hand in hand, on a street that was totally different than the ones she was used to. Colorful, quiet, happy, safe. She didn't know why—perhaps it was because she was with Wyatt?

Where would they live? What would they do? Would Wyatt be a police officer?

Would she be able to re-join the JPL as an astrophysicist? There would be no record of her university degrees, so that would be a challenge.

Would she join her father's hotel empire instead? How could she? He wouldn't know her. She'd have to apply as just a regular job applicant, which would seem weird.

And, she was reluctant to even entertain the idea of sitting her dad down and telling him who she really was and where she was from. She didn't mind interfering with Kennedy to save the world, but was scared at the thought of interfering with her own family. What might that do to the balance of things? To them? To her?

Allison knew, of course, the exact date and time of her parents' and husband's murders. That car trip along the Oregon coast five years ago, when the assassin's vehicle came at them head-on, forcing them over the cliff. She might be able to prevent that now when the time arrived. She could plan to be there, or somehow delay their arrival at that point. But, should she?

Would Majestic 12 even exist? Perhaps, if they succeeded in this mission with Kennedy, he might intervene and disband the group? It was possible. Which, of course, would change everything. There would have been no need for her parents and husband to be killed.

Her husband.

How would she feel when she saw him again? She wasn't sure. All she knew now was that she loved Wyatt, and her heart was telling her that those feelings were stronger than she'd ever felt about Jack. Or, anyone else before Jack.

Suddenly, she jerked awake. A moment of turbulence, stronger than the innocent little jolts that had been poking at her.

Allison sat up straight and glanced at her watch. It was 5:45. Fifteen minutes to go. She was angry at herself for sleeping so long. How could she have allowed her mind to cut it so close?

She looked out the window. They were over the Geneva area now, the Alps off to one side and the Jura range on the other. Mountains framing the entire Geneva zone.

The scene wasn't a calm one, though.

The splendor of the landscape was tainted by ferocious dark clouds, symptoms of a system that had them surrounded. Swirling, angry clouds that seemed alive, fingers reaching outwards, flirting with the wings of the sleek jet.

The plane began its descent. She felt it instantly in the seat of her pants.

Cole started circling the plane as well, getting ready to be at the exact coordinates Allison had given him. She gazed down at the ground—her trained pilot's eyes estimated that they were already at around 15,000 feet.

Allison turned her head and looked back at the others.

The cardinal and his aide were gazing out the window, no doubt well aware that the moment of truth was close. They seemed calm, resigned.

Senator Hartford just smiled and gave her a silent thumbs-up.

Amazingly, the four CERN scientists were still tapping away at their keyboards. At seeing that, Allison gasped and jumped out of her seat.

"Put those laptops away! Now! We can't take a chance on the hard drives being erased by the magnetics. That's why we gave you lead-lined cases, for God's sake!"

The scientists sheepishly obeyed.

Wyatt had nodded off and began to stir at the sound of her outburst.

She gently shook his shoulder. "Get ready, Wyatt. We're close now."

Suddenly, the jet lurched to its port side, knocking Allison down over Wyatt's lap. Then, the plane just fell like a rock, straight down.

Seemingly powerless and helpless, gravity worked its magic. Wyatt reacted quickly, wrapping his arms tightly around her waist to keep her from flying upwards into the ceiling.

The jet shook and groaned with each unnatural move it made. Allison felt a sense of panic rising in her chest. They were being buffeted around by a storm system, and it felt to her as if they'd also hit an air pocket.

Then, as suddenly as it started, the turbulence stopped. To a collective sigh of relief from the already nervous occupants of the plane, the craft levelled off and the flight was once again smooth and calm.

Allison guessed that they had fallen to about the 8,000-foot level.

They needed to be at 9,000.

She stole a glance at her watch: 5:50. Ten minutes to go.

She pushed up on Wyatt's lap and steadied herself back into the aisle again.

"Are we okay?"

"I think so, Wyatt. Just some turbulence."

As if on cue, just to destroy her confidence, it happened again.

This time, the plane went into a violent slide to the starboard side, the aluminum and titanium airframe shaking and screaming in a way that made Allison think that the plane was falling apart at its seams.

A tense voice came over the speaker. Cole's.

"Allison, we've run into a problem. Can't hold the plane at this level. Dangerous area of turbulence. Ascending to 20,000 and heading for our alternate airport, Luxembourg. Sorry."

She reached down and quickly unfastened Wyatt's seatbelt. Then, she grabbed him by the hands and yanked him out of his seat.

"Follow me!"

She staggered toward the cockpit, holding onto seatbacks to steady herself, and stopped at a locked cabinet installed in the bulkhead. She reached into her pocket, pulled out a key, and unlocked the door.

Allison knew which shelf to go to. The object was anchored against the wall in a Velcro strap.

She pulled out the Colt 45 pistol, spun the cylinder, and clicked it back into place…then held it out in front of her, pointed down at the floor.

Wyatt sputtered, "What the…"

She glared at him. "Just follow my lead."

Allison's stomach was in her throat as she felt the jet begin its ascent. She glanced at her watch: 5:55. Five minutes to go.

She raced into the cockpit and rammed the barrel of the pistol into the back of Cole's head.

"I don't have time to argue or explain, Cole. Put the plane at 9,000 feet and head for those coordinates I gave you."

Cole spun his head around. His face bore the shock Allison had expected.

Dave jumped up from the co-pilot's seat, but Wyatt promptly shoved him back down again. "Stay where you are, buddy."

Cole yelled, "What the fuck are you doing, Allison? I'm the captain here. It's my decision. It's not safe."

"Cole, I won't ask again. I'll put a bullet in your head, trust me."

"You won't fire that gun in here, not at this height.'"

Allison glanced at the altimeter. "We're lower than 10,000 feet, so there won't be any depressurization."

"You need us to fly this thing."

"No, I don't. I can fly this in a pinch and you know it."

Cole turned his head back to the controls and went silent.

"Cole, this is life or death! Do it, or I'll kill you here and now! Believe that, for your own sake!"

Cole exhaled slowly, then reluctantly went to work.

The Gulfstream jet shuddered and shook as it descended back down to Allison's commanded height. As soon as they reached the 9,000-foot level, Cole expertly manipulated the controls, sending the plane into a sharp turn to starboard.

Allison and Wyatt held on tightly to the pilots' seatbacks as turbulence grabbed hold of the plane once again.

"Okay! We're ten seconds from your damn coordinates!"

Allison stared at her wristwatch and counted down.

Suddenly, she felt a violent pull, just as if someone had grabbed her from behind. Her body slammed into the wall of the cockpit. She was aware of Wyatt bouncing off the opposite wall.

Allison felt as if she was back in her dream state.

The turbulence ended, replaced by a hypnotically swirling purple light that seemed to completely surround the outside of the plane. Strangely, it was starting to infiltrate the inside of the cockpit as well.

Without warning, the jet was sucked upwards, its nose aimed straight towards the sky—or at least in the direction where Allison thought the sky was supposed to be. The sophisticated plane was now completely vertical and in serious danger of losing lift.

Allison and Wyatt tumbled out of the cockpit and rolled together down the aisle of the cabin, bouncing off seat frames and overhead bins.

After a few long seconds, the plane effortlessly eased itself back down to a level position again, almost as if some unseen force had intervened. The purple light began to fade and Allison saw what she thought was the setting Sun streaming through the cabin windows.

From her prone position at the rear of the jet, she began to crawl towards Wyatt, who was desperately holding onto the anchored legs of one of the seats halfway up the cabin.

Then, Allison stopped crawling, lowered her head, and retched.

CHAPTER 58

Nothing was better than a vacation in New York City. The Empire State Building, Times Square, and the World Trade Center. The hustle and bustle of the city, the iconic cab drivers, and, to Allison's delight, Fifth Avenue.

But, what delighted Wyatt the most was just standing on the street staring up at the Twin Towers of the World Trade Center. Nice to see them again, and they were just so darn shiny and new.

The construction of the North Tower was just completed a year ago and the first tenants had moved in within the last few months. But, the South Tower wouldn't see any signs of life until next year; there was still major work being done on the banks of elevators.

It was a warm spring morning and the leaves on the trees were in full bloom—after all, it was the month of May. Bountiful flower baskets adorned all of the major downtown streets, and the hordes of office workers rushed to their duties, seemingly with a happy bounce in their steps.

It was 1971...and life was good.

Suddenly, Allison yelled out, "Lisa! Eric! Get back here!"

Wyatt dashed ahead and grabbed the little rascals by the backs of their jackets.

Matching jackets, of course.

Lisa and Eric were twins.

Both were giggling as he held them close, making faces at their mom.

Eric was always the mouthy one, and today was no exception. "Mommy, you're no fun. We were just running around. Daddy didn't mind."

Allison caught up to them, out of breath. "Well, your dad is just a big kid himself, that's why."

Wyatt pouted. "Hey, now, that's not fair."

Allison cracked a warm smile. "But…that's one of the reasons I love you, I guess."

Lisa piped up. "Mommy, don't you love us, too?"

She bent down and hugged her little princess. "You know I do."

Eric wiggled his way in close to her as well, transforming the scene into a group hug.

Wyatt smiled down at them. His lovely little family.

The twins were seven years old now, and growing up faster than he wanted them to. They were blonde, blue-eyed, and cute as buttons. He knew where the blue eyes had come from: Allison, and, on his side, Willy. But, they weren't as scintillating as her magnificent blue orbs. More garden variety blue, like Willy had.

Allison's eyes were still the most unusual he'd ever seen, and he guessed he would never see a pair like them again. They always caught people by surprise. He could tell whenever anyone met her for the first time—a look came across their faces that was hard to describe.

Allison stood up and slipped her arm around Wyatt's waist.

"I watched you staring at the towers. It is spooky to see them again, isn't it?"

Wyatt nodded. "It is indeed. I wonder if they'll still come down in thirty years' time."

Allison looked up and shielded her eyes with her hand. "Yes, I wonder about that, too. So much has changed already. Only time will tell what the stars hold for us all. You and I will be old folks then, anyway." She tickled him around the stomach. "Well, especially you."

"Hey, I'm only fifty-three!"

"Yeah, but that means you'll be eighty-three in 2001. You'll be an old fart, Wyatt—but still darn cute. I'll feed and bathe you, don't worry."

He tickled her back and she giggled, sounding very much like the twins.

"You are kind of adorable when you tease me—you're lucky I'm a good sport."

"Yes, you are, dear."

Wyatt winced. "But, you're right. It's even worse when you think about the year we came from. It's hard to believe that back in 2015…or should I say *ahead* in 2015…I was forty-five. If I live long enough to get back to that year again, I'll be ninety-seven!"

Allison smiled. "It is weird. But, look at it this way—the new 2015 will probably be a much safer place than it was when we were there before. And, even though you and I may not live to see that year, our children probably will, and we can take some solace in knowing that what we did made the world better for them."

They walked along, hand in hand—Eric and Lisa laughing from behind, holding onto their parents' belts.

Suddenly, Wyatt put on the brakes. They were in front of the window of an electronics store. A television was tuned in to a news station, and a speaker above the doorway broadcast the sound to those on the street.

Several other people had stopped as well, watching and listening to the speech by a face familiar to all Americans. Indeed, familiar to the entire world.

Robert Francis Kennedy, President of the United States of America.

Affectionately known as "Bobby."

Eric and Lisa didn't like the fact that they'd stopped. They were jumping up and down, pleading to go back to the hotel so they could swim in the pool.

Wyatt knelt down and raised his index finger to his mouth. "Shh... Daddy and Mommy want to listen to the man on TV. If you're quiet for a few minutes, we'll let you have two swims in the pool today instead of just one. And, maybe...ice cream cones, too?"

They both squealed with delight. Ran their fingers along their lips. Eric whispered, "Our mouths are zipped, Daddy."

Wyatt stood up and turned his attention back to the television in the store window. Allison held onto his hand, and together they focused their attention on the handsome politician.

"...and I'll have another economic forecast for you next month. I promised when I became your president back in 1969, that you would hear from me at least monthly. I try to use these sessions to give you my perspectives on current events. I think it's important that we work together as Americans, and no citizen of this country should ever be kept in the dark.

"Speaking of which, I know all Americans have been wondering if I will seek re-election next year, and I can announce today that I've made my decision. I will indeed be campaigning for a second term as your president. I made my decision independent of any undue influence, although most of you know that my brother, John, is quite persuasive. He certainly succeeded in convincing all of you to elect him to two terms. We Kennedys are known for being competitive, so I'm obligated by family doctrine to do my best to keep up with my big brother. He's happy that I've made this decision, and promises to help

with my campaign. I'll hold him to that promise.

"And, needless to say, Ethel, and our eleven children, are supportive as well. But, I warn you, the White House is going to need a major redecorating after our gang finally leaves.

"Now, regarding the subject of Southeast Asia, the war between North Vietnam and South Vietnam continues unabated, but the United States of America will maintain its policy of a 'hands off' stance. My brother withdrew our military advisors from South Vietnam in 1964, and at the same time he used his power of 'executive order' to outlaw any future use of conscription, known by most of you by its more familiar term…the 'draft.'

"The last time America used the draft was back in the 1950s during the Korean War, and I vow never to use it again. I also vow that I will not allow the United States to get mired in foreign conflicts where our interests are not in danger of being impacted. Vietnam is a war we will not become involved in, but we will continue to use our influence with China to try to bring the conflict to a peaceful resolution. China is the only nation North Vietnam will listen to, and we're hoping for a breakthrough soon.

"On another serious note, I wanted to bring everyone up to date on the major projects that were authorized back in 1963, during my brother's presidency.

"We've made major progress on the scientific advancements that President John F. Kennedy announced. There are two major projects that are nearing completion. Both of them are known in scientific terms as Large Hadron Colliders. The United States is a major partner in the CERN complex being constructed under the Swiss/French border, near Geneva.

"The other project is right here at home, virtually identical to CERN. It's being built under a portion of the Mojave Desert in Nevada. I know that the science is hard for most people to digest, but I can promise you that both of these facilities will offer the possibility of technological advancements beyond anything any of us could have ever dreamed of.

"Most Americans who work for large companies are familiar with mainframe computers that are contained in separate sealed-off rooms in their office buildings. But, soon, Americans will have small versions of these computers right in their very own homes, connected to other computers around the world. Hard to imagine, I know. This is not science fiction—it is a real possibility, and very soon.

"I won't go into too much detail right now, but the possibilities are very exciting, as well as the physics experiments that will be conducted from these two underground facilities. Experiments that will help us more clearly understand the universe that surrounds us.

"The Geneva and Mojave facilities will do identical work, identical experiments, and will actually communicate with each other electronically. However, I am proud to

say that the Mojave center in Nevada will be the larger of the two, and will take the lead in experimentation.

"In addition, there are certain aspects of the LHC which will offer a sophisticated defense capability for the United States. John Hartford, my new National Security Advisor, is working closely with the Pentagon to ensure that we enjoy the maximum benefits of this marvelous facility for our country.

"I would be remiss if I didn't extend my sincerest thanks and appreciation to our Facility Director, Doctor Allison Fisher, our nation's most esteemed astrophysicist. Doctor Fisher is, in my view, a true American hero. She and her husband, Wyatt, and their twins, Eric and Lisa, reside in Palm Springs, California, close enough to the Mojave center for Allison to oversee our investment.

"But, Allison and her family also have a holiday home in Canada, which allows her the convenience of being close to our Canadian partners, who have just this week announced the construction of their own version of the Large Hadron Collider. Allison will be working closely with our counterparts in Ottawa to ensure that the specifications match what exist in Geneva and Mojave. She will be a busy girl, indeed, and has my full support."

Wyatt couldn't resist. As soon as he saw Allison's photo pop up on the television screen, he leaned down and kissed her on the lips.

"My beautiful celebrity wife."

Allison grinned. "Don't you ever forget it!"

RFK had moved on to another subject.

"…and those petitions have been submitted and reviewed. Congress has also made their views known to me, and filed their own submissions. I have considered them all carefully and objectively, despite this matter being extremely personal for me.

"But, I have decided that I cannot, in all conscience, pardon the individuals who conspired to assassinate my brother back in 1963. All of those convicted were in high positions of trust in this country, and two of them were elected officials. They abused the trust our citizens and government placed in them, and their crimes are unpardonable.

"All five individuals were convicted of high treason in 1966 and sentenced to life at the Fort Leavenworth Military Prison in Kansas. There they will remain until they die, and this office will not consider any more petitions for pardons.

"The United States of America is the world's greatest democracy, and the will of the people cannot, under any circumstances, be allowed to be circumvented. If we tolerate heinous acts such as these individuals conspired to carry out, we will surely cease to be the 'home of the brave, and the land of the free.' As your president, I will not allow that to happen. God bless you all, and God bless America."

Allison uttered only one word. "Wow."

Wyatt nodded, and whispered, "Powerful words. America isn't even close to being the country we remember."

She squeezed his hand. "We did this, Wyatt. We did this."

"Yes, indeed we did. It's ominous to think about. We've rewritten the history books. Some famous names will never reach the high offices they did in the old books. That alone convinces me that we singlehandedly saved the world. And, the ripple effect of those corrupt politicians being in prison and not influencing events, means that certain horrific moments that we knew of may never come to pass now."

Allison wrapped her arms around his waist and pulled him in close.

"So, are you ready to visit your parents now?"

Wyatt's mouth suddenly felt like sandpaper.

He grimaced. "I guess I've put this off long enough. I'm now only a couple of months away from being born. Cutting it close. After that, I can't take the chance of contact between us.

"So, it's now or never."

CHAPTER 59

They were cruising along I-81, northward to Syracuse. It was a good four and a half hour drive from New York City, but Wyatt wished it was more like ten hours.

He was preparing himself to finally meet his parents, something he'd put off ever since the leap of time back to 1963. But, he knew no amount of time would make any difference. It was now 1971, and this visit was long overdue.

He was on the verge of seeing them again, and they wouldn't have a clue as to who he was.

A surreal thought.

He'd done his homework already and knew they were both alive and well. And, considerably younger than he was, which was unsettling to think about.

Willy and Helen lived in the suburbs just outside Syracuse. Willy was a professor at Syracuse University's College of Art and Helen was, as far as Wyatt could determine, a housewife.

So, their lives were different now, but had still followed along similar lines. Wyatt's time travel back to 1963 hadn't changed the fact that his father had fought in the Korean War in the 1950s and suffered the ill effects of having been beamed by the alien craft. In that respect, he was still the same Willy—with the altered DNA and the acquired art skills, along with all the other talents Wyatt knew he'd acquired.

But, what had changed was that JFK hadn't been assassinated in 1963—and neither had his brother, RFK, in 1968.

Consequently, John served two full terms as president, and Bobby won the election to become John's successor in 1969.

History had changed in a profound way.

The U.S. involvement in the Vietnam War died before it even got started. After meeting with Allison, Senator Hartford, Cardinal Valenti, and the CERN scientists, JFK moved quickly to withdraw all military personnel from South Vietnam. As a result, there was no draft and America didn't have to deal with the heartbreak of seeing 50,000 American boys coming home in body bags.

Because there wasn't a draft, neither was there the exodus of draft-dodgers from the United States. No migration of thousands of angry young Americans to Canada. The mood in the country was entirely different now than it had been in the previous time when Willy and Helen had lived it.

Instead of sneaking off and starting a new life in Nelson, Canada, the happy couple simply remained in their hometown of Syracuse. Wyatt thought it was weird that, if he asked them today, they probably wouldn't even have any idea where Nelson was.

But, Willy was still an artist…so he'd cultivated that skill acquired from his new DNA. Even better than that, he was teaching art at a university. Wyatt was able to easily imagine his dad as an art professor. He had that way about him—a charming humility that his students would find endearing.

He felt her hand rubbing his knee.

"Are you okay?"

Wyatt smiled at her. "Yeah, I'm just fine. A little pensive perhaps, but…"

"But, what?"

Wyatt was silent for a few seconds.

"Well, I do want to see them, but I'm wondering what the point is. I can't tell them who I am, and we're not going to have any kind of relationship. I'll be a stranger to them and they will be to me, too. I'm seeing them before I was even born. And, then, in two months' time when I burst onto the scene as an infant, I won't ever be able to see them again. Can't take the chance on getting too close to myself."

Allison turned her head around to check on the twins. They were both asleep in the backseat. While they probably wouldn't clue in to what she and Wyatt were talking about, she was glad they were fast asleep anyway, just in case.

"You know you don't mean that. They're still your parents. I know it feels odd, but I think you do want to see them, even if it's only for just this once.

"It hurts me a bit to hear you talk like that. I wish I were in your position, able to see my parents one last time, alive and happy."

Wyatt felt a pang of conscience. He reached over and squeezed her hand. "I'm sorry—that was insensitive of me."

She wiped a tear from her eye. "It's okay—apology accepted."

He took his eyes off the road for a second and glanced at her. "We considered all the big things on the world stage that would change by what we did, but we didn't consider how things could change at every other level, too."

She nodded. "Reminds me of that movie, *Final Destination.* Fate sometimes intervenes to have its way even when we thwart it. My parents ended up dying anyway and, ironically, from a car crash, just like in 2010. Our intervention, in reality, cut their lives short by forty-two years. By a miserable drunk driver. Someone who was supposed to have been killed during the Vietnam War, but our intervention allowed him to live."

"Did your hard drive tell you much about the guy?"

She shook her head. "No. All I had was the complete record of military deaths. He was supposed to have died in the war in 1968, but instead he got drunk and killed my parents that year. Which is strange—one death was prevented, but it was replaced by two other deaths in that very same year.

"Now, take that statistic and multiply it outwards. Just think of it. There were 50,000 American men killed in Vietnam, but we changed all that. Some of those who were supposed to die might have turned out to be great people, with careers, inventions, and families. But, others, like this drunk driver, wouldn't have turned out quite so well. How many people who were alive in our era, are now dead in this era just because of the people we saved? And, how does that change the future?"

Wyatt rolled down his window and savored the caress of the wind in his hair. "I'm sorry about your parents, Allison. I know you would have loved to have seen them again. It would have warmed your heart, after losing them before."

She pulled a tissue out of her purse and blew her nose. "It just goes to show—never put off the things that you know are important. We always think there's another day, or another year. Sometimes, there isn't.

"We came back here in 1963, and I could have looked my parents up then. But, like you, I put it off—probably because of how daunting the prospect was. How weird it was going to be. Then, by the time 1968 rolled around, it was too late for me. They were dead…again. That's why I'm glad you're finally doing this."

"You're right. I'm ashamed of myself. I promise you I'll treasure the moment."

He saw the exit sign for Syracuse and took the off ramp. "We're close now—only about ten minutes away. So, what's our storyline again?"

Allison pinched his cheek. "What would you do without me to coach you on our nefarious activities?"

Wyatt laughed. "Not much—and I should be good at this stuff. I used to be a police chief and a Mountie!"

"Yeah, but I don't think subterfuge ever came naturally to you, my dear. So, our cover story is that we're traveling through New York on vacation. I'm pretending to be a representative of Veteran's Affairs. Bobby gave me some pretty authentic-looking identification; well, since he's the president, I guess it's about as good as it gets.

"Anyway, while we're traveling through New York, I'm supposed to be doing my duty by checking in with some of the veterans of the Korean War who live in the state. When I phoned to make the appointment, your mom answered. She bought the story. And, she sounded the same, Wyatt—even though she's a lot younger. The same sing-song voice, cheerful tone. It was weird talking to her, recognizing her voice, but knowing she didn't recognize mine at all."

Wyatt grimaced. "That's the part I know is going to bother me. But, I'm just going to suck it up and realize that this is just the way it is. And, thank my lucky stars that they're alive, and I'm able to see them. Gonna remind myself that you didn't get that chance."

Wyatt turned right on Highlands Parkway, then left on Watkins Drive. "This is it. We're looking for number 207."

Allison whispered. "There's something we haven't talked about yet, Wyatt. We need to do that sometime. And, prepare for it, especially for the sake of the kids. I don't know what it means, or what effect it might have. We just don't know—which is why I warned you against coming in contact with yourself after you're born. Time travel has so many weird possibilities to it. We won't know the answer to this until the year 1977 arrives."

Wyatt felt a knot in the pit of his stomach.

He whispered back. "You're kinda scaring me. What are you getting at?"

"My parents died in 1968. It's now 1971. I wasn't born until 1977. I won't be, now."

*****

They were saying their goodbyes when the phone rang. Helen answered it, and told Allison it was for her.

"Oh, I'm so sorry, Helen. I gave your number as to where I could be reached. I hope you don't mind?"

"Oh, not at all, dear. An important government person like you, I'm guessing you probably never have a moment's rest. We have a second phone plugged in on the covered porch in the back. You can take your call out there for some privacy."

Allison gave Helen a quick hug, then hurried out onto the back porch.

She wasn't gone long. About five minutes. Wyatt examined her face closely when she came back in. Hard to tell, but she seemed to be wearing a slight smile.

Eric and Lisa were entertaining themselves in the hallway with a Fox Terrier named Mazie. The three of them were rolling around together, the kids giggling their heads off. Wyatt made a mental note to buy them a puppy when they got home.

Even though they were ready to go, Wyatt didn't want to. The visit had gone very well, better than he'd expected. As soon as he met them, the butterflies in his stomach disappeared. He felt instantly comfortable, felt at home.

Willy and Helen were younger than he was now, but he still felt like a little kid in their presence—the way most kids felt around their parents, even after they'd grown up. In this case, it was extra strange, though, with the age difference.

Helen was still his mother—pretty as a flower, and the perfect hostess. And, just like back in 2015, she fawned over her husband. But, she was perfectly capable of putting him in his place when he said something stupid. Just like in 2015.

Willy was still his father. Handsome, strong, caring. Showed an interest in everything, just the way he had back in 2015.

But, this time around, they didn't have the father/son bond. He remembered how they teamed up to rescue Helen from the kidnappers. They were an unbeatable team then at a time of incredible stress, just like they had been during his growing-up years. Willy was his dad, and time travel didn't change that. But, the sad part was, only Wyatt knew that.

Willy was sipping his coffee and staring at him.

"Are you sure we haven't met somewhere before?"

"No, Mr. Carson, I don't think so."

"What's your last name?"

Helen slapped him on the shoulder. "Don't be so nosy, Willy!"

Wyatt quickly thought of a fake name. "It's okay, Mrs. Carson. I don't mind. My last name is Burke. Wyatt Burke."

Willy shook his head. "You look so familiar to me. In fact, we even look alike—we could be brothers."

"Well, I'll take that as a compliment, Mr. Carson."

"Call me Willy."

"Okay, Willy."

Helen jumped in. "And, you folks can call me Helen."

Allison smiled. "It's been so nice to visit with you. And, I'm glad to hear that Veterans Affairs is treating you okay, Willy. If you need anything at all, make sure to get in touch with our Washington office."

"Can't I just call you?"

She shook her head. "No, I'm leaving the VA. New job."

"You look familiar, too. Have I seen you on TV?"

"I don't think so. I have one of those familiar faces, though."

Willy laughed. "No, you don't! Those eyes are amazing. I don't think I've ever seen anyone with eyes like that before."

Helen struggled out of her seat and walked over to Wyatt. She leaned down and gave him a kiss on the cheek.

"It was so nice of you all to drop by for a visit. I know it was a VA duty on Allison's part, but it's wonderful that she brought her lovely family along with her."

Wyatt couldn't help but stare at Helen's baby bump. He gestured with his hand. "Sit down, Helen, sit down. You look like you're ready to give birth at any moment."

"No, I'm fine. It feels better when I get up and move around a bit. And, I'm not due until June or July, so I still have to put up with this for a while. But, I wanted to ask you something. I love your name. It's so hard to pick baby names—would you mind very much if we used it?"

Wyatt chuckled. "I'd be honored if you named your baby Wyatt. That's great! I'm thrilled!"

Helen eased back down into her chair again, with Willy's help.

"Oh, I'm so glad. Okay, then, if one of them is a boy, we'll name him Wyatt. What a great name! I might even call him Wy for short."

"One of them?"

"Yes. Didn't we tell you? We're having twins!"

*****

Willy wouldn't let them leave without showing them his art studio. He led them out the back door to a converted garage in the rear.

It felt like déjà vu.

A studio in a garage behind the house.

Weird.

The cavernous studio was filled with finished sculptures, as well as quite a few in their early stages. One corner of the building was set up classroom style, with tables, chairs, and a chalkboard.

Willy explained. "I bring some of my students here for classes once in a while."

Allison walked around a large table and suddenly stopped, staring down at the floor.

"What's this, Willy?"

Wyatt and Willy went over to join her.

A massive ball was sitting on the floor, carved with what looked like canyons and mountain peaks. It was solid granite. And, it was darn familiar.

"Oh, that. I really don't know what it's going to be yet. I get these urges once in a while, as most artists do. Then, I just go with my instincts. So, I can't answer you yet. Come back and visit again, and maybe by that time I'll know what it's supposed to be!"

Allison smiled, and winked at Wyatt.

Suddenly, Wyatt noticed something off in the corner of the studio. It was about four feet in height, covered with a tarpaulin. It jarred a memory in his brain.

He walked over to it, and gently pulled off the tarpaulin.

Déjà vu.

A soldier in battle, kneeling. Wrinkled and torn uniform, helmet on his head. His face was so alive, so torn with anguish. The eyes were closed and actually squinting, pinched; as if in pain, in fear, or…maybe blinded?

He was grasping a machine gun in both hands, the index finger of his right hand pulling tightly against the trigger. The gun was pointed towards the sky. There was drool of some sort seeping out of the soldier's mouth, draping over his chin.

The only parts of his body that weren't covered in military fatigues were his face and his hands.

The statue was both beautiful and vocal. It was screaming out something, seemingly a message of anguish and abject fear.

The skin on the face was transparent. The bone structure of the skull displayed itself in full shocking horror. The hands gripping the machine gun were the hands of a skeleton.

*****

They had just crossed the Canadian border at Buffalo, starting the next leg of their vacation—a trip across Canada to their summer home in Nelson, British Columbia.

They hadn't said much to each other since leaving Willy and Helen. The twins were once again fast asleep in the backseat, and Allison knew that Wyatt was wrapped up in his thoughts. Seeing his parents again had to have been a wonderful experience for him—yet, at the same time, sad.

He would never see them again.

His eyes were focused on the road, and his jaw and clenched lips betrayed his concentration.

She broke the ice—reached over and ran her fingers through his hair.

Wyatt flashed her a quick smile.

"What are you thinking about, Wyatt?"

He sighed. "I was thinking that up until a couple of hours ago, I was an 'only child.' Now, I'm going to have a twin brother or sister. Someone who I'll never meet."

Wyatt shook his head. "It's just too weird. How did our coming back to 1963 change that part of my life?"

"Well, think of it this way. We changed the course of history. A less stressful life for Americans, no draft-dodgers on the run, more relaxed. Hormones might have been impacted beneficially in some people, and reproduction might have become enhanced as a result. What we changed by coming back affected more things than we could have imagined. Some things for the better and, I'm sure, some things for the worse, too. And, some more subtle than overt."

Wyatt adjusted the rear view mirror to take a quick peek at the twins in the back. Then he turned towards Allison and whispered, "That Korean War statue of himself. It's still just as macabre as the first time I saw it. It was unsettling to see it again."

"Yes, it seems that he sculpted it a lot earlier in his life this time around. As well as that granite ball—we know it represents Gargantuan. He doesn't know what it is, but we do. Everything seems to have accelerated a bit. Instead of waiting decades like before, he's sculpted these things now."

Wyatt reached over and rubbed her bare knee. "Okay, let's talk about something else—like, maybe, how nice your skin feels?"

Allison smiled at him. "Are you getting horny, babe?"

"Yes, I am. Good thing the hotel room I've rented for us tonight has two bedrooms!"

"That sounds good to me. Can you drive a little faster?"

They both laughed.

"Oh, you haven't told me what that phone call was about."

"No, I didn't. But, it's pretty exciting. That was Cardinal Valenti. As you know, he started up the Arizona observatory sooner than the timeline we came from. And, he's spent the last eight years building the Lucifer telescope. He phoned to tell me that it's now in full operation, several decades sooner than it was before.

"But, what's interesting is that there are now satellites in the sky that shouldn't be there for another couple of decades or so. He's picked them up with the early testing of Lucifer. LANDSAT 7; NOAA 17; GoldenEye; Galaxy 14; and even the Hubble Space Telescope. These are just a few that he was able to identify so far. And, none of those were launched earlier than 1990. He's still calibrating Lucifer, so it's not even operating at full efficiency or distance yet, but he was so excited at this discovery about the satellites that he had to call me. Neat, eh?"

"I guess—but what does it mean?"

Allison laughed. "We had a good chuckle over that. They may be up there, but we have no capability on the ground of communicating with them. We have those satellites now, but we don't have the technology yet to talk to them or even receive information. So, they're pretty useless. The cardinal and his team are pretty excited about this, though. And, he and the CERN scientists that came back with us have all of the specifications on their hard drives, so it should only take a year or so before we have the first means of communication with those futuristic satellites."

Wyatt threw his cigarette out the window. "By coming back, we sure advanced Earth more than we ever realized, huh? But, how did those damn things get up there? This 1960s society didn't launch them—we did, years from now."

"The cardinal's not sure. But, he thinks our wormhole expanded a bit and pulled the satellites back with us. So, now we get to enjoy the benefits of that. Our observation and understanding of outer space will be decades ahead now."

Wyatt grinned. "I think Bobby should give us all 'medals of honor.'

Whaddaya think?"

Allison stretched her arms out in front of her. "We do deserve something, I agree. Maybe just a cryptic footnote in the history books would be nice—some little notation that most people wouldn't understand, but we would know."

"Well, you work for the government. Get on that, will you? Don't forget—the victors always get to write the history books. And, it sounds like we're the victors here.

"And, hey…I'm gonna be a twin. Try to top that!"

CHAPTER 60

Wyatt loved their summer home. It was on the shores of beautiful Kootenay Lake close to downtown Nelson; so close that they could walk it.

They'd bought the house four years ago in an estate sale for a couple who had lived and loved there for fifty years.

It had needed updating badly, but Wyatt was good with his hands and it didn't take him long to develop the property into their dream home. He hired local contractors for some of the tough stuff, but was proud that he'd done a lot of the work himself.

And, he had time on his hands.

With Allison's busy career running the Mojave Desert LHC complex, he was a proud house-husband. Regular trips back and forth between Nelson and their home in Palm Springs had become a way of life for the Carson family.

On extended trips, he tutored the twins himself in harmony with their curriculum, but they never really needed much tutoring.

They'd been labelled as "gifted" by the California school system and at times Wyatt was overwhelmed with how much knowledge they were able to absorb. They were particularly proficient with mathematics and he could easily see that perhaps a career like Allison's was in their futures.

Usually, they flew from Los Angeles to Calgary, then rented a car to make the rest of the trip to Nelson. But, this time, because of the planned stopover in Syracuse, they'd decided to make it a family road trip.

They'd been living on the highways and byways for three weeks now, and he was glad that they could finally relax at their lake home for a while before making the long trek back to California.

So far, he hadn't missed police work. Although, he knew that as the kids got older and didn't need him as much, he would probably start having a mid-life crisis of some sort.

Wyatt was proud of how clever and resourceful Allison was, and of the important work she was doing. He also wanted her to be proud of him and he knew that she was.

For now.

But, once his "Mister Mom" duties were no longer needed, would she look at him the same way? Would he look at himself the same way?

In the previous life he'd lived back in the future, he enjoyed stimulating and responsible positions with the RCMP, and as Chief of Police for Nelson. But, all that experience was now wiped out. His record didn't exist. He couldn't just pop into the RCMP and apply for a senior position; likewise, with the Nelson police force.

And, he was too old now to attend the police academy to start all over again.

Allison, on the other hand, was in a different position entirely. Her revelations and knowledge that were used to convince JFK to begin building identical CERN complexes in Switzerland and Nevada, decades ahead of time, had set her up in good stead.

JFK used his influence to recreate her degrees, because he trusted her and wanted her in charge of the Mojave installation.

And, after JFK finished his two terms, RFK took over and continued the trusting relationship between Allison and the Kennedy family.

Her career was set for life.

Which was a good thing for her and for the entire Carson family. But, it made Wyatt begin to question his own future usefulness. What would he do to fulfill his need for stimulation once his fathering duties were over?

He knew that he was probably overthinking everything, but that was just the way his mind worked. The old detective brain still had its juice.

Renovating the lake house had been stimulating for him. Maybe he could do more projects like that, which he was sure would be both fun and satisfying. And, lucrative.

He strolled along the side of the house, down to the sandy beach. Walked onto the dock and gazed up at the sky. It was nice not to see streaks of chemtrails poisoning the atmosphere.

Before they'd regressed to 1963, it had been a long time since he'd seen a perfectly blue sky. Back in 2015, that had been a rarity with those damn planes spewing their mess across the horizon. All designed to hide the incoming Gargantuan from the eyes of the unsuspecting public. Wyatt suspected, though, that in the coming decades chemtrails might once again become common, depending on how successful the early development of CERN facilities proved to be.

He was hoping that by the time 2015 rolled around again, the threat from Gargantuan would be minimal, and the need to hide it would no longer be required.

The future would unfold now as it was meant to, because it was impossible to speculate as to what this advanced science could do for them. According to Allison, the possibilities were endless now that they'd gotten such a head start.

Wyatt walked along the dock back to the beach area. He smiled when he saw the twins' shovels and pails sitting alongside the collapsed ruins of yesterday's sandcastles. It was going to be another warm day, so he looked forward to helping them build new ones this afternoon.

Allison came out onto the porch and waved at him.

"Hey there, beach bum! Do you want to take a walk downtown with the kids? I told them we'd pop into the ice cream shop."

"Sounds good to me. I'll be right in."

He stole one last look at the sky before heading inside.

Yep, it was going to be a picture-perfect day.

He entered the kitchen and passed by the twins, who were sitting at the kitchen table. At first, he thought they were coloring but then noticed they had pencils in their hands, both scribbling furiously. He walked over to the table and peeked over their shoulders.

It was a familiar sight.

Each of them had already filled three pages, and were working on their fourth. Seemingly in unison. Numbers, symbols, and letters, with no rhyme or reason to them.

"Are you guys ready for ice cream?"

No answer. They just kept scribbling.

Wyatt walked down the hall and into the bedroom, where Allison was pulling on a pair of jeans and a sweater.

She smiled at him. "Ready for our walk?"

He wrapped his arms around her waist and gave her a kiss.

"They're doing it again."

"Who? What?"

"Eric and Lisa. The scribblings."

Allison frowned. "Oh, no."

"It's been getting more frequent. Remember, the first time was about six months ago? Then, it stopped. But, it started again. Now, it's a weekly thing. They go into their little trances and their pencils just start flying across the pages."

"Didn't you tell me you discussed it with their teacher?"

"Yeah, but she just said it was common for "gifted" children to do these things once in a while."

Allison pulled up the sleeves on her sweater. "Well, that may be true. They've both been tagged as having genius IQs. And, math seems to be their specialty."

Wyatt nodded. "Just like their mom."

She laughed. "Hey, I can't even figure out what they're doing, so I think they're beyond me!"

"Maybe we just need to accept that this is a sign of their altered DNA. I have that remote viewing skill, you have the power of mind-reading, and our kids have these genius math abilities. Our fathers passed things down to us, and now we've passed some things along to Eric and Lisa. It is what it is, I guess."

Allison nodded. "There are worse things parents could worry about. We're pretty lucky that our kids are loving and sensitive little angels. If they have some extra skills, all the better.'"

"Maybe it's just the detective in me, but I wish I could figure out what all those scribblings mean. They seem to be jotting down the exact same things—like they're in sync."

"Well, remember, Wyatt, they are twins. Most twins tend to be in sync with each other on a lot of things."

"True. But, it's still weird. Okay, let's go for that walk."

Suddenly, the phone rang. Wyatt dashed into the living room and picked up the handset.

"Hello?"

"Hi, Wyatt. It's Cardinal Valenti."

"Oh, hi there, Cardinal. Nice to hear from you. How are you?"

"Busy, busy. But, that's a good thing. I wanted to try to get in a game of golf this afternoon. The weather here in Arizona is great right now, but it looks like duty is calling and I'll have to pass."

"Oh, that's too bad. Hey, Allison was telling me that the Lucifer telescope is now up and running?"

"It sure is. I'm excited about that, but it keeps discovering new things every day now that its calibration is finished. That's what I want to talk to

Allison about."

"Okay, I'll put her on."

Wyatt handed her the phone and then walked into the kitchen, to the coffee percolator. One more cup of coffee wouldn't hurt.

He smiled to himself when he remembered that back in 2015 he'd always used a Keurig machine. Now, he had to get used to the old-fashioned way of making coffee. Which he didn't mind, because it tasted so much better. But, it took a hell of a lot longer.

He listened in on Allison's side of the conversation.

"My God! What the hell?"

"We can't get to them! It could take years!"

"Yes, we have all the specifications on the hard drives. It's a start, but NASA and the JPL will have to pull out all the stops. If they can do that, I guess it's possible."

"Well, I could fly down in a couple of days."

"Alright, then. I'll see you in Florida."

Allison put down the phone and wearily ran her fingers through her long hair.

Wyatt walked back into the living room. "That doesn't sound good. What's wrong?"

"Oh, Wyatt, I have to fly down to Cape Canaveral in Florida. We're all meeting there. A bit of a crisis that needs a herculean effort from everyone. RFK's orders."

"Okay, we'll drive to Calgary tomorrow. You can catch a flight to Florida and I'll just continue the drive back to California with the kids."

"I'm so sorry. I was looking forward to just relaxing here for a week or two."

"It's okay. We'll come back again after your crisis is over. So…what is it?"

Allison sighed. "Oh, it's horrible. Lucifer has picked up the International Space Station. It's up there, along with those satellites I told you about. There are three astronauts and three cosmonauts onboard. As far as they're concerned, they're in the year 2015."

"What the fuck…"

"Exactly. What the fuck. Our wormhole expanded more than we realized."

"They'd all be dead by now. We came back here eight years ago."

"Valenti doesn't think so. He thinks the wormhole didn't fade out as we thought it would. He thought at first that it was just the calibration of

Lucifer that caused a delay in seeing these satellites and the ISS. But, now he's convinced that the wormhole is still alive. It's been bringing objects back a few at a time. Which means, since the ISS has just been seen now, we still might have time to save them. The eight years we've spent here are equal to only a few minutes in 2015."

"That alone is hard to fathom. But, how could this have happened? That wormhole was supposed to have just been sudden and temporary."

Allison nodded. "That's what we thought. But, remember, the science was largely untested. It looks like we've unleashed something that we didn't totally understand. Now, we have to try to save those folks."

"Can't NASA just send up a rocket or a shuttle?"

She shook her head. "The ISS was launched in 1998. This is 1971. There are no shuttles, and certainly no ability for a rocket to dock with the ISS. Back in 2015, the only methods of getting astronauts to and from the station were on Russian Soyuz spacecraft. The United States stopped their shuttle program around 2005 and deferred to their partners, the Russians, to get people there and back. Their craft were designed to dock perfectly with the space station. They fit like a glove.

"And, as for supplies, the only ships capable of delivering those were the SpaceX Dragon ship, and the Russian Progress craft. Both were unmanned spacecraft designed specifically for the complex docking procedure."

"God, those poor souls."

"Yes, they're stranded up there. So, we have several problems. We don't have the technology to communicate with them. We can't supply them with food, water, or fuel. And, we don't have any spaceships capable of bringing them home."

"Why does the ISS need fuel?"

"It maintains an orbit at between 205 and 270 miles above the Earth's surface. But, without an occasional re-boost, it goes into gradual freefall. Starts slipping out of its orbit. So, it has to constantly turbo boost itself back to where it wants to be. If it slips too low in its orbit, Earth's gravity will just suck it down."

"What about oxygen and electricity?"

"It gets its breathable air from an oxygen generator. A Russian made device. So, that's not a problem unless it breaks down. As for day-to-day electricity, that all comes from solar panels. The biggest concerns right now are food and water, as well as the fuel needed to keep it in its upper orbital range.

"The ISS uses about 20,000 pounds of liquid hydrogen each year, so hopefully they have enough left from their last fill-up to last them a while. If they run out, they'll start falling.

"As for food and water, they should have enough to last up to six months but of course we don't know how long it's been since the last grocery run.

"So, we have a very tight deadline."

"You're going to build a spacecraft?"

Allison nodded. "Yes. We have the detailed specs on our hard drives for the Soyuz spacecraft. It'll be a rush job and it won't be perfect, but, it's the only chance we have.

"We have to hope in the meantime that it doesn't fall out of its orbit. That space station is the size of a football field. If it does come down, a good portion of it won't burn up—it'll pose a real danger to populated areas, depending on where it hits."

Wyatt couldn't believe what he was hearing. Six astronauts had come back in time with them—on a delayed reaction basis. And, they were probably wondering why no one from the ground was talking to them anymore.

"This wormhole thing—it's giving me a headache trying to understand it."

"I know. We're all learning more now that we've unleashed it. All I can tell you is that it was designed to transfer objects that had their own magnetic fields. So, anything electric or powered that was of sufficient size to have a tangible field.

"My plane fit the bill, and we calculated that we would transfer back and the wormhole would die out. But, it didn't. For some reason, it continued to expand into the atmosphere, hovering, hesitating, and then expanding again. It seems to have a life of its own now.

"The CERN physicists had also calculated a 'fallback' scenario back in 2015. That, if it did somehow expand after transferring us, it would simply slam into Earth's magnetosphere and die out. Well, there was a small chance that wouldn't happen and it looks like 'lady luck' wasn't with us.

"The Earth's magnetosphere back in 2015 had thinned considerably, and from time to time had cracks in it—openings that allowed solar radiation to enter the planet's atmosphere. Valenti thinks that the wormhole found a nice big crack and penetrated through it beyond the magnetic shield.

"Ergo, we now have futuristic satellites and the International Space Station. Just like in Jurassic Park, nature finds a way, huh?"

"And, of course, each of those large objects have electronically-generated magnetic fields, just like my jet did. So, they would automatically get sucked into the wormhole and transferred back to the era that was calibrated by us. They're just appearing a little late due to the erratic nature of the wormhole."

Wyatt rubbed his forehead. "My headache's getting worse. Okay, then, we have no choice but to get you on a plane to Cape Canaveral so you astrophysicists and engineers can build a new spaceship in record time."

With sarcasm in her voice, Allison replied, "Yep, no sweat at all."

"Let's go for our walk. We promised those kids ice cream, and I think when we get back I want a nice tall scotch…or maybe a martini."

"Me, too!"

Wyatt walked out of the living room and into the kitchen. The twins had left their posts, sheets of paper scribbled with random symbols scattered across the table.

They were now standing side by side out on the porch. Eric's right arm was linked through Lisa's left, and they each had their free arms extended up in the air. As if reaching for the stars.

They weren't swaying or shuffling their feet as kids tended to do. They were standing as still as toy soldiers.

Wyatt felt Allison's arm around his waist.

She whispered. "What are they doing?"

"I don't know. Maybe a game they invented; like, 'I Spy' or something like that?"

Allison called out to them. "Kids! We're gonna go get some ice cream now!"

They whirled around in unison. And, yelled out in unison. "Hooray! Ice cream!"

*****

Wyatt pointed. "Look, that's where my spanking new police station was."

Allison turned around and gestured up towards the hills surrounding the town. "And your lovely log home was right up there, overlooking the lake."

They were strolling down Baker Street, which looked a lot different than they remembered it. The bustling town of 11,000 people in 2015 was barely 3,000 in 1971. And, it probably wouldn't change very much over the next few decades. By traveling back to 1963, they had sealed Nelson's fate. It would never become the town that it was.

Wyatt's voice bore a tinge of regret. "Right about now, this year, the draft-dodgers would have been flocking here, never to go back to the States again. They would have started businesses and raised their families, causing this town to boom. There will be no boom now. It will just remain a logging town until that industry grinds to a halt. Then, there will be nothing."

"It will be different, Wyatt, but that's a pessimistic view. Society seeks out new ways to survive and thrive—it always has. This is such a beautiful area of the world. I can easily predict that tourism will probably receive serious attention if they have nothing else to draw from. It was already a tourist center in 2015, so there's no reason why that won't happen again."

"True, but the draft-dodgers developed most of that. They were creative folks, and very independent. They never lost their spirit. This town won't have any draft-dodgers or their descendants now. We've killed that for them."

"Something will fill the void, hon. I'm confident of that. In the meantime, we can just enjoy having a summer home in a quiet mountain town. I'm happy with that."

Wyatt wrapped an arm around her shoulder. "Me, too. I'm just in a pensive mood today, I guess. One thing I'll miss, though, are all those artsy shops the Americans opened up here. They gave the town real character. Maybe I should start up an arts and crafts store?"

Allison giggled. "You don't have a creative bone in your body, my dear. That's one thing you didn't inherit from your dad. But, I love you anyway, because you're my big tough Mountie!"

Wyatt laughed.

He suddenly realized that they'd lost track of the kids.

He spun around, his stomach in knots.

The twins were standing in the middle of the sidewalk about twenty feet behind them. Arms linked together once again, free arms extended upwards.

"What on earth are they doing?"

Allison started walking back to them. "They're just kids, Wyatt. Children love to pretend."

Wyatt followed close behind. "I guess you're right. I need to learn how to be more laid back like you."

"I'll teach you, don't worry. I may need a few years, but I'm willing to invest the time. You're worth it!"

*****

It was martini time. Bombay Sapphire Gin, dry, straight up, three olives…and very dirty. They were sitting in their bright red Adirondack chairs on the covered porch, watching as the twins built their new sandcastles.

It was a warm afternoon, but being that it was only May the lake was far too cold to swim in yet. The kids waded in just a few feet to fill their little pails with water, shrieking in shock each time the water level hit their knees. Then, they'd run back to the sand and pour the water into the intricate moats they'd built around their castles.

Wyatt leaned across to Allison and gave her a kiss. "I'm so glad you're my wife."

She kissed him back. "You're one darn lucky man. I hope you know that!"

Wyatt laughed. "Yeah, you remind me every single day!"

She rubbed his knee. "Who knew that life back in the sixties could be so nice? I'm so glad we're no longer in the twenty-first century. This is perfect. And, we've made it a better world, too."

"Except for the fact that you have to make a quickie spaceship now."

"Well, that's just another challenge. I'm looking forward to the excitement. We'll get it done. We have all we need on our computers. We'll get those astronauts home."

Wyatt swung around and hung his legs over the arm of the chair. "I envy you. The stimulation. The excitement. I don't have that anymore."

"Wyatt, you're raising our kids. And, you're my husband." She giggled. "Two of the most stimulating things in the world!"

He laughed. "True, especially the 'husband' part. But, I worry about the future. I need more."

She laid her hand across his knee. "I don't want to do this forever. I'd rather do something with you. Wait until I finish this spaceship project, okay? Then, I'll leave it all behind. I'll do something else. Hey, we could move here and open up a small hotel—I do have experience at that, as you know. We'd be the catalyst for a tourist rush we know is inevitable. We could be the ones to get it all started."

"Okay, that sounds good to me. Do I get to be the boss?"

"No, of course not!"

They both laughed, and turned their attention back to the kids.

All of a sudden, the twins started kicking down their sandcastles, stomping them into oblivion.

Wyatt chuckled. "They must be getting bored."

Together, they waded back into the water, heads down, studying the lake bottom. Lisa suddenly bent over and lifted up a round yellowish stone. It was a big one and she struggled to get it out of the water and onto the sand.

Eric was searching, too. He copied his sister, but chose a large black rock instead. Almost perfectly round just like Lisa's. He hefted it back to the sand and positioned it a couple of feet to the left of the yellow one. Then, he went back and hauled out another one—quite a bit smaller this time. Eric laid that one just below the yellow one.

The three rocks together formed an obtuse triangle.

Wyatt felt his mouth go dry. The triangle thing was darn familiar.

Allison had been paying close attention as well. She got up from her chair and stepped off the porch and onto the beach. Didn't say anything to the twins. Just bent down and looked at their display.

Eric and Lisa didn't say anything either. They sat in the sand and stared expressionless at what they'd done.

Allison walked back up to the porch and planted herself in front of Wyatt, hands on her hips.

"Did you see what they did?"

Wyatt nodded, slowly.

"Look familiar to you?"

Wyatt nodded his head again. He opened his mouth, but no words came. None could describe how he felt at that very moment.

Suddenly, the phone rang from inside the house.

Allison yanked open the screen door. "I'll get it. It's probably Valenti again."

Wyatt continued watching the kids, trying hard to push the memory out of his mind of what he and Allison had seen in Willy's studio many moons ago.

Three heavy, sculpted balls, arranged in the shape of an obtuse triangle.

One represented the Sun.

Another was Earth.

And the third ball, which was about five times the size of the Earth sphere, was Gargantuan.

Wyatt remembered that moment. The moment of truth.

The display in the sand just created by his innocent little children had approximately the same scale.

He tilted his head towards the doorway, hoping to pick up part of Allison's phone conversation.

He couldn't hear a thing.

He stood up, opened the squeaky screen door that had seen better days, and went looking for her in the living room.

The phone conversation had ended.

She was sitting on the edge of the couch, forehead resting in her hands.

"Are you okay, hon? Who was that?"

She looked up at him, tear stains on her lovely cheeks. Her face was as white as a sheet.

The words came out of her mouth in a hoarse whisper.

Words that a little voice in Wyatt's head warned him in advance he was going to hear. A little voice he'd tried hard to block.

But, he couldn't block out Allison's voice.

And, he never would, for as long as they both should live.

She whispered, "It's...coming. Gargantuan hitched a ride."

THE END

THE AUTHORS

PETER PARKIN

Peter was born in Toronto, Canada, and after studying Business Administration at Ryerson University he embarked on a thirty-four year career in the business world, primarily spent in the executive ranks. He retired in 2007 after serving as the Chief Operating Officer of a major national company. When he's not writing novels, Peter is active serving as a Director on four corporate boards. He has two grown sons and two grandsons and resides near the city of Calgary, on the threshold of the Rocky Mountains of Western Canada. Find out more about Peter by visiting his website. http://www.peterparkin.com.

ALISON DARBY

Alison is a life-long resident of the West Midlands region of England. She studied psychology in college and when she's not juggling a busy work life and writing novels, she enjoys researching the wonders of astronomy. Alison has two grown daughters who live and work in the vibrant city of London. Alison resides in an historic home in the charming town of Tettenhall, U.K.